THE SOLDIER
SHE COULD
NEVER FORGET

BY
TINA BECKETT

THE DOCTOR'S
REDEMPTION

BY
SUSAN CARLISLE

Born to a family that was always on the move, **Tina Beckett** learned to pack a suitcase almost before she knew how to tie her shoes. Fortunately she met a man who also loved to travel, and she snapped him right up. Married for over twenty years, Tina has three wonderful children and has lived in gorgeous places such as Portugal and Brazil.

Living where English reading material is difficult to find has its drawbacks, however. Tina had to come up with creative ways to satisfy her love for romance novels, so she picked up her pen and tried writing one. After her tenth book she realised she was hooked. She was officially a writer.

A three-time Golden Heart finalist, and fluent in Portuguese, Tina now divides her time between the United States and Brazil. She loves to use exotic locales as the backdrop for many of her stories. When she's not writing you can find her either on horseback or soldering stained glass panels for her home.

Tina loves to hear from readers. You can contact her through her website or 'friend' her on Facebook.

Susan Carlisle's love affair with books began when she made a bad grade in math in the sixth grade. Not allowed to watch TV until she'd brought the grade up, she filled her time with books and became a voracious romance reader. She has 'keepers' on the shelf to prove it. Because she loved the genre so much she decided to try her hand at creating her own romantic worlds. She still loves a good happily-ever-after story.

When not writing Susan doubles as a high school substitute teacher, which she has been doing for sixteen years. Susan lives in Georgia with her husband of twenty-eight years and has four grown children. She loves castles, travelling, cross-stitching, hats, James Bond and hearing from her readers.

THE SOLDIER
SHE COULD
NEVER FORGET

BY
TINA BECKETT

MILLS &
BOON

Published in Great Britain 2015
by Mills & Boon, an imprint of Harlequin (UK) Limited,
Eton House, 18-24 Paradise Road, Richmond, Surrey, TW9 1SR

© 2015 Tina Beckett

ISBN: 978-0-263-24700-8

Harlequin (UK) Limited's policy is to use papers that are natural,
renewable and recyclable products and made from wood grown in
sustainable forests. The logging and manufacturing processes conform
to the legal environmental regulations of the country of origin.

Printed and bound in Spain
by CPI, Barcelona

Dear Reader,

Sometimes life gives us second chances: a dream job we passed up for something else, a return trip to a childhood home, a first love that was lost many years ago. And sometimes…sometimes we come to understand why things happened the way they did in the past.

Thank you for joining Jessi and Clint as they unexpectedly come face-to-face after years apart. As Jessi struggles to understand what went wrong between them Clint wrestles with the demons that haunt him. And maybe, through the power of forgiveness and with an approving nod from fate, they can rediscover a love they thought long dead.

Clint and Jessi's journey has a special place in my heart. I hope you enjoy reading their story as much as I loved writing it!

Much love

Tina Beckett

To my children. You bring me joy, every single day.

PROLOGUE

Twenty-two years earlier

"Jess. Don't cry."

The low words came from behind her, the slight rasp to his tone giving away his identity immediately.

Jessi stiffened, but she didn't turn around. Oh, God. He'd followed her. She hadn't realized anyone had even seen her tearful flight out of the auditorium, much less come after her. But they had. And those low gravely tones didn't belong to Larry Riley, who'd had a crush on her for ages, or her father—*thank God!*—but Clinton Marks, the last person she would have expected to care about what she thought or felt.

"I—I'm not."

One scuffed motorcycle boot appeared on the other side of the log where she was seated, the footwear in stark contrast to the flowing green graduation gowns they both wore—and probably topping the school's list of banned attire for tonight's ceremony.

The gown made her smile. Clint, in what amounted to a dress. She hoped someone had gotten a picture of that.

He sat beside her as she hurried to scrub away the evidence of her anguish. Not soon enough, though, because cool fingers touched her chin, turning her head toward him. "You're a terrible liar, Jessi May."

Somehow hearing the pet name spoken in something other than his normal mocking tones caused hot tears to wash back into her eyes and spill over, trailing down her cheeks until one of them reached his thumb. He brushed it away, his touch light.

She'd never seen him like this. Maybe the reality of the night had struck him, as well. In a few short hours, her group of friends would all be flying off to start new lives. Larry and Clint would be headed for boot camp. And her best friend would be spending the next year in Spain on a college exchange program.

They were all leaving.

All except Jessi.

She was stuck here in Richmond—with an overly strict father who'd come down hard when he'd heard Larry was gearing up for a career in the army. The papers weren't signed yet, but they would be in a matter of days. She'd done her best to hide the news, but her dad had been bound to find out sooner or later. He didn't want her involved with a military man. Kind of unreasonable in a place where those kinds of men were a dime a dozen.

Maybe she should have picked an out-of-state college, rather than choosing to commute from home. But as an only child, she hadn't quite been able to bring herself to leave her mom alone in that huge house.

"What's going on, Jess?" Clint's voice came back to her, pulling her from her pity party.

She shrugged. "My dad, he… He just…" It sounded so stupid to complain about her father to someone who flouted authority every chance he got. If only she could be like that. But she'd always been a people pleaser. The trait had gotten worse once she'd been old enough to realize her mom's "vitamins" were actually antidepressants.

Instead of the flip attitude she'd expected from Clint, though, his eyes turned this cold shade of gunmetal gray that made her shiver. His fingers tightened slightly on her chin. "Your father what, Jess? What did he do?"

Her teeth came down on her lip when she realized what he was saying. There'd been rumors about Clint's family, that his father was the reason he was the way he was.

Her dad was nothing like that.

"He didn't do anything. He's just…unreasonable. He's against me being with people like you or Larry."

His head tilted. "Me…and Larry." His mouth turned up at the corners. "I see your dad's point. Larry and I are definitely cut from the same cloth."

They weren't. Not at all. Larry was like her. He was all about good grades and toeing the line. Clint, however, lived on the edge of trouble—his skull tattoo and pierced ear making teachers shake their heads, while all the girls swooned.

Including her.

His words made her smile, though. "You're both going into the army."

"Ah, I see. Your father wouldn't like me, though, in or out of the army."

Her smile widened. "He's protective."

He made a sound low in his throat that might have been a laugh. "The thing is…" his eyes found hers again and a warm hand cupped the back of her neck "…I didn't know I was even in the running. So I'm neck and neck with Larry *straight-A* Riley."

Something hot flared low in her belly. Clint had never, ever given the slightest hint he was interested in her. And yet here he was. Beside her. The only person to notice her walk off the stage and slip out the door after getting her diploma. The only one who'd followed her.

"I—I… Did you want to be?"

"No."

The word should have cut her to the quick, except the low pained tone was somehow at odds with his denial.

"Clint…?" Her fingertips moved to his cheek, her eyes meeting his with something akin to desperation.

Another sound rumbled up from his chest, coming out as a groan this time. Then, something she'd never dreamed possible—in all of her eighteen years—happened.

Clinton Marks—bad boy extraordinaire—whispered her name. Right before his mouth came down and covered hers.

CHAPTER ONE

"Chelsea's new doctor arrived today." The nurse's matter-of-fact words stopped her in her tracks.

Jessica Marie Riley blinked and turned back to the main desk of the Richmond VA hospital, where her twenty-one-year-old daughter had spent the past two months of her life—a frail shell of the robust soldier who'd been so proud of toughing it out at army boot camp.

It had always been just her and Chelsea against the world. They'd supported each other, laughed together, told each other everything.

Until she'd returned from her very first tour of duty as a former POW...and a different person.

"He did?" Jessi's stomach lurched. Her daughter's last doctor had left unexpectedly and she'd been told there was a possibility she'd be shuffled between the other military psychiatrists until a replacement could be found.

Maria, the nurse who'd admitted Chelsea and had shown a huge amount of compassion toward both of them, hesitated. She knew what a sore spot this was. "Dr. Cordoba had some family issues and resigned his commission. It really wasn't his fault."

Jessi knew from experience how devastating some family issues could be. But with the hurricane that had just gouged its way up the coast, her work schedule at Scott's

Memorial had been brutal. The shortage of ER doctors had never been more evident, and it had driven the medical staff to the brink of exhaustion. It also made her a little short on patience.

And now her daughter had lost the only doctor she'd seemed to bond with during her hospitalization.

Jess had hoped they'd finally get some answers about why Chelsea had spiraled into the depths of despair after coming home—and that she'd finally find a way to be at peace with whatever had happened in that squalid prison camp.

That tiny thread of hope had now been chopped in two. Anger flared at how easy it was for people like Dr. Cordoba to leave patients who counted on him.

Not fair, Jess. You're not walking in his shoes.

But the man wasn't walking in hers, either. He hadn't been there on that terrible day when her daughter had tried to take her own life.

She couldn't imagine how draining it was to deal with patients displaying symptoms of post-traumatic stress disorder on a daily basis, but Jessi had been handed some pretty awful cases herself. No one saw her throwing in the towel and moving on to some cushy private gig.

Maria came around the desk and touched her arm. "Her new doctor is one of the top in his field. He's dedicated his life to treating patients like your daughter—in fact, he transferred from California just to take over Dr. Cordoba's PTSD patients. At least until we can get a permanent replacement. He's already been to see Chelsea and reviewed her chart."

Top in his field. That had to be good, right? But if he was only temporary...

"What did he think?"

This time, the nurse wouldn't quite meet her eyes. "I'm

not sure. He asked me to send you to his office as soon as you arrived. He's down the hall, first door on your left."

Dr. Cordoba's old office.

The thread of anger continued to wind through her veins, despite Maria's encouraging words. This was Chelsea's third doctor. That averaged out to more than one a month. How long did this newest guy plan on sticking around?

A sudden thought came to her. "How did the hospital find this doctor so quickly?"

"This is what he does. He rotates between military hospitals, filling in…" The sound of yelling came from down the hallway, stopping Maria's explanation in its tracks. A woman headed their way, pushing a wheelchair, while the older gentleman in the seat bellowed something unintelligible, his fist shaking in the air.

"Excuse me," said the nurse, quickly moving toward the pair. She threw over her shoulder, "Chelsea's doctor is in his office. He's expecting you. Just go on in." Her attention shifted toward the agitated patient. "Mr. Ballenger, what's wrong?"

Not wanting to stand there like a gawker, Jessi stiffened her shoulders and headed in the direction Maria had indicated.

First door on the left.

All she wanted to do was skip the requisite chit-chat and go straight to Chelsea's room. But that was evidently not going to happen. Not until she met with the newest member of Chelsea's treatment team.

Feeling helpless and out of control was rapidly becoming the norm for Jessi. And she didn't like it. At all.

She stopped in front of the door and glared at the nameplate. Dr. Cordoba's credentials were still prominently displayed in the cheap gold-colored frame. The new guy really was new.

Damn, and she'd forgotten to ask the nurse his name. It didn't really matter. He'd introduce himself. So would she, and then he'd ask her how she was. That's what they always did.

Tell the truth? Or nod and say, "Fine," just like she did every other time someone asked her?

She lifted her hand and rapped on the solid wood door.

"Come in." The masculine drawl coming from within was low and gruff.

The back of her neck prickled, the sensation sweeping across her shoulders and down her arms, lifting every fine hair in its path. If she had to pick a description to pair that voice with, she'd say impatient. Or sexy. Two words you didn't want associated with an army psychiatrist. Or any psychiatrist, for that matter. And certainly not one charged with her daughter's care.

He's probably fat and bald, Jess.

Comforted by that thought, she pushed the lever down and opened the door.

He wasn't fat. Or bald.

His head was turned to the side, obscuring most of his face, but the man seated behind the gray, military-issue desk had a full head of jet-black hair, the sides short in typical army fashion, while the longer top fell casually across his forehead. Jessi spied a few strands of gray woven through the hair at his temple.

He appeared to be intently studying his computer screen. Something about his profile tugged at her, just like his voice had. She shook off the sensation, rubbing her upper arms as she continued to stand there.

He had to be pushing forty, judging from the lines beside his eyes as well as the long crease down the side of his left cheek. The result of a dimple utilized far too many times?

Something in her mind swirled back to life as if some hazy image was trying to imprint itself on her consciousness.

"Feel free to sit," he said. "I'll be with you in a minute."

She swallowed, all thoughts of new doctors and balding men fading as worry nibbled at the pit of her stomach. Was something wrong with Chelsea? She tried to open her mouth to ask, but the words were suddenly stuck in her throat. Maybe that's why Maria wouldn't quite meet her eyes. Had Chelsea made another suicide attempt? Surely the nurse would have said something had that been the case.

Pulling one of the two chairs back a few inches, she eased into it, her gaze shuffling around the room, trying to find anything that would calm her nerves.

What it landed on was the nameplate on the doctor's desk. Not Dr. Cordoba's. Instead…

Jessi froze. She blinked rapidly to clear her vision and focused on the letters again, sliding across each one individually and hoping that an *a* would somehow morph into an *e*.

Her gaze flicked back to the portion of his face she could see. Recognition roared to life this time.

She should have realized that prickling sensation hadn't been a fluke when she'd heard his voice. But she would never have dreamed…

Images of heated kisses and stolen moments in the grass beside the creek near her high school flashed through her head.

God. Clinton Marks. A ghost from her past…a rite of passage.

That's all it had been. A moment in time. And yet here he was, sitting across from her in living color.

Worse, he was evidently her daughter's new doctor. How was that possible?

Maybe he wouldn't recognize her.

When his gray eyes finally swung her way, that hope dropped like a boulder from a cliff. A momentary burst of shock crossed his face, jaw squaring, lips tightening. Then the familiar mocking smile from school appeared, and his gaze dropped to her empty ring finger.

"I should have recognized his last name," he said. "Me and Larry. Neck and neck…"

His murmured words turned their shared past into a silly nursery rhyme. His next words shattered that illusion, however. "Still married to him?"

She swallowed. "Widowed."

Larry had died in a car accident a few months after their wedding. Right after he'd discovered from a mutual friend that she'd been seen returning to the auditorium with Clint the night of graduation. He'd asked her a question she'd refused to answer, and then he'd roared off into the night, never to come home.

"I'm sorry."

Was he? She couldn't tell by looking at him. The Clinton Marks of twenty-two years ago had worn this exact same mask during high school, not letting any kind of real emotion seep through. The earring was gone, and his tattoo was evidently hidden beneath the long sleeves of his shirt, but he still projected an attitude of blasé amusement. She'd seen that mask crack one time. And that memory now kept her glued to her chair instead of storming out and demanding that the "punk" who'd slept with her and then left without a word be removed from her daughter's case immediately and replaced with someone who actually cared.

Someone who had at least a modicum of empathy.

He did.

She'd seen it.

Experienced it.

Had felt gentle fingers tunnel through her hair, palms cupping her face and blotting her tears.

She sucked down a deep breath, realizing he was waiting for a response. "Thank you. He's been gone a long time."

And so have you. She kept that to herself, however.

His gaze shifted back to something on his monitor before fastening on her face once again. "Your daughter. There's no chance that…?"

"I'm sorry?" Her sluggish brain tried to sift through his words, but right now it seemed to be misfiring.

"Chelsea. Her chart says she's twenty-one."

It clicked. What he was saying. The same question Larry had asked her before storming off: *Is the kid even mine?* Pain slashed through her all over again. "She's my husband's."

His jaw hardened further. "You didn't waste much time marrying him after I left."

She was sure it would have seemed that way to him. But Clint had been already on his way out of town. Gone long before he'd actually left. There had never been any question of him staying, and he'd used protection that night, so surely he knew Chelsea couldn't be his. But, then, condoms had been known to fail.

"You weren't coming back. You said so yourself." The fact that there was a hint of accusation in her voice didn't seem to faze him.

"No. I wasn't."

And there you had it. Clinton Marks was the same old looking-out-for-number-one boy she remembered. Only now he was packed into a man's body.

A hard, masculine body with a face capable of breaking a million hearts.

He'd broken at least one.

Only she hadn't admitted it at the time. Instead, she'd moved on with her life the day he'd left, doing everything in her power to erase the memory of that devastating night. She'd thought she'd succeeded with Larry. And she *had* loved him, in her own way. He'd been everything Clint hadn't. Kind. Dependable. Permanent.

And willing to give up his career to be with her.

Three months later they'd married, and she'd become pregnant.

And Jessi certainly loved the child she'd made with him.

In fact, that was why she was here: Chelsea.

"It was a long time ago..." Her gaze flicked to the nameplate, and she made a quick decision about how to treat this unexpected meeting. And how to address him. "Dr. Marks, if you think that what happened between two kids—and that's all we were—will hinder your ability to help my daughter—"

"Are we really going to do this, Jessi May?" His brow cocked as the name slid effortlessly past his lips. "Pretend that night never happened? I'm interested in treating Chelsea, not in making a play for you, if that's what you're worried about."

Her face heated. "Of course I'm not."

And he was making it perfectly clear that he had no more interest in her now than he had all those years ago.

"I only asked about her parentage because I would need to remove myself from her case if it turned out she was... not Larry's."

In other words, if Chelsea were his.

What a relief it must be to him that she wasn't.

What a mess. Not quite a love triangle, but almost.

There was one side missing, though. Larry had been in-fatuated with her. She'd been infatuated with Clint. And Clint had loved no one but himself.

Which brought her back to her current dilemma. "My daughter is sensitive. If she thinks you're treating her to work your way up some military ladder, you could damage her even more."

"I'm very good at what I do. And I'm not interested in going any further up the ladder."

The words weren't said with pride. In fact, there was an edge of strain behind them.

She believed him. The word *Colonel* in front of his name attested to decades of hard work. She knew from her father's days in the army that it took around twenty years to make that particular rank. Her dad had made it all the way up to general before his death five years ago.

In fact, her father was why she and Clint had wound up by the creek. When he'd realized Larry was headed for a military career her dad had gone off on her, using her mom's depression as ammunition for his position. The night of graduation had brought home all the changes that had been about to happen. Everyone she cared about had been on their way out of her life.

Only Larry had changed his mind at the last minute, inexplicably deciding to study at a local community college and take classes in agriculture instead.

Her glance went back to Clint, whose jaw still bore a hard edge of tension.

Me and Larry...neck and neck.

And Larry had stayed behind. With her.

The only one who knew about her dad besides her girlfriends was… "Oh, my God. You told him, didn't you? You told Larry about my father."

He didn't deny it. He didn't even blink. "How is he? Your father?"

"He's gone. He died five years ago." The pain in her chest grew. They may never have seen eye to eye about a lot of things, but she'd loved the man. And in spite of his shortcomings, he'd been a tower of strength after Larry had died and she'd been left alone, pregnant and grieving.

"I'm sorry." Clint reached across the desk to cover her hand with his. "Your mom?"

"She's okay. Worried about Chelsea. Just like I am."

He pulled back and nodded. "Let's discuss your daughter, then."

"The nurse said you've already seen her, and you've read her chart, so you know what she tried to do."

"Let's talk about that, and then we'll see her together." He pulled a yellow legal pad from a drawer of his desk and laid it in front of him. He was neat, she'd give him that, and it surprised her. Around ten pencils, all sharpened to fine points, were lined up side by side, and a single good-quality pen was at the end of the row. Nothing else adorned the stark surface of his desk, other than his nameplate and his computer monitor. So very different from the scruffy clothes and longish hair she remembered from their school days. And she'd bet those motorcycle boots were long gone, probably replaced by some kind of shiny dress shoes.

Maybe that had all been an act. Because the man she saw in front of her was every bit as disciplined as her father had been.

She shook herself, needing to gather her wits.

The only thing she should be thinking about was the here and now...and how the Clint of today could or couldn't help her daughter.

What had happened between them was in the past. It

was over. And, as Clint had said, what they should be concentrating on was Chelsea.

So that's what Jessi was going to do.

If, for some reason, she judged that he couldn't help in her daughter's recovery, then she would call, write letters, parade in front of the hospital with picket signs, if necessary. And she would keep on doing it, until someone found her a doctor who could.

CHAPTER TWO

CLINT FORCED HIMSELF to stare over her shoulder rather than at the mouthwatering jiggle of her ass. The woman was no longer the stick-thin figure he'd known once upon a time. Instead, she boasted soft curves that flowed down her body like gentle ocean swells and made his hands itch to mold and explore.

Forget it, jerk. You're here for one thing only. To help Jessi's daughter and others like her.

No one had been more shocked than he'd been to realize the beautiful woman sitting across from him, worry misting her deep green eyes, was none other than the girl he'd lusted after in school.

The one he'd kissed in a rare moment of weakness, her tears triggering every protective instinct in his body.

The woman he'd handed off to the boy she'd really wanted—the one she'd married.

Unfortunately for Clint, he still didn't seem to be immune to her even after all these years.

He'd wanted to protect her.

Only he hadn't been able to back then. He couldn't now.

The only thing he could do was his job.

They reached Chelsea's room, and he shoved aside a new ache in his gut. The one that had struck when he'd realized the young woman's age was close enough to a certain deadly encounter to make him wonder whose she was.

Three months earlier and this story could have had a different ending.

No. It couldn't.

He'd done what he'd had to do back then—left—and he had no regrets.

Jessi glanced back and caught his look, her brows arching in question.

Okay, maybe he had one regret.

But it was too late to do anything about that now.

His fingers tightened on Chelsea's chart, and he started to push through the door, but Jessi stopped him. "I've been hearing things about the VA hospitals, Clint. You need to know up front that if I feel like she's not getting the treatment she needs here, I'll put her somewhere else."

His insides turned into a hard ball. He cared about his patients. All of them. No matter what the bean counters in Washington recommended or the hospital administration at whatever unit he was currently assigned to said or did, he treated his patients as if they were his comrades in arms…which they were. "It doesn't matter what you've heard. As long as I'm here, she'll get the best I have."

"But what if the hospital rules tell you to—?"

One side of his mouth went up. "Jessi May, always worried about something. Since when have you known me to play by anyone's rules?" A question they both knew the answer to, since he'd challenged almost every regulation their high school had been able to come up with.

"Would you please stop calling me that?"

His smile widened. "Is it a rule?"

"No." Her whole demeanor softened, and she actually laughed. "Because it'll just make you worse."

"I rest my case."

A nurse walked down the hallway, throwing them a curious look and reminding him of the serious issues Jessi was facing.

He took a step back. "Are you ready?"

"I think so."

Clint entered the room first, holding the door open for her.

Sitting in a chair by the window, his patient stared out across the lawn, not even acknowledging their presence. Hell, how could he not have seen the resemblance between the two women?

Chelsea had the same blond hair, the same pale, haunted features that her mother had once had. Only there was no way the young woman before him today could have survived basic training while maintaining that raw edge of vulnerability, so it was new. A result of her PTSD.

It affected people differently. Some became wounded and tortured, lashing out at themselves.

And some became impulsive and angry. Hitting out at others.

Clint wasn't sure which was worse, although as a teenager with a newly broken pinkie finger, he could have told you right off which he preferred.

Only he'd never told anyone about his finger. Or about his father.

And when he'd found Jessi crying outside the school building because of something her own father had done… he'd thought the worst. Only to have relief sweep through his system when it had been something completely different.

He drew a careful breath. "Hi, Chelsea. Do you remember me from earlier today?"

No reaction. The waif by the window continued to stare.

He glanced at her chart again to remind himself of the medications Dr. Cordoba had prescribed.

He made a note to lower the dosage to see if it had any effect. He wanted to help Chelsea cope, not turn her into a zombie.

Jessi went over to her daughter and dropped to her knees, taking the young woman's hands in hers and looking up at her. "Hi, sweetheart. How are you?"

"I want to go home." The words were soft. So soft, Clint almost missed them.

Jessi hadn't, though. Her chin wobbled for a second, before she drew her spine up. "I want that, too, baby. More than anything. But you're not ready. You know you're not."

"I know." The response was just as soft. She turned to look back out the window, as if tuning out anything that didn't get her what she wanted.

Clint knew Chelsea's reaction was a defense mechanism, but having her own daughter shut her out had to shred Jessi's insides even though she was absolutely doing what was right for Chelsea.

He pulled up a chair and sat in front of the pair, forcing himself to keep his attention focused on his patient and not her mother. "I'm going to adjust some of your medications, Chelsea. Would that be okay?"

The girl sighed, but she did turn her head slightly to acknowledge she'd heard him. "Whatever you think is best."

He spent fifteen minutes watching the pair interact, making notes and comparing his observations with what he'd read of her past behavior.

She'd slashed her wrists. Jessi had found her bleeding in the bathtub and had fashioned tourniquets out of two scarves—quick thinking that had saved her daughter's life.

A couple of pints of blood later, they'd avoided permanent brain and organ damage.

Unfortunately, the infusion hadn't erased the emotional damage that had come about as a result of what her chart said was months spent in captivity.

Trauma—any trauma—had to be processed mentally and emotionally. Some people seemed to escape unscathed, letting the memory of the event roll off their backs. Others were crushed beneath it.

And others pretended they didn't give a damn.

Even when they did.

Like him?

Jessi had coaxed Chelsea over to the bed and sat next to her, arm draped around her shoulders, still talking to her softly. He got up and laid a hand on her shoulder.

"I'll give you a few minutes. Stop in and talk to me before you leave the hospital." He didn't add the word *okay* or allow his voice to change tone at the end of the phrase, because he didn't want to make it seem like a request. Not because he wasn't sure she'd honor it, but part of him wondered if she'd head back to the front desk and demand to have another doctor assigned to the case.

Clint had to somehow break the tough news to Jessi that she was stuck with him for the next couple of months or for however long Chelsea was here. There just wasn't anyone else.

So it was up to him to convince her that he could help her daughter, if she gave him a chance. Not hard, since he believed it himself. Clint had dealt with all types of soldiers in crisis, both male and female, something Dr. Cordoba had not. It was part of the reason Clint had agreed to this assignment. His rotations didn't keep him anywhere for more than six months at a time. Surely that would be long enough to treat Chelsea or at least come up with a plan for how to proceed.

If he'd known one of Dr. Cordoba's toughest cases was

Jessi Spencer's daughter, though, he wouldn't have been quite so quick to agree to return to his hometown.

Being here was dangerous on a number of levels.

Jessi's not the girl you once knew.

He sensed it. She was stronger than she'd been in school. She'd had to be after being widowed at a young age and raising a daughter on her own. And according to the listing on Chelsea's chart, Jessi was now an ER physician. You didn't deal with trauma cases all day long without having a cast-iron stomach and a tough emotional outlook.

He'd seen a touch of that toughness in his office. Her eyes had studied him, but had given nothing away, unlike the Jessi of his past, who'd worn her heart on her sleeve.

Just as well. He was here to treat the daughter, not take up where he'd left off with the mother. Not that he'd "left off" with her. He'd had a one-night stand and had then made sure her beau had known that to win her heart he had to be willing to give up his dreams for her.

Evidently he had.

That was one thing Clint wouldn't do. For anyone.

If he could just keep that in mind for the next couple of months, he'd be home free. And if he was able to help Chelsea get the help she needed while he was at it, that was icing on the cake.

He corrected himself. No, not just the icing. It was the whole damn cake. And that was what he needed to focus on.

Anything else would be a big mistake.

"And how long will that be?" Jessi's mouth opened, then snapped back shut, before trying again. "I don't want Chelsea's next doctor to give up on her like..."

Her voice faded away as the reality of what she'd been

about to say swept through her: *Like Dr. Cordoba did. Like Chelsea's father did when he took off into the night.*

"Are you talking about Dr. Cordoba?"

She blinked. Had he read her mind? "Yes."

"He didn't give up on her." His voice softened. "His wife is very ill. He had to take a job that allows him to be home with her as much as possible. He couldn't do that and continue working long hours here. He knew his patients deserved more than that."

Oh, God. Her ire at the other doctor dissolved in a heartbeat. She'd been so caught up in her own problems that she hadn't even stopped to think that maybe he had been dealing with things that were every bit as bad as hers were. Maybe even worse. "I…" She swallowed. "I don't know what to say. I'm so sorry."

The events of the past months were suddenly too much for her, and her heart pounded, her stomach churned.

Please, no. Not now.

She'd had two panic attacks since Chelsea's hospitalization, so she recognized the signs.

Pressing a hand to her middle, she tried to force back the nausea and took a few careful breaths.

"I thought you should know." Clint leaned forward. "If you're worried about me suddenly taking off, don't be. I'll give you plenty of notice."

This time.

The words hung in the air between them, and for a horrible, soul-stealing second she thought he was hinting for her not to get her hopes up.

"I'm not expecting you to stay forever." The sensation in her chest and stomach grew, heat crawling up her neck and making her ears ring. Her vision narrowed to a pinpoint. And then it was too late to stop it. "I think I'm going…"

She lurched to her feet and somehow made it through

the door and to the first stall in the restroom before her gut revolted in a violent spasm, and she threw up. She'd been running on coffee and pure adrenaline for the past several weeks, and she hadn't eaten breakfast that morning. The perfect set-up for an attack.

That had to be the reason. Not finding Clint sitting behind that desk.

Again and again, her stomach heaved, mingling with tears of frustration.

When she finally regained control over herself, she flushed the toilet with shaking hands before going to the sink, bending down to rinse her mouth and splash water over her face. She blindly reached for the paper-towel dispenser, only to have some kind of cloth pressed into her hand.

Holding the fabric tightly to her face and wishing she could blot away the past two months as easily as the moisture, she sucked down a couple more slow breaths, her heart rate finally slowing to some semblance of normality.

"Thank you." She lifted her head, already knowing who she'd find when she opened her eyes. "You shouldn't be in here."

"Why? Because it's against the rules? I thought we'd already sorted all that out." He added a smile. "Besides, I wanted to make sure you were okay."

The words swirled with bitter familiarity through her head. They were the same ones he'd said the night of their high-school graduation ceremony when she'd suddenly veered away from the rows of chairs and rushed out into the parking lot and then down to a nearby creek. Thankfully neither her dad nor mom had seen her. And an hour and a half later, when the ceremony had been over and the reception had been in full swing, she'd returned. With the

lie that Clint had told her to use trembling on her tongue…
that she'd been sick with nerves.

Her dad had bought it, just like Clint had said he would.

Only when she'd said it, it had no longer been a lie, because she had felt sick. Not because of nerves, but because
the boy she'd always wanted—the boy she'd lost her virginity to—would soon be on his way to the airport, headed
for boot camp. Leaving her behind forever.

"It's just the shock of everything."

"I know."

She shivered and wrapped her arms around herself.
Clint made no effort to take off his jacket and drape it
around her. It was a good thing, because she'd probably
dissolve into a puddle all over again if he did.

"Have you eaten recently?"

"What?"

"I get the feeling you're running on fumes along with a
heaped dose of stress. Which is probably why—" he nodded at the closed stall "—that just happened."

Leave it to him to point out the obvious. "I can eat later."

He nodded. "Yes. Or you could eat while we go over
some treatment options. I skipped breakfast this morning
and could use something, as well. Besides, some carbs will
help settle your stomach."

Before she knew it, she found herself in the hospital
cafeteria with a toasted bagel and a cup of juice sitting in
front of her.

A hint of compassion in his voice as he detailed the
treatments he'd like to try told her this wasn't going to be
an easy fix. It was something Chelsea would be dealing
with for the rest of her life. He just wanted to give her the
tools she needed to do that successfully.

It was what Jessie wanted, as well. More than anything.
As a mom, she wanted to be able to make things better, to

take away her daughter's pain. But she couldn't. She had to trust that Clint knew what he was doing.

He certainly sounded capable.

"And what if she tries to do something to herself?" She set the bagel back down on the plate, unable to leave the subject alone.

"I'll take steps to avoid the possibility." He steepled his fingers and met her gaze with a steadiness that unnerved her. The man was intimidating, even though she knew he wasn't trying to be. Despite his reassurances, she still wasn't convinced Clint was the man for the job. Especially considering their history—which, granted, wasn't much of one. On his side, anyway.

What other option did she have, though? An institution? Bring her home and hope Chelsea didn't try to take her life again?

No. She couldn't risk there being a next time.

She'd do anything it took to help bring her daughter back from wherever she was. That included seeing Clint every day for the rest of her life and reliving what they'd done by the bank of that creek.

Decision made.

"I want you to keep me informed of every move you make."

One brow quirked. Too late she realized he could have taken her words the wrong way. But he didn't throw a quick comeback, like he might have done in days gone by. Instead, he simply said the words she needed to hear most: "Don't worry, Jessi. Even if we have to break every rule in the book, we're going to pull her through this."

And as much as the word *we* made something inside her tingle to life, it was that other statement that reached out and grabbed her. The one that said the old Clint was still crouched inside that standard issue haircut and neat-as-a-pin desk. It was there in his eyes. The glowing intensity that said, despite outward appearances, he hadn't turned into a heartless bureaucrat after years of going through proper channels.

He was a rule-breaker. He always had been. And just like his bursting into the ladies' restroom unannounced, it gave her hope, along with a sliver of fear.

She knew from experience he wasn't afraid to break anything that got in the way of what he wanted. She just had to make sure one of those "things" wasn't her heart.

CHAPTER THREE

Jᴇꜱꜱɪ ʜᴀᴅ ᴊᴜꜱᴛ finished suturing an elbow laceration and was headed in to pick up her next chart when a cry of pain came from the double bay doors of the emergency entrance.

"Ow! It hurts!"

A man holding a little girl in his arms lurched into the waiting area, his face as white as the linoleum flooring beneath his feet. The child's frilly pink party dress had a smear of dirt along one side of it, as did her arm and one side of her face. That had Jessi moving toward the pair. The other cases in the waiting room at the moment were minor illnesses and injuries.

The man's wild eyes latched on to her, taking in the stethoscope around her neck. "Are you a doctor?"

"Yes. How can I help?"

"We were at a… She fell…" The words tumbled out of his mouth, nothing making sense. Especially since the girl's pained cries were making the already stricken expression on his face even worse.

She tried to steer him in the right direction. "She fell. Is this your daughter?"

"Yes. She fell off a trampoline at a friend's house. It's her leg."

Like with many fun things about childhood—climbing

trees, swimming in the lake, riding a bike—danger lurked around every corner, ready to strike.

Jessi brushed a mass of blond curls off the girl's damp face and spoke to her. "What's your name?"

"Tammy," she said between sobs.

She maintained eye contact with her little charge. "Tammy, I know your leg must hurt terribly. We're going to take you back and help fix it." She motioned to one of the nurses behind the admission's desk. Gina immediately came toward them with a clipboard.

The girl nodded, the volume of her cries going down a notch.

"Let's take her into one of the exam rooms, while Nurse Stanley gets some information."

It wasn't standard protocol—they were supposed to register all admissions unless there was a life-threatening injury—but right now Jessi wanted to take away not only the child's pain but the father's, as well.

Maybe Clint wasn't the only one who knew how to break a few rules.

But she had to. She recognized that look of utter terror and helplessness on the dad's face. She'd felt the same paralyzing fear as she'd crouched in the bathtub with her daughter, blood pouring out of Chelsea's veins. She'd sent out that same cry for help. To God. To the universe. To anyone who would listen.

And like the distraught father following her to a treatment room, she'd been forced to place her child in the hands of a trained professional and pray they could fix whatever was wrong. Because it was something beyond her own capabilities.

But what if it was also beyond the abilities of the people you entrusted them to?

Raw fear pumped back into her chest, making her lungs ache.

Stop it.

She banished Clint and Chelsea from her thoughts and concentrated on her job. This little girl needed her, and she had to have her head in the game if she wanted to help her.

"Which leg is it?" she asked the father.

"Her right. It's her shin."

"Did she fall on the ground? Or which part of the trampoline?"

She asked question after question, gathering as much information as she could in order to narrow the steps she'd need to take to determine the exact nature of the injury.

Gina followed them into the room and was already writing furiously, even though the nurse hadn't voiced a single question. That could come later.

"Set her on the table."

As soon as cold metal touched the girl's leg, she let out an ear-piercing shriek that quickly melted back into sobs.

As a mother, it wrenched at her heart, but Jessi couldn't let any of that affect what she did next. Things would get worse for Tammy before they got better, because Jessi had to make sure she knew what she was dealing with.

"Gina, can you stay and get the rest of the information from Mr...?" She paused and glanced at the girl's father.

"Lawrence. Jack Lawrence."

"Thank you." She turned back to her nurse. "Can you do that while I call Radiology?"

Once she'd made the call, she made short work of getting the girl's vitals, talking softly to her as she went about her job. When she slid the girl's dress up a little way, she spied a dark blue contusion forming along her shin and saw a definite deformation of the tibia. The bone had separated.

Whether they could maneuver the ends back in place without surgery would depend on what the X-rays showed.

Within fifteen minutes, one of the radiology techs had whisked the five-year-old down the hall on a stretcher, her father following close behind. His expression had gone from one of fear to hope. Sometimes just knowing it wasn't all up to you as a parent, that there were others willing to pitch in, made a little of the weight roll off your shoulders.

So why did she still feel buried beneath tons of rubble?

Because Chelsea's injury went beyond the physical to the very heart of who she was. And Jessi wasn't sure Clint—or anyone else—could repair it. There was no splint or cast known to man that could heal a broken spirit.

A half hour later Tammy and her father were back in the exam room, and an orthopedist had arrived to take over the case. The urge to bend down and kiss the little girl's cheek came and went. She held back a little smile. She didn't need to break *all* the rules. Some of them were there for a reason.

Hopefully, Clint knew which ones to follow and which ones to break.

He did. She sensed it.

He wouldn't go beyond certain professional boundaries. Which meant he would try to keep their past in the past. If one of them stepped over the line, he'd remove himself from Chelsea's case.

Should she talk to Chelsea about what had happened down at the creek—tell her she'd gone to school with Clint? Not necessary. He appeared to have a plan. Besides, if she heaped anything else on her daughter, she might hunker further down into whatever foxhole she'd dug for herself. She needed to give Clint enough time to do his job.

"Jessi?" Gina, the nurse from the earlier, caught her just

as she was leaving her patient's room. "You have a phone call on line two."

"Okay, thanks." It must be her mom, confirming their dinner date for tonight. She'd promised to update her on Chelsea's condition, something that made her feel ill. With her father gone, Jessi and Chelsea were all her mother had left. And though her mother was no longer taking antidepressants, she'd been forgetful lately, which Jessi hoped was just from the stress of her only granddaughter's illness.

Going to the reception desk, she picked up the phone and punched the lit button. "Hello?"

Instead of the bright, happy tones of her mother, she encountered something a couple of octaves lower. "Jess?"

She gulped. "Yes?"

"Clint here."

As if she hadn't already recognized the sound of his voice. Still, her heart leaped with fear. "Is something wrong with Chelsea?"

"No. Do you have a minute? I'd like to take care of some scheduling."

"Scheduling?"

A low, incredibly sexy-sounding hum came through the phone that made something curl in her belly.

"I want us to talk every day."

"Every day?"

About Chelsea, you idiot! And what was with repeating everything he said?

"Yes. Our schedules are probably both hectic, but we can do it by phone, if necessary."

"Oh. Okay." Was he saying he didn't want to meet with her in person? That he'd rather do all of this by phone? She had no idea, but she read off her schedule for the next five days.

A grunt of affirmation came back, along with, "I'll also want to meet with you and Chelsea together."

"Why?"

"Didn't Dr. Cordoba have family sessions with you?"

She shook her head, only realizing afterwards that he couldn't see it. "No, although he mentioned wanting to try that further down the road."

"I believe in getting the family involved as soon as possible, since you'll be the one working with her once she's discharged."

Discharged. The most beautiful word Chelsea had heard in weeks. And Clint made it sound like a reality, rather than just a vague possibility. So he really was serious about doing everything he could to make sure treatment was successful.

A wave of gratitude came over her and a knot formed in her throat. "Thank you, Clint. For being willing to break the rules."

Was she talking about with Chelsea? Or about their time together all those years ago.

"You're welcome, Jess. For what it's worth, I think Chelsea is very lucky to have you."

Her next words came out before she was aware of them forming in her head. But she meant them with all her heart. "Ditto, Clint. I think Chelsea and I are the lucky ones."

"I'll call you."

With that intimate-sounding promise, he said goodbye, and the phone clicked in her ear, telling her he'd hung up. She gripped the receiver as tightly as she could, all the while praying she was doing the right thing. She was about to allow Clint back into her orbit—someone who'd once carried her to the peak of ecstasy and then tossed her into the pit of despair without a second glance. But what choice did she have, really?

She firmed her shoulders. No, there was always a choice. She may have made the wrong one when she'd been on the cusp of womanhood, but she was smarter now. Stronger. She could—and would—keep her emotions in check. If not for her own sake, then for her daughter's.

CHAPTER FOUR

THE FIRST FAMILY counseling session was gearing up to be a royal disaster.

Jessi came sliding into Clint's office thirty minutes late, out of breath, face flushed, wispy strands of hair escaping from her clip.

He swallowed back a rush of emotion. She'd looked just like this as she'd stood to her feet after they'd made love. He'd helped her brush her hair back into place, combing his fingers through the strands and wishing life could be different for him.

But it couldn't. Not then. And not now.

"Sorry. We had an emergency at the hospital, and I had to stay and help."

"No problem." He stood. "I have another patient in a half hour, so we'll need to make this a quick session."

"Poor Chelsea. I feel awful. I'm off tomorrow, though, so I'll come and spend the day with her."

When they walked into Chelsea's room, the first thing he noticed was that the lunch she'd been served an hour ago was still on a tray in front of her, untouched. At the sight of them, though, she seemed to perk up in her seat, shoveling a bite of mashed potatoes into her mouth and making a great show of chewing.

Manipulating. He'd seen signs of it earlier when he'd

tried to coax her to talk about things that didn't involve the weather.

Her throat worked for a second with the food still pouched inside one cheek. She ended up having to wash the potatoes down with several gulps of water. She sat there, breathing as hard as her mother had been when she'd arrived a few moments ago.

"Enjoying your meal?" he asked, forcing his voice to remain blasé. So much for showing Jessi how good he was at his job.

As if this was even about him.

He ground his teeth as his frustration shifted to himself.

Chelsea shrugged. Another bite went in—albeit a much smaller one this time.

Not polite to talk with my mouth full, was the inference.

Well, she'd run out of the stuff eventually. And since she was pretty thin already, he was all for anything that would get food into her system. That was one of the comments on the sheet in her file. She didn't eat much, unless someone wanted to interact with her in some way. The staff had taken to coming to her room and loitering around, straightening things and making small talk. It was a surefire way to get that fork moving from plate to mouth.

He decided to give her a little more time.

Jessi stood there, looking a little lost by her daughter's lack of greeting. He sent her a nod of reassurance and motioned her to sit in one of the two nearby chairs and joined her.

"Let's go ahead and get started, if that's okay with you, Chelsea."

Chew, chew, chew.

She moved on to her green beans without a word. Okay, if that's the way she wanted to play it, he'd go right along with it.

He turned to Jessi, sorry for what he was about to do, but if anything could break through her daughter's wall it might be having to face some hard, unpleasant subjects. "Since Chelsea's busy, why don't you tell me what led her to being here."

Right on cue, Jessi's eyes widened. "You mean about the day I called…"

"Yes."

Her throat moved a couple of times, swallowing, probably her way of either building up the courage to talk about the suicide attempt or to refuse.

"Well, I—I called Chelsea's cell phone to let her know I was coming home early. It rang and rang before finally going over to voice mail. I was going to stop and pick up some Thai food—her favorite…" Jessi's eyes filled with tears. "I decided to go straight home instead, so we could go out to eat together. When I got there… Wh-when I got to the house, I—"

"Stop." Chelsea's voice broke through, though she was still staring down, a green bean halfway to her mouth. "Don't make her talk about it."

Whether the young woman wanted to spare her mother's feelings or her own, Clint wasn't sure. "What would you like to discuss instead, then?"

There was a long pause. Then she said, "What you hope to accomplish by keeping me here."

"It's not about us, Chelsea. It's about you."

"Where's Dr. Cordoba?" Her head finally came up, and her gaze settled on him.

"He went to work somewhere else."

"Because of me." The words came out as a whisper.

Clint shook his head. "No, of course not. He made the decision for personal reasons. It had nothing to do with you."

Jessi's chest rose and fell as she took a quick breath. "We all just want to help, honey."

"Everything I touch turns to ashes."

"No." Jessi glanced at him, then scooted closer to her daughter, reaching out to stroke her hair. "You've been through a lot in the past several months, but you're not alone."

"I am, Mom. You have no idea. You all think I'm suffering from PTSD, because of my time in that camp, don't you? Dr. Cordoba did. But I'm not."

Clint glanced at Jessi, a frown on his face. "You tried to take your life, Chelsea. Something made you think life wasn't worth living."

The girl's shoulders slumped.

"Does this have to do with your pregnancy?"

Two sets of female eyes settled on him in shock.

Hell. Jessi hadn't known?

It was right there in Chelsea's medical chart that her physical exam had revealed she'd given birth or had had a miscarriage at some point. He'd just assumed...

His patient went absolutely rigid. "I want her to leave. Now."

"But, Chelsea..." Jessi's voice contained a note of pleading.

"Now." The girl's voice rose in volume. "Now, now. *Now!*"

Jessi careened back off her chair and stumbled from the room as her daughter's wails turned to full-fledged screams of pain. She was tearing at her hair, her food flung across the room. Clint pressed the call button for the nurse and between the two of them they were able to administer a sedative, putting an end to Chelsea's hysterical shrieks. Her muscles finally went limp and her eyes closed. He stood staring down at her bed for a few moments, a feeling of unease settling over him as it had each time he'd met with Chelsea. There was something here. Something more than what was revealed in her records.

And it involved that pregnancy. She'd been calm until the moment the subject had come up.

It was time to do a little more digging. But for now he had to go out there and face Jessi. And somehow come up with something to say that wouldn't make things worse than they already were.

"I didn't know."

Clint came toward her as she leaned against the wall twenty feet away from Chelsea's door. Her stomach had roiled within her as the nurse had rushed into the room and the screams had died down to moans, before finally fading away to nothing. All she wanted to do was throw up, just like she had during a previous visit, but she somehow held it together this time.

"I'm sorry, Jess." Clint scrubbed a hand through his hair, not touching her. "I'd assumed she told you."

"She hasn't told me anything. Could it have been while she was a prisoner?"

"I'm not sure. This is the most emotion I've seen from her in the past week. We hit a nerve, though. So that's a good thing."

"I can't imagine what she went through." She leaned her head against the wall and stared at the ceiling.

Chelsea's convoy had been ambushed during a night patrol by enemy forces disguised as police officers. The group had been held for four months. Chelsea had said they'd all been separated and interrogated, but she'd had no idea one of the prisoners had died until she and the rest of those rescued had been flown home.

Jessi sighed and turned back to look at him. "The army

debriefed her, but I was never told what she said, and I—I was afraid to press her too much. She seemed to be doing fine. Maybe that in itself was a warning sign."

"There was no way you could have known what she was going to do." Clint pushed a strand of hair off her cheek.

She wasn't sure she could stand seeing her daughter in this much pain week after week. And a pregnancy...

Had her daughter been raped during her captivity? The army had said there was no evidence of that, but then again Chelsea wasn't exactly a fount of information. "I think I'm doing more harm than good by going in there with you."

"Let's see how it goes for the next week, okay? Chelsea was admitted under a suicide watch. That gives you permission to make decisions regarding her health care. She could still open up."

"She doesn't even want me here, Clint. You heard her." Jessi's head still reverberated with her daughter's cries for her to get out.

"That was the shock talking. She didn't expect me to ask that particular question. At least she's getting it out, rather than bottling it all up inside."

His eyes narrowed as he looked at her face. "How long's it been since you've done something that hasn't revolved around your job or Chelsea?"

She thought for a second. "I can't remember."

"The last thing she needs is for you to break down as well, which is where you're headed if you don't take some down time."

She knew he was right. She'd felt like she'd been standing on the edge of a precipice for weeks now, with no way to back away from it.

Before she could say anything, he went on. "You said you're off tomorrow. Why don't you go out and do something fun? Something you enjoy?"

"I need to spend the day here with Chelsea."

"No. You don't. She'll understand. It might not be a bad idea to give her a day to think through what just happened."

She hesitated. "I don't even know what I'd do." Chelsea might need a day to think, but the last thing Jessi wanted to do was sit at home and let her brain wander down dark paths.

"Tell you what. I don't have anything pressing tomorrow. Why don't we do something together? It's fair season. There's probably something going on in one of the nearby counties."

"Oh, but I couldn't. Chelsea—"

"Will be fine."

Conflicting emotions swept through her. The possibility of spending the day with Clint dangled before her in a way that was far too attractive. "I'm not sure…"

"Is it because I'm her doctor?"

"Yes." He'd given her the perfect excuse, and she grabbed at it with both hands.

"That can be remedied."

Panic sizzled through her. He'd hinted once before that he might drop her daughter's case.

"No. I want you."

He paused, then shook his head and dragged his fingertips across her cheek. "Then you have to take care of yourself."

She nodded, unable to look away from his eyes as they locked on her face. Several emotions flicked through them, none of them decipherable.

"I'll try."

"How about I check the local schedules and see if I can find something for us to do? Something that doesn't involve a hospital."

Guilt rose in her throat, but at a warning glance from him she forced it back down. "Okay."

He nodded and let his hand fall back to his side. "Are you going to be okay tonight?"

Was he asking her that as a psychiatrist or as a man?

It didn't matter. The last thing she wanted was to jeopardize her working relationship with the one man who might be able to get through to her daughter. She needed to keep this impersonal. Professional. Even though his touch brought back a whole lot of emotions she hadn't felt in twenty-two years.

But she had to keep them firmly locked away. Somehow.

"I'll be fine. Just call if there's any change, okay?" She was proud of the amount of conviction she'd inserted into her voice.

"I will. I'm off at ten, but the hospital knows how to reach me if there's a problem." He took a card from his desk and wrote something on the back of it, then handed it to her. "I'll give you a yell in the morning, but until then, here's my cell phone number. Call me if you need me."

If you need me.

Terrifying words, because she already did. More than she should. But she wouldn't call. No matter how much that little voice inside her said to do just that.

CHAPTER FIVE

CLINT STEPPED ONTO the first row of metal bleachers and held his hand out for her. Grasping his fingers, and letting him maneuver through the crowd of seated spectators, they went to the very top, where a metal brace across the end provided a place for their backs to rest.

She watched the next horse in line prance into the arena, ears pricked forward in anticipation. Three fifty-five-gallon drums had been laid out to form a familiar triangle.

Barrel racing.

The speed event looked deceptively easy, but if a horse knocked over a barrel as it went around it, the rider received a five-second penalty, enough to cost a winning ribbon.

"I used to do this, you know. Run barrels."

"I know you did."

Her head swiveled to look at the man sitting next to her, completely missing the horse's take-off.

"You did?"

He smiled. "I came to the fair on occasion. Watched a few of the 4-H events."

The thought of Clint sitting on one of these very bleachers, watching her compete, was unnerving. How would she have missed him with the way he'd dressed back then? He hadn't exactly looked the part of an emerging cowboy.

Exactly. She would have noticed him.

Which meant he'd never actually seen her race. She settled back into place.

"I didn't realize you were interested in 4-H."

His gaze went back to the arena. "I wasn't."

Something about the way he'd said that…

"Do you still have your trophy?" He was still looking straight ahead, thankfully, but her gasp sounded like a gunshot to her ears, despite the noise going on around her.

The metal brace behind her groaned as more people leaned against it. Jessi eased some of her weight off it.

"How did you know I…?" She'd only won one trophy in all her years of entering the event.

"I happened to be in the vicinity that day."

How did one *happen* to be in the vicinity of the fair? It spanned a large area. And the horse arena wasn't exactly next to the carnival rides or food.

"You saw me run?"

"I saw a lot of people compete."

Okay, that explained it. "So you came out to all the horse events?"

"Not all of them. I had a few friends who did different things."

Like run barrels? She didn't think so. Neither did she remember him hanging out with any of her 4-H friends. And the only year she'd won the event had been as a high school senior.

The next horse—a splashy brown and white paint—came in, and she fixed her attention on it, although her mind was going at a million miles an hour. The rider directed the horse in a tight circle near the starting area and then let him go. The animal's neck stretched forward as he raced toward the first barrel, tail streaming out behind him.

"Here!" the rider called as they reached the drum, using

her voice along with her hands and legs to guide the horse around the turn. She did the same for the second and third barrels and then the pair raced back in a straight line until they crossed where the automatic timer was set up. Nineteen point two three seconds.

The announcer repeated the time, adding that it put the horse and rider into second place.

Clint leaned closer, his scent washing over her at almost exactly the same time as his arm brushed hers. The dual assault made her mind blank out for a second. So much so that she almost missed his question. "I always wondered. Why do some of them start with the left barrel rather than the one on the right?"

Play it cool, Jessi.

"B-because horses have a dominant side, kind of like being right- or left-handed."

"Interesting. So your horse was right-handed?"

She swallowed. So he *had* seen her. She'd hoped maybe he'd heard that she'd won from a friend, rather than having been there in the flesh. What did it matter? So he'd seen her race. No big deal.

But it was. And she had no idea why.

"Yes, she was."

Neither of the next two horses beat the time of the leader. Despite her wariness at coming out today, and her horror at realizing he'd watched her the day of her win, she could feel the muscles in her body relaxing. He'd been right to suggest she take a day off.

A *real* day off.

"Do you think Chelsea—?"

"The hospital will call me if they need me. We're both off duty today."

She frowned. "She's my daughter, Clint. I can't help but worry about her."

"I'm not asking you to put her from your mind. I'm asking you to enjoy your day. It's what she would want."

She sighed. "She did seem happy when I told her where I was going." Jessi had insisted on stopping to see Chelsea before they'd left, although she hadn't told her that she and Clint were going together.

"Exactly." He bumped her with his shoulder again. "And she's probably going to ask what you did. So let's make it good."

Jessi's eyes widened. How was she supposed to respond to that?

She was still trying to figure it out when she heard a weird screech of metal, then Clint's arm was suddenly behind her, crushing her tightly against him.

"Hold on!"

She thought at first it was because a new horse had started the course, but then she sensed something falling, followed by screams.

When she glanced back, she saw that the metal support had broken free—probably from the weight of everyone leaning against it—and was dangling from the far side of the bleachers. And on the ground...

Oh, Lord. Fifteen feet below them were five people who'd evidently tumbled backward off the top seat when the structure had given way. Others were now on their feet in a panic, trying to rush down the stands to get to the ground. One person tripped and landed on another spectator a few rows down.

"Stay here," Clint muttered.

Like hell. "I'm coming with you. I'm a doctor, too, remember?"

Someone in the judges' booth called over the loudspeakers, asking for everyone to remain calm. And also asking for medical assistance.

Clint cautiously made his way down, trying to make sure he didn't trample on anyone, and again holding her hand as he took one step at a time.

By the time they reached the bottom they could hear a siren that cut off just as it reached the wide dirt aisle that separated the main arena from campers and horse trailers. The crowd opened a path to let it through.

One of the victims was now on her feet and waving away offers for help. Another person had disappeared, evidently also unhurt. But the remaining three were still on the ground, although one was sitting up, holding his leg.

"I'm a doctor," Clint said to him. "Can you hold on for a minute while we check the others?"

"Go," the man said, his thin, wiry frame and rugged clothing suggesting he was a farmer or someone who worked with livestock.

Jessi motioned that she'd take the far patient, a woman who was on her side, moaning, while Clint took the last remaining patient, a child, who was writhing on the ground and crying. They pushed through layers of people who wanted to help.

"I'm a doctor, let me through," she said to a man who was kneeling next to the woman. The man backed up to make room in the tight circle.

The EMT vehicle stopped and two medical workers jumped from the back just as Jessi crouched near her patient. The woman was conscious but obviously in a lot of pain.

"Where does it hurt?"

"Brandi," she gasped, ignoring the question and trying to roll onto her back, only to stop with a moan. "My daughter. Where's Brandi?"

Jessi glanced to the side, but couldn't see Clint through

the bodies of onlookers, but his patient had looked to be a little girl.

"How old is your daughter?"

"She…she's five. Pink shorts." Talking was an obvious struggle for her.

That had to be Clint's patient.

"Someone's helping her right now. Where does it hurt?"

"M-My ribs. It hurts to breathe."

Jessi did a quick rundown of the woman's vitals. Everything seemed good, except for a marked tenderness on her right side. "Did you hit your head at all?"

"No. Just landed flat on my side. I couldn't get up."

One of the emergency services workers knelt beside her. "What have you got?"

Jessi glanced at the man, who looked to be almost as young as Chelsea. "Possible rib fractures." She read off the woman's vitals. "How's the little girl next to us?"

"Fractured wrist, but she looks good to go."

Jessi's patient broke down in tears. "Is that her? My daughter?"

It was amazing someone hadn't been more seriously injured or even killed in that fall. But luckily the bleachers had been built on dirt rather than a harder surface like concrete or asphalt.

She turned to the EMT. "Can you ask Dr. Marks if his patient's name is Brandi? It's her daughter, if so."

"Sure. I'll be right back."

Asking everyone to move back as he did so, she finally had a clear line of sight to Clint. He gave her a reassuring wink that made her smile.

God, how familiar that was. And it still made a jolt of electricity go through her system.

The girl was indeed Brandi, and within minutes everyone had been bundled up into two ambulances, which were creeping back between the throngs of horses and people, and soon disappeared. The sirens were off this time, probably trying not to spook the horses and risk more accidents.

Clint grasped her elbow and eased her over to the side. "They're taping off the bleachers."

Her adrenaline was just beginning to dissipate from her system. "I felt the piece of metal give a little bit earlier, but it's been here for ages. I had no idea it could come loose."

"Just an accident."

"Thank God it wasn't worse. How about the person who fell, trying to get down?"

"Evidently they were all okay, since we didn't have any other patients."

With the excitement dying down, people were moving over to the rail next to the arena as the remaining barrel racers moved back into position.

"Do you want something to eat?"

She glanced up at him. "You can eat, after all that?"

He tweaked her chin. "They're all fine, Jess. Let's enjoy the rest of the day."

Their patients may have been fine, but Jessi wasn't so sure about herself. The memory of his hand grasping hers as he'd hauled her up the steps wound around her senses. She missed his touch. Wanted to reach over and…

The cell phone on Clint's hip buzzed. The hospital? Her whole body stiffened as dread rose up to fill her being.

Clint's system went on high alert as he put the phone to his ear.

"Marks here."

"Clinton? Clinton Marks?"

Frowning, he tried to place the feminine voice on the other end of the line. While the light Southern drawl was familiar, it definitely wasn't anyone from the hospital,

because they would have called him "Doctor." If this was
some telemarketer, they were about to get an earful for
scaring Jessi.

And she was scared. He could read it in her stiff posture and the hands clenched at her sides.

He decided to go ultra-formal. "This is Dr. Marks."

"Well, *Dr.* Marks—" there was an air of amusement
to the voice now "—this is Abigail Spencer, Jessi's mom.
Chelsea's grandmother. You remember me, don't you?"

Hell. That's why she sounded familiar.

He mouthed "Your mom" to relieve Jessi's fears, wondering why she was calling him instead of Jessi.

Jessi evidently had the same idea as he did, because
she frowned and checked her phone. Maybe it was dead
or something.

Clint and Jessi's dads had both been stationed at the
same base, so he'd seen her parents quite a bit during his
school years. His memories of Mrs. Spencer were of a
kind woman with blond curls very like her daughter's and
a quiet smile. So very different from his own mother's
tense and fearful posture that had cropped up anytime
she'd heard that front door open. Or how she would place
her body in front of her son's until she had gauged what
mood her husband had brought home with him. He rubbed
a thumb across his pinky. His mother hadn't always been
able to protect him, though.

Which was why the Spencer household had seemed so
strange and alien to him. He'd never been able to shake
the feeling that Jessi's mom had seen right through to the
hurting kid hidden beneath a rebellious leather jacket and
spiked hair. He brought his attention back to Jessi's mom
as the silence over the phone grew awkward. He cleared
his throat. "Of course I remember you. How are you?"

"Anxious to see my granddaughter. But Jessi told me

that's not a good idea right now. I want to ask why. It's been over two months."

He didn't understand what that had to do with him, unless Jessi had used him as an excuse to deflect her visits. But whatever it was, that was between the two of them as far as he was concerned.

"I'm sorry, Mrs. Spencer. I really think you should talk to your daughter about that, because I can't discuss Chelsea's treatment. Jessi would have to give written authorization to—"

A poke to his arm made him look at the woman beside him. She shook her head.

Mrs. Spencer's voice came back down the line. "I can do better than that. Why don't you come over for dinner tonight? Jessi will be here, and we can hash all this out between the three of us." There was a pause. When her voice came back it was on the shaky side. "I'm her grandmother. Don't you think I'm entitled to know what's going on?"

"Again, that's not up to me." He felt like an utter jackass for saying those words to a woman who'd been nothing but nice to him during his time in Richmond, but Jess was staring holes right through him. "Jessi has medical power of attorney at the moment."

"She's trying to protect me, but I don't need protecting." An audible breath came through the receiver. "Won't you please come to dinner?"

There was no way he was going to walk into a situation like that without Jessi being fully aware of what was coming, and he wasn't willing to admit her daughter was standing right next to him. Not without Jess's approval. "Tell you what. Call your daughter and talk to her. If she's in agreement with me coming over tonight, I'll be glad to." How was that for admitting he had no other plans for a Friday evening?

Another poke to the arm, harder this time. "What are you doing?" she whispered.

He gave her a helpless shrug.

Unlike Jessi, he'd never married, instead throwing his whole life into helping others who were dealing with traumatic events stemming from their military service. It had been the least he could do for his dad, who, like Chelsea, had felt all alone.

"Okay, I'll do that." A quick laugh made a warning system go off in his head. "Do you still like corned-beef brisket?"

She remembered that? He'd eaten over at their house exactly once, which was when he'd discovered how overprotective her dad was –the polar opposite of his. And he hadn't liked Clint. At all. Clint had never been invited back to the house again.

"I love brisket." Not that he thought there was a snowball's chance in hell that Jessi would agree to him coming over and talking about Chelsea's condition. If she'd wanted her mom to know how treatment was going, surely she would have told her by now.

"See you around seven, then."

Not quite sure how to answer that, he settled for a noncommittal reply. "Thank you for the invitation, Mrs. Spencer."

The phone clicked off.

He met Jessi's accusing eyes. "Why did you let her invite you to dinner?"

As if he'd had any choice in the matter. One eyebrow went up. "I think the more important question is how did she get my number and why is she calling me, instead of you?"

"I don't know what you—"

Her phone started playing some samba beat that made

him smile. Jessi groaned. "Oh, Lord. How am I going to get you out of this?"

"Don't worry about trying. I can come, if it's okay with you." Why he'd said that he had no idea.

"Hi, Mom. No, I'm…out at the fair." She licked her lips, while Clint handed money to the man in the funnel cake booth. "I know, I'm sorry. It was a spur-of-the-minute thing. A friend invited me."

She listened again, her face turning pink. "No, it's not a *guy* friend."

Pretend feathers all over his body began to ruffle and quiver in outrage as he accepted two plates from the vender. Uh…he could show her he was a guy, if she needed proof. Scratch that. She'd already seen the proof.

"Don't sound so disappointed, Mother." She rolled her eyes and glanced back at him. "You did what? How did you get his number?"

Her lips tightened, and she plopped down on a nearby bench, shutting her eyes for a second. "That's right. I forgot I left his card on the refrigerator. What were you doing at my house, anyway?"

Clint shifted beside her, uneasy about listening in on the conversation.

"Mom, you are going to spoil Cooper rotten. You know he has a weigh-in coming up."

Cooper? He set one of the plates on her lap and kept the other for himself. Did Jessi have another boyfriend? Visions of some muscle-bound hunk lounging in her bed came to mind.

No, she would have said something to him.

And exactly when had he given her the chance? He'd asked about Larry, but not about any other man who might be waiting in the wings.

"What? Clint *already* agreed to come? Wow, he sounds a little desperate, doesn't he?"

She stuck her tongue out at him, just as he took a bite of his fried cake, making him relax in his seat. "Okay, I'm about done here, so I'll start heading back that way. Love you."

He hadn't exactly agreed to go, and he was glad Jessi had heard for herself his side of the conversation. His smile widened. It would seem Mrs. Spencer could play loose and easy with rules, too.

She got off the phone and picked her cake up with a napkin he held out to her.

"Desperate, am I?" He didn't try to hide the wry tone to his voice.

"What could I do? If I said you couldn't come to dinner, she'd make up her own conclusions. And I couldn't exactly admit that you were sitting right next to me, eating funnel cake, could I?"

That part was his fault. He'd been the one to pretend they weren't together.

"So who's Cooper?" He dropped the question as if it were no big deal. Which it wasn't.

"A communal beagle," she said, as she swallowed. "Mmm…that's good stuff."

Also good was the dot of powdered sugar on her lower lip. One he was just able to refrain from licking off.

"A communal…beagle?"

Her tongue sailed across her lip, whisking away the sugar. "Okay, I guess that does sound weird. He adopted me about a year ago…came waddling up to the door and scratched on it. No one ever claimed him, so Mom and I have been caring for him between the two of us. He's on a diet. Supposedly." Stretching her legs out in front of her, she went on, "When I have to work late, Mom takes him to her house. You'll probably meet him tonight. Since you're evidently coming to dinner."

She munched down on another piece of cake, moaning in enjoyment. "That is if you still have room for food after this."

"You haven't asked me if I had plans for the evening."

Her eyes widened. "Oh, God. I'm sorry. Do you?"

"No. But I don't want to make things any harder for you than they already are." The tortured look when she'd discovered her daughter's pregnancy came back to haunt him. "I know this isn't easy, Jess."

"No, it's not." She paused, setting her food back on her plate. "Can you let me set the tone of the conversation? Mom will just worry herself sick if she knew the extent of what Chelsea is facing. And she hasn't seemed herself recently either. She was on antidepressants for several years, so it has me worried."

He frowned, surprised by the information. But people sometimes hid their problems well. "Does she know about the suicide attempt?"

"Yes. But she wasn't there when it happened. She only knew…afterwards."

He touched her hand. "You sure you want me to come?"

"I'm not sure of anything right now. But Mom is right. Chelsea is her granddaughter. One she hasn't seen in over two months. It's time to start letting her know what's going on. I—I just want to feed her the information in bits she can process. She's been through a lot in the past five years."

Since her husband's death.

"I understand." He withdrew his hand and sat up straighter. "I'll let you answer specific questions, and I can fill in any of the medical gaps. How does that sound?"

"Perfect. Thanks so much, Clint."

Well, at least she hadn't thrown his card away. Then

again, she hadn't kept it in her wallet either. "If you're done, I'll take you back to the house. I'm pretty sure you don't want us arriving in the same car."

She handed him her plate and waited until he'd thrown them both in a nearby trash receptacle to answer.

"Probably not a good idea." She smiled and stood to her feet. As they made their way back to the parking area, Clint had one thought. He hoped tonight went a whole lot better than his day had.

Jessi's plans for a relaxing evening at home looked like they were shot to hell. Between helping her mom set the table and dragging her makeup bag from her purse to touch up the dark circles under her eyes, she was getting more and more antsy. It was one thing to spend a few relaxing hours at the fair. It was another thing entirely to eat a meal with him while her mother grilled them about Chelsea's condition, which of course she would.

She'd just put the last swipe of mascara on her lashes when the doorbell rang and Cooper started up with the baying his breed was famous for. She froze, the makeup wand still in her right hand. Sucking down a breath, she quickly shoved it back in the tube, blinked at herself in the bathroom mirror and headed to get the door.

By the time she got halfway down the stairs she saw her mother had beaten her to it, apron wrapped around her waist. The door opened, and Cooper bumbled forward to greet the newcomer.

As Clint bent to pet the dog, Jessi couldn't help but stare. He'd evidently showered as well, because his hair was still damp. Dressed in a red polo shirt that hugged his shoulders and snug black jeans that hugged other—more dangerous—parts, he looked better than any funnel cake she'd ever had. He straightened and went over to kiss her mother's cheek, while Cooper continued to snuffle and groan at his ankles.

His eyes came up. Met hers across the room.

A sting of awareness rippled through her as his gaze slid over her white peasant shirt and dark-wash jeans before coming back up to her face. One side of his mouth pulled up into something that might have been a smile. Then again, it could have just as easily been classified as a modified grimace. Either way, the action caused that crease in his cheek to deepen and her heart rate to shoot through the roof.

Sexy man. Sexy smile. Stupid girl.

Hurrying the rest of the way down the stairs, she grabbed Cooper's collar and tugged him back into the house, while greeting Clint with as much nonchalance as she could muster under the circumstances. "Glad you could make it."

Not that there'd been much choice on either of their parts. Her mom had made sure of that. And right now the woman was the perfect hostess, ushering Clint in and offering him a drink, which he declined. That surprised her. He'd been such a rebel in high school that everyone had assumed that he'd played it loose and easy with alcohol, although she'd never actually seen him touch the stuff.

Her mom glanced at her in question, but Jessi shook her head. She needed all her wits about her if this evening was going to go according to plan. If she could help it, they were going to avoid talking about Chelsea as much as possible, and when her mom pressed for information, she would be honest but gloss over some of the more depressing aspects of her granddaughter's present situation. Like the fact that she either didn't want to talk about what had precipitated her suicide attempt, or she had simply blocked out that portion of her life. Who knew which it was? And it wasn't like Clint had had much time to get to the bottom of things. He'd been her doctor for, what…a little under a week?

"You look lovely," Clint said to her once her mom had gone to the kitchen to put the finishing touches on their meal. Cooper, obviously hoping for a few dropped morsels, puttered along behind her.

"Thank you." She bit her lip. "I'm really, really sorry you got caught in the middle of this."

"It's fine. I haven't had a homemade meal in…" He paused. "Well, it's been a while."

A while since someone had cooked for him? Jessi found that hard to believe. A man like Clint wouldn't have any trouble finding dates. He was even better looking now than he'd been in high school, although she never would have believed that possible. Gangly and rebellious as a teenager, he had filled out, not only physically—which was impressive enough—but he now had a maturity about him that had been lacking all those years ago. Oh, he'd made all the girls, including her, nervous wrecks back then. But as a man—well, she'd be hard pressed to say he wasn't breathtaking in a totally masculine way. From the self-assured smile to the confidence he exuded, he gave her more than a glimmer of hope that this was a man who could help her daughter.

"Have a seat," she told him. "Mom will be back any minute, and I'd like to set some quick ground rules. Like I said earlier, I haven't told her much about Chelsea's behavior—she knows about the suicide attempt, but not much about her time at the hospital. I wanted to keep it simple until I felt like there was some ho—"

Her voice cracked as an unexpected wave of emotion splashed over her, blocking the one word she wanted to believe in.

"Until you felt like there was some hope?" He finished the sentence for her. "There's always hope, Jess. I think we'll start seeing a little more progress in the coming weeks."

He shifted to face her. "Exactly what do you want me to say to your mom? I'm not comfortable with lying."

And yet he'd been the one to suggest she lie to her father about what happened after she'd run out of the gym during graduation all those years ago. To protect himself from her dad's wrath? Or to protect her?

Maybe it had been a little of both.

"I don't expect you to lie. You said there's always hope. If you could just keep that as a running theme when you talk about Chelsea, it would help Mom feel better."

"She's going to ask to see her, you know. Is there a reason you don't want her to?"

"I'm worried about her, like I told you earlier. I want to…be there when she sees Chelsea."

And I want you to have time to work your magic first. She didn't say the words, but she wanted them to be true. She trusted him. Why that was she couldn't say. She hadn't seen them interact that much. But he'd said he'd do his very best for Chelsea and she believed him. She just hoped it was enough.

Five minutes later, they were called into dinner. Cooper settled under the table with his head propped on Clint's right foot, despite all her efforts to deter him.

"He's fine," Clint said. "As long as he doesn't expect me to share any of that delicious-looking brisket."

They all laughed, and Jessi gave a quick sigh of relief. She'd half expected her mom to grill Clint on Chelsea's prognosis from the moment they sat down, but it was mostly small talk as Jessi munched lettuce leaves with nerves that were as crackly as the salad. The feared topic didn't hit until they were halfway through her mom's famed brisket, which, despite being as succulent as ever, was getting tougher and tougher for her to force down.

"Jessi tells me that she thinks Chelsea is dealing with PTSD. Is that what you're seeing, as well?"

Clint dabbed his mouth with his napkin and nodded. "We see quite a number of veterans who come back with issues related to what they've seen and done."

"Does that mean you have some ideas on how to proceed?"

Jessi's eyes jerked to his and found him watching her. She put her fork on the table as she waited for him to answer.

"We're keeping our options open at the moment. I'm still working through the notes from her previous doctor."

"That's right. I forgot you'd just moved home. What perfect timing. Or were you just so homesick that you couldn't bear to stay away any longer?"

Jessi sucked down too much of the water she'd been sipping and choked for a second, but Clint didn't miss a beat. "Doctors are transferred to other locations on a regular basis, just like any other member of the armed forces." He gave a rueful twist of the mouth. "We both know about that, don't we?"

Way to go, Clint. Find something you have in common and use it to evade the real question.

Kind of like he'd done when she'd asked him why he had to leave the day after graduation. "I've already signed the papers, and that's when they told me to show up" had been his answer. She'd bought it at the time. But now? She had a feeling he'd just wanted to avoid her making any demands on him after their shared time together.

Which stung even more now than it had when he'd said the words.

Jessi's mom smiled back. "I'm sure you've done your share of moving, just like we did when Jessi was little." She paused then said, "I'm really glad you're back, though, and that you'll be the one treating Chelsea."

Clint's face registered surprise. "Why is that?"

Cutting into another section of her meat, her mom glanced up with a hint of sadness mixed with what looked like relief. "Because you, more than anyone, know what it's like to live with the effects of PTSD."

CHAPTER SIX

THE ROOM WAS silent for five long seconds.

Clint knew, because he counted every damn tick of the clock. He hadn't told Jessi or anyone else about his dad and the problems he'd had. Could his mom have mentioned it to Abigail or someone else from their past?

Worse, did Jessi know?

Even as the questions ducked through his cerebral cortex, looking for a believable response, he thought he saw pity flit through Jessi's eyes, although right now her mouth was hanging open in shock.

But, eventually, he had to say something. The ache in his pinky finger sprang to life, reminding him of all the reasons he'd decided to join the military and leave Jessi far behind. He clenched his fist to rid himself of the sensation and made a decision.

He was going to tell the truth. Air his dirty laundry—at least about his father. After all these years.

"Yes. I do know."

Jessi's fork clattered to her plate, and her mouth snapped shut. "Mom, I don't think that's an appropriate thing to blurt out at the dinner table."

Wounded green eyes, so like her daughter's, widened. "Oh, I'm sorry. I didn't realize. I just assumed that everyone knew—"

"It's okay," Clint said, his thumb scrubbing across the crooked joint, a habit he used as a daily reminder of why his job was so crucial. Because PTSD didn't affect just the individual soldier…it affected everyone around them, as well. "I didn't talk about my problems much. And for a long time I didn't realize that something could be done."

Jessi finally spoke up. "*You* had PTSD?"

"No. My dad did. It was back when I was in high school."

Differing emotions flickered through her eyes. Sadness. Shock. Then finally the one he'd hoped never to see: guilt.

"Clint, I—" Her tongue flicked across her lips. "You never told any of us."

"Would *you* have?"

He knew she'd catch the inference. That her father— a tough army boot-camp instructor—had been vehement in his opposition to her being involved with anyone in the military. After Mrs. Spencer's words, he now wondered if it was because Jessi's dad and the entire base had witnessed the hell his mom had gone through because of his dad. Because of the way he'd used the bottle to blot out the demons related to his war deployment. It hadn't worked. He'd just created a living hell for everyone around him. Clint wouldn't want any daughter of his to go through what his mom had on a daily basis.

Whatever Mr. Spencer's reasons, it had ended up saving Clint's hide down at that creek. It—and his enlistment papers—had given him the perfect out for leaving Richmond. He'd jumped at the excuse, although he now realized that's all it had been. An excuse. He'd been afraid *of* his dad and *for* his dad. Had run away from the possibility that he might turn out to be just like him. But most of all, he hadn't wanted anyone to know the shame he'd felt.

The irony was, they had known, according to Abigail.

"No," Jessi said. "I wouldn't have shared my secrets with just anyone."

The hint of accusation in her voice was unmistakable. Because she had shared *her* secret with someone: him. But he hadn't returned the favor by telling her his. Maybe because he hadn't wanted to add any more to her plate. Maybe because the only thing he'd wanted at the time had been to erase the pain in her eyes.

Instead, he'd ended up making love to her and adding to his long list of sins. Which included leaving her the very next day. He'd thought it was to protect her.

Not that it had done any good. Jessi's own daughter was now struggling with trauma related to her military service, so he hadn't ended up protecting her from anything. Just his own ugly past and uncertain future.

Little had she known back then that he had harbored a secret crush on her. Maybe it had been part of the whole badass, wanting-to-redeem-himself syndrome. The same reason he'd enlisted. A need to redeem himself and maybe even his father—or at least to make peace with what had happened.

Clint's job, though, had turned into a passion he just couldn't shake. In some small measure he *had* redeemed himself. Each time he was able to help an emotionally wounded soldier have a shot at a normal life, he was somehow giving his father the help he'd never received when he'd been alive. And in doing that—Clint flexed his damaged finger again—he helped protect their sons and daughters.

Abigail broke into his thoughts. "I really am sorry. I just assumed that Jessi knew, since you went to school together."

They'd done more than just that. Which was something

he could not—would not—think about right now. Not with her mom sitting there, looking more than a little mortified.

"It's fine…"

"Don't worry…"

He and Jessi spoke at exactly the same time, which caused everyone to laugh and broke the tension instantly. Even Cooper gave a quick *woof* of approval.

And although he'd been the one to say, "Don't worry," he was worried. More than a little. Because every time he caught Jessi watching him, his gut slid sideways.

"I have some peach ice cream for dessert," Abigail said, "if anyone wants some."

He glanced down at his watch. Almost nine. He could safely take off and claim to have survived the evening. "Thank you, but I probably should be heading home. I have an early morning tomorrow."

He pushed his chair back, dislodging Cooper from his foot in the process. The dog's nails clicked on the hard-wood floor as he slid from beneath the table and pressed his cheek against Clint's calf. Reaching down, he scratched behind the animal's ears.

"Are you sure?" Abigail asked.

"Yes, unless there's something I can do to help clean up."

She smiled. "Not a thing." A quick frown puckered her brow. "I almost forgot. When can I see Chelsea? I don't want to set her treatment back, but if I can just spend a minute or two with her to assure myself that she's really—"

"Of course." He glanced at Jessi for confirmation. "How about if we make it for the next time Jessi and I meet with her? Friday at three?"

Jessi nodded her approval. "It's okay with me. I want to talk to you a little bit about her condition first, though, okay, Mama? I don't want you to be shocked by what she might say…or not say."

"I wasn't born yesterday. I know it's bad. I just want to see her."

"I'll pick you up on my way home from work, then. We can go together." She kissed her mother on the cheek, something that made Clint's chest tighten. Despite Mr. Spencer's heavy-handed ways, this had been a house of love. It was obvious the two women were close. And he was glad. Glad that her teenage angst hadn't left any lasting scars.

His arthritic pinky creaked out a warning shot when he curled his hand around the chair to push it back in.

"Thanks again for dinner, Mrs. Spencer."

"You're very welcome, and I'm glad you came. I already feel better."

As he started for the door, he was surprised to find Jessi right behind him. "I'll walk you to your car."

He opened the door, forgetting about Cooper. The dog bounded out before he could stop him.

"It's okay," Jessi said. "He does it to everyone. He won't go far."

The walk down the driveway was filled with the scent of magnolia blossoms, a smell he remembered well. Unbeknownst to Jessi, he'd sat in front of her house for hours the night of graduation, listening for any sounds of fighting, or worse. It had been hard back then to remember that not every father struck out with his fists.

But there'd been nothing that night. Just the muggy heat and that rich floral scent—something he connected to Jessi every time he smelled it. Even now, memories of the soft carpet of moss he'd felt beneath his hands as he'd supported his weight swirled around him. Of her face, soft and flushed, tilting back as he'd trailed his mouth down her neck.

Damn. He never should have come here.

He quickened his steps, only to have her hand touch his arm as they reached his car. He turned to face her, keys in hand, ready to get the hell out of there. The faster he left, the sooner he could regain his sanity.

Which right now was nowhere to be found. Because all he wanted to do was kiss her. Right in front of her house. To relive a little of the magic he'd experienced all those years ago.

"Why didn't you tell me...back then?" she asked.

He might have known this was why she'd wanted to come with him. "I thought I'd explained that. It was my problem, there was no reason to involve anyone else."

"God, Clint. I bawled my eyes out about my dad's stupid rules without even knowing what you—"

"I didn't tell you because I didn't want anyone to know. Besides, it doesn't matter anymore. It's all in the past."

"And your dad is gone."

His jaw clenched. His father's liver cancer, brought on by years of alcohol abuse, didn't mitigate the fact that Clint wished he'd known sooner how to help him. "So is yours."

"Yes. I'm just glad he's not suffering. The strokes came faster at the end..."

"I'm sorry." He put his arm around her, meaning to give her a quick squeeze and release her. Instead, somehow she wound up against his chest, palms splayed against his shirt, staring up at him with those huge eyes.

The same eyes that did something to his insides every damn time she looked at him. It had happened in high school. And it was still happening now. He leaned back against the car door, still holding on to her.

She bit her lip for a second. "For what it's worth, I'm

glad you were the one—back then. And I'm glad it's you now."

Whoa. If that wasn't a kick in the gut, he didn't know what was. She was glad he'd been the one who'd taken her virginity and not Larry? He'd beaten himself up about that for years afterwards.

And what did she mean, she was happy it was him now? She had to be talking about Chelsea.

"I had no idea who she was, Jess, until you stepped into that room. I swear."

"I didn't know it was you either. Until I saw the name-plate on your desk."

Her fingers came up and touched the line of his jaw, and she smiled. "I never believed that rebel freedom air you put on back in school."

He cocked a brow. "Oh, no? And why was that?"

"Because you looked so lost at times. I just never understood what caused it back then."

Before he had time to tense up, she continued. "Mama is right, you know."

"How's that?"

"You are the absolute best person to be treating Chelsea." She closed her eyes for a second before looking up at him again. "I'm so glad you're here, Clint. So glad you came home."

The squeezing sensation in his chest grew. The tightrope he was toeing his way across was thinner than he'd realized…harder to balance on than he'd expected.

"Promise me you won't drop the case," she added.

That's exactly what he *should* do. Especially now. Bow out and ask someone else to step in. Transfer the hell out of that hospital and go back to California.

A thought came to him. Was this why Jessi was in his arms, staring all doe-eyed at him? "I can't make you that promise. I have to do what I think is in the best interests of your daughter."

"I know. Just promise me that tomorrow, when you walk into that office, you'll still be the one treating her."

He was suddenly aware of her fingers. They were still on his skin, only now they'd moved slightly backward, putting his senses on high alert—along with certain parts of his body. "I'll be there for her."

"Good. Because I think I'm about to do something very, very stupid."

He didn't need to ask what it was. Because he was on the verge of doing something just as stupid.

But it didn't stop him from tugging her closer, neither did it stop his lips from closing over hers in a sudden crazy burst of need.

And once their mouths fused together, he was transported to the past. Twenty-two years, to be exact. He'd been unable to get enough of her. Her taste. The faint scent of her shampoo or body wash, or magnolias—whatever the hell it had been that had filled his senses, intoxicating him more than the booze he'd been offered earlier ever could have.

A faint sound came from her throat. He was fairly certain it wasn't a gasp of protest, since her arms had wound around his neck and her body had slid up his as she'd gone up on tiptoe. He buried his fingers in the hair at her nape, the slight dampness probably due to the Virginia humidity, but it brought back memories of perspiration and bodies that moved together in perfect harmony. Of…

The sound of Cooper's plaintive howl split the air a short distance away, followed by the sound of the front door opening. Abigail's voice called out the dog's name.

Cursing everything under the sun, he let Jessi pull free from his lips, even though the last thing he wanted to do was let her go. He wanted to drag her into the car and drive right to the creek to see if that night had been everything he'd remembered it being.

Abigail's voice called the dog's name again. The bushes shielded them from view, so Clint didn't look. Besides, his gaze was glued to Jessi's pale features.

Even when Cooper decided to lumber over to them, instead of going to the house, he didn't break eye contact.

"Sorry. I'm sorry." The gutted apology as she backed up one step, then two, made his lungs burn. The back of her hand went to her mouth, and she pressed hard. Her feet separated them by another pace, then she reached down to capture Cooper's collar. "Please, don't dump her. This was my fault. Not hers."

As she led the dog back to the front door, Clint gave his head a silent shake. There was no one else. He couldn't leave. Not yet.

Chelsea couldn't afford to lose two doctors in the space of two weeks.

Which meant Clint couldn't afford to start something he would never be able to finish. He'd made love to Jessi once and had barely been able to find the strength to walk away. If it happened twice, there was no hope for him.

So, from now on, he would tread carefully. And keep his distance from Jessi and her mom as much as possible.

CHAPTER SEVEN

CHELSEA WAS TALKING.

Not a lot, but Clint had noticed a subtle shift in her demeanor over the past several days as they met for their sessions. She was more interested and less withdrawn. He wasn't sure what had caused the change, but he was all for it.

Besides, it kept him from having to deal with the devastating consequences of that kiss he and Jessi had shared beside his car. And the suspicious thoughts that had crept into his mind in the meantime.

Had she tried to manipulate him into staying?

No. Jessi wasn't like that. When he'd left all those years ago, she'd never said a word to try to make him change his mind. Yes, she'd made him promise that he'd remain on her daughter's case—right before she'd locked her lips to his, but it wasn't as if she was the only one who'd been thinking along those lines. He'd been just as guilty. And she'd been very careful to maintain her distance ever since. Their consultations were now over the phone—despite their earlier agreement to meet with Chelsea together—and her voice during those calls was brisk and businesslike.

Just like the doctor she was.

And she was smart. She knew exactly the right questions to ask regarding her daughter's state of mind.

According to the nurses, her visits to Chelsea occurred during his off hours. He had no doubt she'd somehow found out his schedule and was purposely coming when he wasn't around.

As grateful as he should be for the breathing space, he found himself irritated at the way he missed her presence.

What else could he do, though? He'd always prided himself on his self-control, because it was something his dad had never had much of. And yet Clint lost it every time he was around Jessi.

Every. Damn. Time.

It had been true twenty-two years ago, and it was still true today. He just couldn't resist her. The good girl that he'd had a secret crush on in high school had turned him into an impulsive, reckless creature. One he feared, because he recognized the beast all too well. He'd looked into impulsive, reckless eyes so like his own during his teenage years.

That raw, angry kid had morphed into a cool, rational man somewhere along the way, and in doing so had found himself. Had found an antidote that worked. But it only functioned if he didn't let anyone get too close.

Today would be the test. Jessi was due here with her mom in a little over an hour. He'd warned himself. Scolded himself. Immersed himself in work. All to no avail.

His heart was already pounding in anticipation of seeing her—trying to justify being with her one more time.

Just one kiss. He could stop anytime he wanted.

Sound familiar, Clint?

Substitute *drink* for the word *kiss* and you had his dad in all his lying glory.

Not good.

His assistant pushed open the door. "Dr. Marks? Miles Branson is here for his appointment. Are you ready for him?"

"Yes, send him in. Thanks, Maria."

As hectic as his morning had been, with two new patients and a flurry of consultations, he shouldn't have had time to think about Jessi at all. But she'd found her way into every nook and cranny of his brain and surged to the forefront whenever he had a free moment.

Like now.

Miles came in and, after shaking Clint's hand, lowered himself into one of the chairs across from him. Another PTSD patient, this particular man had made great strides in his treatment over the past couple of weeks. It could be because of that new baby girl he had waiting at home for him.

"How're Maggie and the baby?" he asked.

"Both beautiful." The smile the man gave him was genuine, and the furrows between his brows seemed less pronounced than they'd been when Clint had arrived. He scrolled through his phone for a second and then handed it over.

Miles's wife and a baby swaddled in a pink blanket lay on a hospital bed. She looked exhausted but happy, while it was obvious their daughter was trying out her new set of lungs, if the open mouth and red, angry-looking face were anything to go by.

"Beautiful. You've got a great pair of girls there." Clint pushed the phone across his desk.

"I'm a lucky man." He smiled again, glancing down at his wife and daughter. "You know, for the first time in a long time I actually believe that."

"I know you do. Are you ready to try for a reduction of your medication?"

"Can I do away with it altogether?"

Clint paused for a second. While his superiors were very conscious of time and money, his only concern was for his patients. He'd been known to ruffle a few feathers along the way, but had still somehow made it up the chain of command. While paroxetine wasn't addictive, like the benzodiazepine family of medications, he still felt it was safer to reduce the dosage gradually while maintaining a regular therapy schedule as they progressed.

In the two years since Miles had first been seen by other doctors, the man had gotten engaged and then married to a wonderful woman who knew exactly what he was battling. And, thank heavens, this man hadn't shown the agitation and anger issues that Clint's dad had.

"Let's knock it down from sixty milligrams a day to twenty and go from there." He grabbed his prescription pad and wrote out a new dosage recommendation. "We'll maintain our sessions, and in a couple of weeks, if all goes well, we'll reduce them even more. How does that sound?"

Miles sat back in his chair, his posture relaxed and open. "It sounds like living. Thanks, Doc."

For the next forty-five minutes they went through the new father's moods and actions, detailing where he'd struggled, while Clint made notes he would transcribe later. Together they made a plan on how to deal with the next several weeks, when having a new baby at home would put more stress on both him and the family.

When they finally parted, he opened the office door to let Miles out and his glance immediately connected with Jessi and her mom, who'd arrived fifteen minutes early for their session with Chelsea. He nodded at the pair, walking Miles over to his assistant's desk and giving a few last-minute instructions on scheduling.

Taking a deep breath, he finally turned and made his way over to the pair in his waiting area. Jessi, dressed in a casual white-flowered dress that stretched snugly across her top and waist, stood to her feet. Flat, strappy sandals showed off pink toenails and dainty feet. He swallowed when he realized he'd been staring. All his misgivings from earlier came roaring back. He shoved them aside.

"Sorry to keep you waiting," he muttered, his voice a little gruffer than he'd expected. But seeing Jessi up close and personal created this choking sensation that closed off the upper part of his throat.

Her mom was the one to break the stare-fest. "We were a little early, at my insistence. I'm anxious to see my grand-daughter."

"I'm sure you are."

Abigail was in a pair of jeans with a white button-down shirt. At almost sixty, she was still a beautiful woman, with high cheekbones and eyes very like her daughter's. And her granddaughter's, for that matter.

"Do you want to meet in my office or head down to Chelsea's room? Jessi gave a little shrug, no longer attempting to look directly at him. Maybe she felt as uncomfortable as he was about this meeting. "Wherever you feel is best."

Her mom spoke up again. "I haven't seen Chelsea's room. Do you think she would mind if we met her there? I'm curious about where she's been staying." She blinked a couple of times. "Not that I'm saying there's anything wrong with the hospital. It looks modern and well cared for."

Not what she'd expected. She didn't say the words, but he could imagine her thoughts.

The VA's reputation had taken a beating in the press over the last year. And not without reason, but the corruption was slowly being weeded out, and Clint hoped the end result would be a system of hospitals the country's servicemen and women could be proud of.

Clint had done his best to make sure his patients received the best treatment possible. And he knew there were a lot of other dedicated doctors who also cared deeply about their patients. The waiting lists were staggering, and, yes, it would probably be much easier to find work in the civilian sector for better pay and a lighter workload. But that wasn't why he did what he did.

"You're fine," he assured Abigail. He turned to his assistant. "Could you call down to Chelsea's room and let her know we're on our way?"

"Of course, Doctor." She picked up her phone and dialed as Clint nodded toward the hallway to their right. "Jessi, you know the way."

She stood and slung the strap of her purse over her arm, making sure her mother was following her. She glanced back at him. "Any last-minute instructions?"

"No. Chelsea's been more open, as I told you over the phone. I think that's an encouraging sign." Not that they'd made definitive steps in her treatment. The new class of antidepressants he'd prescribed was kicking in, though, so he had hopes that as the fog of despair continued to lift, she would start looking to the future, instead of crouching in the past. They had yet to talk about the specifics surrounding her months in captivity. She'd reiterated that she hadn't been tortured or assaulted, but as to what exactly had happened during that time, there was still a large swath of information that was missing. Clint had even tried going through channels and seeing if her superior officers knew anything more. But they were what Clint would label as "careful" with their words. It hadn't been anything in particular that was or wasn't said. It had just been the way the information had been delivered. And every story had been told in an identical fashion.

For Clint, that fact alone raised a huge red flag.

"Nana!" he heard the greeting even before he reached

the room. And the happiness in that one word was apparent. As was the sight of the two women embracing, while Jessi stood back to allow the reunion to happen.

"How's she really doing?" she asked him in a low voice as Abigail sat on the edge of the bed, her arm around her granddaughter.

"Just like I said. She's talking more."

"Any idea yet on the why?"

The why of the suicide attempt.

"We haven't made it that far, yet."

The exchange ended when Abigail waved her daughter over. "Doesn't she look wonderful?"

She didn't, and they all knew it. Still pale and frighteningly thin, Chelsea did not have the appearance of a soldier who'd been through the worst that boot camp had to offer… who had survived a stint as a POW. She looked like a fragile piece of china that might shatter at the slightest tap.

While they talked, Clint grabbed two chairs from an empty room that adjoined Chelsea's and added them to the two that were already against the pale gray walls—Clint had learned how important equalizing the setting was, which was why his office had three identical chairs. One for him and two for those who met him there. His rank was above that of many of his patients, but that didn't mean he had to act the part.

"Dr. Marks?" Jessi's voice interrupted his thoughts.

Although it rankled at some level, he knew it was better for them to address each other in a formal manner in public, although he'd told Chelsea—in vague terms—that he and Jessi had known each other in the past. It was easier to be as truthful as possible, while holding back information that could be deemed harmful to her treatment.

"Sorry," he murmured. He turned to Chelsea. "Do you feel up to sitting with us?"

"Yes." She swung her legs over the side of the bed, waving off her mom, who'd immediately moved to help her. "It's okay. I can do it."

She was in a set of flannel pajamas that Jessi had evidently brought in during one of her other visits. Ideally, he would have liked her to be dressed in normal clothes for their meetings. And in recent days she'd made more of an effort.

So why was today different?

Was she trying to appear fragile, warning away any talk that crept toward painful subjects?

It was too late now to ask her to change, and he didn't want to do anything that would upset Jessi's mom in the process. Besides, he had another client in an hour and a half and he wanted to make sure that Chelsea wouldn't be cut off in the middle of anything important.

They sat in a circle. Chelsea and Abigail glanced at him expectantly, while Jessi's gaze was centered on the folded hands she held in her lap.

"Chelsea, it's been a while since your grandmother has seen you, am I correct?"

The young woman's hand snaked out and grabbed Abigail's. "I'm glad she's here."

"So am I."

He wasn't going to push hard this session, he just wanted to reintroduce the family and make sure everyone knew that their old ways of interacting might not work in this new and different world. Chelsea had gone to war as one person and had come back another. They all had yet to see where exactly that left her mom and grandmother, although the reunion had gone much more smoothly than he would have expected.

Even as he thought it, Abigail pressed her fingertips to her eyes and wiped away moisture that had gathered beneath them. "Oh, no, Nana. Don't cry." Chelsea wrapped her arms around the older woman. "Mom, there's a box of tissues in my top drawer. Would you mind getting me one?"

Jessi jumped up and headed toward the small end table beside the bed. She drew out the top drawer, found the box and withdrew it. Then she stopped. Chelsea was facing away from her mother and couldn't see her, but Clint could. A strange look crossed her face as she peered at something inside that drawer. She started to reach for it then withdrew her hand.

Chelsea, as if realizing something was wrong, swiveled around in her chair. "Can't you find…? Oh, no, Mom. Please don't."

But it was already too late, because Jessi had reached back into the drawer and withdrawn what looked like a wad of tissues. Glancing at Chelsea and seeing the horror in her eyes, he realized that's not what that was. Not at all.

Even as he looked, Jess smoothed down the bottom edge of the thin paper and came forward a couple of steps, only to stop halfway. It was a doll of some sort.

No. Not a doll. A baby. Painstakingly crafted from the tissues in the box in her drawer.

"Chelsea, honey." Jessi's voice dropped away for a second before coming back again. "What is this?"

CHAPTER EIGHT

JESSI SLUMPED IN a chair in Clint's office. "I don't understand. What could it mean?"

Her daughter had refused to talk about the strange item, withdrawing back into her shell until Clint called a halt to the session and let Chelsea crawl back into her bed. She'd silently held out her hand for the doll and laid it carefully back inside the drawer.

The act made Jessi shiver.

She'd sent her mom home with a promise to stop by later, and Clint had ordered the nurse to call him immediately if there was any change.

"I don't know what it means. Maybe she miscarried while she was overseas. Maybe it's something she made as a coping mechanism. There could be any number of explanations, but until she tells us we won't know for sure."

"Will you ask her again tomorrow?"

"I'll see how she is. We may have to work our way toward it slowly." He dragged his fingers through his hair and leaned back in his chair. "It could just be a dead end."

"Who makes a doll out of a box of tissues? It just doesn't seem...normal."

When he stared at her, she closed her eyes. "Sorry. That didn't come out right. It's just that everything seemed to explode out of nowhere two months ago."

"I know. It just takes time."

"What if she never gets better? What if she's like this for the rest of her life?"

He reached across and covered her hand with his. "Thoughts like that aren't going to help anyone."

"Did you struggle with those kinds of thoughts during high school? About your dad? Did *he* ever get better?"

When he went to withdraw his hand with a frown, she grabbed at his fingers, holding him in place.

"Oh, God, Clint, I'm so sorry," she whispered. "I'm just worried about Chelsea."

"I know." He laced his fingers through hers. "I gave her a sedative, so she should sleep through the night. We'll start fresh in the morning."

"I want to be there when she wakes up."

He studied her for a minute or two, before shaking his head with what looked like regret. "I don't think that's a good idea, Jess. When you and your mom left, she was agitated and withdrawn. I don't want those memories to be the ones that resurface when she opens her eyes. Give her a day."

"A day?" She couldn't believe he was asking her to stay away from the hospital for an entire day. "I'm not the only one worried. Mom is, as well."

"I'll call you as soon as I see her. Are you working tomorrow?" He let go of her hand and reached for one of his pencils, jiggling it between his fingers as if he needed something to keep him busy. Or maybe it was a hint that he needed to get back to work.

"I'm on the afternoon shift, starting at three. I'd better get out of your hair." She stood to her feet, then thought of something. "What if you get a call in the middle of the night?"

"If something serious happens, I'll be in touch."

"Promise?"

"Promise." He must have read her dubious smile, because one side of his mouth curved into that familiar half smile. "Would you like me to pinkie-swear, as well?"

Despite her worry, she found her own lips twitching. "Would you, if I asked you to?"

"Yes."

Something icy hot nipped the air between them. She held her breath and then released it in a long stream. "Or you could come and spend the night at the house. Just in case."

Why on earth had she asked that? It was too late to take back the offer, although she could clarify it. "On the couch, of course."

His eyes softened, but he shook his head. "I have to work for a couple more hours. Besides, I don't think my staying with you would be a good idea, Jess. Things never quite remain that simple between us. And I meant what I said about taking myself off the case if I think my objectivity has been compromised."

Oh, Lord, that's right. He'd intimated that he'd hand Chelsea over to someone else if things got too personal between them. "I wasn't asking you to sleep with me. Not this time."

She'd gone that route once before, asking him to make love to her by the creek, desperately needing a few minutes out from beneath her father's thumb.

"I don't remember complaining the last time you did."

No. But then again she hadn't seen him volunteering to hang around the next day—although it had probably been too late for him to back out of boot camp by that time. And who was to say he would stick around in Richmond now? Some servicemen loved the adventure of a new place every couple of years. Not Jessi. Once she'd gotten to high school, her father had finally seemed willing to settle down and stay until she graduated. Then she'd married Larry, who hadn't known she'd had a dalliance with his friend. Not until that last day of his life.

She blocked out the thought and concentrated on the here and now as Clint got up and opened the door to his office.

She walked through it and then hesitated on the other side. "So you'll call me tomorrow."

"As soon as I have some news. Yes."

They said their goodbyes, and already his manner was more aloof. Businesslike.

Once she got to the front door of the hospital she lifted her chin and made a decision. If Clint could keep his personal life separate from what happened at the hospital, then she could, too. For everyone's sakes, she was going to have to learn to take her cues from Clint, adopting that same professional demeanor whenever she was here.

No matter how hard it was starting to be.

The suicide had come out of nowhere, and while it hadn't been one of Clint's patients it brought home the thin line he was walking with Chelsea and Jessi. The entire hospital was on edge because of it.

It wasn't easy for any doctor to lose a patient, no matter what anyone said. True impartiality was hard to come by at the best of times…and with Jessi it seemed to border on the impossible.

He'd felt the anguish radiating from every pore of her body when she'd lifted that macabre paper figure out of her daughter's drawer. And it had taken a lot of self-restraint to remain in his seat, observing Chelsea's reactions, and not rush over to make sure the woman who wasn't his patient was okay.

While he and Jessi hadn't been involved emotionally in the past—a thought he stubbornly clung to, no matter what his gut said—there could be nothing at all between them now.

Not just because of his patient. Not just because of his and Jessi's past. But because of his job and his own personal baggage.

Once they found a replacement for him, he was headed back to San Diego. It was either that or request that his transfer to Richmond be made permanent, something he couldn't see happening. He was the one they called on for temporary assignments. It's what he wanted. Moving around a lot kept his mind on the job at hand, rather than highlighting his lack of a personal life. And the unlikelihood that he'd ever have much of one.

Not that he hadn't tried. He'd been in serious relationships. Twice. But both times the woman had left, saying she felt he was withholding himself emotionally.

He had been. Somehow he could never quite let his guard all the way down. His every move was calculated. Controlled. And that's the way he liked it.

He was very aware that wasn't what most women looked for in a man. He was just not husband material.

Because of his dad?

Hell, the second Jessi had mentioned his father in his office he'd tried to yank his hand away, very aware that his crooked finger was right there for her to see. And ask about. The last thing he wanted to talk about was his past. Jessi's father might have been a pain-in-the-ass drill sergeant—but at least he'd loved her enough to care about who she saw. What she did.

His cell phone beeped. When he glanced at the caller ID, he winced. Jessi. The very person presently haunting his every thought. And it was already midmorning.

He was supposed to have called her to let her know how Chelsea was.

He pressed the answer button and bit out an apology. "Sorry, Jess. We've been swamped and I hadn't had a chance to call you yet."

She brushed aside his apology with a cleared throat. "Was she okay when she woke up?"

Despite the worry in her tone, her voice flowed over him, soothing away some of the worst parts of his morning. A few muscles in his jaw relaxed.

"I haven't had an in-depth conversation with her. Just a few minutes of small talk as she ate breakfast. We're due to have a therapy session at two."

"But she's okay."

He realized what she was looking for, and all the day's heartache came roaring back. "She doesn't seem to be obsessing over what happened yesterday. I'll call you when I've talked to her again."

"Hmm." She didn't say anything more.

"I know I promised. I'm sorry." He gritted his teeth.

"No, it's just that I have to be at work at three, and I'll probably be just as swamped with patients as you seem to be, since it's a holiday."

Ah, yes. Father's Day. Something he tried to forget every year. He glanced down at his left hand, where the crook in his finger reminded him of a whole childhood of fear and unhappiness. That wasn't the only reason he wasn't crazy about this particular day. At this point in his life, he didn't see himself ever carrying the title of father, even if he found someone and married her. He was close to forty, and had never really given kids much of a thought.

Maybe he should ask Jessi if the day held any special significance for Chelsea, though...good or bad. He should be prepared for any eventuality.

"Will Father's Day add to Chelsea's stress levels?"

There was silence over the line for a long minute. "No. Larry died before she was born. She only knows him through pictures." There was something sad about the way she said it.

He forced the next words out even as his insides tightened. "You didn't have much time together."

"No, we didn't. The worst thing is he might still be alive if someone hadn't…" The words ended on a strangled note.

Something burned in his gut. "If someone hadn't what, Jess?

"It doesn't matter. What does is that I have a wonderful daughter from our union. That's what made the hard times after his death bearable."

The image of Jessi mourning her husband was enough to make that burning sensation tickle the back of his throat. She'd had a daughter with the man. And as much as he told himself he didn't care, the cold reality was that part of him did—the same part that had leaped when he'd first realized who Jessi was and had wondered if Chelsea might be his.

But she wasn't. And if he was going to do his job, he had to remember that and keep on remembering it.

"About my session with her. How about if I send you a text, rather than trying to call? That way you can check in when you've got a free moment."

"That would be fantastic. Thank you, Clint. But please do call if something changes. I'll set my ringer to vibrate just for your number. If it does, I'll know it's important, and I'll find a way to answer, or I'll call you right back."

The tension in his gut eased and something warm and dangerous took its place. She was going to be listening for his call and his call only.

Okay, idiot. It's in case of an emergency. It's not like she's putting your number on speed dial or anything.

"So you have the number here, if you have any questions or need something, right? I remember you said my card was on your refrigerator." He glanced at the business card on his desk, since he hadn't quite memorized his Richmond number yet. "Or do you need me to read it off to you again?"

"Nope. I've already programmed it into my phone. In fact, I have you on speed dial," she said. "Just in case."

CHAPTER NINE

FATHER'S DAY SHOULD be outlawed.

Or at least the giving of gifts involving any type of motor should be banned. So far that afternoon, Jessi had treated a leg that been kissed by a chain saw, a back injury from an ATV accident and a lawn mower that had collided with a lamppost before bouncing back and knocking its new owner unconscious. Not to mention assorted other minor injuries. And she still had two hours to go until the end of her shift. The one thing she hadn't seen had been the screen on her cell phone lighting up or feeling its vibration coming from the pocket of her scrubs.

All was silent with Clint and her daughter.

Sighing, she grabbed the next chart and headed for the curtained exam room. Patient name: William Tuppele. Complaint: the words *fishing hook* and *earlobe* ran through her head before she blinked and forced her eyes to read back over that part.

Okay. So it wasn't just things with motors that should be banned from this particular holiday.

When she entered the room, a man dressed in hip waders with a camo T-shirt tucked into them sat on the exam table. And, yep, he was sporting a shiny new piece of jewelry.

She looked closer and gulped. Had something behind his ear just moved?

Stepping farther in the room, she glanced again at his chart. "Mr. Tuppele." She omitted the words *How are you?* because it was pretty obvious this was the last place the man wanted to be. Instead, she aimed for cheeky. "Catch anything interesting today?"

Instead of smiling, the man scowled. "Great, I get a nurse who thinks she's a comedienne."

She bristled, but held out her hand anyway. "I'm Dr. Riley. How long have you been like this?"

"About an hour." His gaze skipped away from hers, his words slurring the slightest bit. "My son caught me with his hook. It was his first fishing trip."

"Hmm." She kept the sound as noncommittal as possible, but from the way his face had turned scarlet and—she tried not to fan herself openly—the alcohol fumes that bathed every word the man spoke, she would almost bet there was no "son" involved in this particular party. Rather, she suspected a male-bonding episode that had gone terribly wrong.

Hip waders and booze. Not a good combination. They were lucky no one had drowned. "Did someone drive you to the hospital?"

She certainly didn't want to let a drunk loose on the roads.

"One of my buddies. He's down in the waiting room."

Jessi could only hope the *buddy* had been less generous when it came to doling out those cans of beer to himself. She made a mental note to have someone check on his friend's sobriety level.

She sat on her stool just as the worm—and, yes, it was indeed a piece of live bait—gave a couple of frantic wiggles. Lord, she did not want to touch that thing, much less have to handle it. But the best way to remove a fishing hook was to cut off the end opposite the barb and push the shank on through, rather than risk more damage by pulling it back out the way it had gone in. That barb acted like a one-way door. They went in, but they didn't want to come out.

The worm moved again.

"Hell," said the man. "Can you please get this damned thing off me? It stinks."

And it's creeping me out.

Mr. Tuppele didn't say the words, but she could well imagine him thinking them, because the same thoughts were circling around in her head, too. Maybe this was the worm's way of exacting revenge on anglers everywhere.

And maybe she could call one of the male nurses.

Ha! And give her patient a reason for his earlier sexist remark. Hardly. "When was your last tetanus shot?"

"Haven't been to a doctor in twenty years. Wouldn't be here now if one of my…er, my son hadn't been so squeamish about taking it out himself. "Is my ear going to be permanently pierced? I don't cotton to men with earrings and such."

She smiled despite herself, tempted to match his it-was-my-son fib and tell him that, yes, he would be permanently disfigured and might as well go out and buy a couple of nice dangly pieces of jewelry. But she restrained herself. "No. I knew a man who had his ear pierced in high school but had to stop wearing an earring when he went into the military. It's all healed up now."

At least she assumed that's when Clint had stopped wearing the single hoop in his ear, because there was no sign of it now. And how was it that she had even noticed that? Or remembered what he'd worn back then?

She'd kind of liked his earring, back in the day.

"Good. Don't need anyone getting any strange ideas about me."

Too late for that, Mr. Tuppele. She already had a few ideas about him. And they went much deeper than men sporting earrings. "Let me set up. I'm going to call in a nurse to give you a shot to numb your ear."

"I don't need it numbed. I just need that damned thing out."

"Are you sure?" The rest of the staff was going to thank her patient for sparing them the need to get close to that wriggler.

"Just do it."

"Okay." Trying not to shudder, she got her equipment together, praying the worm died before she had to deal with it. As disgusting as she found it, she felt a twinge of pity for the creature. It hadn't been its choice to be cast into a river for the first hungry fish to gulp.

Gloves in place, she squirted some alcohol on the wound in back of his ear, waiting for the string of cuss words to die down before continuing. She grabbed her locking forceps and clamped the instrument right behind the worm. If the barb had gone all the way through his ear, she could have just cut it off and backed the hook out, worm and all. But while there was a tiny bit of metal showing in the front of the lobe, the barb was still embedded in the man's flesh. It was going to hurt, pushing it the rest of the way through. She got a pair of wire cutters and took a deep breath, then moved in and cut the eye, leaving as much shank as possible behind that worm.

"Okay, I'm going to have to push the barb through the front, are you sure you're okay?"

"Fine."

Holding the front of the man's earlobe with her gloved fingers, she used the forceps to push hard, until the barb popped through.

The man yelled out a few more choice words, but he'd

held remarkably steady. Having a hook shoved through your ear was evidently a surefire way to sober up. Fast.

"All right, the worst part is over. I just need to pull the hook the rest of the way out." Holding a tray beneath his ear so she wouldn't have to touch the worm, she removed the forceps and used them to grasp the barb in front. Then she pulled steadily, until the worm plonked onto the instrument tray and the hook was the rest of the way through his ear.

Praying the creature didn't find his way off the counter and onto the floor, she set the tray down and used a piece of antiseptic soaked gauze to sponge away the blood and dirt from the front and the back of the man's ear and then took a piece of dry gauze and applied pressure to stop the bleeding. "Can you hold this here? We'll need to get you a tetanus shot as well as some antibiotics, just in case."

Mr. Tuppele did as she asked and squeezed his earlobe between the two sides of gauze. But when she carried the worm over to the garbage can, the man stopped her with a yelled "Hey!"

She turned toward him, still holding the tray. "Yes?"

"That thing dead?"

She glanced down. It wasn't moving any more, thank God. "I think so."

"Touch it to make sure."

Horror filled her to the core. She hated fishing. Hated bugs. Broken bones, bullet wounds, she could whiz through with ease, but anything that wiggled or crawled or stared with cold-blooded eyes she was just not into. "I'll let you do the honors." She held out the tray and let the man jab the worm with a finger while she cringed. Thankfully it remained limp, even after two more pokes.

"Damn. I was hoping to use that one again."

Again? Hooking himself once hadn't been enough?

She gave a mental eye roll. "Sorry about that. It was probably the alcohol."

"There ain't that much in my blood."

And... Okay.

Dumping the worm and the cleaning gauze into the trash bin, she turned back to face him. "I'll have the nurse come in with the shot and your prescription. Make sure you see your doctor if that ear puffs up or doesn't seem to be healing after a couple of days. Or if you develop a fever."

She took the gauze from him and checked his ear, before pressing tiny round bandages over the front and back of the puncture wound. "You can take those off in a couple of hours."

The man managed to mumble out a "Thank you."

Her phone buzzed, making her jump.

Clint. It had to be.

Patting the man on the back and telling him to take care, she went out and gave instructions to the nurse and asked her to send someone out to check on his buddy. By that time her phone had stopped ringing. "Anyone else waiting for me?"

The nurse grinned. "Not at the moment. But the new barbecue grills are probably being fired up even as we speak."

"Heaven help us all."

Hopefully, that wave of patients would come through after she was off duty. She forced out a laugh, even though she was dying to grab her phone and call Clint back. He knew she was on duty. Knew she'd get back to him as soon as she could.

The nurse got the injection ready and carried it into the room, leaving Jessi alone in the hallway. She took out her phone and glanced at the readout, even though she knew who it was.

C. Marks.

Hitting the redial button, she leaned a shoulder against the wall, an ache settling in her back at all the bending she'd done today.

"Marks here."

"Clint? It's Jessi. What's up?"

"Just calling to see how much longer you were on duty."

Jessi glanced at her watch. "I have another half hour, why?"

"I thought we might get together and talk about Chelsea."

"Is something wrong?"

"No, she's fine. No major developments, but no setbacks either. I just haven't eaten, and I assume you haven't either. Would you like to go somewhere? Or I could come to the hospital and eat with you in the cafeteria."

She grimaced, glancing at the room she'd just come from. "No. The food here isn't the best, and I'm not really hungry. I could do with a shake, though, while you get something else."

She was still puzzling over his sudden change of heart.

"A shake sounds fine. How about we get it to go?"

Okay, she hadn't thought this far ahead. "And go where?"

"We could go to the park on the east side."

The park? She glanced out at the streetlights that were already visible in the darkening sky. "Sounds like a plan."

"Good. I'll meet you at the front entrance of the hospital, okay?"

"I'll be there."

Maybe somehow in that period of time she could shake off all thoughts of sitting inside Clint's car in a dark park, sipping on a milk shake. Or the fleeting images of what they could do once they finished their drinks and had said all they needed to say.

A warning came up from the depths of her soul, reminding her of days gone by and how badly he'd broken her heart. But only because she'd let him.

You can't head down that road again, Jess.

No, she couldn't.

Well, if her heart could make that decree, then she could somehow abide by it.

So she would have to make one thing very clear to herself before he came to pick her up. She would not kiss Clinton Marks again. Not in the dark. Not in a park.

The impromptu rhyme made her smile.

And if *he* kissed her instead?

As much as she might wish otherwise, if that ever happened, then all bets were off.

Because she might just have to kiss him back.

"YOU USED TO have an earring in high school."

A swallow of his milk shake went down the wrong way, and Clint gave a couple of rough coughs before turning in his seat to stare at her. In the dim light of the parking lot at a nearby burger joint, he could just make out her questioning gaze. He'd decided against going to the park, worried about being *too* alone with her.

This was more public, although he wasn't exactly sure what he was worried about. Surely they could both handle this situation like adults. Running into each other from time to time was part of adult behavior.

And going to the fair and having dinner with her and her mother?

All part of being back in his hometown. It meant nothing. At least, he'd better make sure it didn't.

And what about her asking about his earring?

Jessi must have changed clothes before leaving the hospital, because she wasn't wearing a lab jacket or rubber-soled shoes but a pair of slim, dark jeans, lime-green T-shirt and a pair of shoes that had a wedged heel. Not what he would consider doctor gear at all. In fact, she looked much more like the teenager he'd known in high school than a mom with a grown daughter.

He felt like an old fuddy-duddy in comparison, still

in his shirt and tie. He could have sworn the kid at the drive-through window had eyed Jessi with interest. Clint had thrown the teen a glare in return, which had felt like something Jessi's actual father might have done.

When had he turned into such a square?

Maybe when he'd seen the emotional wounds of those returning from battle. And how they reminded him of his own.

"I did have an earring. I took it out the night before I reported for boot camp."

The night of their graduation. The night he'd made love to Jessi. It had marked the end of an era for him, a journey from childhood to becoming a man. Removing the earring that night had been something the old Clint wouldn't have done. He'd have reported to boot camp and waited until someone ordered him to take it out. But he hadn't. After watching Jessi's house for a while that night, he'd gone home—avoiding the after parties and festivities that had gone along with graduation—and stared at himself in the bathroom mirror. God, he'd wanted to stay in Richmond that night. For the first time he'd thought of doing something other than running away. And it had been all because of Jessi.

Instead, he'd unhooked the small gold hoop and pulled it from his ear. As if that one act would give him the courage to walk away when everything inside him had been yelling at him to stay and fight for her, shoving aside his fears about what might happen if he did. What kind of life he might drag her into, if he stayed.

But, even if he'd decided to risk it all for her, Jessi was already spoken for, at least according to Larry and all their friends.

The image in the mirror that night had told him which of them had had a better shot of giving Jess a good life.

The choice had been obvious—at least to him. He had just been a screwup from a dysfunctional family, his finger a constant reminder of what that brought.

He hadn't wanted that for her.

So he'd let her go. An act his teenage self had decided was the mature thing to do. He still had that old hoop in a box somewhere.

Jessi unexpectedly reached up, her fingers cool from holding her frozen drink as they touched his chin. Using gentle pressure, she turned his head to the right, leaning over to look. Her breath washed across his skin, the scent of vanilla catching hold of his senses and making him want to sneak a taste of her mouth.

"Is there still a hole where your earring used to be?"

What was with all the questions? And why had he ever thought sitting in a car—or anywhere else—with her was a good idea?

Just being an adult. Proving he could control his impulses.

He swallowed. "I haven't really looked in a while. Why?"

"We had a guy come into the ER tonight who'd hooked himself while fishing and I had to push the barb all the way through his ear. He was worried his family would think he'd pierced it." She gave a soft laugh. "He wanted to know how long it would take to heal. I told him he should be more worried about the risk of tetanus than a tiny hole."

Her nose wrinkled. "The worst thing was there was still a live worm attached to the end of that hook."

"Well, that had to be an interesting scenario."

"I almost couldn't do it." She let go of him and leaned back in her seat. "Did you ever have to do something and wonder if you'd be able to get through it?" She made a sound in her throat. "Never mind. Of course you have."

He could think of two at the moment. One was leaving her behind twenty-two years ago. And the other was not touching her now, when everything inside him was straining to do just that. "I think everyone eventually gets a case like that. Or at least wonders if the patient would be better off with another doctor."

Jessi suddenly bent to get her milk shake. In the process the lid came off, dumping the cup, and half of its contents, right onto her lap.

He moved to grab it just as her cry of dismay went up. "Oh, no. Clint, I'm so sorry. Your car."

"I'm more worried about you turning into a block of ice." He sent her a half grin as he tried to scoop some of the shake back into the cup. It only ended up sloshing more onto her shirt and jeans.

"Don't move." He got out of the car, cup in hand, and strode into the restaurant to throw it away, exiting a few seconds later with a fresh empty cup and a handful of napkins.

Together they corralled most of the spillage between the paper cup and a spare lid, and then sopped up the remainder with the pile of napkins.

"I always was the clumsiest girl in high school."

"Don't do that."

"What?"

"You used to cut yourself down for things, even when they weren't your fault."

He could always remember some self-deprecating comment or other she would throw out there in school, making everyone laugh and passing it off as a big joke. But there had always been a ring of conviction to the jibes that had made him wonder if she didn't actually believe all the "I'm such a klutzo" and "Wow, am I ever a nerd" statements.

She glanced up at him, her hand full of napkins. "Everyone did that. Even you."

Yes, he had. And he knew for a fact that he'd believed most of what he'd said. Maybe that's why it bothered him so much when she did it.

"Let's get you home."

"I'll pay for whatever it costs to clean your seats."

He shook his head. "They're leather. I'll just wipe them down with a damp rag. They'll be fine. You, however, might need to be hosed off." He said it with a grin to show he was joking.

"Thanks for being so understanding," she said, as he gathered up the rest of the trash and got out of the car once more to throw it all away.

Understanding? Hell, he was barely holding it together. He put the car in Drive and followed her directions to her house. "Come on in while I change. We can talk about Chelsea over coffee, if that's okay?"

"Sounds good."

No, it didn't. It sounded idiotic. Impulsive. And he should leave. Now. But something drove him to open his car door and follow her up the steps to her house.

It's just coffee. She hasn't propositioned you. You're her daughter's doctor, for God's sake.

He was the one who'd called to arrange this meeting in the first place.

Which meant he should have asked her to come to his office, not a fast-food joint.

But surely Jessi had patients who were acquaintances or the children of acquaintances during her years of working in the ER. And it would make sense that she might meet them in the hospital cafeteria or a coffee joint to catch up later. It was kind of hard to work in a town where you grew up—no matter how large—and never expect to run into anyone you knew.

Only Jessi was more than an acquaintance.

And what they'd had was more than a quick hello and goodbye.

That was years ago. They'd spent a little over an hour down by a creek, hopped up on hormones and the thrill of graduating from high school. And she'd been distraught by her father's unbending rules.

It was in the past. All of it.

And that kiss beside his car at her mother's house a week ago?

Fueled by memories of that shared past. It wouldn't happen again. Not if he could help it.

She unlocked the door, glancing behind her as if to make sure he was still coming. "I'll get you that rag if you want to wipe the seat down while I change. I'll leave the front door open."

"Sounds good." And if he were smart, he'd leave the rag just outside the door afterwards and take off in his car before she could come back out of her bedroom.

And that would be just as unprofessional as kissing her had been.

At least that was his mental excuse, because after wiping up the few drops of milk shake from his seat he found himself back inside her house, calling up the stairs to her and asking her what she wanted him to do with the rag.

"Just put it in the sink and have a seat in the living room. I'll be down in a few minutes."

Instead of doing as she asked, he rinsed out the rag and hung it over a towel bar he found in her utility room. Then he spotted the coffee machine on one of the counters and a huge glass jar filled with those single-serving coffee filters that seemed to be all the rage nowadays. He had one of the machines at home himself. The least he could do was make the coffee while he waited. He'd just found the mugs when Jessi came traipsing back into the kitchen, this time dressed in a white floral sundress similar to the one she'd worn during dinner at her mom's, her feet bare, hair damp as if she'd showered.

He tensed, before forcing himself to relax again.

Of course she'd had to rinse off. She'd had a sticky drink spilled in her lap. It meant nothing.

"Sorry, Clint. I didn't intend you to get the coffee ready, too."

"No problem. I just thought I'd save you a step." He realized something. "Where's Cooper?"

"At Mom's. He's a communal pet, remember? I get him tomorrow."

"Ah, right."

She reached in a cabinet. "What do you take in your coffee?"

"Just sugar."

She set a crystal bowl down and then went over to the refrigerator and pulled out a container of milk. "Help yourself."

"Thanks."

They worked in silence until the coffee was done and they'd moved into Jessi's living room, which was furnished with a huge sectional and a center ottoman. Pictures lined the fireplace mantel and as he took a sip of his coffee he wandered over to them. There were several snapshots of Chelsea doing various activities and one of a more formal military pose. She was soft and natural in every photo except the last one, since official portraits were supposed to be done sans smile. But even in that one there was a spark of humor lighting her eyes that the woman back at the VA hospital lacked.

There was one picture of Jessi and Larry in their wedding attire. Both of them looked so young. Larry would be forever ageless, never having had a chance to really grow up and become a man.

He might still be alive if someone hadn't...

Her earlier words came back to mind. If he *were* still alive, Clint would probably not be standing here in her living room right now.

He probably shouldn't be, regardless.

And the sight of the two of them smiling up at each other sent something kicking at his innards. A slight jabbing sensation that could have been jealousy but that made no sense. He'd been the one who'd left. What had he expected Jessi to do? Dump Larry and wait for him to come back for her?

He hadn't. He'd never set foot in Virginia again until now. And if he'd known who Chelsea was before he'd agreed to come, he doubted very seriously he would be standing here now.

"Clint?"

Her voice reminded him that he was still staring at the picture. "Sorry. Just seeing how Chelsea was before she deployed." He turned and sat on the shorter leg of the sofa perpendicular to her. "She smiled a lot."

"Yes. She was happy. Always. Which is why it's so hard to see her like this and not know how to help her."

"I'm sure it is." He took another sip of his coffee, wishing he hadn't added quite so much sugar.

"Did she talk at all today?" Jessi tucked her legs up under her, smoothing her hemline to cover her bare knees.

"She shared a little about what her days in captivity had been like. What she did to pass the time."

"You said on the phone there weren't any breakthroughs. You don't consider that one?"

That was a tricky question to answer. Because while it was technically more than Chelsea had told him in the past, she'd spoken without emotion, as if she were using the information itself as one more blockade against questions that might venture too close to painful subjects. Like that macabre tissue paper baby she kept in her nightstand.

"It does help to know a little about what went on. But she's not talking about her captors or about her rescue. Just about what she did. Reciting her ABCs and having conversations inside her head."

Jessi slumped. "It's been almost two and a half months."

He didn't mention that sometimes the effects of PTSD lasted a lifetime. His dad, instead of getting better, had slowly sunk into a pit filled with alcohol, drawing away from those he'd known and loved. And when he or his mom had tried to force the issue... Yeah, that was something he didn't want to talk to Jessi about.

"I know it seems like forever. But she was held for four months. It takes time. Sometimes lots of it."

She stared down at her cup for several long seconds before glancing up with eyes that held a wealth of pain. "It sounds so terrible for me to say this out loud, but I'm afraid to have her home again. Afraid the next time she tries something I won't get there in time to stop her."

Clint set his coffee cup down on a tray that was perched on an ottoman between the two seating areas. He went over to sit beside her, setting her coffee aside as he draped his arm around her shoulder and drew her close. "Jess, you're dealing with some aftereffects yourself. Maybe you should talk to someone."

She lifted her head. "I'm talking to you."

"I mean someone objective." The second the words came out of his mouth he wished he could haul them back and swallow them whole. He tried to clarify his meaning. "It would be a conflict of interest for me to treat you both."

He realized that explanation wasn't any better when she tried to pull away from him. He squeezed slightly, keeping her where she was. "I'm not explaining myself very well." Hell, some psychiatrist he was. He couldn't even have a coherent conversation with this woman.

"No, it's okay." She relaxed, and her arm snaked around his waist with a sigh. "I'm being overly sensitive."

No, she wasn't. And Clint was drawing closer and closer to a line he'd sworn he wasn't going to cross with her. But with her head against his chest and her hand curled around his side, her scent surrounded him. *She* surrounded him.

Her fingers went to his left hand and her head lifted slightly, staring at something. Then she touched his damaged finger. She bent a little closer. "What happened?"

Damn. He tried to laugh it off. "An old war wound."

"You never mentioned going to war."

He hadn't. That particular war had been fought here on American soil. Not even his father had known what he'd done to his son with that hard, angry squeeze.

"I was making a joke. A bad one." He shrugged. "It's not important."

Her head went back to his chest, but her finger continued to stroke his crooked pinkie, the sensation strangely intimate and disturbing on a level that was primal.

He needed to get up and move before either of them did something they would regret.

Then she lifted his hand to her mouth and kissed his finger, the delicate touch ramming through his chest and driving the air from his lungs.

Her tongue trailed across the skin, and his hand tightened slightly on her shoulder. He wasn't sure whether or not it was in warning. And if it was, was he warning her not to stop? Or not to continue? His body responded to the former, rejecting the latter. Because he did want her to continue. To keep on kissing him with those featherlight brushes. And not just there. Everywhere.

"Jess," he murmured. "I think I should move back to the other seat."

She stopped, still holding his hand. "Does that mean you're going to?" Her whispered words were as much a caress as her touch had been.

Heat swirled through him.

"Not if you keep talking to me in that tone of voice."

She let go of his hand and moved hers a little bit higher, smoothing over his biceps until her palm rested on his shoulder. And when she looked up at him, he was lost.

Decision made.

He was going to kiss her. Just like she'd kissed him. Softly. Gently. And with just enough contact to drive her wild.

CHAPTER ELEVEN

IT WAS AS if the past twenty-two years had rewound themselves.

The second his lips touched hers, Jessi was back by the creek, her only worries her father's strict rules and getting to school on time. And it felt so good. So carefree.

If only she'd known how free she'd been back then.

But she could experience it again. With the same man. Just for a little while.

She'd always thought Clint had been invincible all those years ago. But her mom's comment about his father and discovering that crooked little finger showed her he wasn't. He was just as human as she was. Back then...and maybe even now.

Jessi threaded her fingers through his hair, hearing Clint's low groan as he moved to deepen the kiss, shifting her until she lay half across his lap, one of his hands beneath her shoulders, his other splayed flat on her stomach. It was that hand that made her go all liquid inside. It wasn't doing anything special but it was between two very sensitive areas of her body, both of which were doing their damnedest to coax his fingers to slide their way.

A gentle touch of his tongue was enough to get her full attention.

Yes!

Surely he wouldn't stop this time. It had been ages since she'd been with somcone. So long that the slightest movement of his body had her eagerly lapping up the sensations like a person deprived of food and water, and desperate for any sign of relief.

She was ready for that kind of relief. For him.

Clint.

And here he was, in her house. And there was absolutely no one around. Not her mom. Not Chelsea.

Just the two of them.

So she pressed closer to him, deepening their kiss, his soft lips making her feel dizzy with need.

And finally…finally, the hand at her waist woke up, his thumb drawing little circles on her belly that had her moaning with anticipation, arching up into it with a mental plea that he evidently heard. Because with a single movement it slid up and over her right breast, that circling thumb finding her nipple without hesitation. Her sundress had a built-in bra, but it was thin, just a shelf of netting with a piece of elastic beneath it, so his touch was heady and intimate, arcing straight down to her toes and then back up again.

When his fingers moved away, she whimpered in protest. His mouth slid from hers, depriving her of another point of contact.

"Clint…"

His hand moved to the back of her head, supporting it as the scrape of his chin along her cheek put him at her ear. "I don't want to stop."

The moment of truth. She sensed he was giving her time to compose herself, to give her a chance to put an end to things even while telling her he didn't want to.

She made a dangerous decision.

"Then don't."

His fingers tightened on the back of her head. Then

his other hand went to the thin strap on her sundress and tugged it down her arm, leaving one shoulder bare.

There was a slight hesitation, then that wicked thumb went to work, brushing the joint where her shoulder met her arm. "Is this what you want?"

"More." The word came out as a shaky whisper. She hardly dared to believe she was goading him to continue. But this was exactly what she needed. To have someone just sweep aside her normal code of conduct and make her...*feel* again.

"How about this?" His fingertips moved higher, trailing from beneath her jaw down the side of her neck and along her collarbone. Light ticklish touches that made her ache and squirm.

She wanted him everywhere at once, kissing her mouth, cupping her breast, filling her with his heat where it counted the most. So she took his hand and placed it on her breast, where she wanted it.

"You read my mind, Jess." The words came out in a half growl that made her shiver.

He ducked beneath the edge of her sundress and found her bare skin. He paused then curved his palm over her, the light friction on her nipple sending a low sound up her throat.

"Hell, woman. You need to warn a man before you go braless."

Encouraged by the rough words, she bit her way up his jaw and then smiled against his mouth. "My dress has a bra. You just missed it."

"Could have fooled me." His thumb and forefinger captured the tight bead and gave a gentle squeeze that made her squirm again. "But in that case..."

He removed his hand and urged her off the couch and onto her feet, while he sat, legs splayed.

"Wh-what are you doing?"

"I want to see you—all of you—but at the rate I'm going, I'm not going to make it that far." A quick flash of teeth accompanied the words.

She smiled back at him, his meaning giving her a shot of courage and daring her to tease him back. "I think I can help with that. What would you like to see first?" Balling the skirt portion of her dress, she slid the hem part way up her thighs, keeping her attention focused on his face.

A muscle worked in his jaw, and he placed his hands flat on his thighs. "Let's start from the top. And work our way down. Just like we did in school."

The reminder of how his hands had trailed from her face to her breasts and finally down to that last forbidden place made hot need spurt through her. And the way his knuckles turned white as his long fingers dug into his thighs told her that need wasn't one-sided.

"Okay, let's do that." She let go of her skirt and trailed the back of her right hand down her neck, like he'd done moments earlier, only she didn't stop at her collarbone. Instead, she dragged her fingers along the edge of her bodice—one strap still draped over her arm. The second strap flipped down.

"Next?" she asked, waiting for direction.

"Peel it down. Slowly." The low words weren't abrupt and bossy, rather they coaxed her to do his bidding. Dared her to cross a threshold to a room she'd never entered before. Her times with Larry had been good, but they'd been to the point. Vanilla sex that had been a sharing of hearts and minds, even if it hadn't been superimaginative. Then again, they'd had such a short amount of time together, there hadn't been a chance to venture much further than that.

And that wasn't something she was going to think about.

Not when Clint was right here, holding the door open and asking her to step through it.

This was what she wanted—what she expected from Clint. Wild and raw and real…echoes of the rebellious boy he'd once been. The one who had whispered to a matching defiance within her, drawing it out and fulfilling her in ways she never would have imagined.

So she crossed her arms and took a strap in each hand and pulled with slow, steady pressure that made the fabric of her dress roll back on itself, revealing the upper swell of her breasts. She kept going until she got to the most crucial part, then hesitated.

"Jess." The whispered word shifted her eyes back to his. But he wasn't looking at her face. He was staring at the half-exposed portion of her body, the heat in his expression taking away the last of her inhibitions. She tugged, and he swallowed.

"You have no idea how much I want to drag you down here and finish this."

"Then do it." She let her arms go to her sides, making no attempt to hide herself from him.

He reached behind him and retrieved his wallet from his pants. Her mouth watered, thinking he was going to pull a condom out and do exactly what she'd suggested. And a packet did appear, but he made no move to haul her down onto the couch.

"Here or in your bedroom?"

"It doesn't matter." It was the truth. She wanted him. Badly, and she didn't care where it happened, as long as it happened. And soon.

He smiled again and set the condom on his thigh, making her tighten inside. Because six inches north of that packet was a bulge that left no question as to whether or not he wanted her.

"Does that dress have a zipper?"

It took a second for the question to register, and when she glanced up at him she saw that he knew exactly where she'd been looking. That he'd meant for her to measure the distance between possibility and reality. Because nothing was for sure until he slipped that protection over himself and thrust into her.

"Yes."

"Can you reach it?"

She nodded, her now shaking fingers going to the side of her dress, finding the pull tab then sliding it down to her hips, her other hand holding the rest of the garment in place.

"Let it go," he murmured, his meaning clear.

Releasing her grip, the fabric slid to the floor, leaving her standing in front of him clad only in her panties.

She expected him to tell her to remove those as well, but instead his fingers went to the button of his slacks and undid it.

"Once those come off, honey, it's all over." His bald words made the breath stall in her chest. As did the fact that he was sliding his own zipper down and ripping the condom open.

She wanted to do that. "Wait."

Wary eyes moved to her face. Oh! He thought she was stopping him.

Hurrying to correct him, she said, "Let me."

He took the condom from the packet. "Next time."

Next time!

Her lips parted as he drew the waistband of his briefs down and exposed himself. And unlike her, Clint had no inhibitions. None. Not the last time they'd been together. Not this time. His eyes burned into hers as he sat there. He toyed with the open condom.

The nub at the apex of her thighs tightened, making her squeeze her legs together, aching for some kind of relief.

She licked her lips. "Put it on."

"First your panties."

Hurrying to do as he asked, she hooked her thumbs into the elastic and started to bend over to slide them down, only to have him interrupt her. "Watch me as you do it."

Shifting her focus back to his face, she finished, stepping out of her underwear and standing back upright.

"Beautiful," he murmured. "Even more now than then."

He finally rolled the condom down his length, and took himself in hand. "Now come here, honey."

She moved between his still splayed legs and shuddered when the fingers of his free hand slid in a smooth move up her thigh and found the heart of her. Just the process of removing her clothing while he'd watched had made her body moist and ready.

"Hell. Just like I remember."

By the time he'd finally touched her by the creek, she'd been shaking with desire. One flick of his finger had sent her over the edge. She'd been so embarrassed, only to have him shush her and tell her how much he liked it. When he'd finally entered her, she had already been riding the crest of that same wave, shattering right along with him.

The Clint of today slid one finger inside her, wringing a moan from her. He stayed there, just like that, not moving. She shuddered, needing him so badly she couldn't speak.

"Spread your legs for me."

Somehow, she shuffled her legs farther apart.

"Perfect." He sat up straight, the pressure of his finger inside her holding her right where she was, putting his face dangerously close. Too late, she realized that was what he'd been aiming for all along. "How much will it take this time, Jess?"

Another reference to their first time together.

He added a second finger and pushed deep, using the pair to edge her hips closer. Suddenly off balance, she was forced to clutch his shoulders. "How much, Jess?" he repeated.

Then, as she watched, he moved his mouth until it was pressed against her…and let his tongue slide right across her.

It was as if he'd lit a fuse inside her. Her nails dug into his shoulders and every muscle in her body stiffened as what he was doing blotted out everything except the sensation of his tongue moving backward along her in a slow, drawn-out motion. The fuse ran out of line in a millisecond, and she detonated, crying out as his fingers finally moved, pumping inside her while she convulsed around them.

Then she was in his lap, his hands gripping her butt as he thrust hard into her, filling her beyond belief. She wrapped her hands around his neck, her mouth going to his ear as she rode him furiously, whimpering as her climax continued to crash all around her. He gave a muttered oath and then jerked his hips forward, holding her tight against his body as he strained upward for long seconds, the pressure inside her causing a new wave of convulsions.

When his muscles finally went limp, his arms encircled her back, thumb gliding along her spine.

She drew a deep, careful breath, registered Clint's heavy breathing and smiled, the problems of the day melting as his scent mixed with her own and filled her head. She nuzzled his cheek and then went back to his ear.

"I guess I'm not the only one who went up pretty fast."

His fingers tightened around her, although his voice was light. "Is that a complaint?"

"No. It was sexy, watching you lose control."

He drew her mouth back to his and kissed her long and deep. "Is that so? In that case, maybe we should find out which one of us holds out longer...the second time around."

CHAPTER TWELVE

"It's just been a long time, and I was upset."

Not the first words a man wanted to hear when he woke up after a night of passionate lovemaking. But there they were, and Clint was at an obvious disadvantage, since he was lying on her couch, an afghan draped over his privates, while Jessi hovered above him, already dressed, looking both worried and...

Hungry.

It was there in her eyes as they slid over his body and then darted back to his face, as if she was doing her damnedest not to look at him.

They'd never even made it back to her bedroom last night, instead using the long L-shaped couch to its full advantage.

Well, if she thought he was going to make it easy for her...

He slid up and propped himself up one of the throw pillows as he eyed her right back.

"Well, that's a hell of a good morning."

She took a step closer. "Sorry. I just don't want you to think..."

"That last night meant something other than great sex?"

Her eyes widened. "That's not what I was going to say."

"So it did mean something," he said, not sure which he preferred.

"No." She held out a hand to stop him from saying anything else. All that did, though, was give him a way to reach out grab her wrist.

She half laughed, half screamed. "Clint, stop. I'm trying to be serious."

"Oh, honey, so am I."

She let him drag her to the sofa and haul her down on top of him, where a certain area of his body was already displaying its delight at this turn of events.

"Wait. Let me finish my thought."

Leaving his fingers threaded in her hair, he looked at her, knowing his next words were not what he wanted to say at all. Hell, he didn't want her to say *anything* except what she wanted him to do to her. But he forced the words out. "Okay, so talk."

She drew an audible breath. "I just didn't want you to think last night had anything to do with Chelsea."

Her eyes trailed away from him, but the words themselves hit him in the chest like a bucket of ice water, sluicing away any hint of desire and leaving a cold trail of suspicion in its wake.

A sour taste rose up in his throat.

"I hadn't thought that at all, Jess." He rolled until she was wedged between him and the back of the couch as he stared at her. "Until just this very second. Did last night have something to do with her?"

"No! Yes. There are just things that you don't know. About how her father…about how Larry died. Not even Chelsea knows. But if someone from our past sees you, I'm afraid she could find out."

"I think you'd better tell me, then."

Jessi's eyes filled with tears. "A few months after we

got married he told one of his friends I was pregnant. Well, the friend had seen us—you and me—leave graduation together and come back within minutes of each other. It got him thinking. He suggested Larry ask me whose child I was carrying." There was a pause before she continued. "We had a huge fight, and he accused me of sleeping with you. When I wouldn't deny it, he said Chelsea probably wasn't even his."

She shifted against the couch, and he eased back to give her some breathing space.

Clint could barely open his mouth. "His death?"

"He stormed off...so very angry. He went to a bar, and then a few hours later his car hit an embankment. He died instantly."

Hell. He felt like the biggest ass in history.

He leaned his forehead against hers, guilt causing his muscles to cramp. One more thing destroyed by his lack of control all those years ago. "Dammit. I'm sorry, Jessi. I had no idea."

So many mistakes: if he hadn't impulsively raced after her that night. If he hadn't stayed there with her and done the unthinkable... If he hadn't left her to deal with it all afterwards.

The small box of baggage from the past morphed into a shiny new trunk of regret.

They remained like that for a minute or two until Jessi gave a little sniff.

He scooted back some more, giving her a chance to compose herself, trying to ignore the quick swipe of palms across damp cheeks. The last thing he wanted to do was hurt her.

Then...or now. But it would seem he'd done both.

And he knew what he had to do to keep from hurting her further.

He sat up and slid off the sofa, conscious of her eyes following his movements as he gathered his clothing and headed for the bathroom just down her hallway. After he'd flushed and washed his hands, he dressed quickly, avoiding his image in the mirror as much as he possibly could, because whenever his eyes met those in the reflection, angry accusations stared right back at him.

How had he let this happen again?

When he was around her, his common sense went out the window, and he let his emotions rule.

Just like his father. He didn't hit, but his actions caused just as much damage. Dammit, they'd culminated in a young man's death. Someone Jessi had loved.

He had to take himself off Chelsea's case. It was no longer about remaining objective but about doing what had served him—and everyone around him—well for the last twenty-two years: staying away from emotionally charged situations.

If he'd known the details about Larry's death, he would have taken himself off Chelsea's case that very first day. This time, though, he wasn't going to let Jessi carry any of the blame for what just had happened between them. Nope, he was going to stuff it into his own bag of blame. One that seemed to swell larger every time he laid eyes on her. When he returned to the living room, Jessi was still there, seated on the sofa, only this time she had a phone to her ear.

"Of course, honey," Jessi said to whoever was on the line. "I'll check with Dr. Marks and see how soon we can arrange it." Her glance met his and she mouthed, "Chelsea."

Jessi's daughter was calling her? Right now?

He sat beside her, suddenly very aware of all inappropriate things they'd done in this house last night.

The second she clicked off the phone, she finally looked at him. Really looked at him. "Chelsea wants to talk about something." She licked her lips as if afraid of saying the next words. "She wants us both to be there."

Please, don't quit yet.

The words chanted through her skull as Clint dropped her off at Scott's Memorial to pick up her car and then waited for her to follow him back to the VA hospital.

They hadn't said much once she'd got off the phone, and the interior of his car had been filled with awkward silence and a sense of dread that had blocked her stomach and clogged her throat.

How could she have been so stupid to think last night wouldn't have any serious repercussions? Her only excuse was that it had felt so good to be in his arms. So right.

Only it wasn't right.

The timing had always been lousy when it came to her and Clint. If he'd stayed all those years ago, she never would have married Larry. But she never would have had Chelsea either.

And just like last time Clint wouldn't be there for the long haul. As soon as they'd found a replacement for him, he'd be gone.

He would waltz out of her life once again.

It's just not meant to be. It never was.

The words trailed through her head as if dragged on a banner behind a plane for all the world to see.

Her subconscious rejected them, though, cutting the line and watching as the lettering fell to the ground in a swirl of white canvas and belching smoke.

Before she had a chance to come to any conclusions, Clint pulled to a stop in one of the few parking spaces that had another spot beside it. She slid her car next to his and took a couple of deep breaths before she got out and went to where he stood, waiting. "You won't say anything, will you?"

Clint looked at her as if she had two heads. "About what? Larry? Or about us having a second one-night stand?"

A flash of intense hurt zinged through her chest, making her gasp for air.

As if realizing what he'd done, he hooked his index finger around hers. "Sorry, Jess." He gave a squeeze before letting her go. "I seem to spend a lot of time issuing apologies nowadays."

She tipped her chin back. "Let's just see what she wants." The words came out sharper than she'd meant them to, but maybe that was a good thing. She could put her armor back in place and pretend last night had meant nothing. "We can discuss everything else later. If we could avoid arriving at her room at the same time, that would make me feel more comfortable."

"So you want me to hide out in my office for a few minutes before joining you."

Saying it like that made Jessi realize how cheesy and paranoid the idea sounded. "You're right. Let's just go together."

Once they got to Chelsea's room, they found her seated on the bed, that eerie tissue-paper baby on top of the nightstand. Jessi tensed. That had to be what she wanted to talk about.

She leaned down and kissed her cheek. "Hi, sweetheart."

Chelsea grabbed her around the shoulders, wordlessly hugging her tight for a minute or two. Then she whispered, "I'm sorry for putting you through what I have for the past couple of months. I love you, Mom. Always remember that."

A chill went over her at the solemn words. She stood up and glanced at Clint. "All that matters is that you start feeling better."

"I think I will as soon as I get something off my chest."

Once they were all seated, Clint started things off with some light conversation, never even hinting that he'd been with Jessi in anything other than a professional capacity. Instead, he asked about Jessi's day at work yesterday, subtly guiding her to tell the fishhook-in-the-ear story. Chelsea actually laughed right on cue.

"You hate worms," her daughter said.

"I do. I still remember you bringing in a jar of dirt for me on Mother's Day. Little did I know that that you and Grandpa had spent hours digging up earthworms to put in it."

Chelsea grinned again. "You screamed when one of them dug through the dirt and slithered along the inside of the jar. Grandpa laughed and laughed."

Jessi smiled at the memory of Chelsea and her dad's conspiratorial glances at each other as they'd handed her their "gift."

"You always were the fearless one."

"Not always." Chelsea's smile faded. "I need to tell you something. Something about when I was held in Afghanistan."

"Okay." She glanced at Clint, but he simply nodded at her.

Setting the doll in her lap, Chelsea took a deep breath. "You were right about my pregnancy. I was expecting when I was captured. I hadn't told anyone because it meant a ticket straight home—and I didn't want that. The whole thing was so stupid. It was an accident. I kept meaning

to do something—say something—but I put things off…
and put things off." Her eyes came up. "And then we were
ambushed."

Jessi's heart contracted. "Did they…did they do something to you, honey?"

"No." Chelsea glanced up at the ceiling her eyes filling
with tears and spilling over. "I mean, they didn't hurt me
physically. They isolated me and made me change into a
long, loose tunic. Then they wrote a script and forced me
to read it in front of a camera."

Jessi had never heard about any message, but she didn't
say anything, just let Chelsea continue talking.

"As one month turned into two, the isolation started to
get to me, and I began talking to the baby. Every day. I
went from just wanting her to go away to needing her for
my own survival."

Her?

Oh, God, had they made Chelsea deliver the baby and
then stolen it from her? Was that what the doll was all
about?

When Chelsea's words stopped, Clint voiced the question that Jessi couldn't bring herself to ask.

"What happened to the baby?" The line of his jaw was
tight, as if he too was struggling with his emotions right
now.

"She died."

"Oh, Chelsea…" Her mind went blank as she tried to
find the words to say. But there was nothing.

"She died, and I couldn't do anything to save her."

"Your captors didn't help?"

She shook her head. "I didn't want them to know I was
pregnant, because I wasn't sure how they'd react to an un-
married woman carrying a child. So I hid my condition. It
wasn't hard under the robes. I was in my cell most of the

time, and I figured once I delivered, they'd let me keep her, or maybe even let us go."

Clint spoke up. "How far along were you when you were captured?"

"Around three months." She turned to glance at him. "I lost track of time after a while, but I think she was born around four months into my captivity."

Too small. Without the help of modern medicine the baby wouldn't have had much chance to survive.

Chelsea continued. "She came in the middle of the night. She was so tiny. And absolutely perfect." Her fingers caressed the doll. "She never even cried. I held her for a long, long time, praying for her to take a breath." Her voice broke for a second, but then she continued. "After a while, I knew she was dead, and I was afraid if anyone found out, I'd be killed, too—and I didn't want anyone other than me touching her. So I tore off a piece of my robe and wrapped her in it, then I scratched a hole in the dirt floor of my cell with my fingernails and buried her. I was rescued less than a week later."

A couple more tears trickled free, and Jessi reached over and held her hand, her own vision blurry.

"I'm so, so sorry, Chelsea." Her daughter had dealt with all of this by herself. There'd been no one there to help her...no one to comfort her. Her own heart felt ready to shatter in two.

A box of tissues appeared on the tiny table in front of them. Chelsea took several of them and wiped her eyes and then blew her nose before turning to look at her.

"Once she was gone, I realized just how alone I was. I couldn't even mark my baby's grave. And if I died there, I would be just like her. Dumped in a shallow grave somewhere. No one would even know I existed. After I got home, I started thinking maybe that would be for the best.

That the baby should have survived. Not me. That I should be the one forgotten, instead of her."

Clint leaned forward. "You wouldn't have been forgotten, Chelsea. People would have grieved deeply, just like you grieved for your baby. You have a mother who loves you. A grandmother. Comrades in your unit. And you're right where you should be. You're here. Alive. Everything you did while in that cell had to be done. It gave you a chance to survive. Gave you a chance to make sure your baby would never be forgotten.

"If you had died, her memory would have died with you." He paused, keeping his gaze focused on her. "And yet look at what's happened. Your mom now knows about her. I know about her. You'll probably talk to more people about her as you live your life. She won't be forgotten. Your very survival makes that a certainty."

Chelsea seemed to consider his words for a minute, and then nodded as if coming to a decision. "I'd like her to have a grave here in the States. A marker with her name on it."

"Of course we'll do that." Jessi wondered if the ache in her heart would ever stop. She'd been about to be a grandmother of a baby girl who might have survived, given access to modern medical facilities. But those were things she could never say to Chelsea—*would* never say to her. They would decide together whether to tell Chelsea's paternal grandparents. Larry's parents were still alive, and Jessi and Chelsea kept in touch with them regularly. As for her mother...

They could think through all that later. The important thing was that Chelsea was talking. Working through things she hadn't told another soul.

She had to ask. "Does the father know?"

"No. I never told him, and there seems to be no point

now." She licked her lips. "And he could get in serious trouble if the truth were made known."

"Why?"

"He's an officer, and I'm not. We weren't supposed to get involved with each other to begin with."

Jessi shot Clint a glance that was probably just as guilt-filled as she feared. But he wasn't looking at her. At all.

"Did you love him?"

"No. And he didn't love me. It just happened. Neither of us meant for it to, and we've never gotten together again. It was just the one time."

God. Chelsea could have been describing exactly what had happened years ago, only with different players. And Chelsea was right about one thing. Larry had found out and the consequences had been disastrous. And so very permanent.

Her stomach clenched and clenched.

And unlike Chelsea, she hadn't learned from that mistake all those years ago. She'd gone right back and done it again.

Jessi hadn't been able to resist Clint.

She never had. He'd been just as taboo as that officer Chelsea had spoken of.

Chelsea glanced at Clint. "You told me during our first meeting that you were here to help me get through this. So I'm ready to try. I promise to work really hard."

Clint stiffened visibly in his seat.

Chelsea, totally unaware of the strained dynamics in the room, kept on talking. "Did you go through boot camp, Dr. Marks?"

"I did." Nothing in his voice betrayed his feelings, but Jessi knew. She knew exactly the struggle going on inside him right now.

"Then you know a soldier agrees never to leave a wounded comrade behind."

He gave a quick nod.

"I may not be missing a limb or have any visible external injuries except these…" she held out her wrists, showing the scars "…but I am wounded. So please, please don't leave me behind."

CHAPTER THIRTEEN

THEY WERE MAKING PROGRESS.

It came in fits and starts, but the past week had seen Chelsea come further than she had since she'd been at the hospital.

And Clint was still on her case, even though in his heart of hearts he knew he shouldn't be. But Chelsea's words had reached to the heart of who he was as a soldier, and he knew that he would have wished more than anything that someone had been there for his father. But they hadn't. He'd dealt with his demons alone. That's not what he wanted for Chelsea.

Besides, since that session, Jessi had been careful to keep her distance, speaking to him only when he asked her something during joint sessions or when he saw her in the halls at the VA hospital. It was like she was walking on eggshells around him.

Well, so was he, around her. And the edges of those shells were beginning to feel damn uncomfortable beneath his feet.

But as long as he could maintain things for another few weeks, they should be fine. Chelsea had gotten her wish not to be abandoned "like her baby." And she was gradually starting to believe that none of what had happened had been her fault. She'd soon be discharged and start doing her sessions on a weekly outpatient basis—which meant he'd be seeing even less of Jessi.

And that made his chest tighten in ways he'd never thought possible. In fact, he hadn't felt this way since...

Since the day he'd left her twenty-two years ago.

Just like he'd leave her again once his transfer papers went through.

And, yes, he was prepared to put in for one, even though a little voice inside of him whispered that when this was all over—when Chelsea was no longer his patient—he could ask Jessi out on a real date and woo her the way he'd once dreamed about.

Except nothing had changed. Not really.

He was still not the right man for her. He was still too cautious—too afraid to let himself be with any one woman.

Besides, Jessi had already experienced the worst parts of coming from a military family, having a daughter who'd served and come back with serious issues. Did she really need to be involved with a man who dealt with wounded soldiers day after day? Wouldn't it just remind her of all she'd gone through with Chelsea?

Never had he felt the weight of responsibility more than he did right now.

"Dr. Marks?" One of the nurses popped her head into the room. "Peter Summers just called. He's asking for a refill of his methadone prescription."

Another complicated case.

He sighed. Peter's maintenance dosage of the drug was dependent on his showing up for his sessions, the last two of which he'd missed. A longtime addict, methadone was meant to replace cravings. The treatment regimen was highly regulated and required sticking to a precise schedule. That meant outpatient sessions and progress reports. Clint would have followed those guidelines even without the corresponding laws, just because it was the right thing to do.

Hell, it didn't seem like he'd been too worried about doing the right thing when he'd been rolling around on Jessi's couch.

And thoughts like that would get him nowhere.

"Would you mind calling him and setting up a new appointment? Tell him he can't have a refill without coming in."

Consequences. Larry's tragic death came to mind. The consequences of his fling with Jessi.

Well, someone else besides him might as well learn the meaning of the word.

"Will do." The nurse jotted something down onto the paper in her hand. "Oh, and I didn't know if you knew, but there's someone waiting to see you. At least, I think she is. She's come down the hallway and almost knocked on your door twice before going back to the waiting room and just sitting there."

He glanced at his planner. He wasn't scheduled to see anyone for another couple of hours. "Any idea who it is?"

"It's Chelsea Riley's mother."

His throat tightened. Jessi was here to see him? Had almost knocked on his door twice?

"Is she still here?"

The nurse nodded. "She's in the main waiting area."

He pushed his chair back and climbed to his feet. "Has she been to see Chelsea yet?"

"No, that was the strange thing. She came straight here without asking anyone anything." She shrugged. "I thought you might like to know."

"Thank you." He shoved his arms into his sports jacket. "If I'm not in my office when you get hold of Peter Summers, could you leave me note with his next session date? Or let me know what he said?"

"Sure thing."

With that, the nurse popped back out of the room, leaving him to struggle with whether to go down to the waiting area and talk to Jessi or to pretend he knew nothing about it and either wait for her to come to him or to leave, whichever she decided.

Consequences, Clint. You have to do more than talk the talk—you have to be willing to walk the walk. Even if it means walking away.

Despite his inner lecture, he wandered down the hallway—like the idiot he was—and found her in the waiting area, just like Maria had said.

Jessi's head was down, her hands clasped loosely between her jeans-clad knees. She could have been praying. Hell, maybe that's what he should be doing right now. Because just seeing her was like a fist to the stomach. A hard one. Hard enough to leave him breathless and off balance.

And all those emotions he'd worked so hard to suppress boiled up to the surface.

The waiting room was full, only five or six seats empty in the whole place and neither of them next to where Jessi was perched. He moved in, catching the eye of an older man, who, although gaunt, still sat at stiff attention. Clint nodded to him, receiving the same in return. He finally got to where Jessi was seated.

"Jess?"

She glanced up, the worry in her green eyes immediately apparent. She popped to her feet. "I was just coming to see you."

"I know. One of the nurses told me."

Her teeth came down on her lower lip. "I figured it

must look weird. I just couldn't get up the nerve to…" She glanced around, bringing back the fact that the room was full and now more than one or two sets of eyes were following their exchange with interest.

"I'll take you back to the office," he said. "And I'll run down to the cafeteria and get us some coffee." He wasn't sure how smart it was to be alone with her. But as long as he kept the door unlocked, they'd be fine. At least, Clint hoped so.

He went to the cafeteria and ordered their coffees. She liked hers with milk, something he shouldn't remember, but did. He dumped a packet of sugar into his own brew and headed back to his office.

When he pushed through the door, he noted she still wore the same haunted expression she'd had earlier. Setting her coffee on the desk in front of her, he went around to the other side and slid into his office chair. "What's going on, Jess?"

"It's Mom. I—I felt like I had to tell her about…about Chelsea's baby, since she and my mom are close." She blinked, maybe seeing something in his face that made her explain further. "I'd already talked to Chelsea about it. She knew I was going to tell her."

"And how did your mom react?"

Her clenched fingers pressed against her chin. "That's just it. She's in the hospital. And I don't know what to tell Chelsea. I know she's going to ask as soon as I go in there."

Shock spurted through his system. "What happened?"

"I think I told you, she hasn't been quite herself lately. Anyway, when she heard the story, she seemed to be handling it okay, then she suddenly started feeling a weird pressure in her chest." Jessi blew out a breath. "It turns out one of her arteries is 90 percent blocked. She needs bypass surgery. She'd been having symptoms for about a month, but didn't want to worry me."

He immediately went to reach for her hand then stopped when Jessi slid hers off the top of the desk and into her lap.

Keeping her distance. Asking for his professional opinion.

Of course that's what it was. She'd already told him what she needed to. She wanted to know whether or not she should tell her daughter about what had happened. She hadn't come to him for comfort or anything else.

Just medical advice about her daughter…his patient.

Right now, though, the last thing he wanted to do was think this thing through. What he wanted was to get out of his chair, walk around the desk and grab her to his chest, holding her while she poured out her heart.

Impulse control.

With his recent track record, holding her was exactly what he shouldn't do.

He took a sip of his coffee and let the heat wash down his throat and pool in his stomach, adding to the acid already there. "I think you should tell her the truth about your mom's condition. Maybe not the events preceding the attack but that her doctor found a blockage in an artery and has decided it needs to be addressed as quickly as possible."

"So you don't think I should tell her about Mom knowing what happened with the baby?"

"Not unless she asks you point-blank. The truth might eventually come out, but I don't think you need to hurry into any kind of explanation right now. That can wait until after the surgery. When your mom—and Chelsea—are better."

The truth might eventually come out.

Great advice, Marks, considering your and Jessi's current situation. And what had happened to her late husband once that truth had indeed come out.

None of that mattered at the moment. "When is the procedure scheduled?"

"They want to do it as soon as possible. This afternoon, in fact."

He sat back in his seat. "Maybe it's good that this happened when it did. At least you were with your mom at the time and knew what to do."

"Did I, Clint? What was I thinking, just blurting something like that out?"

"You said she'd been having symptoms for a while. Besides, I'm sure you didn't 'blurt it out.' You were doing what you thought was best for your mom and for Chelsea."

Like he was doing, by continuing to treat Jessi's daughter? Actually, yes. Nothing had happened to suggest that this couldn't all work out for the best as far as Chelsea was concerned.

"I just never dreamed it might lead to—"

"I know." He paused. "Do you want me to be there when they do the procedure?"

"Don't you have patients?"

Not a direct refusal. More like a hesitation...trying to feel him out, maybe?

"I have one more to see in about an hour and a half. What time is her surgery scheduled for?"

"Five." Her hands came back onto the table and wrapped around her mug.

"I'll be done in plenty of time to get to the hospital." He waited until her eyes came up and met his. "Unless you don't want me there."

There, if she wanted reassurance, he would give it to

her. And he had a feeling she could use a friend right now, even if they could never be anything more than that.

"I'd actually like you to be there, if it's not too much trouble."

"Of course it's not."

This time her fingers crept across the desk and touched the top of his hand. He turned his over so it was palm up and curled his fingers around hers.

"Thank you so much, Clint. I know it's hard after everything that went on between us."

"Not hard at all."

They sat there in silence for a few long seconds, hands still gripping each other's. Only now he'd laced his fingers through hers, his thumb stroking over her skin.

A few minutes later she left—with his promise to be at the hospital before her mom's procedure.

And somehow in that period of time he was going to give himself a stern pep talk about what he should and shouldn't do as he sat with her in the waiting room.

And all he could do was hope that—for once—his heart decided to cooperate.

CHAPTER FOURTEEN

JESSI PACED THE waiting room of the hospital an hour into her mom's surgery, her chaotic thoughts charging from one subject to another. Her daughter had been so upset by the news that she hadn't asked if Jessi had told her about the baby.

Or asked any deeper questions about why Jessi had told Clint before she'd told her.

That was good, because the last thing she needed to do was heap one more tricky situation onto the pile.

And tricky was the best way she could think of to characterize her and Clint's relationship.

There was no way she could be falling for Clint all over again. They hadn't seen each other in over twenty years. But as they'd worked together, treating patients at the fair, there'd been a feeling of rightness. A rightness that had continued when they'd made love at her house a week later.

Except feelings didn't always mean anything, at least where she was concerned, because she'd always had a thing for Clint. Even back in high school.

It didn't make a difference then, Jessi, and it's not going to make a difference now. He's going to leave. Just you wait and see.

All those confused feelings had to do with Clint being her first. After all, you never really forgot your first love, right? And she *had* loved Chelsea's father. Very much. If it hadn't been for their argument, Larry would still be alive. Would she even be giving Clint a second glance if he were?

Something else she didn't want to think about because it just made her feel that much worse.

The man in question was seated in one of the cushioned chairs in the hospital waiting room, elbows on his knees, watching her pace. She went over to him. "How do you think it's going?"

One corner of his mouth turned up. "You mean since the last time you asked me? All of five minutes ago?" He patted the chair next to him. "Why don't you sit down? Wearing a hole in the linoleum isn't going to help anyone right now."

She blew out a breath, worry squeezing into every available brain cell and wiping away any other thoughts. Plopping down in the chair, she leaned back and closed her eyes. "What if Mom or Chelsea finds out what we've done?"

"Where did that come from?" His arm went around her shoulders and eased her closer.

"I just don't want to make anything worse for either of them."

"No one's going to find out."

"Larry did." She was immediately sorry she'd said it when his body stiffened.

"Sorry, Clint. I'm just worried."

"I know." He sighed. "You need to stop pacing."

Her eyes opened, and she cranked her head to the right to look at him. "I already did."

"Not there." He nodded at the floor, then his fingers went to her temple and rubbed in slow circles. "I mean up here. You're driving yourself crazy. Nobody's going to find out, unless one of us tells them. And I don't see that happening."

"Thank you," she murmured. "You've been a lot cooler about all of this than I have any right to expect."

He chuckled. "Cool, huh? I don't know if I would call it that, exactly."

She wasn't sure what he meant by that, and she was too nervous to try to figure it out right now. All she knew was that she was glad he was there with her.

Jessi leaned into Clint a little bit more, allowing herself to absorb a little of the confident energy he exuded. That energy was something that had drawn her to him as a high school student, and it wasn't any less potent now.

"How long are they going to be?"

"Jess, it takes time. The doctors felt pretty sure going in that everything was going to run according to plan."

"Yes, but anything could happen." Even as she said it, she allowed her eyelids to slide together, letting his clean scent wash through her, canceling out the sharp bite of disinfectant and illness that came with being at a hospital. She was used to those smells, for the most part, but right now, when she was worried about her mother, they were reminders that sometimes things went wrong, and people died.

"It could, but it probably won't. I think she's going to be just fine."

His words were so inviting, offering up a reality that was in stark contrast to the gloomy paths her own thoughts were circling.

"I hope you're right."

This time when her eyelids slid closed, she allowed them to stay like that, lulled by his easy assurances.

Maybe because that's what she wanted to believe.

Either way, she found herself emptying her mind of

anything that didn't revolve around the man beside her. And of how right, and good, and...restful it felt to be with him right now.

Dangerous to let him know that, though.

A hand squeezing hers brought her back. She blinked, the harsh glare of the overhead lights flooding her system.

Heavens, she'd fallen asleep. While her mom was undergoing bypass surgery.

"Jess, the doctor is heading this way."

She jerked her head off his shoulder so fast she thought it was going to bounce to the floor and roll down the hall. Dragging her attention to the present, she glanced past the wide door of the waiting room to see that her mom's doctor was indeed striding toward them, no longer wearing his scrubs.

Standing, she waited for him to reach her, vaguely aware that Clint had climbed to his feet beside her, his fingers at the small of her back as if knowing she still needed that connection.

Even before the doctor reached them, he flashed a thumbs-up sign and a smile. "Everything went really well, better than we could have hoped for, actually," he said. "The harvested vein went in without a hitch and her heart is going strong. She should feel better than she's felt in quite a while. Her other arteries still look pretty good. With a change in diet and exercise, hopefully they'll stay that way for a long time to come."

Relief rushed through her system. "So she's going to be okay?"

The doctor nodded. "Absolutely. Barring anything unforeseen, we'll release her in the next few days. She'll need someone home with her for about a week after that. We checked her insurance, and it'll cover a home nurse."

"Thank you so much. When can I see her?"

He smiled. "She's in Recovery at the moment. You know the routine. Once she's moved into a room, we'll let you see her." For the first time his glance slid smoothly to Clint. "But just you right now."

The touch at her back moved away.

Chelsea hurried to make the introductions, but left out why Clint was there, waiting with her.

The surgeon held out a hand. "Dr. Marks, good to meet you. I served as an army doc before moving over to private practice. I appreciate all you do for our military."

She tensed, wondering if Clint would question why he'd moved when there was so much need—much like she'd done when she'd heard about Dr. Cordoba resigning his commission. All Clint said, though, was, "I'm happy to do it. The country needs both civilian and military doctors. I'm glad you were there for Jessi's mom."

If Dr. Leonard thought it was strange that Clint was there with her or that he'd called her by her first name, he gave no hint of it. He simply nodded and let them know he'd send a nurse out to get Jessi when her mother was settled in. Then he turned around and headed back the way he'd come.

She glanced up at Clint. "Thanks for waiting with me. If you need to get back to the hospital, I understand."

"I already told you, I'm done for the day. I'll stay and make sure everything is okay."

"Thanks again." She bit the side of her lip. "Sorry for falling asleep on you. I can't believe I did that."

His fingers touched her back again. "You've been carrying a lot of weight around on those strong shoulders, Dr. Riley. Maybe it's time you let someone else help with the load from time to time."

Was he offering his services in that regard? And if he was, did she dare let him?

Maybe she already had just by accepting his offer to be here during the surgery.

"I'm sorry you've gotten dragged into my family's problems. Both in high school and now."

He turned her and laid his hands on her shoulders—ignoring everyone else in the room. "No one 'dragged' me." He squeezed softly before letting her go. "Either then or now. I'm here because I want to be."

And later, after Chelsea was better. Would he still be there?

Something she didn't dare even think about at the moment. Because who knew when that would be. It could be years before Chelsea was well enough to function without the help of someone like Clint. Although she imagined the emphasis would be on counseling later, if there came a time that she didn't need medication to help her cope.

And Jessi knew how things worked in the military. Clint would be transferred out of here, either sooner or later, whereas she had settled her life in Richmond for the long haul. Her mom and daughter were here—not to mention Cooper—and she couldn't imagine leaving them.

Not even for Clint?

She stepped back a pace, not willing to face that question quite yet. Besides, there was nothing between them other than what boiled down to a couple of one-night stands.

One-night stands.

Why did that explanation make her throat ache in a way it hadn't all those years ago?

Hadn't it? Her subconscious whispered the question into her ear, but Jessi raised a hand and swished it away, making Clint frown.

"You okay?" he asked.

"Yes. Just relieved." She took another step back. "Seriously, you don't have to sit here with me. I'm sure you've got other things to do."

His frown grew deeper. "If you're worried about Chelsea or your mom finding out, don't. I won't tell them I was here unless you want me to."

"No!" She cleared her throat and lowered her voice when she realized a couple of pairs of eyes in the waiting room had shifted their way. "I don't want to have to explain why."

Because she wasn't even sure of the answer, and she was afraid to look too closely at the possibilities. She might just discover something she was better off not knowing.

She'd already had her heart broken. Not once. But twice. Once by Clint and once by her husband's accusations. She didn't want to risk another crack in an already fragile organ.

Clint's voice was also low when he responded. "I already said I wouldn't say anything. So don't worry about it."

But he sounded a little less confident than he had a few minutes ago, when he'd assured her that her mother would be just fine.

"Thanks."

They both sat down, but this time without talking, and Clint didn't put his arm back around her. She tried to tell herself she was glad. But deep inside it made her feel lonely, yearning for something she was never going to have.

And what was that exactly?

A relationship with Clint?

Those four words caused a shudder to ripple through her. Her arms went around her waist, even though the waiting room wasn't chilly.

God, she hoped that's not what she was looking for.

Because that wasn't on the cards for her or for Clint. Going down that road would be a recipe for disaster.

She would do better on that front, starting now. Despite her earlier thoughts, she needed to start relying on Clint less than she currently was.

The problem was, Jessi honestly didn't know how she was going to back away when the time came.

Because that crack in her heart was just waiting for an excuse to widen. And she had a feeling it was already far too late to stop that from happening. The crowbar was there in hand, poised and ready.

Or maybe it wasn't her hand that wielded that power at all.

What if, in the end, Clint was the one to decide if her heart came apart in jagged pieces or remained intact?

When the nurse finally came down to tell her her mom was awake and ready to see her, Jessi was relieved to be able to walk away from her spinning, panicked thoughts… and to put her attention firmly where it should have been all along: on her mom and Chelsea…and off Clint.

CHAPTER FIFTEEN

THE SUN WAS peeking out from between heavy storm clouds. Both figuratively and literally. At least as far as Chelsea was concerned. A good omen.

Jessi's mom was home and recovering after her bypass surgery. Clint had seen Jessi in passing, but she had her hands full at the moment with her job, her mom and her daughter.

Which brought him back to the item on his desk.

Transfer papers.

Or rather a request to terminate his temporary assignment in Richmond and head back to Cali, where, from what he'd read on the internet that morning, all was sunny and bright. Not a cloud in sight.

And, hell, he could use a little more light right now to clear his head.

To sign or not to sign, that was the question.

No, it wasn't. He'd eventually put in that request. It was only a matter of time. And willpower.

Willpower he'd been sorely lacking in the past several weeks. To stay would be a mistake. Something he'd convinced himself of time and time again.

His presence here in Richmond brought back memories of not-so-happy times for all of them.

How many times had Jessi mentioned Larry's name?

Hell, he hadn't even known the man had died when he'd arrived here, much less the reason for it. And Jessi had been carrying that around for all these years.

And being here with her was a definite reminder of his own bitter childhood. People from his past knew more than he'd realized—judging from Mrs. Spencer's comments at dinner. They'd evidently talked amongst themselves about his father's problems.

And Clint's explosive reactions when he was around Jessi? Also reminders of what a lack of control could cause—had caused. He might have enjoyed it at the time, but there were consequences for everything in this life.

He'd have to leave some time or other. Why not now? Chelsea was scheduled to be released from the hospital next week. She'd continue her sessions as an outpatient... a victory he should be cheering, instead of acting like he was about to be shot off to the moon, never to be heard from again.

Maybe he'd request deployment instead. That should take him far enough away. Or he could just let the army decide where he was needed, rather than ask to return to San Diego.

Chelsea popped her head in, as if she'd heard his thoughts. "Have you heard anything about my grandmother yet?"

He slid the transfer papers beneath a file folder, not willing to let her see it. No need to cause a panic. It would take time for the orders to go through, anyway.

"No, just that she's been released." He smiled at her. "And you really should learn to knock, young lady. I could have been with a patient."

He motioned at the chair across from his desk.

Her lips twisted. "You're right. Sorry."

"No problem." He tapped the eraser end of his pencil

on the smooth gray surface of the desk, the hidden papers glaring at him from their hiding place. "As I was saying, your grandmother seems to be doing pretty well, according to your mom. She just has to take it easy for a few weeks."

Just like he did. He'd seen firsthand the problems that jumping into something with both feet could bring.

"Hmm…"

"And what does that sound mean?" He forced a light smile, although it felt like the corners of his mouth were weighted down with chunks of concrete.

Chelsea's own light attitude vanished. "I was hoping to do something, but I guess it can wait until Nana's feeling better."

"Anything I can help with?"

"I'm not sure. Maybe. I was telling Paul that I'd like to hold a memorial service for my…for the baby. He said he'd like to come. So did some of the others in our group."

Paul Ivers, a young man who'd moved over to sit by Chelsea during one of their group sessions. When had this particular conversation taken place?

"I don't see why that couldn't happen at some point."

"I'd want you there as well, if that's okay. You've helped me so much."

"I haven't done anything, Chelsea. You've come this far under your own power. I've just been here to listen and facilitate."

"Maybe you don't think you've done much, but I do. And you said you knew each other before. I asked Mom about that, and she said you, she and my dad were all in school together. My dad's not here anymore, so it would mean a lot if someone who knew him came."

Me and Larry, neck and neck.

He'd been a stand-in for the man back then. The last thing he wanted was to be one now.

Was that what he'd been when he'd made love to Jessi back at her house? A stand-in for a man who was dead and gone? A man whose death he'd helped cause?

"Please, Dr. Marks?" Chelsea's voice came back again.

Clint sat there, conflicted. He believed in keeping his word whenever possible, something his father had never seen fit to do.

In fact, a lot of the strict rules governing his life had come about because of his dad's poor judgment. Maybe that wasn't such a bad thing. Those rules had served him well, until he'd come back to Richmond. "I can't promise anything, Chelsea, but if I'm still here, I'd love to come."

Her eyes widened then darkened with fear. "You're thinking of leaving?"

He hurried to put her mind at ease. "I simply meant if you hold the service five years from now, there are no guarantees I won't have been transferred somewhere else by then."

His buzzer went off before he had time to think.

When he answered, his assistant said, "Mrs. Riley is here."

His already tense muscles tightened further. Hearing Jessi referred to as Mrs. anything stuck in his craw.

Jessi Marks. Now, that had a nice ring to it.

No, it didn't.

Hell. This day was turning out to be anything but the good omen he'd hoped for fifteen minutes earlier. It was morphing into a damned nightmare.

"Oh, good," said Chelsea. "We can ask her what she thinks."

Perfect. He had a feeling Jessi was going to love this almost as much as he did.

He responded to his assistant, rather than to his patient. "Send her in."

Jessi scooted through the door, her face turning pink when she spied her daughter sitting in one of the chairs. Then her eyes crinkled in the corners. "Hi, sweetheart. I was just headed down to see you."

"Were you?" Chelsea's lips slid into a smile. "Guess you decided to stop by and see my doctor first."

Pink turned to bright red that swept up high cheekbones like twin beacons of guilt.

Chelsea waved away her mother's discomfiture and stood up to catch her hand. "Anyway, I'm glad you did, because we have something to tell you."

"We do?"

"You do?"

He and Jessi both spoke at once, then their eyes met. Hers faintly accusing as she met him stare for stare. She was the first to look away, though.

Chelsea blinked as she glanced from one to the other. "I don't actually mean 'we' because I kind of sprang this on Dr. Marks."

That was one way of putting it.

She glanced at him again. "Is it okay if I tell her?"

"That's completely up to you." He had to force the words out as invisible walls began to close in around him. So much for his quick, silent escape. What a damn mess. No matter which way he spun, seeking the nearest exit, he only dug himself in deeper and deeper.

Pulling her mom over to the chairs, they both sat down, then Chelsea told Jessi what she'd told him, in almost exactly the same way. As if she'd been rehearsing the words over and over until she'd got them perfect.

His insides coiled tighter.

Once her voice died away there was silence in the room, except for Clint's phone, which gave a faint pinging sound as it received a message of some type.

Jessi licked her lips, her gaze flicking to Clint for a mere second before going to rest on her daughter. "I think that's a lovely idea."

"I asked Dr. Marks about letting the group come...and I invited him, as well. He said he'd be there, if he was still in Richmond."

"'Still in Richmond'?"

The words curled around a note of hurt, the sound splashing over him in a bitter wave.

This wasn't how he'd wanted her to hear the news.

Chelsea's hand covered her mother's. "No, I mean he said that if I had the service five years from now, he might have been transferred somewhere else by then."

Jessi's body relaxed slightly.

Did she care that he might move away?

Of course not. She had to know as well as he did how utterly foolish it would be for them to go any further than they already had. And she'd withdrawn a little over the past week, changing their working relationship into one of professionals who were collaborating on a patient they had in common. Only to Jessi she was no patient. She was her daughter—someone she loved with all her heart and soul. He saw the truth of it each time the women looked at each other and in the way Chelsea touched her mom, as if needing the reassurance of her presence.

To be loved like that would be...

Impossible. For him, anyway.

And he needed to pull himself together before someone realized how jumbled his emotions had become.

"Of course I'll be there." The words came out before he had time to fully vet them. So he added, "If I can."

"When do you want to do this?" Jessi's voice became stronger, as if she saw this as a way for her daughter to close this chapter in her life and move on to the next one.

One that Clint hoped with all his being would be full of laughter and happiness. This family deserved nothing less, they'd been through so much over the years.

He did not need to add more junk to the pile. They both had enough to deal with right now. He decided to change the subject. "How's your mom?"

"Good. The home nurse is with her this morning. She's getting stronger every day. In fact, she said today that finding out…er…finding out about her blockage might have been one of the most positive, life-affirming experiences she'd ever gone through. She feels tons better and is raring to get out of bed and go back to work on her garden and play with Cooper." Jessi shook her head and squeezed Chelsea's hand. "I think I know where you got your stubbornness from."

"Mine?"

Laughing, Jessi said, "Okay, mine, too."

That was one thing Clint could attest to. This was one strong trio of women, despite the momentary flashes of pain that manifested themselves in physical reactions: Abigail's heart blockage. Chelsea's suicide attempt. Jessi's reaching out to an old flame during a crisis?

Yes. That was exactly it.

It should have made him feel better—set his mind at ease about leaving in the months ahead. Instead, a cold draft slid through his body and circled, looking for a place to land. He cleared his throat to chase it away. It didn't work. It lay over him in a gray haze that clung to everything in sight, just like the morning dew. What it touched, it marked.

And that mark was…

Love.

He reeled back in his seat for a second, trying to process and conceal all at the same time.

He loved her? Heaven help him.

How could he have let this happen? Any of it? All of it?

He had screwed up badly. Had let his emotions get the best of him, just like he always had when he was around this woman.

The transfer papers seemed to pulse at him from beneath the binder with new urgency. The sooner he did this the better.

And his promise to Chelsea?

"What do you think Nana would want me to do?" Even as his own thoughts were in shambles, Chelsea's were on the brink of closing old wounds and letting them heal.

"I think Nana would want you to be happy, honey."

"Can we have the service next week, then? I don't know how long the members of the group will keep coming to sessions. We can have a private memorial for just our family later, if Nana feels up to it."

"We can have it anytime you want."

And in that moment he knew he had to see this through. He had to be there for Jessi, just as she had to be there for Chelsea. Abigail wasn't up to taking on that role yet. And Larry was no longer there.

And he wanted to. Wasn't that what love was about? Sacrificing your own comfort and well-being for someone else's?

Like he'd done once upon a time?

He peered into the past with new eyes. Eyes that saw the truth.

He'd loved her even then. Even as he'd been preparing to hand her over to another man. One whose father didn't drink himself into a rage and let his fists do the talking.

A normal, mundane life.

Something Clint hadn't been able to give her. Because back then he'd had anger issues, too. Toward his father, who'd dished it out. Toward his mom, who'd sat there and taken it. Toward the world in general, for turning a blind eye toward what had been going on in homes like his.

The military had helped him conquer most of his anger, but only because it had instilled discipline in its place, and had channeled his negative energy into positive areas.

But his life still wasn't peaceful. It was filled with patients like Chelsea, who scrabbled and clawed to find some kind of normalcy.

Jessi had been through enough. She'd deserved better than him back then, and she still did today.

She deserved a professor or architect or poet. A man who brought beauty into her life. Not memories of days gone by.

I'm going to have to give her up all over again.

And he was going to have a few more scars to show for it.

He realized both pairs of female eyes were on his face, both wearing identical expressions of confusion. One of them had said something.

"I'm sorry?"

Chelsea bit her lip. "I asked if next Sunday would work for you? Or do you have other plans?"

"No. No plans." Once he'd said it, he realized he could have come up with an excuse. Like what? A date? That would go over really well with Jessi. Besides, he'd meant what he'd thought earlier. He wanted to be there for her... and for Chelsea. Like the family he'd never had?

Maybe. Maybe it was okay to pretend just for a few hours—to soak up something he'd never be able to have in real life.

Like a wife and daughter?

Yes.

Even if they both belonged to a man who could no longer be there for them.

So he would act as a stand-in once again. For an hour. Maybe two. And he could pray that somehow it was enough to get him through the rest of his life.

CHAPTER SIXTEEN

SHE WANTED TO hold Clint's hand, but she couldn't.

Not in a cemetery, while mourning a tiny life that had been snuffed out before its time. Standing next to him would have to be enough.

Only it was so hard. Hard to remain there without touching him.

Curling her fingers into her palms, she forced them to stay by her sides as a chaplain she'd never met talked about life and death...commemorating a granddaughter she'd also never met.

A hand touched hers. Not Clint's, but Chelsea's. Her daughter's fingers were icy cold, her expression grim, eyes moist with grief as the minister continued to speak.

"In the same way this marker serves as a reminder that a tiny life was placed into Your loving arms, we, like Marie Elizabeth Riley, need to place our trust and hope in You, the Author and Finisher of our faith, that we will one day see her as she was meant to be. Whole and full of life..."

The sudden rush of tears to eyes that had been dry took Jessi by surprise, overriding whatever else the chaplain was saying. She fumbled in her purse, letting go of Chelsea's hand for a second as she searched for a tissue.

Clint, still, solemn and heartbreakingly handsome in a dark blue suit, pressed a handkerchief into her trembling hands. She glanced up at him to find him watching her, something dark and inscrutable in his gray eyes. Was he irritated at her for blubbering? But this baby would have been her first grandchild...would have probably survived if Chelsea had had access to health care.

And that was another thing that had driven her daughter crazy with guilt. All those what-ifs. *If* she had just spoken up...*if* she'd admitted she was pregnant, instead of fearing a reprimand or, worse, of being sent home in flurry of paperwork and inner shame...*if* she'd told her captors the truth. The baby's father had never been notified. Chelsea saw no reason to cause trouble for a man with whom she'd had a one-night stand.

Jessi knew what that was like. She'd had two of them. Both with the same man.

The chaplain asked everyone to bow their heads, so Jessi closed her eyes. And felt a hand to her right clasp hers once again. Chelsea.

And then, out of nowhere, warm fingers enveloped her other hand, lacing between hers.

Clint.

Oh, God. The tears flowed all over again. She'd wanted to hold his hand, and he'd not only read her mind, he'd found a way to accomplish the impossible.

A flicker of hope came to life in her chest.

Maybe it wasn't impossible. He had certainly made love to her like she'd meant something to him.

Then again, he'd done the same thing all those years ago. Maybe it was different now. They were both older. Wiser. They'd both lived through things many people never had to experience.

She tightened her grip around both hands, allowing herself to feel connected to him in a way that had noth-

ing to do with sex. Or need. But was something deeper.
More profound.

No.

Not happening.

And yet he'd made the impossible possible.

As the prayer went on, Clint gave her hand a quick
squeeze, then released it.

When she peeked between her lashes, she saw that she
wasn't the only one who had a male hand linked with hers.
The young man next to Chelsea stood so close their shoulders and arms touched. And his index finger was twined
around her daughter's.

She swallowed. Maybe, just maybe, she could let herself believe. Just like the chaplain said.

The seed took root and spread throughout her being,
twisting around her heart and lungs until she wasn't sure
where they started and the belief ended. Maybe that was
the way it was meant to be.

She could talk to Clint. Somehow find out if he felt the
same way. Surely he did. Otherwise why would he have
held her hand?

Because she'd been crying? Maybe. That was why it
was important to talk to him. And she would. Just as soon
as the service was over, and she'd made sure her daughter
was okay. Her mom was at home. They still hadn't told
Chelsea about the circumstances behind the heart episode,
and they'd both agreed to keep that quiet. Her mom also
felt it was best for her to stay at home for this particular
event. Neither of them wanted anything to mar the service. And although Jessi trusted Clint not to say anything,
one of them could inadvertently let something slip without realizing it.

The prayer ended, and Chelsea took the white rose in
her hand and gently kissed the bloom, then placed it across

the bronze marker that had been set in the lush grass beside Larry's grave. Grass that hadn't needed to be turned up, since there was no body to bury this time. The back of Jessi's throat burned. Larry would have loved his daughter. And his granddaughter, if he'd been able to see past his own hurt and pride. Two lives, needlessly lost.

But at least there was now a place where Chelsea could come and remember—along with a concrete bench that had been placed at the foot of the graves, a gift from her mother. She hoped they could come here each year and remember.

The service ended with a flautist from their church playing "Amazing Grace," the light, bright sound of the instrument giving the hymn a sense of hope and peace. It's what Chelsea had wanted, and as her daughter moved to stand beside the same young man as before, a quick glance was shared between the two of them. Jessi looked at him a little more closely. Surely it was a good thing that her daughter was beginning to look past the pain in her heart and see a future that was brimming with possibilities.

Like Jessi herself was?

When she gave Clint a sideways look, she saw that his attention was also on the pair. She could have sworn a flash of envy crossed his expression before disappearing. His gaze met hers, and he nodded to show her he had noticed, then he leaned close, his breath brushing across her ear as he murmured, "Try not to worry. Paul's a good man."

Words hung on the tip of her tongue, then spilled past her lips. "So are you, Clinton Marks."

His intake of breath was probably not audible to anyone except him, but even so he froze for several seconds at her comment, while his brain played it over and over in that same breathy little whisper.

She thought he was a good man?

Emotion swelled in his throat, and he forced himself to stand up straight before he did something rash right in front of her late husband's grave. Like crush her in his arms and kiss her like there was no tomorrow. Tell her that he loved her and would always be there for her.

As the last notes of the song died away, people began to filter out of the cemetery. Chelsea leaned over to Jessi and said, "I'll see you later on at Nana's?"

"I probably won't be there for a few hours, okay? There's something I need to do first," said Jess.

"Okay." The two women embraced for several long seconds then broke apart. Paul walked her daughter over to her car and held the door open, leaning over to tell her something before closing it.

"What do you have to do?" Clint asked.

If he was smart, he'd say his goodbyes right now before he got caught up in some kind of sentimental voyage that would end with him dragging her back to his place.

"I thought we might go back to my house for a little while."

He waited for her to tack a valid reason on to the end of that phrase. But she didn't. Instead, she simply waited for him to respond to the request. One that had come right on the heels of her other shocking comment.

He should end it right now. Cut her short before she could say anything else with a brusque, "Not a good idea and you know it."

Right. He could no more bring himself to say something like that than the moon could grow an oxygen-rich atmosphere. Or maybe it could, because right now he was having trouble catching his breath and his head felt like it was ready shut down.

He glanced back at the markers, Larry's name biting

deep into his senses and grinding them into something he no longer recognized. Needing to get away before it took another chunk from him, he said, "Sounds good. Are you ready?"

"Do you want to follow me back?"

Honey, I'd follow you anywhere, if I could.

Maybe things weren't as dire as he'd painted them. Would it be so bad if he and Jessi somehow tried to make a go of things?

That paper on his desk came to mind. He could just tear it up and dump it in his waste can, and no one would be the wiser.

The thought grew as they walked to the parking lot together. With no one else around, Clint took her hand again, gripping it with an almost desperate sense of reverence. This woman did it for him. She met him right at his point of deepest need. And she had no idea.

And if she wanted to go back to her place and discuss Chelsea's case, he was going to be crushed with disappointment. Because he wanted her. In the past. Right now in the present. And in the days that stretched far into the future.

Whether or not any of that was possible was another matter. But maybe he shouldn't worry about leaping right to the end of this particular book. Maybe he should turn one page at a time and savor each moment as it came.

Because who knew how long anything in this life was going to last? Wasn't today a reminder of that?

He saw her to her car and smiled when he did the exact same thing young Paul had done. Opened her door for her and then leaned across it. Only instead of saying something, he kissed her. Right on the mouth. Right in the middle of a public parking lot.

And he didn't give a rip who saw him.

One page at a time. And he was loving the current chapter because, instead of a quick peck and retreat, Jessi's lips clung to his for several long seconds. When he finally forced himself to pull back, she gave him a brilliant smile. "I think we're on the same page."

A roll of shock swished through him. Coincidence. It had to be. Unless Jessi had suddenly become a mind-reader.

Then again, he found it pretty damned hard to hide his feelings from this particular woman. They bubbled up and out before he could contain them. That's what had gotten him into trouble when they'd been in high school and again a couple of weeks ago. It was impossible to be near her and not want to touch her. Hold her. Make love to her.

He didn't respond to her words, just said, "I'll meet you at your house." Because if he was wrong, if she wasn't feeling the same deep-seated need that he was, he'd end up eating his words and feeling like a fool.

The fifteen-minute drive seemed to take forever, but finally she pulled into the driveway of her house. They got out of their cars and stared at each other for a minute before coming together.

Then he was reaching for her and dragging her into his arms, kissing her with a fervor he had no business feeling. But she kissed him back just as hard, her hands winding around his neck, going up on tiptoe so she could get closer.

Her tongue found his, leaving no doubt in his mind where her thoughts were headed. And that was fine by him, because his had been there for hours...weeks.

"Keys." His muttered words were met with a jingle, then he swept her up in his arms and strode to the front door. "Unlock it."

It gave him a thrill to note that her hands shook as she twisted around to do as he asked, because he knew his were trembling just as hard, along with every other part of his body. Half in anticipation of what was to come and half in fear that somehow it was all going to fall apart before they got inside…before he got the chance to strip her clothes from her body—in her bedroom this time—and drive her to the point of no return.

Because he was already there. There was no turning back from the emotions that were throbbing to life within him. He couldn't bring himself to say them, so he would show her instead. With his mouth. With his hands.

With his heart.

And hope that somehow she'd be able to decipher their meaning.

He kicked the door closed, trying not to trip when Cooper suddenly appeared, barking wildly and winding around him. He let Jessi down long enough for her to let the dog out into the backyard before hauling her back up into his arms. This time he lifted her higher so that his mouth could slant back over hers, his fingers digging into the soft flesh of her thighs, her waist. Right on cue, her arms went back around his neck and she held on tight.

Clung as if she were drowning.

Well, so was he.

"Bedroom," he muttered against her mouth. Could he not get anything out other than one- and two-word sentences?

Evidently not.

And if she was going to stop this parade, she had the perfect opportunity to drag her lips from his and tell him to put her down, that they were going to sit on that long sofa and talk.

She didn't. "Down the hallway, first door on the right."

Then she was kissing him again, her eyes flickering shut even as his had to remain open to avoid tripping over furniture or running into a wall as he made his way down the hallway and arrived at her bedroom. He paused in the doorway and eyed the space, noting the frilly pillows on the bed and the hinged frame that held two pictures on the nightstand. One of Jessi with another man. And one of her holding that man's baby.

Larry.

His chest tightened, and he pulled back slightly, rethinking this idea.

"What's wrong?" Her breathless reply washed over him.

He nodded at the nightstand, and she glanced in that direction and then tensed before looking back up at him. She shook her head. "It's okay, Clint. He's been gone a very long time."

She didn't say that she didn't love him, or that Larry wouldn't mind if he could see them.

Just that the man had been gone a long time.

He stood there, undecided. Could he lie in that bed and thrust inside her, while her dead husband watched them?

"Take me over there," she murmured.

He didn't want to. Wanted to suggest they go back to the familiar sofa in the living room. But his feet had ideas of their own. He carried her over to the small table and watched as she tipped the frame over onto its front so that the pictures were no longer visible.

"Better?" she asked, one corner of her mouth curling.

It was. A little, anyway. "Yes."

"Okay, now put me on the bed—" her fingers sifted through the hair at the back of his neck, sending a shiver over him "—and take off all my clothes."

"Your wish—" he wiped Larry from his mind and dropped her from where he stood, then smiled at the squeal she gave as she bounced on the mattress and lay there staring up at him "—is my command."

She licked her lips. "Then come down here and start commanding me."

CHAPTER SEVENTEEN

BEFORE HE COULD do as she asked, Jessi sat up and scooted to the edge of the bed, allowing her legs to hit the floor. Then she grabbed him behind the knees and dragged him forward a step or two, parting her legs until he stood between them.

"I thought I was doing the commanding," he said.

"Changed my mind," she said with a laugh, removing his keys and wallet from his pockets and putting them on the bed. "Because you'll end up having all the fun, like last time."

His brows went up. "I don't remember hearing any complaints."

"That's because there weren't any." Reaching for his belt buckle, she slid the loop out in one smooth move that made his mouth water. "And I don't think you'll be hearing any complaints now. At least, not from me."

With the buckle undone, she moved to the button of his dress slacks.

Hell, she wasn't going to hear any complaints from him either. Although his ideas for maneuvering her to the point of no return were not going according to plan.

Or maybe she'd had the very same thoughts about him.

His flesh twitched.

And he was already too far gone to back out now.

Down went his zipper. "Wait."

She stopped and met his eyes. "Am I doing something wrong?"

No, she was doing everything exactly right. And that was the problem. He really *was* too far gone. His body was pumping with anticipation. Too much too soon and he was going to have trouble not letting go in a rush. It was why he hadn't let her touch him last time.

"No, honey." His hand tangled in her hair, resisting the urge to drag her forward and show her exactly what he meant. "I just don't want you to do anything you don't want to do."

One perfectly arched brow went up an inch, and she licked her lips. "And if I want to?"

Even as she said it, she peeled apart the edges of his slacks and pushed them down his hips, until they sat at midthigh.

No trying to hide what she did to him at this point, because it was right there in front of her. Her hands moved around to the backs of his thighs, sliding over his butt and grabbing the elastic waistband of his briefs. "Are you ready?"

Oh, he was ready all right. But he wasn't so sure he was ready for what she wanted.

Dammit, who was he kidding? He was a man. He wanted it. Wanted every last thing she could think of doing to him.

And he wanted it now.

"Do it."

That was all it took. She dragged his underwear down in one quick tug, her nails scraping over his butt in a sensual move that set all his nerve endings on high alert.

He bobbed free, inches from her face. Her thumbs brushed along the outsides of his legs as her hands curled around the backs of his thighs, holding him in place. Then she leaned forward without hesitation, her mouth engulfing him in a hot, wet rush that made him grunt with ecstasy.

She remained like that for several seconds, completely still, her eyes closed, nostrils flaring as if the sensation was heavenly.

Hell, lady, you should be standing in my shoes.

He struggled like a wild man to contain the warning tingle, using every bit of ammunition in his bag of tricks to keep from erupting right then and there. Tangling his hand in her hair, he dragged her backward until he popped free. "Damn, woman. You're going to get more than you bargained for if you keep that up."

She laughed. "Haven't I told you? I love bargains. Especially when I get more bang for my…buck."

The pointed hesitation before she said that last word made his flesh tighten in anticipation. A silent promise to give her exactly what she wanted: a hard, fast bang that was, oh, so good.

Just like last time.

But this time he wanted to draw out his pleasure. And hers.

So, keeping his fingers buried in her hair, he drew her forward again, watching as she slowly opened her mouth.

Yes!

He edged closer, dying to feel her on him, then pulled away at the last second. He repeated the parry and feint several times with a slow undulation of hips that was a blending of obscene torture—emphasis on the torture. At least for him.

She clenched the backs of his thighs, trying to tug him closer, while he remained just out of reach. "Clint. Please…"

"What do you want, Jess?"

"Right now? I want you."

That was all it took. He pushed her backwards on the bed, knocking the frame off the end table in the process, and shoved her full skirt up around her hips. Black satin panties met his hungry eyes. He jerked them down and then kicked his way out of the rest of his clothes, cursing when one foot got hung up in the waistband of his briefs. Once free, he tossed a condom packet onto the bed and lay down, hauling her on top of him, until she was straddling him, her skirt pooling around her hips.

"You wanted to be in control, Jess? You've got it."

Her eyes trailed from the straining flesh outlined beneath the fabric of her skirt up his bare chest, until her eyes met his. "In that case, do you want me clothed? Or unclothed?"

Unclothed. His mind screamed the word, mouth going dry. He had to force himself to say, "Your game. Your rules."

She gave him a slow smile. "Mmm. I like the idea of making my own rules." Taking her skirt in hand, she pulled the black silk up his erection in a long, slow move that made him rethink his assessment. Then she let it slip back down the way it had come.

Okay, clothed was pretty hot, too. Especially when she continued to hold his gaze, and he knew she could spot every muscle twitch in his cheek, discern every time he had to hold himself in check. Like now, when myriad sensations began to gather in his chest. In his gut…

"Jess…" It was meant to be a warning, but her name came out as a low hum of air.

One of her hands crawled beneath her skirt and found him. And the tactile awareness of being able to feel what she was doing but not see it made the act seem secretive and forbidden. An exotic ritual that defied time and space.

She slid forward and shifted her hips up and over his ready flesh. He braced himself, but she didn't come down on him in a rush, as he'd expected. Instead, she brushed him across her skin, back and forth, her eyes closing, lips parting. He swallowed hard when he realized what she was doing—using him on her body, giving herself pleasure, rocking her hips in time with her hand.

Holy hell. This was as hot as her mouth had been.

Worse.

Because then she'd only been pleasuring him. Now she was bringing both of them to new heights of throbbing awareness. Every cell in his body wanted to thrust home and end the torment. He could just slide up and inside her in one fast move, and she would probably let him... probably welcome him. But the shifting expressions on her face were too entrancing to do anything but lie there and take whatever she wanted to dish out.

"God, Jess. You're killing me here."

"What do you want?" She turned his earlier words around and pushed them back at him.

Only he knew exactly what he wanted. "I want you to make yourself come."

Her fingers tightened, and her movements became quicker, bolder, her breasts straining beneath her shirt as she brushed herself against him—or brushed him against herself—he didn't know which it was and didn't care. He was dying to cup her, to scrape his thumb across those hard nipples now visible even through her blouse and bra, but he wanted this round to be all hers.

All around him, he felt her slick heat. Lust spiraled through him, growing stronger with each stroke, even as her movements became more purposeful. Reaching sideways, Clint found his wallet and the condom just inside it. He wrapped his fingers around the plastic wrapper, gripping it tight, hoping he'd still have the sanity to use it when the time came.

Jessi's breathing quickened, her teeth coming down on her lip as her body continued to feign the motions of sex. Good sex. The kind of sex that didn't come along every day, with every woman.

No, there was only one woman he'd ever shared this kind of connection with.

Her body stiffened suddenly, pressing hard against him. Then she went off with a cry, her body pulsing against the tight need of his erection. Tearing into the packet, he reached beneath her skirt and sheathed himself in a rush before plunging into her and losing himself in the continued contractions of her orgasm.

Using her hips, he pulled her down onto himself as hard as he could, already too far gone to try to last any longer. Instead, he pressed upwards in greedy thrusting motions as he allowed himself to plummet mindlessly over the cliff of his own release, falling, falling, until there was nowhere else to go.

Nothing registered for several seconds—or it might have been minutes. Hours, even.

When he could finally breathe again, finally think, he gathered her to his chest, his fingers sliding up through the damp strands of her hair and holding her close.

"Remind me not to put you in charge ever again."

"So you *are* complaining." She snuggled closer.

"Never."

He kissed her brow, her taste salty with perspiration, and allowed his eyelids to finally swing shut…no longer afraid he was going to miss something crucial.

With one last sigh, he propped his chin on her head and allowed his body to relax completely.

Something tickled the side of her arm.

There it was again. It wasn't Cooper, because he was in the living room, and the bedroom door was shut.

Her mind reached out to grasp something, only to have it shift away uneasily. The sensation returned. A light rhythmic stroke trailing up toward her shoulder now.

Her eyes opened to find someone standing beside the bed, watching her.

Clint.

"Hello, sleepyhead. I fed Cooper and let him out. Hope that was okay."

"Mmm..."

Since his voice sounded as rough as hers felt, she wasn't the only one who had fallen asleep after the second time they'd made love.

In her bed. In her house. And the second time he'd undressed her slowly. Carefully. Kissing his way down her body in a way that had made her heart melt, even while her senses had been kicking into high gear.

Like now. Only it was her heart that was soaring, rather than her libido. Because Clint was still here. He hadn't hightailed it out of here like she'd half expected. The hope she'd grasped earlier continued to grow, picking up speed as she finally acknowledged the possibilities that this might just work out between them.

"Hey, yourself. What time is it?" She rolled onto her back to look at him fully.

"About five in the afternoon." A hand reached up to scrub the stubble on his jaw. "Do you have to work?"

Work? At a time like this?

"Have you been walking around the house like that?" The man had fed Cooper and let him out...stark naked?

He smiled. "Why? Does it bother you?"

"Define bother."

He laughed. "So, about work..."

"No. No work, but I need to check on Chelsea and my mom, like I told them I would."

"I thought you might. Otherwise I would have let you sleep. As it was, if Cooper hadn't scratched at the door, I was going to wake you in a completely different way." He found one of her hands and linked his fingers through hers.

She closed her eyes, happiness flowing over her. "Wow. You're up for a third round?"

"Believe me, I'm up for all kinds of things. Round or otherwise." A quick glance down showed he was already up and ready.

"Mmm." She let out a sigh as a thought came to her. Talk. That's what she'd meant to do at some point, only she'd gotten sidetracked. She dipped a toe into the water. "Do you think Chelsea and Paul are going to start seeing each other?"

"I think it's a possibility. Why? Is that a problem?"

"Do you think it's a good idea?"

"Don't know. They've both been through some tough times. They'll either be able to support each other, or they'll drag each other down."

A shiver went over her. "I hope I never have to live through anything like the past couple of months ever again. How do you deal with patients who are in such pain on a daily basis? I think it would eat at my heart." She hesitated before continuing. "And after what happened with your dad..."

Lifting his hand to kiss it, his crooked little finger

caught her attention. She changed her aim and kissed that knuckle instead.

He stiffened at her act. "My dad is the reason I'm in this line of work."

Pulling away, he reached down and picked something up off the floor. She frowned, and then saw it was the picture frame he'd knocked off. Flipping it over, he went to put it on the nightstand then stopped, his jaw tightening as he stared at it.

"Clint?"

He shook his head, throat moving for a second. Jessi swiveled her eyes to look at the frame.

The glass on Larry's side had broken, a series of jagged, cobweb-looking cracks distorting his features and obscuring half of his face.

When she glanced back at Clint he looked...stricken. That was the only word she could think to describe it.

She reached out a hand. "Hey, it's okay. It's only a cheap frame. I can get another one."

He set it on the table but wouldn't quite meet her eyes.

Something was wrong. Very wrong.

"Jessi, I need to tell you something."

A wave of foreboding licked at her toes, then her ankles. Soon it was waist deep and rising.

She reached out to touch him, but the second she did, he backed away and found his trousers, sliding into them and fastening them before he looked at her again.

"I was going to wait and tell you later, but this seems as good a time as any." A muscle worked in his jaw. "They've found a permanent replacement for Dr. Cordoba. He arrives in two weeks."

She wasn't sure what this had to do with them. "Chelsea will continue her sessions with him, then."

"Yes." He scooped his dress shirt from the floor and pushed his arms through the sleeves.

Why was he getting dressed? This was good news. They wouldn't have to hide their relationship anymore.

Right?

"So that means we'll be able to see each other with-out—"

"No." His lean fingers moved quickly to button up his shirt. "We won't. I'm putting in my transfer papers. You knew this was only a temporary assignment. Just until they found another doctor. I'm going back to San Diego."

What? Her mind screamed that word over and over and over until it was hoarse with grief and confusion.

He'd made love to her last night as if he couldn't get enough. As if she really meant something to him. And now he was leaving?

Shades of the past came back to haunt her. Hadn't he already done this once before? Screwed her and then taken off without a backward glance?

The ominous wave was still rising, faster than ever, splashing up her neck and cresting over her head until she couldn't breathe. Horror washed through her at all she'd done with him last night, at how truly and freely she'd given herself to him.

In. Love.

And he'd felt nothing. *Nothing.*

As the silence drew out, he finally broke it by saying, "I should have told you before..." He motioned at the bed.

He hadn't been willing to change his life for her twenty-odd years ago so why had she thought he would now?

Sitting up and not bothering to cover her nakedness, she glared at him, welcoming the anger—because it kept away the tears. "Yes, you should have. But, then, you wouldn't have had one last trip down memory lane, would you?

Treating patients isn't the only thing you're good at, Dr. Marks. You're also an expert at using people, and then ditching them when you've had what you wanted."

She climbed to her feet and stood there. Refusing to be vulnerable. Refusing to care what he did.

Only she knew deep inside it was a lie. The cracks in the picture frame now mirrored the ones in her heart, splitting wide open and spilling everything inside her into the dust that had become her life.

"Jess, that's not the way this—"

"No!" If he said one more word she was either going to burst into tears or slap him across the face with all her might. "Just go. Have Chelsea's new doctor call us when he arrives."

He grabbed the rest of his clothes and shoved his bare feet into his dress shoes. "I'm sorry, Jess."

Tossing her head, she bit out a quick reply. "Don't be. It was a blast from the past. We had our own mini high school reunion right here in my bedroom, but now it's time to pack up and get back to our own lives, in our own cities."

She didn't ask him exactly when he was leaving. She didn't want to know.

Clint's throat moved as he looked at her for another minute. Then he said, "Goodbye, Jessi."

With that, he turned around and walked out of the bedroom, his receding footsteps on the hardwood floor marking his location and searing the message into her brain. There was no slowing of his pace, no hesitation as the front door opened and then closed.

Clint was leaving. And this time he wasn't coming back.

CHAPTER EIGHTEEN

A WEEK WAS all it took to change his life forever.

He'd filed expedited transfer papers, asking them to put him wherever they needed him, preferably deployed overseas. He wound up at the VA hospital in New Mexico instead.

It might as well have been the other side of the world.

He sat at a desk that looked exactly like his previous one and wondered how he'd gotten here. Aimless. Rootless. And, thus far, patientless. They were letting him get settled in.

Right. Like that's what he needed. More time to think about what had happened that night in Jessi's bedroom.

He'd been all set to tell her how he felt, and then he'd picked up that frame and seen the damage he'd caused.

To her marriage. To her life.

At that moment he'd felt as shattered as that glass.

Being with Jessi again had wreaked havoc with his insides, turning him back into that impulsive screwup he'd been in high school.

He couldn't risk messing up her life a second time. Neither could he ask her to pick up and move away the next time he got his transfer papers. Jessi's life was in Richmond. With Chelsea and her mom—and those two graves.

Clint's place was with his patients. The one thing he knew he was good at.

She'd be okay without him. Seeing Chelsea get better would give her hope for a new beginning. He'd soon be relegated to the past again—where he belonged.

His phone rang. He glanced at the readout and his mouth went dry, his blood pressure spiking.

A Richmond area code.

Only it wasn't Jessi's number. He didn't recognize it. Damn it!

When would the hope finally die? It was over. He'd ended it himself—and she hadn't been sorry to see him go. She'd not said one word to discourage him. Instead, she'd practically shoved him out the door.

Checking the door to his office to make sure it was closed, he pressed the speakerphone button and stared at the open case file in front of him. So much for trying to get up to speed.

"Hello?"

"Dr. Marks?"

He recognized the voice immediately. "Chelsea? Is everything okay?"

"I don't know. I mean, everything's fine with me. It's Mom."

His heart plummeted. "Is she all right?"

"No." There was a pause, and then her voice came through. Stronger. With just a hint of accusation. "I saw you holding hands at the memorial service. How could you just…leave like that?"

"I was transferred. You know how it works."

A curse word split the air, and Clint picked the phone up and put it to his ear, even though he knew his assistant wouldn't be able to hear their conversation through the thick walls.

Chelsea's voice came back through. "You're right. I do know how it works. And there's no way you'd be able to get the okay for a transfer that fast unless you asked for it to be expedited. Or unless you'd been sitting on it this whole time."

"What does it matter? The Richmond hospital was a temporary assignment."

"Did I say something? Do something?"

"No." He hurried to set her mind at ease. "This had nothing to do with you, Chelsea. I'm proud of how hard you've worked on your recovery. You've faced the past head-on and now you're ready to move into the future."

A laugh came over the phone, but it was without humor. "That's what you always told us during group, wasn't it? That we had to face the past and see it for what it was without running or hiding from the truth. But in the end that's not what you did, is it?"

Hell, how had a tiny slip of a girl managed to read him so well? He had run. He'd taken one look at that broken glass, and instead of facing his fears, instead of talking to Jessi about everything that had happened, he'd turned tail and run.

Because he was afraid to face the future. Afraid his past would somehow catch up to him and splash its ugliness on to Jessi.

In reality, he'd been looking for an excuse to flee ever since he'd seen her sitting in his office that first day.

Why? Because he loved her, and just like back in high school he'd hightailed it out of town rather than having the courage to tell her how he felt and let her decide what to do with that information.

"What happened between me and your mother isn't any of your business."

"Sure it is. She's. My. Mother." She took an audible

breath. "When I was in trouble, you never hesitated to bleed every detail of my therapy to her, because…she had a right to know the truth. She's listed as my next of kin. Well, guess what, Doctor, that works both ways. I'm her next of kin. I have a right to know. Did you even care about her at all?"

He swallowed. "Yes."

"Well, she cares for you, too. She's been smiling and saying all the right things, but she's not okay. She looks awful."

"I'm sorry."

"Not good enough. You might outrank me, but I'm going to tell you straight up what I think."

He smiled despite himself. "There's no question you and your mom are related."

"Yeah? Well, here it is. You're no better than a common deserter."

Shock rolled through him. "Excuse me?"

"You heard me. When the battle inside your head got tough, you turned around and walked away, instead of acting like a soldier and facing it, the way you told us to do. She's not the enemy, Dr. Marks. I don't know what it is you're fighting, but I suggest you figure it out and come back and face it. Otherwise you'll regret it for the rest of your life."

She looks awful.

He'd rushed off so sure that he was doing the right thing and saving the woman he loved a whole lot of pain.

What if he'd ended up *causing* her pain instead?

Hell. He was an idiot. "Reprimand noted and accepted."

"Good. You said you cared about her. Do you love her?"

He smiled, making a decision he should have made

twenty-two years ago. "I think your mom deserves to hear that from the source, don't you?"

"Then get back here and tell her. Because I'm pretty sure she loves you, too."

Jessi pulled her sticky scrubs away from her midsection, fanning the fabric against herself as she headed into the parking lot. It was an hour past the end of her shift, and she was only now able to leave the hospital.

A gang war had seen her dealing with multiple gunshot wounds. Two had died en route to the hospital and another three had needed surgery. One of them had a broken finger in addition to other more serious wounds, but that small injury had been the one that had made her finally break down and admit the truth. That she missed Clint. Terribly.

She had a feeling Chelsea knew something was wrong, and her mom—almost completely recovered from her surgery a month ago—had also cast some worried looks her way. She had no idea why. She'd been acting cheerful, even if that's all it was. An act.

Straightening her back, she quickened her pace. This was ridiculous. How long was she going to keep mooning over something that was never going to happen? She needed to pull herself together and forget about...

Keys in hand, she paused halfway across the parking lot. Someone in uniform stood near where she'd parked her car, the tall military bearing painfully familiar. How many times had she seen that stance?

Her dad. Her daughter. In a military town, it was impossible not to recognize the proud upright posture. Only this went beyond that. This was...

Clint.

Oh, God. Something inside her urged her to turn around and dash back to the safety of the hospital.

No. She was not going to let what that man did or didn't do dictate her actions and emotions any longer. So she walked toward him, trying not to look directly at him as she did so, afraid he'd see the misery in her eyes.

When she reached her car she saw that she was right, he was standing right next to it. She'd have to pass in front of him to get to the driver's door.

"I thought you'd left," she said, her voice sounding as chipper as ever.

"I did." He didn't move. Didn't crack a smile at her tone. "I came back."

Her heart took a swan dive. What? Had he decided he hadn't tortured her enough?

She swallowed. "Why?"

"Because I'm done running. When you told me about Larry and his death, it was like a hole opened up and swallowed me whole. If I hadn't followed you that day…if I'd let him chase you outside instead, you'd still be one big happy family."

He drew in an audible breath. "And then I broke that frame, Larry's frame, and it was as if the universe was sending me a message. That I'd screwed up your life once before, and I could very well do it again if I stayed."

Her own breath caught in her lungs before whooshing back out. "Why didn't you say something?"

"I thought I was doing you a favor."

"Well, you didn't. I—" He cut her off with a finger pressed across her lips.

"Let me finish, while I still have the nerve. I came back to tell you I love you. I have since high school when I found you crying beside the creek." He paused. "I gave you up once, thinking it was for your own good, but I'm not going to do it again. Unless you tell me to go."

She pushed his hand away.

"Twice." The correction came out before she could stop it. "You gave me up twice. Why should I believe you this time?"

"Because it's the truth, Jess. I swear it." He took a step forward.

She tried to force herself to move back, but she couldn't. She just stood there, staring up at him. Maybe the summer heat had gone to her head and he was a mirage. After all, he didn't look hot at all.

Okay, so he looked superhot in that uniform, but not in the way she'd meant it.

"So what changed your mind this time?"

She had to know he hadn't just come back on a whim. That he was here for the long haul this time.

"That's a complicated question. I've never been truly terrified of anything—not even my father. But you scare me, Jess. The fear that I might not be good enough for you because of my past. Larry's death just seemed to echo that fear. It took a wise young woman to set me straight."

She frowned, until something clicked. "Chelsea."

He nodded. "Yes. She challenged me to come back and face my fears. So here I am. This is my battleground, and I'm not going to retreat. Not this time. Unless you tell me to."

He was handing her the power. Just like the last time they made love. Only this time it wasn't a game, and she had to be very sure of her heart. Trust that he wasn't going to leave, this time. That he wasn't going to take off like Larry and do something crazy, instead of sitting down and talking out their problems.

Did she trust him?

Yes. If he had the guts to face his fears, then she owed it to herself—and him—to do the same.

"Well, I guess we're at an impasse, then," she said in as

serious a voice as she could manage, when all she wanted to do was throw herself into his arms and kiss him until neither of them could breathe. "Because I'm not going to tell you to leave. And you're evidently not going to leave on your own."

His eyes clouded for a second, but he stood firm. "No, I'm not."

"Then you'll just have to stay." She thought of something. "Wait. What about your transfer?"

"It hasn't been officially approved, it was still in the works, but they let me move early. My current contract is almost up, so I can resign my commission—go into private practice—if that tilts the odds in my favor. We wouldn't have to move. Ever. We could stay right here in Richmond."

This time she did throw herself at him, wrapping her arms around his neck. "Those odds were already tilted once I saw you standing here. I love you, too, Clint, no matter what you decide to do. You do so much good for people like Chelsea. And if the paperwork on your transfer goes through before you can cancel it, I'm coming with you."

He grabbed her up and held her tight—so tight that she felt the air rush from her lungs. She didn't care.

She loved this man. More than she ever had.

Leaning down, he caught her mouth in a kiss that held a wealth of love and longing. "There's only one thing I want to do right now."

She laughed. "Really? Can it wait until I've had something to eat?"

"It could, but…" He withdrew and reached inside the jacket of his uniform, pulling out a small jeweler's box.

Her hands went over her mouth, afraid the sun and heat were still playing tricks on her. "Clint?"

He snapped the box open to reveal a ring. Small and

twinkling and perfect. "It was my grandmother's. Mom gave it to me before I went into the service. She said I might need it one day. She was right." He smiled. "I'd get down on one knee, but I'm afraid I'd be seared permanently to the pavement if I did. Damn, I'm screwing this all up. I should have waited to ask you to marry me until dinner, when we could have champagne, or until I had the ring resized—"

"No. This is the perfect place. The perfect ring. And you're the perfect man for me." Tears gathered in her eyes. "And I accept your proposal, Colonel Clinton Marks."

He kissed her again. Then Jessi unhooked the chain from her necklace and let him slide the slender ring onto it, where it dangled in the hollow of her collarbone. Fingering it while heat waves danced over the black tar surface of the parking lot, she blinked. "Where's your car?"

"Someone offered me a lift."

She could guess who that might be. "Chelsea again?"

"Yes."

"So you've been standing in the parking lot for over an hour?"

"Not quite. I had a little help tracking your movements."

Ahh…so that's why Chelsea's text—asking her to let her know the second she got off work—had been waiting for her when she'd switched her phone back on.

She clicked the button to unlock her car. "I guess we should put her out of her misery, then."

"Already done. I told her if you weren't home in an hour to assume we were out celebrating somewhere."

"Oh? You were that sure of yourself, were you?"

He grinned. "You have no idea what I've been through over the past month. I wasn't sure of anything, least of all myself."

"So what kind of celebration were you thinking of?"

He slid into the passenger seat and waited for her to join him. "I was thinking of something small and private."

"Interesting." Her pulse rate sped up, despite her earlier words about eating something. "So whose turn is it to be in charge this time?"

He eased his fingers deep into her hair and turned her face toward him. "How about if from now on we make sure it's an equal partnership?"

"Yes," she breathed as he leaned down to kiss her again, allowing her senses to begin that familiar climb. "That's the perfect solution."

EPILOGUE

"Do you, Jessica Marie Riley, take Clinton Shane Marks to be your lawfully wedded husband?"

Clint faced Jessi as she said the words that would legally bind her to him. Only they were already bound by cords much stronger than anything the minister could say.

Jessi had convinced him that the broken frame didn't represent what he'd done to her life all those years ago. Instead, it symbolized a breaking free from the mistakes of the past in order to face a future that was clean and new. They were getting a second chance, and Clint didn't intend to waste one second of it.

After they'd repeated the rest of the vows, he gripped her hands and let the emotion of doing so pour over him in a flood. And it was okay. No more shoving them behind a wall and hoping they'd stay there. He wasn't his father. He knew how to control those unhealthy feelings, while giving himself over to the ones that made two people into one.

"You may kiss the bride."

"Gladly." He wrapped his arms around Jessi's waist and reeled her in. "Love you," he whispered against her lips.

"Love you, too," she mouthed back.

Only then did he allow himself to really kiss her, putting his heart and soul into the joining of their lips.

"Whooo…" The sound came from the seats behind them, growing in volume the longer the kiss went on.

Clint smiled and leaned back, allowing his hands to slide down her arms until he was clasping her fingers once again. His grandmother's small diamond glittered up at him, a promise of the future. A promise further evidenced by the ultrasound in a drawer in his office desk. Jessi was expecting. A surprise to both of them. And for someone who'd thought he'd never be a father, it was another emotional first. A good one, though.

Jessi squeezed his hands and then turned to motion Chelsea and her new fiancé up to the front.

Paul had proposed just a week ago, and Chelsea had accepted, so there would be more wedding bells in the future. And probably more births along this crazy path they were all on. Her daughter hugged her long and hard, while Paul shook Clint's hand and wished him well.

Then Clint wrapped his arm around his new bride, while the minister introduced them as Mr. Clint and Mrs. Jessica Marks.

Smiles and cheers from some army buddies and their families and friends came from all around them.

This was where he belonged. He'd faced his deepest fears and they hadn't destroyed him. They'd given him hope.

Hope for a future filled with happiness as well as trials, but, most important, love.

"Shall we?"

Jessi grasped his hand and ran down the aisle, half dragging him along with her.

"What's the rush, Mrs. Marks," he asked.

They reached the door and pushed through it. "I've been waiting all morning for the chance to smash a piece of wedding cake all over your face."

"That's more exciting to you than us getting married?"

"No." She threw him a happy grin. "It's what comes after that has me all worked up."

"Dare I ask what that is?"

"You could, but you might not want me to explain in a public venue."

He laughed, his heart lighter than the frothy layers of his bride's cream-colored dress that fluttered around her knees.

"Then lead on, woman. We've got a cake to cut."

* * * * *

Look out for Tina Beckett's next Medical Romance™
HER PLAYBOY'S SECRET
Available in July 2015
Don't miss this final installment of the
fabulous MIDWIVES ON-CALL *series!*

THE DOCTOR'S
REDEMPTION

BY
SUSAN CARLISLE

Published in Great Britain 2015
by Mills & Boon, an imprint of Harlequin (UK) Limited,
Eton House, 18-24 Paradise Road, Richmond, Surrey, TW9 1SR

© 2015 Susan Carlisle

ISBN: 978-0-263-24700-8

Printed and bound in Spain
by CPI, Barcelona

Dear Reader,

For years I have been fascinated with the concept of Mardi Gras and the tradition behind it. Most people only know of wild, free-spirited times in New Orleans. When Kathy Cooksey, a friend of mine, moved to Louisiana I learned that there is more to the season than what I've seen on TV. During a visit to her house my children and I enjoyed a family atmosphere of parades and King Cake. Boy, did we attend parades! Sometimes as many as three a day. Even my youngest would holler, 'Hey, mister, throw me some beads!'

I later learned that Mobile, Alabama, was the first city in America to celebrate Mardi Gras. At the Mardi Gras Museum located there I discovered the behind-the-scenes events of the local society. I learned about krewes. Another friend and I attended one of the balls and had the pleasure of seeing the King and Queen, along with their court, which I describe in the book.

Laura Jo and Mark's story takes place during the Mardi Gras season. As medical personnel they help, but they also get in on the fun. It is a time of high revelry and— for them—a chance for change. Mardi Gras is about living high and then giving something up for Lent. As you read Laura Jo and Mark's story you will see that they did just that and found life was all the better. I hope you enjoy their story and the Mardi Gras season surrounding it.

If you would like to make your own King Cake and gumbo you can find the recipes on my website at www.SusanCarlisle.com. I also love to hear from my readers.

Susan

Books by Susan Carlisle

Heart of Mississippi
The Maverick Who Ruled Her Heart
The Doctor Who Made Her Love Again

Snowbound with Dr Delectable
NYC Angels: The Wallflower's Secret
Hot-Shot Doc Comes to Town
The Nurse He Shouldn't Notice
Heart Surgeon, Hero...Husband?

**Visit the author profile page
at millsandboon.co.uk for more titles**

**Praise for
Susan Carlisle**

'Shimmering with breathtaking romance amid the medical drama, spectacular emotional punch, a believable conflict and vivid atmospheric details *NYC Angels: The Wallflower's Secret* is sure to thrill Medical Romance readers.

—*GoodReads*

To Kathy Cooksey and Jeanie Brantley.
Thanks for sharing Mardi Gras with me.

CHAPTER ONE

THE PARADES WERE what Laura Jo Akins enjoyed most about the Mardi Gras season in Mobile, Alabama. This year was no different. She placed a hand on the thin shoulder of her eight-year-old daughter, Allie.

Her daughter smiled up at her. "When does the parade start?"

"It should already be moving our way. Listen. You can hear the band."

The faint sound of a ragtime tune floated from the distance.

Allie looked up at Laura Jo. "Can we stay for the next one too?"

The sure thing about Mardi Gras was that the parades kept coming. The closer the calendar got to Fat Tuesday the more heavily the days were filled with parades. Sometimes as many as four a day on the weekends.

"No, honey. They're expecting me at the hospital. We'll watch this one and then we have to go."

"Okay, but we get to see one another day, don't we?"

"Maybe on Wednesday. Next Monday and Tuesday you'll be out of school for a long weekend. We'll be sure to watch more then."

"Why can't I be in one?" Allie asked, turning to look at Laura Jo.

It had been a constant question during last year's Mardi Gras season and had become more demanding during this one. "Maybe when you get older. For now we'll just have to watch."

As the banner holders at the head of the parade came into sight the crowd pushed forward, forcing her and Allie against the metal barriers. A bicycling medical first responder or mobile EMT circled in front of them then rode up the street. He looked familiar for some reason but, then, most of the medical help during the carnival season were employed at the hospital where she worked. Dressed in red biking shorts and wearing a pack on his back, he turned again and pedaled back in their direction. Laura Jo squinted, trying to make out his features, but his helmet obscured her view.

Members of the medical community volunteered to work during Mardi Gras to help out with the crowds. Most of the nurses and doctors gave up their days off during the season to work the parades. It wasn't required but many enjoyed being a part of the celebration. Laura Jo knew most of the employees at Mobile General, at least by face. Although she couldn't place the rider, he looked just fine in his formfitting pants. He must bike regularly.

"Look, Mommy." Allie pointed to a group of people who had come through the barriers and were entertaining the crowd standing on both sides of the street. They were dressed in clown-type outfits and were riding three-wheeled bikes with bright-colored fish attached to the side.

Laura Jo smiled down at her daughter. "That's the Mystic Fish."

They made a circle or two in the open parade area and then disappeared into the crowd across the street from her and Allie. Laura Jo knew from years of watching parades that they would appear somewhere else along the parade route.

"What's a mystic fish?" Allie asked.

"You know what a fish is. In this case it's a club or group of people. It's also called a krewe. Because they meet in secret they are mystic or mysterious. It's all just fun."

"Are you in a queue?"

"It's krewe. Like a crew member. And, no, I'm not." She placed a hand on her daughter's head. "I have you to take care of, work at the shelter and at the hospital. No time."

Laura Jo understood being a member of a krewe. Her family had been participants all her life. In fact, they had been a part of the largest and most prestigious krewe in Mobile. She'd been one of the Mobile society that had celebrated her coming of age at carnival time. But no more.

The noise level increased as the first high-school band approached. She positioned Allie between her and the barrier so Allie could see. As the first ostentatiously decorated float rolled by the spectators pressed closer to them. The float was designed in a dragon motif and painted green, purple and gold with piles of beads hanging off pegs. Members of the krewe were dressed in costumes and wore masks.

She and Allie joined those around them in yelling, "Throw me something, mister."

Raising their hands along with everyone else, she and Allie tried to catch the beads, plastic cups with the krewe name printed on them or stuffed animals that were being thrown from the float. Bands playing and music blaring from large speakers mounted on the floats made it difficult to hear.

One krewe member made eye contact with Laura Jo and pointed at Allie. He threw a small stuffed gorilla to

Laura Jo, which she handed to Allie, who hugged it to her and smiled up at the grinning man. The float moved on.

When a strand of brightly colored beads flew through the air in Allie's direction from the next float, Laura Jo reached to catch them. She couldn't and they were snatched by the man standing behind her. He handed them to Allie. She smiled brightly at him. That was one of the special things about Mardi Gras in Mobile. It was a family affair. Any age was welcome and everyone saw that the children had a good time. Twenty minutes later a fire truck that signaled the end of the parade rolled by.

The man standing next to them shifted the barrier, creating an opening. A few people rushed through in an effort to snatch up any of the goodies that had fallen on the pavement.

"Mama, can I get those?" Allie pointed out into the street, now virtually empty except for a few children.

Laura Jo searched for what Allie was asking about. On the road lay a couple of plastic doubloons. "Sure, honey. There won't be another parade for an hour."

Allie ran through the opening and ran in the direction of the strand of gold and silver disks. In her exuberance to reach her target she stumbled and fell, stopping herself with her hands. Laura Jo gasped and rushed to her. Allie had already pushed herself up to a sitting position. Tears welled in her eyes but she'd not burst into sobs yet. There was an L-shaped hole in the thin material of her pants and a trickle of blood ran off the side of her knee.

"Oh, honey," Laura Jo said.

"My hands hurt." Allie showed Laura Jo her palms. The meaty part looked much like her knee.

"Friction burns." Laura Jo took one of Allie's wrists and raised her hand, blowing across it. Here she was a registered nurse with not a bandage to her name. Allie's injuries were going to require far more than what Laura Jo was doing.

"Can I help here?" a deep male voice said from above them.

Laura Jo glanced up to see the bike medic she'd admired earlier. She'd been so adsorbed with Allie she'd not noticed him ride up.

"Do you have any four-by-fours? Some antibiotic cream?" Laura Jo asked.

The man gave her a curious look then stepped off the bike. He slung the red pack off his back and crouched down on his haunches. "Let me see what I can do."

Laura Jo looked at him through moisture in her eyes. She knew him. Or more accurately knew who he was. Mark Clayborn. She'd had no idea he was back in town. But, then, why would she? "If you'll just share your supplies I can handle it. I'm her mother and a nurse."

"I appreciate that but I need to treat your daughter since it happened at the parade. I'll have to make a report anyway."

She gave him room. Years ago she'd been very enamored of Mark Clayborn. Just young enough to hero worship him, she'd often dreamed of "what if" when he'd glanced her way. Which he never had, unless it had been to smile at the gaggle of young maids in his queen's court. He'd had it all. Good looks, social status, education and a bright future. And to top it off he'd been Mardi Gras King that year. Every girl had dreamed of being on his arm and she'd been no different. She had watched him so closely back then no wonder he seemed familiar.

Allie winced when he touched the angry skin of her knee.

Laura Jo's hands shook. As an emergency room nurse she'd seen much worse, but when it came to her own child it was difficult to remain emotionally detached. Still, she should be the one caring for Allie. She'd been her sole caretaker and provider since her daughter's father had left Laura Jo when she was three months pregnant. Having been pushed aside before, she didn't like it any better now than she had then. No matter how irrational the reaction.

"So what's your name, young lady?" Mark asked Allie.

She told him.

"So, Allie, what have you liked best about Mardi Gras this year?"

Allie didn't hesitate to answer. "King Cake."

He nodded like a sage monk giving thought to the answer. "I like King Cake, too. What's your favorite? Cinnamon or cream cheese?"

"Cinnamon."

"I'm a fan of cream cheese. So have you ever found the baby?"

"Yeah, once. I had to take a cake to school the next week."

"So you baked one?"

"No, my mother did." She pointed at Laura Jo.

Mark glanced at her with a look of respect but there was no sign of recognition. Even though their families had known each other for years he didn't remember her. The last she'd really heard, he'd been in a bad car accident and had later left for medical school.

"You mom didn't get it from a bakery?"

"No. She likes to make them." Allie smiled up at Laura Jo. "She lets me put the baby inside."

Allie continued, telling him how she liked to stand beside Laura Jo as she rolled the pastry out. She would wait patiently until it was time to put the miniature plastic baby into one of the rolls before Laura Jo braided them into a cake. When it came out of the oven Allie begged to be the one to shake the green, purple and gold sugar on top.

"Well, that sounds like fun. Are you ready to stand?"

Laura Jo couldn't help but be impressed. Mark had cleaned up Allie with little more than a wince from her.

He placed a hand below Allie's elbow and helped her to stand then said to Laura Jo, "Keep the area clean. If you see any infection, call a doctor right away or take her to the ER."

Laura Jo rolled her eyes. "I'm a nurse, remember?"

"I remember, but sometimes when it's someone we love our emotions get in the way."

That was something close to what her father had said when she'd announced that she was marrying Phil. "He's only interested in your last name and money." Her father had gone on to say that Phil certainly wasn't worth giving up her education for. When she'd asked how her father knew so much about Phil he admitted to having had someone check into his background. That Phil had already been married once and couldn't seem to hold down a job. "He's not good enough for you. Not welcome in our home," had been her father's parting words.

She'd chosen Phil. Even though she'd soon learned that her father had been right, the situation had created a rift between Laura Jo and her parents that was just as wide today as it had been nine years earlier. She had sworn then never to ask her parents for help. She had her pride.

Taking Allie's hand, Laura Jo said, "Let's go, honey. I'm sure we have taken enough of the medic's time."

"Bye," Allie said.

Mark bent and picked up the doubloons off the pavement and placed them carefully in Allie's hand. "I hope you find a baby in your next cake. Maybe it'll bring you luck."

Allie grinned back at him with obvious hero worship.

"Thank you." She led Allie through the barrier. "Bye."

That would be it for the reappearing Mark Clayborn. He had been a part of her life that was now long gone. She wouldn't be seeing him again.

Mark had never planned to return to Mobile to live permanently, but that had changed. He'd worked hard to make LA home. Even the few times he'd come back to Alabama he'd only stayed a few days and then gone again. When his father's houseman had phoned to say Mark Clayborn, Sr. had suffered a stroke, Mark could no longer refuse not to make southern Alabama his home again. His mother was gone and his brother was in the military with no control over where he was stationed. Mark was left no choice. Someone needed to live close enough to take care of his father.

Pulling up the circular drive framed by a well-manicured yard in the center of the oldest section of homes in Mobile, Mark stopped in front of the antebellum mansion. This house had been his home for the twenty-five years before he had moved to LA. Now just his father lived here. Mark had chosen to take up residence forty-five minutes across the bay in the Clayborn summer house in Fairhope, Alabama. He had joined a general practice group made up of five doctors. The clinic was located in the town of Spanish Fort, which was halfway between Mobile and Fairhope. He lived and worked close enough to take care of his father and far enough away that memories of the past would remain murky instead of vivid.

It had been carnival season when he'd left for LA. He'd been riding high on being the king. His queen had been his girlfriend for the last two years and one of the most beautiful girls in Mobile society. He'd gotten his pick of medical fellowships that had allowed him to only be a few hours away in Birmingham. Gossips had it that he and his queen would ride off into the happily-ever-after as soon as he finished his fellowship. Mark had not planned to disappoint them. That was until he and Mike had decided they needed to drive to the beach after the krewe dance on Fat Tuesday night.

How many times since he'd been back had he picked up the phone to call and see how Mike was doing? How many times had he not followed through? He'd seen Mike a few times over the years. Those had been brief and uncomfortable meetings. Mark had always left with another wheelbarrow of guilt piled on top of the mountain that was already there.

He and Mike had made big plans. They had both been on their way to Birmingham, Mark to complete his fellowship and Mike to earn his Master's in Business. They would return to town to set up a clinic practice, Mark handling the medical end and Mike overseeing the business side. They'd even talked about their families building homes next door to each other. But after the accident Mike's longtime girlfriend had left him. Those dreams vanished. Because of Mark.

As time had gone by it had become easier to satisfy his need to know how Mike was doing by asking others about him. Often when Mark had spoken to his father he'd ask about Mike. His father had always encouraged him to call and talk to Mike if he wanted to know how he was doing. Mark hadn't. That way the guilt didn't become a throbbing, breathing thing.

Mark pushed the front doorbell of his father's house then opened the door. He was met in the high-ceilinged hall by John, the man who had worked for Mark, Sr. since Mark, Jr. had been a boy.

"Hi. How's he doing today?"

"Your dad has had a good day. He's out by the pool."

Mark headed down the all-too-familiar hall that led through the middle of the house and out onto the brick patio with the pool beyond. His father sat in a wheelchair in the sun, with his nurse nearby, reading a book. Mark winced at the sight. It hurt his heart to see the strong, commanding man brought to this by a stroke. Only with time and patience and massive amounts of physical therapy would he regain enough strength to walk again. At least his father had a chance of getting out of the chair, unlike Mike, who had no choice.

Mark circled his father so he faced him. "Hi, Dad."

His white-haired father gave him a lopsided smile. "Hello, son."

Fortunately his mind was still strong. His nurse closed her book and after a nod to Mark made her way toward the house.

Mark pulled a metal pool chair close so he could sit where his father could see him. "How are you doing today?"

"Fine. Emmett has been by to tell me what went on at the board meeting. He said you didn't make it."

"No, I had patients to see. We've talked about this already. You've put good people in place to handle the company. Let them do it."

"It's not the same. We need a Clayborn there."

"I know, Dad."

His father continued. "I'm glad you stopped by. I wanted to talk to you about attending the krewe dance next week. I can't go and our family needs to be represented. You're the only one to do it."

Mark had always enjoyed the fanfare and glamour of The Mystical Order of Orion dance, the visit from the king and queen and their court. But after what had happened twelve years ago he was hesitant to attend. He took a deep breath. "It's not really my thing anymore but I know it's important to you to keep up appearances."

"You were king. That is and was a high honor. You owe it to the krewe, to the Clayborn name to attend."

"I know, Dad. I'll do my duty."

"This used to be your favorite time of the year. You need to let yourself off the hook, son. It wasn't your fault."

Maybe everyone thought that but Mark sure didn't. He carried the horror of what had happened to Mike with him daily. Now that he was back in Mobile it was more alive than it had ever been. Time hadn't healed the wound, only covered it over.

Mark had dinner with his father then headed across the bay to Fairhope, a small township where the family summer home was located. When he'd arrived in Alabama he'd needed a place to live. Staying in Fairhope gave him a house of his own, a safe haven. Since he was working at a clinic in Spanish Fort, a city just north of Fairhope, living there was convenient.

Entering the large dark room with hardwood paneling, Mark walked through to the family-style kitchen. There he pulled a drink out of the refrigerator and went out to the deck. Mobile Bay stretched far and wide before him. He could see the tall buildings of the city in the distance. The wind had picked up, rustling the shrubbery around the deck. A seagull swooped down and plucked a fish out of the water near the end of the pier. No, this wasn't LA anymore.

Mark had agreed to pitch in and work the parades as a first responder when one of his new partners had said that they did that as a public service during Mardi Gras season. He'd agreed to do his part but had expected that it would be in some of the surrounding smaller towns. When he'd been assigned the parade in downtown Mobile he hadn't felt like he could say no. He needed to be a team player since he'd only joined the medical group a few months earlier. Despite the parade location, Mark had enjoyed the assignment. Especially helping the young girl. Her mother had been attractive. More than once since then he'd wondered where she worked.

He'd spent the rest of the parade scanning the crowd. His chest still contracted at the thought he might see Mike. He'd spent years making a point of not thinking about the automobile accident. Now that he was back it seemed the only thing on his mind.

His cell phone rang. He pulled it out of his pocket. "This is Dr. Clayborn."

"Hey, Mark, it's Ralph. We need you again the day after tomorrow if you can help us out. Afternoon parade in Dauphine."

He didn't mind working a parade in Dauphine. It was on his side of the bay. As long as it wasn't in Mobile. There the chance of facing his past became greater. "Yeah, I'm only seeing patients in the morning. Will I be on a bike again?"

"Not this time. I just need you at the med tent. It'll be set up in the First Baptist Church parking lot."

"I'll be there."

"Marsha?" Laura Jo called as she and Allie opened the door of her best friend's apartment Wednesday afternoon.

"Hey, we're back here," a voice came from the direction of the kitchen area located in the back of the apartment.

She followed Allie down the short hallway to find Marsha and her son, Jeremy, decorating a wagon with purple, green and gold ribbons.

Marsha looked up as they entered. "You know Mardi

Gras almost kills me every year. I say I'm not going to do anything next year then here I am, doing even more."

Allie had already joined in to help Jeremy with the decorations.

"I know what you mean. It makes working in the ER interesting. I've enjoyed my day off but I'll pay for it, no doubt, by being on the night shift. I appreciate you letting Allie spend the night."

"It's not a problem. I love her like my own." She ruffled Allie's hair.

Laura Jo had met Marsha at the Mothers Without Partners clinic. Phil had lived up to all her father's predictions and more when he'd left her pregnant and cleaned out their bank account to never be seen again. Even after all these years he hadn't even checked to see if he had a son or daughter. Marsha's husband had died in a fishing accident. She and Marsha had hit it off right away. Circumstances had brought them together but friendship had seen to it that they still depended on each other.

They'd shared an apartment for a few months and had traded off their time watching the kids while the other had worked or gone to school. They had their own apartments now but in the same complex and Marsha was more like family than the one Laura Jo had left behind.

They had joined forces to help other mothers who didn't have anyone to fall back on. They had convinced the city to sell them an old home so these women would have a place to live and receive help while they were getting their lives in order. The deadline to pay for the house was looming. Finding the funding had become more difficult than Laura Jo had anticipated.

Marsha announced, "I heard from the city contact. He said we had to move soon on the house or the city will have to announce it's for sale. They can't hold it forever."

Laura Jo groaned. That wasn't what she wanted to hear. "How much time do we have?"

"Week or two. At least until things settle down after Mardi Gras. We've got to come up with a good way to raise a lot of money. Fast. I know you don't want to do it but you do have the contacts. Maybe you could put on a party dress and go pick the pockets of all those society friends you used to hang around with."

Laura Jo shook her head. "That's not going to happen. We'll have to find another way."

What if she had to face her mother and father? Worse, have them see her asking for money. That's what they had thought she'd be doing if she married Phil. That's what he'd wanted her to do, but she'd refused. After her fight with her parents she and Phil had gone to Las Vegas that night to get married.

When they'd returned Phil had left to work on an oil rig. Three weeks later he'd come home. A week later all his pay had gone and he'd admitted he'd been fired. He'd made noises about looking for a job but in hindsight she didn't think he'd ever really tried. Things had got worse between them. The issue that finally snapped them had been Laura Jo telling him she was pregnant. Phil's snarling parting words were, "I didn't sign on for no kid. You can't put that on me. Having you is bad enough."

Marsha gave her questioning look. "You know I'm kidding but…"

"I'll come up with something." She checked her watch. "Now, I have to get to the hospital." Stepping toward Allie, Laura Jo said to Marsha, "I'll meet you at the parade tomorrow evening."

"Sounds like a plan."

Laura Jo leaned down and kissed Allie on the head. "See ya. Be good for Marsha."

"I will," Allie replied, then returned to what she was doing.

"Thanks, Marsha." Laura Jo called as she went up the hall.

Six hours later, Laura Jo was longing for her dinner and a moment to put her feet up. She wasn't going to get either anytime soon. Working in a trauma one level hospital meant a constant influx of patients, not only the regular cases but Mardi Gras's as well, which brought out the revelers and daredevils. Weekend nights were the worst and the place resembled a circus with not enough clowns to go around. Everyone had their hands full. The doors were swishing open regularly with people coming in. The constant ringing of the phone filled the area, blending with the piercing scream of ambulance sirens.

As she stepped back into the nursing station the phone rang again. Seconds later the clerk called out, "Incoming. Sixty-seven-year-old male. Heart attack. Resuscitating in transit. Child with head trauma behind that. ETA ten."

"I'll take the heart. Trauma six." Laura Jo hurried to set up what was needed before the patient arrived.

Minutes later the high-pitched sound of the ambulance arriving filled the air and Laura Jo rushed outside. The double rear doors of the vehicle stood wide open. Usually by this time the EMTs would be unloading the patient.

Looking inside, she immediately recognized the EMT working over the patient but not the other man. Then she did. *Mark Clayborn.* Again he was wearing red biking shorts and a yellow shirt of a first responder.

Mark held the portable oxygen bubble away from the

patient as the EMT placed the defibrillator paddles on the patient's chest. The body jerked. The beep of the machine monitoring the heart rate started and grew steadier. Putting the earpieces of the stethoscope that had been around his neck into place, Mark listened to the man's heart. "Let's get him inside," he said with a sharp tone of authority. He then made an agile jump to the ground, turned toward the interior of the ambulance and helped bring out the patient on the stretcher.

Although confused by why he had been allowed in the emergency vehicle, she still followed his lead. It was against policy to ride in the back unless you were part of the EMT staff. But now wasn't the time for questions. She stood aside while the two men lifted out the stretcher. The wheels dropped to the pavement and Laura Jo wrapped her hand around the yellow metal frame and pulled. Mark kept his fingers on the pulse point of the patient's wrist while the EMT pushed.

They had reached the doors when Mark said, "We're losing him again."

Tall enough to lean over and push on the patient's chest, he began compressions. Another nurse met them and gave oxygen. Laura Jo kept moving ahead, her arm burning. To her relief, they got the patient into the trauma room. There Mark and the EMT used the defibrillator once again. Seconds later the monitor made a beep and the line went from straight to having peaks and valleys. After they gained a steady pulse, she worked to place leads to the monitors on the patient. The ER doctor rushed in.

Mark and the EMT backed away with exhausted sighs, giving the ER doctor, Laura Jo and the other staff members space to work. For the next twenty intensive minutes, Laura Jo followed the ER doctor's instructions to the letter.

Finally they managed to stabilize the patient enough to send him to surgery.

Laura Jo had to talk to the family. They must be scared. When she asked the admission clerk where they were she was told exam room five.

"Why are they in an exam room?"

"The man's granddaughter is being evaluated."

Laura Jo headed for the exam room. It shouldn't have surprised her that Mark was there, too. He came out as she was preparing to go in.

"Well, fancy meeting you here," he drawled in a deep voice that made her think of a dark velvet night.

"It's not that amazing really. I work here."

"I figured that out. So how's your daughter? Healing nicely?"

"She's fine. A little tender but fine."

"Good. By the way, I'm Dr. Mark Clayborn."

"Yes, I know who you are. As in the Clayborn Building, Clayborn Bank, Clayborn Shipping."

He gave her a studying look. "Do I know you?"

"I'm Laura Jo Akins. Used to be Laura Jo Herron."

"Herron? My parents used to talk about the Herrons. Robert Herron. Real estate."

She looked away. "Yes, that's my father."

He had pursed his lips. "Well, that's a surprise. Isn't it a small world?"

Too small for Laura Jo's comfort. It was time to change the subject. "Thanks for helping out. Now I need to talk to the family." She gave the door to the exam room a quick knock and pushed it open.

It turned out that she was wasting her time. "The nice Dr. Clayborn" had updated them and also seen to Lucy, their little girl, but they appreciated Laura Jo coming in. By the time she'd returned to the nursing station things

seemed to be under control in the ER. All the exam and
trauma rooms were full. The critical cases were being
cared for. Those waiting were not serious.

"Why don't you take your supper break while you can?"
the lead nurse said.

"Are you sure?"

"It's now or never. You know the closer we get to Fat
Tuesday the merrier it gets around here."

Laura Jo laughed. "If merry is what you want to call
it. Okay, I'll go."

"I'd rather call it merry otherwise I think I might cry,"
the lead nurse said with a grin.

Laura Jo grabbed her lunch box. It had become a habit
to pack a lunch when money had been so tight even before Phil had left. Reaching the cafeteria, she scanned the
room for an empty table. The busy ER translated to a full
room. As soon as a table opened up she headed for it. Before she could get to it Mark slid into one of the two seats
available. Disappointed, she stopped and looked around
for another spot.

He waved her toward him. "You can join me, if you
like."

Laura Jo looked at him. Did she really have a choice?
She was expected back in the ER soon. "Thank you."

He grinned at her. "You don't sound too excited about
it."

What was he expecting her to say? *You're right, I'm not?*
"I have to eat. The ER won't stay calm for long."

"It did look a little wild in there. I've certainly had
more than my share this evening. I haven't done this much
emergency work since I was on my med school rotation.
Don't see many head trauma and heart attacks in family
practice."

Laura Jo pulled her sandwich out of the plastic bag. "I

understand that the girl was sitting on top of her father's shoulders and toppled off. When the grandfather saw what had happened he had a heart attack."

"Yeah. Thank goodness it all happened within running distance of the med tent. For a few minutes there wasn't enough of us medical personal around to handle all that was going on. I'm just glad the girl has regained consciousness and the grandfather is stable."

"The girl will be here for observation for at least one night and the grandfather for much longer, I'm afraid."

He took a large bite of his hamburger and they ate in silence for a while before he asked, "So you knew who I was the other day. Why didn't you say something?"

"There just didn't seem a right moment."

"So you've seen a lot of Mardi Gras."

She straightened her back and looked directly at him. "I'm not that old."

He grinned. "I'm sorry, I didn't mean to imply that."

Laura Jo had to admit he had a nice smile. She grinned. "That's not what it sounded like to me."

"I was just trying to make pleasant conversation and didn't mean—"

"I know you didn't." Still, it would have been nice if he'd at least thought she looked familiar. She'd been invisible to her parents, unimportant to her husband and just this once it would have been nice to have been memorable. But, then, it had been a long time ago.

"So do you attend any of the krewe festivities?" He chewed slowly, as if waiting patiently for her answer.

"No. I don't travel in that social circle anymore." She took a bite of her sandwich.

"Why not? As I remember, the Herrons were a member of the same krewe as my family."

"I'm an Akins now."

"So Mr. Akins isn't a member either, I gather."

"No, and Mr. Akins, as you put it, isn't around to be a member."

"I'm sorry."

"I'm not. He left years ago."

"Oh, I thought…"

"I know. For all I know, he's alive and well somewhere."

Having finished his meal, Mark leaned back in his chair and crossed his arms over his chest. "Well, it has been a pleasure running into you, Ms. Atkins."

Laura Jo stood to leave. "You, too, Dr. Clayborn. We do seem to keep running into each other."

"Why, Ms. Akins, you don't believe in serendipity?"

"If I ever did believe in serendipity, that would've been a long time ago. Now, if you'll excuse me, I need to get back to work."

CHAPTER TWO

ON SATURDAY AFTERNOON Mark made his way through the side streets of Mobile, working around the parade route, which was already blocked off. It was one more week before Mardi Gras weekend and there would be a large parade that afternoon and another that night in downtown Mobile.

Throughout the week in the surrounding towns parades were planned, culminating in three or four per day until the final one on Fat Tuesday. Then Ash Wednesday would arrive and end all the revelry.

He'd been assigned to work in the med tent set up just off Government Street at a fire station. He'd wanted to say no, had even suggested that he work one or two of the parades in a nearby town, but he'd been told that he was needed there. His gut clenched each time he crossed the bay but his partners wouldn't like him not being a team player during this time of the year. Plus, Mark had no desire to admit why going into Mobile bothered him.

All he hoped for now was a slow day, but he didn't expect it. He wanted less drama than the last time he'd worked a med tent a few days earlier. Still, there had been some interesting points.

Dinner with Laura Jo Akins had been the highlight. He had at least found out she wasn't married. And she seemed to be anti-krewe for some reason. He had no doubt that she'd grown up on the social club festivities of a krewe, just like him. Why would she have such a negative view now? Or was her pessimistic attitude directed toward him? Did she know about the accident? His part in it?

Laura Jo Akins also appeared to be one of those women who knew her mind and stood her ground, but it also seemed there was a venerable spot to her, too. As if she hid something from the world. What was that all about?

Mark looked over the crowd again. At least she took his thoughts off worrying that he might see Mike at a parade. He looked forward to seeing her pixie face if they ever met again. People were creatures of habit and usually showed up in the same places to watch the parades. He wasn't sure why she interested him so, but she'd popped into his head a number of times over the past few days.

He had been at the med tent long enough to introduce himself to some of the other volunteers when he looked up to see none other than Laura Jo walking toward the tent. She caught sight of him about the same time. He didn't miss her moment of hesitation before she continued in his direction. He smiled and nodded at her. She returned his smile.

A few minutes later he was asked to help with a woman who was having an asthma attack in the unseasonably warm weather. It was some time later before he had a chance to speak to Laura Jo.

"I believe we might be caught in some Mardi Gras mystical mojo," he said, low enough that the others around them couldn't hear.

"I don't believe any sort of thing. I'm more of the dumb luck kind of person," she responded, as she continued to sort supplies.

He chuckled. "Didn't expect to see me again so soon, did you?"

She spun around, her hands going to her hips. "Did you plan this?"

"I did not," he said with complete innocence. "I was told when and where to be."

"I thought maybe with the Clayborn name..."

What did she have against the Clayborns? Did she know what he'd done? If she did, he couldn't blame her for not wanting to have anything to do with him. "Excuse me?"

"Nothing."

"Dr. Clayborn, we need you," one of the other volunteers called.

Mark had no choice but to go to work.

Half an hour later, the sound of a jazz band rolled down the street. Because the med tent was set up at the fire station, no one could park or stand in front of it. Mark and the others had an unobstructed view of the parade. Thankfully there was no one requiring help so they all stepped out toward the street curb to watch. Laura Jo seemed to appreciate the parade. She even swayed to the music of "Let the good times roll."

He wandered over to stand just behind her. "You enjoy a good parade as much as your daughter does, I see." Mark couldn't help but needle her. She reacted so prettily to it.

"Yes, I love a good parade. You make it sound like it should be a crime."

"And you make it sound like it's a crime that I noticed," he shot back.

"No crime. Just not used to someone taking that much notice."

"That's hard to believe. You mean there's no man who pays attention to you?"

"Getting a little personal, aren't you, Doctor?" She glanced back at him.

"No, just making conversation."

"Hey, Mom."

They both turned at the sound of Laura Jo's daughter's voice. She was with another woman about Laura Jo's age and there was a boy with them about the same height as the daughter.

Before her mother could respond the girl said to Mark, "I know you. You're that man who helped me the other day. Look, my hands are all better." She put out her hands palms up. "My knee still hurts a little." She lifted her denim-covered knee.

"And I know you." He smiled down at her. "But forgive me, I've forgotten your name."

"Allie."

He squatted down to her level. "I'm glad you're feeling better, Allie." Standing again, he glanced in the direction of the woman he didn't know. Laura Jo must have gotten the hint because she said, "This is Marsha Gilstrap. A friend of mine." She looked toward the boy. "And Jeremy, her son. I thought ya'll were going to watch the parade over on Washington."

"We wanted to come by and say hi to you," Allie said.

Laura Jo gave her daughter a hug then looked down at her with what Mark recognized as unbounded love. He liked it when he saw parents who really cared about their children. Her actions hadn't just been for show when her daughter had been hurt at the parade. She truly cared about her child. He recognized that love because his parents had had the same for him. That's why his father had insisted Mark not get involved with Mike's case after the accident. His father had feared what it might do to Mark's future. He been young enough and scared enough that he'd agreed, despite the guilt he'd felt over leaving the way he had. Now he didn't trust himself to get close enough to care about someone. If he did, he might fail them, just as he had Mike. He hadn't stood beside Mike, whom he'd loved like a brother, so why would he have what it took to stand by a wife and family?

A float coming by drew Allie's attention. Mark put a hand on her shoulder. "Come on. This is a great spot to watch a parade."

Allie looked at her mother in question. Laura Jo took a second before she gave an agreeable nod but he got the sense that she didn't want to.

Allie glanced at the boy. "Can Jeremy come, too?"

"Sure."

Jeremy's mother, in contrast to Laura Jo, was all smiles about the boy joining them.

"We'll just be right up here if you need us." Mark made an effort to give Laura Jo his most charming smile.

He nudged one of the volunteers out of the way so that the children had a front-row place to stand. A couple of times he had to remind them not to step out beyond the curve. Because they were standing in front of the fire station, there were no barriers in place. After a few minutes Laura Jo and her friend joined them.

"Thanks, we'll take these two off your hands," Laura Jo said, as if she was helping him out. What she was really doing was trying to get rid of him.

"Look at the dog. How funny." Allie squealed. The dog was wearing a vest and a hat. "I wish I had a dog to dress up. Then we could be in a parade."

Laura Jo placed her hand on top of Allie's shoulder. "Maybe one day, honey."

There was something in the wispy tone in the girl's voice that got to him. It reminded him of how he'd sounded the first time he'd asked if he could be in a dog parade. When he and his brother had participated in a parade it had been one of the greatest pleasures of his childhood. He could surely give that to Allie without becoming too involved in her and her mother's lives. "You could borrow my dog. Gus would be glad to let you dress him up," Mark offered.

"Could I, Mom?" Allie looked at Laura Jo as if her life depended on a positive answer.

"I don't know."

"I think Allie and Gus would make a great pair." He had no doubt Laura Jo hated to say no to something her daughter so obviously wanted to do. But why was he making it his job to see that Allie had a chance to be in a parade? Was it because Laura Jo was a hard-working mother who couldn't do this for her daughter and it was easy enough for him to do? It would be a great memory for Allie, just as it had been for him.

"Please, Mom."

"Fairhope has a parade on Sunday evening that I believe dogs are allowed in. Why don't you and Allie come and meet Gus that afternoon? You could bring some clothes for him and see how he likes them."

Laura Jo gave him a piercing look that said she wasn't pleased with the turn of events.

In a perverse way he liked the idea he was able to nettle her.

"Allie, I don't think we should take advantage of Dr. Clayborn's time."

"Please, call me Mark. And I don't mind." He really didn't. Since he'd been back in town he had kept to himself. It would be nice to spend the afternoon with someone. "I'm sure Gus will be glad to have the company. I've not been around much the past few days. Marsha, you and Jeremy are welcome, too."

"Thanks. It sounds like fun but I can't. Jeremy can if Laura Jo doesn't mind," Marsha said, smiling.

Laura Jo shot Marsha a look as if there would be more to say about this when they were alone.

"Mom, please," Allie pleaded. "Please."

"Won't your wife mind us barging in? Won't your children be dressing him up?"

"No wife. No children. So there's no reason you can't."

"Then I guess we could come by for a little while but I'm not making any promises about the parade." Laura Jo looked down at Allie.

"Great. I'll expect you about two. Here's my address." He pulled out a calling card, turned it over and, removing a pen from his pocket, wrote on it. "I'll have Gus all bathed and waiting on you."

Allie giggled. "Okay."

Mark looked at Laura Jo. "See you tomorrow."

She gave him a weak smile and he grinned. He was already looking forward to the afternoon.

Laura Jo wasn't sure how she'd managed to be coerced into agreeing to go to Mark's. Maybe it was because of the look of anticipation on Allie's face or the maternal guilt she felt whenever Allie asked to do something and she had to say no because she had to go to work or school. Now that she was in a position to give her child some fun in her life, she couldn't bring herself to say no. But going to Mark Clayborn's house had to be one for the record. She didn't really know the man. She'd admired him with a young girl's hero worship. But she knew little about the man he had become. He'd been nice enough so far but she hadn't always been the best judge of character.

She'd searched for a sound reason why they couldn't do it. Marsha certainly hadn't been any help. It was as if she had pushed her into going. For once Laura Jo wished she had to work on Sunday. But no such luck.

Allie was up earlier than usual in her excitement over the possibility of being in the dog parade. Jeremy had been almost as bad, Marsha said, when he ran to meet them at the car later that day.

"So are you looking forward to an afternoon with the handsome, debonair and rich Dr. Mark Clayborn?" Marsha asked with a grin.

They'd had a lively and heated discussion over a cup of coffee late the night before about Mark. Marsha seemed to think she should develop him as an ally in funding the single mothers' house. Laura Jo wasn't so sure. That was a road she'd promised herself she'd never go down again. She wasn't ever going to ask her parents or her society friends for anything ever again. That certainly included Mark Clayborn.

After today she didn't plan to see him again. This afternoon was about Allie and seeing a smile on her face. That only. Allie had been begging for a dog for the past year but they didn't have a lifestyle that was good for taking care of a dog.

Laura Jo pulled her aging compact car off the winding, tree-shaded road into the well-groomed, riverbed-pebbled drive of the address she'd been given. The crunch made a familiar sound. Her own family's place just a few miles down the road had the same type of drive, or at least it had the last time she'd been there.

The foliage of the large trees with moss hanging from them gave the area a cozy feel. Soon she entered an open space where a sweeping, single-story beach house sat with a wide expanse of yard between it and the bay beyond.

"Do you see Gus?" Allie strained at her seat belt as she peered out the window.

"Now, honey, I don't want you to get your hopes up too high. Gus may not like being dressed up." Laura Jo didn't want to say "or you." Some owners thought their dogs loved everyone when they often didn't.

"He'll like it, I know he will."

"I think he will, too," Jeremy said from the backseat.

Laura Jo looked at him in the rearview mirror and smiled. "We'll see."

She pulled to a stop behind a navy blue high-end European car. To Mark's credit, it wasn't a sports car but it was finer than Laura Jo had ever ridden in, even when she'd still been living with her parents.

Her door had hardly opened before Allie ran toward a basset hound, whose ears dragged along the ground. Not far behind him strolled Mark. For a second her breath caught. He had all the markers of an eye-catching man. Tall, blond wavy hair and an air about him that said he could take care of himself and anyone else he cared about. It was a dazzling combination.

She'd been asked out a number of times by one of the men at the hospital, but she'd never had a man both irritate her and draw her to him at the same time. That was exactly what Mark Clayborn did.

He looked down with a smile at Allie, with her arms wrapped around Gus, and Jeremy, patting him, then at Laura Jo.

Her middle fluttered. If it wasn't for all the baggage she carried, her inability to trust her judgment of men, maybe she might be interested. She'd let Allie have her day and make a concerted effort not to see Mark again.

"Hey. Did you have any trouble finding it?"

"No trouble. I knew which one it was when you told me you lived in Fairhope."

"Really?"

"I remember passing it when I was a kid." She'd been aware all her life where the Clayborn summer home was located.

He glanced back to where the children played with the dog. "I think they're hitting it off."

Laura Jo couldn't help but agree.

"Allie, did you bring some clothes for Gus? I got a few things just in case you didn't," Mark said, strolling toward the kids and dog.

"They're in the car."

"I'll get them, honey," Laura Jo called, as the kids headed toward the large open yard between the house and bay. "Don't go near the water and stay where I can see you."

She walked to the car and Mark followed her. "You're a good mother."

Laura Jo glanced at him. "I try to be."

"So when did Allie's father leave?"

Laura Jo opened the passenger door then looked at him. "When I was three months pregnant."

Mark whistled. "That explains some of your standoff-ishness."

She pulled a large brown sack out of the car and closed the door with more force than necessary. "I'm not."

"Yeah, you are. For some reason, you don't want to like me, even when you do."

She was afraid he might be right. Thankfully, squealing in the front yard drew their attention to the two children running around as a dog almost as wide as he was tall chased them.

Mark checked his watch and called, "Allie and Jeremy,

we need to get started on what Gus will wear because the parade starts in a couple of hours."

The kids ran toward them and Gus followed.

"Why don't we go around to the deck where it's cooler? We can dress Gus there," Mark said to the kids.

Mark led the way with the kids and Gus circled them. Laura Jo hung back behind them. Mark was good with children. Why didn't he have a wife and kids of his own? She imagined she was the only one of many who didn't fall at his charming feet.

The deck was amazing. It was open at one end. Chairs and a lounge group were arranged into comfortable conversation areas. At the other end was an arbor with a brown vine that must be wisteria on it. Laura Jo could only envision what it would look like in the spring and summer, with its green leaves creating a roof of protection from the sun. She'd love to sit in a comfortable chair under it but that wasn't going to happen.

"Allie, why don't you and Jeremy pull the things you brought out of the bag while I go get what I bought? Then you can decide how to dress Gus."

Allie took the bag from Laura Jo. With the children busy pulling feather boas, old hair bows, purple, green and gold ribbon from the bag, Laura Jo took a seat on the end of a lounge chair and watched.

Mark quickly returned with an armload of stuff.

"I thought you only got a few things," Laura Jo said.

He grinned. Her heart skipped a beat.

"I might have gotten a little carried away." He looked directly at her. "I do that occasionally."

For some reason, she had the impression he might be talking about sex. She hadn't had a thought like that in forever. Not since Phil had left. He'd made it clear that she hadn't been wanted and neither had their child.

Mark added his armload to the growing pile on the deck.

"Okay, Allie, I want you and Jeremy to pick out a winning combination. They give prizes for the funniest dog, best dressed, most spirited and some more I don't remember. Let's try to win a prize," Mark said, as he joined them on the planks of the wooden deck and held Gus. "I'll hold him while you dress him."

Laura Jo scooted back in the lounge to watch. It was a February day but the sun was shining. It wasn't long until her eyes closed.

She didn't know how long she'd been out before Mark's voice above her said, "You'd better be careful or you'll get burned. Even the winter sun in the south can get you."

"Thanks. I'm well aware of that. Remember, I've lived here all my life."

"That's right, a Herron."

"Who is a Herron, Mommy?"

"They're a family I used to know."

Mark's brows rose.

"Now, let me see what ya'll have done to Gus while I was napping," Laura Jo said quickly, before he could ask any more questions in front of Allie.

Mark didn't question further, seeing that Laura Jo didn't want to talk about her family in front of Allie. But he would be asking later. Allie didn't even know who her grandparents were? There was a deep, dark secret there that he was very interested in finding out about. Why hadn't he recognized Laura Jo? Probably because she had been too young to take his notice. His mouth drew into a line. More likely, he had been so focused on his world he hadn't looked outside it.

"My, doesn't Gus look, uh…festive?"

Mark couldn't help but grin at Laura Jo's description.

Festive was a good word for it, along with silly. His dog wore a purple, gold and green feather boa wrapped around his neck. A dog vest of the same colors was on his body, bands on his ankles and a bow on the end of his tail. This being the one thing Allie had insisted he needed. Mark was amazed the Gus was as agreeable as he was about that.

Allie pronounced him "Perfect."

"I think we should be going if we want to make the start time."

"Start time?" Laura Jo asked.

"For the Mystic Mutts parade."

"I don't think—"

"We can't miss it. Isn't that right, Allie and Jeremy?"

"Right," both children said in unison.

Great. Now she was being ganged up on.

"Come on, Mommy. We have to take Gus," Allie pleaded.

Laura Jo glared at Mark. "I guess I don't have much of a choice."

Allie and Jeremy danced around her. "Yay."

"Let me get Gus's leash and we'll be all set." Mark went inside and returned with a lead.

As they rounded the house and headed toward the cars he looked at Laura Jo's. It was too small for all of them.

"I don't think we can all get in my car," Laura Jo said from beside him.

Mark stopped and looked at hers again. "I guess I should drive."

"You don't sound like you really want to do that. We could take two cars but I'm sure parking will be tight."

Mark's lips drew into a tight line. The thought of being responsible for Laura Jo and the kids gave him a sick feeling. Children had never ridden in his car. Since the accident he'd made it a practice not to drive with others in the car if he could help it. Often he hired a driver when he went out on a date. Unable to come up with another plan, he said, "Then we'll go in my car. Please make sure the children are securely buckled in."

Laura Jo gave him an odd look before she secured Allie and Jeremy in the backseat. Gus found a spot between them and Allie placed an arm around him. Laura Jo joined him in the front. Mark looked back to check if the children were buckled in.

"Is there a problem?" Laura Jo asked.

If he kept this up he would make them all think he was crazy. He eased his grip on the steering wheel and let the blood flow back into his knuckles. "No. I was just double-checking they were okay."

Laura Jo shook her head as she ran a hand across the leather of the seat. "Worried about having kids in your fancy car?"

"No."

"Nice," she murmured.

"Like my car?"

"Yes," she said, more primly than the situation warranted, as she placed her hand in her lap.

He grinned. At least this subject took his mind off having a carload of passengers. "It's okay to say what you think."

"I wouldn't think it's very practical. The cost of a car like this could help a lot of people in need."

"I help people in need all the time. I also give to charities so I don't feel guilty about owning this car." Taking a fortify breath, he started it and pulled away from the house. At the end of the drive, he turned onto the road leading into town.

"I'm just not impressed by fancy cars and houses.

People with those think they can tell you what to do, how you need to live. Even look down on others."

He glanced at her. "That's an interesting statement. Care to give me some background?"

"No, not really."

"Well, you just insulted me and my family and yours as well, and you won't even do me the courtesy of telling me why?"

"I'm sorry I insulted you. Sometimes my mouth gets ahead of my brain." She looked out the side window.

Yes, he was definitely going to find out what gave her such a sour view of people with money. He'd always prided himself on the amount he gave to charities. He had nothing to be ashamed of where that was concerned. Standing beside someone he loved when there was a disaster was where he failed.

A few minutes later he pulled the car into a tight space a couple of blocks from the parade route. It was the only spot he could find after circling the area. How had he gotten through the short drive without breaking into a sweat? Amazingly, talking to Laura Jo had made him forget his anxiety over driving. "This is the best I can do. We'll have to walk some."

Laura Jo saw to getting the children out. He leashed Gus and then gave him over to Allie. The girl beamed.

"I checked the paper this morning and the start of the parade is at the corner of Section and Third Street."

They weaved their way through the already growing crowd. As the number of people increased, Mark took Gus's leash from Allie and made sure that space was made for the dog, children and Laura Jo. A few times he touched her waist to direct her through a gap in the crowd. At the first occurrence she stiffened and glanced back at him. When he did it again she seemed to take it in her stride.

Mark was pleased when his little party arrived at the starting line without a loss of personnel. He looked at Laura Jo. "Why don't you wait here with the kids while I check in?"

"We'll be right over here near the brick wall." She took Gus's lead and led Allie and Jeremy to the spot she'd indicated.

"I'll be right back."

"You hope." She smiled.

It was the first genuine one he'd seen her give. It caught him off guard. It took him a second to respond. "Yeah."

Fifteen minutes later he had Gus, Allie and Jeremy signed in for the parade. He found Laura Jo and the kids waiting right where she'd said they would be. She had her head down, listening to something that Jeremy was saying. The angle of her head indicated she was keeping an eye on her daughter at the same time. Once again he was impressed by her mothering skills. The women he'd gone out with had never shown any interest in being mothers. He'd always thought he'd like to be a father, but he wouldn't let that happen. What if he ran out on them, like he had Mike, when the going got tough? He couldn't take that chance.

There was nothing flashy or pretentious about Laura Jo. More like what you saw was what you got. He'd grown up within the finely drawn lines of what was expected by the tight-knit Mobile society. He hadn't met many women who'd seemed to live life on their own terms. Even in California the women he'd dated had always worn a false front, literally and physically.

Laura Jo's face was devoid of makeup and she wore a simple blouse and jeans with flats. She reminded him of a girl just out of high school. That was until she opened her mouth, then she left no doubt she was a grown woman who could defend herself and her child. Nothing about her indicated she had been raised in one of local society's finest families.

Allie said something and Laura Jo turned her head. Both mother and child had similar coloring. Pretty in an early-spring-leaves-unfolding sort of way. Easy on the eye. Why would any man leave the two of them?

If he ever had a chance to have something as good in his life as they were, he'd hold on to them and never let them out of his sight. He sighed. What he saw between Laura Jo and Allie wasn't meant for him. It wasn't his to have. He'd taken that chance from Mike and he had no right to have it himself. What they had he couldn't be trusted with.

"Hey, there's Dr. Clayborn," Allie called.

Mark grinned as he joined them. He ruffled Allie's hair. "That's Mark to you. Dr. Clayborn sounds like a mouthful for such a little girl."

Allie drew herself up straight. "I'm a big girl."

Mark went down on one knee, bringing himself to eye level with Allie. "I apologize. Yes, you are a big girl. Big enough to walk with Gus in the parade?"

"Really, you're going to let me take Gus in the parade?"

"Yes, and Jeremy, too. But I have to come along with you."

She turned to Laura Jo. "Mommy, I'm going to get to be in the parade."

"I heard, honey, but I don't know."

"I'll be right there with them the entire time." Mark reassured Laura Jo.

The look of hesitation on her face gave him the idea that she didn't often trust Allie's care to anyone but her friend Marsha.

He reached for Gus's leash and she handed it to him. The nylon was warm from her clasp. "She'll be perfectly safe. We'll meet you and Jeremy at the car when it's over. The parade route isn't long."

"I guess it'll be okay." She looked at Allie. "You and Jeremy do just what Mark tells you to do." Laura Jo pinned Mark with a look. "And you turn up with my daughter and Jeremy at the end of the parade."

"Yes, ma'am." He gave her a smile and a little salute. "I'll take good care of them, I promise. Let's go, kids. We need to get in line."

Laura Jo watched as Mark took her daughter's much smaller hand in his larger one and Jeremy's in his other one. Gus walked at Allie's heels as they were swallowed up by the crowd.

What was it about Mark that made her trust him with the most precious person in her life? She'd never allowed anyone but Marsha that privilege. Maybe it was the way he'd care for Allie's knee, or his devotion to the grandfather and later the girl he'd cared for. Somehow Mark had convinced her in a few short meetings that he could be trusted. Now that she was a mother she better understood how her parents had felt when she had insisted on going off with someone they hadn't trusted.

Alone, she made her way through the crowd to the curb of a street about halfway along the parade route. Taking a seat on the curb, she waited until the parade approached. For this parade there would be no bands involved. All the music would come from music boxes pulled in carts by children. The floats would be decorated wagons and dogs of all shapes and sizes.

Twenty minutes later the first of the parade members came into view. Not far behind them were Allie, Jeremy and Mark. Laura Jo stood as they approached. She'd never seen a larger smile on Allie's face. Mark and Jeremy were grinning also. Gus was lumbering behind them, looking bored but festive. Allie held his leash proudly.

She screamed and waved as they came by. Allie and Jeremy waved enthusiastically back at her. Mark acknowledged her also. As they came closer he stepped over to Laura Jo and said, "The kids are having a blast."

Laura Jo smiled.

An hour later Laura Jo stood waiting outside Mark's car. Anxiousness was building with every minute that passed. Something had to have gone wrong. Mark and the children should have been there by now. Had something happened to one of the kids? She shouldn't have let them out of her sight. Was this how her parents had felt when she'd run off with Phil?

He had been a master of manipulation. Before they'd got married he'd made her believe he had a good job and he would take care of her. "Don't worry about what your parents think, I'll take care of you," he would say. The worst thing was that he'd made her believe he'd loved her.

Had she let Mark do the same thing? Persuade her to let the kids be in the parade. Had she made a poor character judgment call again? This time with her daughter? Her palms dampened. She'd promised herself to be careful. Now look what was happening. She headed in the direction of where the parade had ended, and soon recognized Mark's tall figure coming in her way. He pulled a wagon on which Gus, Allie and Jeremy rode. With relief filling her chest, she ran toward them.

Mark was red-faced. Jeremy wore a smile. Allie looked pleased with herself as she held Gus's head in her lap. The dog was wearing a crown.

"Where have ya'll been? I was getting worried." Laura Jo stopped beside them.

"Mommy, we won first place for the slowest dog in the parade." Allie beamed.

Laura Jo gave her a hug. "That's wonderful, honey."

"Sorry we made you worry. I should have given you my cell number. Gus also got slower after the parade. I carried him halfway here until I saw a kid with a wagon. I had to give him fifty dollars for it so I could haul Gus back."

At the sound of disgust in Mark's voice Laura Jo couldn't help but laugh. His look of complete exasperation and her sense of relief made the situation even more humorous.

"I'm glad someone thinks it's funny." Mark chuckled.

Laura Jo had to admit he was a good sport and he'd certainly made her daughter happy. Every time she tried to stop laughing she'd think of Mark begging a boy for his wagon and she'd burst out in laughter again. It had been a long time since she'd laughed hard enough to bring tears to her eyes.

"If you think you can stop laughing at me for a few minutes, we can load up this freeloader…" he gave the dog a revolted look "…and get him home."

"Had a workout, did you?" Laura Jo asked, trying to suppress the giggles that kept bubbling up.

"Yeah. No good deed goes unpunished."

"Whose idea was it to be in the parade?"

"Okay, it was mine."

Laura Jo burst into another round of snickers.

"Mommy, are you all right?" Allie looked at her in wonder.

"Oh, honey. I'm fine. I'm just glad you had a good time." She looked over the top of her head and grinned at Mark. Had it really been that long since Allie had seen her laugh?

Mark scooped Gus up in his arms. "If you'll get the door, I'll get this prima donna in the car."

Laura Jo's snort escaped as she opened the door. Allie climbed in next to the dog then Jeremy clambered in. Laura Jo saw they were buckled in. Mark put the wagon in the trunk and slapped the lid down harder than necessary.

"So you plan on being in another parade anytime soon?" she asked him, as she took her place in the front seat.

Mark sneered at her as he started the car. Laura Jo's smile grew. Before they left the parking spot, he twisted to study the children. As he turned the first corner, she looked back to find both of the children asleep. Most of the people at their end of the parade had left already, which made it easy for him to maneuver out of town and back to his home.

As they drove down the drive, Laura Jo said, "Thanks for going to so much trouble for Allie. She had the time of her life."

"You're welcome. Despite Gus being in slow motion, I enjoyed it. I've been a part of a number of parades in my time but never one like today's."

Laura Jo grinned. Something she seemed to have been doing more of lately. "Well, I appreciate it. I'll get the kids loaded up and we'll get out of your hair."

"Mommy, I'm hungry."

Laura Jo sighed and looked back at her daughter. "I thought you were asleep."

"I bet they are hungry. They've had a busy day. I've got some hot dogs I could put on the grill," Mark suggested, as he pulled the car to a stop.

"You've already done enough. I think we had better go." Laura Jo didn't want to like him any more than she already did, and she was afraid she might if she stayed around Mark much longer. The picture of him pulling the dog and Allie and Jeremy put a warm spot in her heart. He wasn't the self-centered man she'd believed he might be.

"Can't I play with Gus a little while longer?" Allie pleaded.

"Face it, you're not going to win this one." Mark grinned.

"You're sure about this?" Laura Jo realized she'd lost again.

"Yeah. It'll be nice to have company for a meal."

"Okay," she said to Mark, then turned and looked at Allie. "We'll stay for a little while longer but when I say it's time to go, we go without any argument, understood?"

"Yes, ma'am," Allie said, and Jeremy, who had awoken, nodded in agreement.

Laura Jo opened the door for Allie while Mark did the same for Jeremy and Gus.

"If you both give your mom and me just a few minutes, we'll have the hot dogs ready. Why don't you guys watch the parade on TV? Look for us."

"Do you think they'll have it running already?" Laura Jo asked.

"They should. When I told friends on the West Coast that we had Mardi Gras parades on TV they were amazed." Mark turned to the kids again. "I'll turn the TV on and we'll give it a look."

They all followed Mark through the front door of the house. Laura Jo studied the interior. The foyer had an easy, casual feel to it but every piece of furniture was placed so that it reminded her of a home decorating magazine. From the entrance, it opened into a large space with an exterior glass wall that gave the room a one-hundred-and-eighty-degree view of the deck area and the bay. Full ceiling-to-floor green-checked curtains were pushed back to either side of the windowed area. The late-afternoon sunlight streamed into the room, giving it an inviting glow.

Overstuffed cream-colored couches faced each other. A table with a chess set on it sat to one side of the room.

Opposite it there was a large-screen TV built into the wall, with bookshelves surrounding it. Comfortable-looking armchairs were placed throughout the room. The house gave her the feeling that a family had lived and loved here.

"What a wonderful room," Laura Jo whispered.

"Thanks. It's my favorite space."

She turned, startled, to find Mark standing close. She had been so caught up in the room she hadn't noticed him approach.

"I'll turn the TV on for the kids then get started on those dogs. You don't need to help. You're welcome to stay with them."

"No, I said I would help and I will. After all, I haven't carried a dog around town all afternoon," she said with a grin.

"You're not going to let that go, are you?" He gave her a pained look.

She shook her head. "The visual is just too good to let go of."

He picked up a remote and pushed a button. The TV came on. The kids had already found themselves a place on a sofa. After a few changes of channels he stopped. "I do believe this is ours."

"You guys stay right here. Don't go outside," Laura Jo said.

Mark headed toward the open kitchen Laura Jo could see off to the left. She followed. It was a modern and up-to-date space that was almost as large as her entire apartment. She ran a hand across the granite of the large counter in the middle of the room with a sigh of pleasure. "I wish I had a place like this to cook. I bet you could make a perfect king cake on this top," she murmured, more to herself than Mark.

"You're welcome to come over anytime and use it. I

get nowhere near the use out of it that I should." Mark put his head in the refrigerator and came out with a package of hot dogs.

"Thanks for the offer. But I don't really have time to do a lot of cooking." She wished she did have. Even if she did, she wouldn't be coming here to do it.

"That's not what Allie led me to believe." He picked through a drawer and found some tongs.

"I'd like to but I don't think we'll be getting that friendly."

He came to stand across the counter from her. "Why not? You might find you like me if you'd give me a chance."

"We're from two different worlds now and I don't see us going any further than we did today."

"What do you mean by two different worlds? Our parents have been acquaintances for years. I don't see that we are that different."

Had she hurt his feelings? No, she couldn't imagine that what she thought or felt mattered that much to him. But he had been nice to Allie and he deserved the truth. "I have nothing to do with that society stuff anymore."

"I had no idea you were such a snob, or is it narrow-mindedness?"

"I'm not a snob and it has nothing to do with being narrow-minded and everything to do with knowing who the Clayborn family is and what they represent. I want no part of that world again."

"Once again, I think I have been insulted. Do you know me or my family well enough to have that opinion? What have we done to you?" His tone had roughened with each sentence. "I think I deserve to hear you expound on that statement."

"Well, you're going to be disappointed."

Mark's brows came together over his nose.

"Instead, why don't you tell me what has you living on this side of the bay when I know the other side is thought to be the correct one?"

He placed some hot dog buns on the counter. "I needed a place to stay when I moved back and no one was staying in the summer house. It's no big mystery."

"That's right. I remember hearing talk that you were in a bad accident and left town afterwards."

He winced. "Yeah, I left to do my fellowship in California."

"Well, do tell. I am surprised. I would have never thought a Clayborn would live anywhere but Mobile."

"And for your information, my brother and I both moved away. I came back because my father had a stroke and needs someone close."

"I'm sorry to hear about your father." And she was. It was tough to see someone suffer that way. She remembered Mr. Clayborn, Sr. being a larger-than-life man whom everyone noticed when he came into the room. Much like Mark. She admired Mark for giving up his life in California to return home to care for his father. In comparison, she lived in the same town and didn't even speak to her parents.

"He had a bad stroke but he is recovering. Working every day is over for him but at least he's alive."

"Mommy," Allie called. "I'm hungry."

Mark shrugged. "I guess we'd better save this conversation for later. If you really want to help, why don't you get the plates and things together while I get these hot dogs on the grill? The plates are in that cabinet—" he pointed to one to the right of the stove "—and the silverware is in that drawer." He indicated the one right in front of her. "Condiments in the refrigerator. What few there are." He went out the side door of the kitchen without another word.

What Mark didn't realize was that she was through having any type of conversation about her past. Why she'd told him so much she had no idea.

CHAPTER THREE

MARK STARTED THE gas grill and adjusted the flame, before placing the hot dogs on the wire rack above it. He glanced back into the house through the window of the door. He could just see Laura Jo moving around.

She had a real chip on her shoulder about the world in which they had been raised. For a moment there he'd thought she might open up and tell him why but then she'd shut down. Why did it matter to him anyway?

Maybe it was because for some reason he liked the brash, independent and absolutely beautiful woman, especially when she laughed. He couldn't get enough of that uninhibited embracing of life. Would she act that way in bed?

Whoa, that was not where he was headed. He didn't really know her and what he did know about her was that she'd sooner sink her teeth into him than allow him to kiss her.

Just what was going on between her and her family? He knew of the Herrons. They were good people but Laura Jo had certainly had a falling out with them. She hadn't even told Allie she had grandparents living in town. Who did that? It just didn't make sense.

He'd enjoyed his afternoon with the children. It had been tough to drive with them in the car but he'd done it.

He'd had a taste of what it would be like to have a child in his life and he rather liked it. In fact, he liked it too much.

Laura Jo made another trip by the door. He jerked around when she called from the doorway, "Hey, do you need a platter for those?"

"Yeah." Why did he feel like he'd just been caught in someone else's business? What was going on between her and her family wasn't his problem.

"Where do I find it? I'll bring it to you."

She looked so appealing, framed by the door with the afternoon sun highlighting one side of her face. The urge to kiss her almost overwhelmed him. He'd like to prove that they weren't different in the areas that mattered. He had to say something to get rid of her until he regained his equilibrium. "Cabinet below the plates."

Laura Jo disappeared into the house again. A few minutes later she came out and stood beside him. Her head reached his shoulders. She was close enough that he smelled a hint of her floral shampoo but not near enough that they touched. He was aware of the fact that all he had to do was take a half step and her body would be next to his.

"You might want to turn those. They look like they're burning."

Great. He had been so focussed on her that he wasn't thinking about what he was doing. "So now you're going to come out here and start telling me how to cook my hot dogs. Do you like to be bossed?"

She took a step back. Her eyes turned serious. "No. I don't. I'm sorry." She moved to leave.

He caught her wrist. "Hey, I was just kidding. They're just hot dogs."

Laura Jo pulled her arm out of his grip. "I know. But I

need to get us some drinks. I saw the glasses when I was looking for a bowl." With that she was gone.

This was a woman better left alone. She had more hang-ups than he did and, heaven knew, he had plenty.

Twenty minutes later, Allie and Jeremy were picnicking, as they called it, in front of the TV so they could watch another parade. Mark had persuaded Laura Jo to join him on the deck. This was what he remembered it being like when he'd been a kid. He liked having people around. Being part of a family. Could he ever have that again?

He and Laura Jo ate in silence for a while, but not a comfortable one. Mark worked to come up with a subject they could discuss. Finally, he asked, "So you remembered me from years ago, so why don't I remember you?"

She grinned. "Oh, I don't know. Maybe because the only person you saw was Ann Maria Clark."

He had the good grace to turn red. "Yeah, we were a hot item back then."

"That you were. There was no reason you'd see a simple lady-in-waiting."

His gaze met hers. Something about her tone made him think she might have liked him to notice her. "You were in her court?"

She nodded. "I was."

"I can't believe it."

"Well, it's true."

"We were that close all those years ago and it took a skinned knee at a parade for us to get to know each other."

She fingered the hot dog. "Life can be strange like that."

"That it can."

"I thought you two would get married," Laura Jo said, more as a statement of fact than someone fishing for information.

"That had been the plan but things changed."

"That happens. Especially where people are concerned." She sounded as if she was speaking about herself more than him.

It was time to change the subject. "Have you and Jeremy's mom been friends for a long time?"

"No. We only met a few years ago."

Well, at least he was getting more than a one-word answer.

"She works at the hospital?"

Laura Jo gave him a speculative look. "Are you interested in her?"

"I'm just trying to make conversation. Maybe learn a little more about you."

Laura Jo placed her half-eaten hot dog on the plate in front of her. She looked at him from across the table for a second before saying, "We met at a group for mothers without partners. Her husband had died. We became friends, at first because we needed each other, then we found we liked each other."

"So she was there when you needed someone." He knew well what it was like to be alone and need someone to talk to. There had been no one when he'd arrived in LA. He had been lonely then and, come to think of it, he'd been lonely in Mobile at least up until the last week.

"Your parents weren't around?"

"No. Hers had died. Mine...well, that's another story. That's why Marsha and I are trying to open a house for mothers who are on their own."

"So how's that going?"

"The city has agreed to sell us a house at a good price that would be perfect but we're running out of time to raise the money."

"Maybe I could be of some help. Atone for my car."

"A check for three hundred thousand would be great."

She grinned at him as if she was making a joke but he could see hope in her eyes.

He winced. "That would be my car and at least one or two more."

"I've seen you ride a bike." She grinned.

He threw back his head and laughed. "You'd make me resort to that to get your house?"

"I'd do almost anything. This chance might not come again."

She took a swallow of her drink as if her mouth had suddenly gone dry.

Why did that thought of her in bed, beneath him, pop into his head? He raised a brow.

Her eyes widened. A stricken look covered her face. "You know what I mean."

"I have an idea. We could go to the Krewe of Orion dance together. See some of our old friends. There should be plenty of people there willing to donate. All you'd have to do is get one to agree to support you and then the others would line up to help out."

"I don't think so."

"To going with me or that others would help?"

"To going."

"Do you mind if I ask why?" He caught her gaze.

"That's not my idea of a good time anymore."

What had brought on that remark? He pushed his plate away. "Well, this is a first. A woman who doesn't want to get dressed up and go to a party."

"Not all women like that sort of stuff."

"It's just one night. Attending with me isn't like going to the gallows." He chuckled. "I promise."

"It's still no, thank you." She pushed half of her leftover hot dog bun across the plate.

"Well, I guess you have other plans for the way you're

going to get the money for the house. I'm sorry, I need my car. However, I'll make a donation to the cause."

As if she was all of a sudden concerned about sounding rude, she said, "I do appreciate you trying to help. I'll take you up on that." She stood with plate in hand. "I guess I better get the kids home to bed. They have school tomorrow."

Mark also gathered his plate and joined her as she walked into the house. They found Allie and Jeremy on the couch, Gus snoring between them.

"I'll write that check and help you get them loaded," Mark said as he took her plate and walked into the kitchen. While there he wrote a check. When he returned, Laura Jo already had Allie in her arms. He scooped Jeremy up and followed her out of the house. They worked together to get each child in and secured.

Digging in his front pocket, he pulled out the check and handed it to Laura Jo.

Laura Jo read it. Her eyes widened. She looked at him. "Thank you. This is very generous."

"You're welcome."

"Also thanks for giving Allie today. I don't have much of a chance to do things like this for her."

"I didn't just do it for Allie." They walked around to the driver's door and Laura Jo opened it.

"I know Jeremy also had a good time."

"What about you?"

"Me?'

"Yeah. I was hoping you had a nice day, too."

"I did."

She acted as if it was a foreign idea that he might be interested in her having a good time. "Good. Maybe we could do it again sometime. Just you and me."

"I've already told you. We have nothing in common."

"Nonsense. We have a lot in common. Our childhoods, medicine, parades and laughter. That's more than most people have." When she'd been teasing him about Gus there had been an easiness between them. He wanted to see if she was putting up the front he believed she was. To make her act on her attraction to him. He was tired of being dismissed by her. "I bet if you tried, you could find something you like about me. Maybe this could help."

He wrapped an arm around her waist and pulled her to him. She only had time to gasp before his lips found hers. She didn't react at first, which gave him time to taste her lips. Soft, warm and slightly parted. Then for the briefest of seconds she returned his kiss. His heart thumped against his ribs at the possibilities before her hands spread wide against his chest. She shoved him away, hard.

His hands fell to his sides.

"You had no right to do that," she hissed.

"I can't say that I'm sorry."

She slid behind the steering wheel and before she could close the door he said, "Goodnight, Laura Jo."

"It's more like goodbye." She slammed the door.

Not a chance. Mark watched her taillights disappear up his drive. They'd be seeing each other again if he had anything to say about it. She was the first woman he'd met who had him thinking about the possibilities of tomorrow, even when he shouldn't.

It intrigued him that she put up such a fight not to have anything to do with him. That was except for the moments she'd melted in his arms. Could he get her to linger there long enough to forget whatever stood between them? Long enough to make her appreciate something they might both enjoy?

* * *

Laura Jo couldn't remember the last time a man had kissed her, but it sure hadn't been anything near as powerful as the brief one Mark had just given her. Her hands shook on the steering wheel. Why had he done it? Hadn't she made it clear to him that she didn't want to become involved with him? Had she been giving off a different signal?

It didn't matter why. It couldn't, wouldn't happen again. There couldn't be anything real between them anyway. When she did open up again to a man she would know him well. She wanted someone settled, who wouldn't leave town at any moment. Someone who cared nothing for being involved in Mobile society. From what she knew about Mark so far, he had none of those qualities.

The lights of the cars flickered across the water as she traveled over the low bay causeway back to Mobile.

Thinking about and fretting over Mark was a waste of time. Laura Jo fingered the check he had given her. It was literally a raindrop in a pond to what she needed. She had to find some way to raise the money needed to buy the house. There was also Allie to see about and her job to keep. Mark Clayborn hadn't been hers years ago and he wasn't hers now.

Mark, she'd already learned, was a man with a strong sense of who he was. If she let him into her life he might try to control it, like her father and Phil had. She needed a partner, a father for Allie, someone sturdy and dependable. Until that happened it was her job to make decisions about her life and Allie's. She would never again depend on a man or let him dictate to her.

Marsha was there to greet her when she pulled into the parking area of the apartment complex. She had to have been watching for them. Knowing Marsha, she'd want details of the afternoon and evening. When Laura Jo had called her earlier to inform her that they would be staying a little longer at Mark's for supper, her speculative tone had made Laura Jo feel like she needed to justify her decision.

She'd told Marsha, "Don't get any ideas. There's nothing going on here."

"Okay, if you say so." Marsha hadn't sounded convinced before she'd hung up.

Allie and Jeremy woke when she parked. They got out of the car, talking a mile a minute about the parade and Gus. Marsha grinned over their heads at Laura Jo. "Come in and tell me all about your visit to Dr. Clayborn's," Marsha said, as if to the children but Laura Jo had no doubt she meant her.

"There's not much to tell and the kids have school tomorrow." Laura Jo locked her car.

"I know they have school tomorrow but you can come in for a few minutes."

Laura Jo straightened. Marsha wouldn't let it go until she'd heard every detail but Laura Jo wouldn't be telling her about the kiss. The one that had shaken something awake in her. It wouldn't happen again, even if there was an occasion, which there wouldn't be. She doubted that her path and Mark's would cross again. They didn't even live on the same side of the bay.

Allie and Jeremy ran ahead on the way to Marsha's apartment. She and Marsha followed more slowly.

A few minutes later, Marsha set a glass of iced tea in front of Laura Jo and said, "Okay, spill."

"Mark let the kids dress up Gus, his dog."

"So you're on a first-name basis with the good doc now?"

Laura Jo rolled her eyes. It was starting. "He asked me to call him Mark and it seemed foolish not to."

Marsha nodded in a thoughtful way, as if she didn't believe her friend's reasoning. "So what else did you do?"

"We went to the parade. Mark walked with the kids while I watched." She chuckled.

"What's that laugh for?"

"I was just thinking of the look on Mark's face when he showed up pulling a wagon with the kids and the dog in it he'd bought off a boy."

Marsha gave her a long look. "That sounds interesting."

"It was." Laura Jo launched into the story, her smile growing as she told it.

She ended up laughing and Marsha joined her.

"So you went back to his place?"

"I wish you'd stop saying 'so' like that and acting as if it was a date. The only reason I agreed to go was because Allie wanted to dress up the dog and be in the parade so badly."

"So..."

Laura Jo glared at her.

"You didn't enjoy yourself at all?" Marsha continued without paying Laura Jo any attention.

"I don't even like the guy."

"This is the most you've had to do with a man since I've known you. I think you might be a little more interested in him than you want to admit."

"I think you're wrong." Laura Jo was going to see to it that it was the truth. "There's one more thing and I probably shouldn't tell you this, but he did ask me to the krewe dance."

"And you said no." Marsha said the words as a statement of a fact.

"I did. For more than one reason."

Marsha turned serious. "We could use his contacts."

"I've already told you that I'm not going to do that.

What if I saw my parents and they found out I was there, asking for money. I couldn't face them like that."

"Even at the cost of losing the house? Laura Jo, you've been gone so long I can't imagine that your parents would see it as crawling back."

"You don't know my father. It would be his chance to tell me 'I told you so.' I lived though that once. Not again."

Marsha didn't know that Laura Jo hadn't spoken to her parents since before Allie's birth.

"So I guess we'll put all our hope in that grant coming through."

Laura Jo took a sip of her tea then said, "Yes, that and a moneybags willing to help us out."

"You've got a moneybag in Mark Clayborn."

"Oh, I forgot to show you this." Laura Jo pulled the check Mark had given her out of her pocket."

Marsha whistled. "Very generous. He must really like you."

"No. It was more like I made him feel guilty."

"Whatever you did, at least this will help. We just need to get others to be so kind."

"Now I'm not only indebted to him for giving Allie a wonderful afternoon but for helping with the shelter."

"You don't like that, do you, Ms. I-Can-Do-It-Myself?"

"No, I don't. We have nothing in common. He and I don't want the same things out of life anymore."

"Oh, and you know that by spending one afternoon with him?" Marsha picked up both of their glasses and placed them in the sink. "You do know that people with money also care about their families, love them, want the best for them?"

All of what Laura's Jo's father had said to her just before he'd told her that Phil was no good. Had her father felt the same way about her as she did about Allie? Worry that something bad might happen to her? Worry over her happiness?

"Well, it's time for me to get Allie home."

As Laura Jo and Allie made their way to the front door Marsha said, "We've got to find that money for the shelter. There are worse things in life to have to do than dress up and go out with a handsome man to a dance."

"What handsome man, Mama?"

"No one, honey. Aunt Marsha is just trying to be funny."

Mark was handsome. But what Laura Jo was more concerned about was the way his kiss had made her feel. Had made her wish for more.

Mark came out of a deep sleep at the ringing of his cell phone.

What time was it? He checked his bedside clock. 3:00 a.m. This was never good news. Had something happened to his father?

Mark snatched up the phone. "Hello."

"Mark, its Laura Jo."

The relief that he felt that the call wasn't about his father was immediately replaced with concern for her.

"I'm sorry to call…"

He was wide awake now, heart throbbing. "Are you all right? Allie?"

"Yes. Yes. We're fine. It's a child staying at the shelter. The mother has no insurance and is afraid of doctors. I think the child needs to be seen. Fever, sweating, not eating and lethargic. The mother won't agree to go to the hospital. Will you come?"

"Sure, but will she let me examine the child if I do?"

"I'll convince her that it's necessary before you get here. If she wants to stay at the shelter then she'll have to let you."

"Give me directions."

Laura Jo gave him an address in a less-than-desirable area of the city.

"I'll be there in about thirty minutes."

"Thanks, Mark. I really appreciate this."

The longest part of the trip was traveling the two-lane road between his house and the interstate. Even at this early hour it took him more time than he would have liked. Finally, he reached the four-lane, where he could speed across the two-mile causeway that bisected the bay.

The child must really be worrying Laura Jo or she would never have called him. She'd made it clear she didn't plan to see him again when she'd left his house. He'd thought of nothing but their kiss for the rest of the evening. To hear her voice on the other end of the phone had been a surprise. The child's symptoms didn't sound all that unusual but with a small person it wasn't always straightforward.

He drove through the tunnel that went under Mobile River and came up on Governor Street. There were no crowds now, only large oaks and barriers lining the main street. A number of miles down the street he made a left and not long after that he pulled up in front of what looked like a building that had been a business at one time. The glass windows were painted black and there were dark curtains over the door window. One lone light burned above it. It looked nothing like a place for pregnant woman or children. He could clearly see why they needed a house to move to.

Laura Jo's car was parked near the door and he took the slot next to hers. Picking up his cell phone, he pressed Return. Seconds later, Laura Jo's voice came on the line. "I'm outside."

"I'll be right there."

Mark stood at the door for only seconds before the dead bolt clicked back and Laura Jo's face came into view.

After making sure it was him, she opened the door wider. "I appreciate you coming."

He entered and she locked the door behind him. The room he was in resembled a living room with its couches and chairs spread out. There was one small TV in the corner. At least it looked more welcoming from the inside than it did from the outside.

"Anna's family's room is down this way." Laura Jo, dressed in jeans, T-shirt and tennis shoes, led him down a hall toward the back of the building, passing what he guessed had once been offices. Were families living in nothing more than ten-by-ten rooms?

"Has anything changed?" Mark asked.

"No, but I'm really worried. Anna has been so distraught about the loss of her husband I'm not sure she's been as attentive to her children as she should have been."

"I'll have a look and see what we come up with. Don't worry."

They stopped at the last door.

"Anna isn't a fan of doctors."

"I'll be on my best behavior." He gave her a reassuring smile.

Laura Jo nodded and knocked quietly on the door before she opened it. "Anna, someone is here to check on little Marcy."

Laura Jo entered and he followed close behind. A lone light shone, barely giving off enough light for him to see the room. There was a twin bed shoved into the corner and another at a right angle to that one where two children slept feet to feet. There was also a baby bed but it was empty because the child was in her mother's arms. The woman was reed thin, wide-eyed and had wavy hair. She couldn't have been more than twenty-five.

"Hi, Anna, I'm Mark, and I've come to see if I can help

little Marcy. Why don't you sit on the bed and hold her while I have a look? I promise not to hurt her."

Anna hesitated then looked a Laura Jo.

"I'll sit beside you." Laura Jo led her over to the bed.

Mark went down on one knee and placed his bag beside him. He pulled out his stethoscope. The heat he felt as he put his hand close to the child's chest indicated she was still running a fever.

"I'm only going to listen to her heart and lungs now. Check her pulse." He gave the mother a reassuring smile and went to work. Done, he asked, "How long has she had this fever?"

"Since yesterday," the mother said in a meek voice.

He looked a Laura Jo.

"I had no idea." She sounded defensive and he hadn't intended to make her feel that.

To Anna he said, "I'm going to need to check Marcy's abdomen."

"Let's lay Marcy on the bed. That way she'll be more comfortable," Laura Jo suggested.

Mark moved his hand over the child's stomach area. It was distended and hard. Something serious was, without a doubt, going on. He glanced at Laura Jo. Their gazes met. The worry in her eyes was obvious.

"Anna, thank you for letting me see Marcy." He looked at Laura Jo again and tilted his head toward the door. As he stood he picked up his bag and walked across the room. Laura joined him. He let her precede him into the hall and closed the door behind him.

Laura Jo looked at him.

"Marcy has to go to the hospital."

"I was afraid of that. What do you think the problem is?"

"The symptoms make me think it might be an obstructive bowel problem. This isn't something that can wait. Marcy must been seen at the hospital."

"I'll talk to her." Laura Jo went back into the room.

Mark pulled out his phone and called the ER. He gave the information about Marcy and they assured him they would be ready when he arrived. Finished, he leaned against the wall to wait.

Soon Laura Jo came out, with Anna holding Marcy in her arms.

"Anna has agreed to go to the hospital as long as you and I stay with her," Laura Jo said. "I need a few minutes to let someone know to see about her other children. Will you drive?"

His stomach tightened. He didn't want to but what was he supposed to say, "No, I might injure you for life"?

"If it's necessary," Mark answered.

Laura Jo looked at him with a question in her eyes before he turned to walk down the hallway to the front.

"The car seat is by the front door," Anna said in a subdued voice.

"I'll get it."

He was still working to latch the child seat into his car when Laura Jo arrived.

"I'll get that."

With efficiency that he envied she had the seat secured and Marcy in it in no time. Laura Jo didn't comment on his ineptness but he was sure she'd made a note of it. She would probably call him on it later.

Anna took the backseat next to Marcy, and Laura Jo joined him in front. Before pulling out of the parking space, he looked back to see that the baby was secure and that Anna was wearing her seat belt. "Are you buckled in, Laura Jo?"

"Yes. You sure are safety conscious."

Yes, he was, and he had a good reason to be. Mark nodded and wasted no time driving to the hospital. He pulled under the emergency awning and stopped.

As they entered the building Laura Jo said to Anna, "We'll be right here with you until you feel comfortable. They'll take good care of Marcy here."

Anna nodded, her eyes not meeting Laura Jo's.

They were met by a woman dressed in scrubs.

"Lynn, this child needs to be seen," Laura said.

"Is this the girl Dr. Clayborn called in about?"

"Yes," he said. "I'm Dr. Clayborn." Because he wasn't on the staff at the hospital he couldn't give orders. They would have to wait until the ER physician showed up.

"Exam room five is open. Dr. Lawrence will be right in."

Two hours later Marcy was in surgery. Mark's diagnosis had been correct. Thankfully, Laura Jo had called him or the child might have died. They were now sitting in the surgery waiting room with Anna. With Laura Jo's support, Anna had accepted that Marcy needed the surgery. Mark was impressed with the tender understanding Laura Jo had given the terrified mother. He liked this sensitive side of her personally. What would it take for her to turn some of that on him?

Mark approached the two women and handed each one a cup of coffee from the machine. He slipped into the chair beside Laura Jo. Waiting in hospitals wasn't his usual activity. He'd always been on the working end of an emergency.

While Anna was in the restroom Laura Jo said, "I think you can go. She seems to be handling this better than I thought she would."

"No, I said I'd stay and I will."

"You make a good friend."

Mark's chest tightened. No, he didn't. He'd already proved that. Mike certainly wouldn't say that about him. Mark hadn't even gone to the hospital to see Mike before he'd left town. Laura Jo shouldn't start depending on him.

"You might be surprised."

Laura Jo gave him a speculative look but he was saved from any questions by Anna returning. Soon after that the surgeon came out to speak to them.

The sun was shining when he and Laura Jo stepped outside the hospital. Marcy was doing well in PICU and Anna had insisted that she was fine and no longer needed them there. They left her in the waiting room, dozing. Laura Jo had promised to check on her other children and that she would see to it they were cared for properly.

As he and Laura Jo walked to his car, which he had moved to a parking place earlier, Mark asked, "Where do you get all the energy for all you do?"

"I just do what has to be done."

"You sure have a lot on your plate."

"Maybe so, but some things I can't say no to."

What was it like to feel that type of bond with people? He understood the practical side of doing what needed to be done medically to save a life but it was a completely different concept to support another person emotionally without reservation. Mark understood that well. He hadn't been able to stand beside his best friend when he'd needed him most. He had even ignored his conscience when it had screamed for him to do better. It hadn't gotten quieter when he'd moved back to town but he still couldn't muster the guts to go visit Mike.

"I wish I had your backbone."

"How's that?"

"You face life head-on."

"You don't?"

"What little I have falls short of the amount you have."

"Thank you. That's a nice compliment."

They had reached his car. "How about I buy us some breakfast then take you home? I'm guessing Marsha has Allie."

"Yes. I really need to check on her and Anna's kids. I need sleep. I'm sure you do also. I have to work this afternoon. Don't you have to be at work this morning?"

"I don't go in until two and you need to eat. I'm hungry so why don't you let me get us some breakfast without disagreeing for once?"

She walked to the passenger door. "I'm already too far in debt to you."

"I don't mind that."

She sighed. "I pick the place."

"Ladies choice, then."

A smile spread across her lips. "I like the sound of that."

Had no one ever let her make a choice of where they went? He liked seeing Laura Jo smile. She didn't do it often enough. She was far too serious.

"Where're we going?"

"I'll show you."

She got in the car and put her seat belt on. When he was ready to pull out he looked over at her.

Laura Jo said, "Yes, I have buckled up."

He had to sound crazy to her, or over-the-top controlling, but he just couldn't face hurting someone with his driving ever again. Somehow it seemed easier when he had her in the car with him; she accepted him for who he was. As he drove she gave him directions into an older and seedier part of downtown Mobile. He had last been to the area when he'd been a teen and trying to live on the wild side some.

"It's just down the street on the right. The Silver Spoon."

Mark pulled into the small parking area in front of a nineteen-fifties-style café that had seen better days.

"You want to eat here?"

"Sure. They have the best pecan waffles in town." Laura Jo was already getting out of the car. She looked back in at him. "You coming?"

Mark had been questioning it. He wasn't sure the place could pass a health inspection.

"Yes, I am." He climbed out of the car. "I wouldn't miss it."

She was already moving up the few steps to the front door.

Because all the booths were full, Laura Jo took an empty stool at the bar. She didn't miss Mark's dubious look at the duct-taped stool next to her before he took a seat.

"You don't frequent places like this, do you?"

"I can say that this is a first."

She grinned. "I thought it might be."

Mark picked up a plastic-covered menu. "So I need to have the pecan waffles."

"They're my favorite." She was going to enjoy watching Mark out of his element.

"Then waffles it is. You do the ordering."

"Charlie," she said to the heavy man wearing what once must have been a white apron, "we'll have pecan waffles, link sausage and iced tea."

"Coming right up, Laura Jo," Charlie said, and turned to give the cook her order.

"I see you're a regular," Mark said.

"I come when I can, which isn't often enough."

Charlie put their glasses of iced tea on the counter with a thump.

"I don't normally have iced tea for breakfast." Mark picked up his glass.

"If you'd rather have coffee…" Laura Jo made it sound like a dare on purpose.

"I said I wanted the same as you and that's what I'm having. So how did you find this place?"

"Charlie gave one of the mothers that came through the shelter a job here after her baby was born."

"That was nice. I'm impressed with what you're doing at the shelter."

"Thanks. But it never seems like enough. You know, I really appreciate you helping me out with Anna and Marcy. I hated to call you but I knew I couldn't get her to the hospital and I was uncomfortable with how Marcy looked."

Mark really had been great with Anna and Marcy. He'd stayed to give moral support even when he hadn't had to. Maybe she had better character radar than she believed.

"I'm glad you thought you could call."

She'd been surprised too that she hadn't hesitated a second before picking up the phone to call him. Somehow she'd just known he would come. "Were you always going to be a doctor?"

"I believe that's the first personal question you have ever asked me. You do want to get to know me better."

Laura Jo opened her mouth to refute that statement but he continued, not giving her a chance to do so.

"Yes, I had always planned to go into medicine. My parents liked the idea and I found I did, too. I've always liked helping people. How about you? Did you always dream of being a nurse?"

"No, I kind of came to that later in life."

"So what was your dream?"

"I don't know. I guess like all the other girls I knew we

dreamed of marrying the Mardi Gras king, having two kids and living in a big house."

He looked in her direction but she refused to meet his gaze. "Marrying the Mardi Gras king, was it? So did you dream of marrying me?"

"I don't think your ego needs to be fed by my teenage dreams. But I'll admit to having a crush on you if that will end this conversation."

"I thought so."

"Now we won't be able to get your head out of the door."

Charlie placed a plateful of food in front of each of them with a clunk on the counter.

"Thanks, Charlie." She picked up her fork and looked at Mark. "You need to eat your waffle while it's hot to get the full effect." She took a bite dripping with syrup.

"Trying to get me to quit asking questions?"

"That and the waffles are better hot."

They ate in silence for a few minutes.

"So I remember something about an accident and then I didn't hear much about you after that. I later heard you'd left town. Did you get hurt?"

Mark's fork halted in midair then he lowered it to the plate.

Had she asked the wrong thing? She looked back at her meal. "You don't have to tell me if you'd rather not."

"I wasn't really hurt. But my friend was. I had to leave a few days later to start my fellowship."

"What happened?"

"It's a long story. Too much of one for this morning."

So the man with all the questions was hiding something. Minutes later she finished her last mouthful. Mark said something. She turned to look at him. "What?"

He touched her face. His gaze caught and held hers as he

put his finger between his lips. Her stomach fluttered. She swallowed. Heaven help her, the man held her spellbound.

"You had syrup on your chin."

"Uh?"

"Syrup on your chin." Mark said each word slowly, as if speaking to someone who didn't understand the language.

"Oh." She dabbed at the spot with her napkin. Mark was starting to shatter her protective barriers. "We'd better go."

She climbed off the stool and called, "Thanks, Charlie." She was going out the door as Mark pulled a couple of bills out of his wallet.

Her hand was already on the door handle of his car as Mark pulled into a parking place at the shelter. She needed to get away from him. Find her equilibrium. That look in his eye as he'd licked the syrup on his finger had her thinking of things better left unthought. She stepped out of the car. "Thanks for helping out last night. I don't know how I'll repay you."

"No problem."

"Bye, Mark."

Why did a simple gesture from Mark, of all men, make her run? She had to be attracted to him for that to happen. Surely that wasn't the case.

CHAPTER FOUR

FOUR DAYS LATER, as Laura Jo was busy setting up the med tent on North Broad Street, she was still pondering how to raise the money needed for the single mothers' shelter. The grant they were hoping for had come through, but with a condition that the board match the amount. There were only five more days of Mardi Gras season, then things would settle down. After that the city would place the house on the market. She couldn't let that happen. They had to move out of the too-small building they were in now.

She didn't want anyone to get hurt at the parade but if she was busy tonight it would keep her mind off the issue of money…along with the thoughts of how agreeing to go to the dance with Mark just might solve her problem.

Think of the devil and he shows up. Mark rode over the curb of the street and up onto the grassy lot where the med tent was stationed. His tight bike shorts left little to the imagination and there was nothing small about the man. He unclipped his helmet and set it on the handlebars, before heading in her direction. For a second her heart rate picked up with the thought that he'd come to see her. She wasn't sure if it was relief or disappointment that filled her when he stopped to talk in depth to one of the ER doctors working with her. Mark should mean nothing to her. She shouldn't be feeling anything, one way or another.

Laura Jo returned to unpacking boxes, turning her back to him.

A few minutes later a tenor voice she recognized said, "Hello, Laura Jo."

She twisted, making an effort to act as if she hadn't been aware of where he'd been and what he'd been doing during the past ten minutes. "Hi, Mark. I didn't expect to see you today."

"It would be my guess that if you had you'd have seen to it you were reassigned to another med tent."

"You know me so well," she quipped, returning to what she'd been doing.

"I wish I did know you better. Then maybe I'd understand why I find you so fascinating."

A ripple of pleasure went through her at his statement. She resisted placing a hand on her stomach when it quivered. "It might be that I don't fall at your feet like other women do."

"I don't know about that."

"They used to. I figured now wasn't any different. In fact, I saw and heard the ER nurses swoon when you came in the other day."

"Swoon. That's an old-fashioned word." He leaned in close so that only she could hear. "Did you swoon over me, too, Laura Jo?"

She had but she wasn't going to let him know that. Straightening and squaring her shoulders, she said with authority, "I did not."

He grinned, his voice dropping seductively. "Something about that quick denial makes me think you did."

Her heart skipped a beat. "Would you please go? I have work to do."

He chuckled. "I'm flattered. I had no idea girls swooned over me."

I bet. Laura Jo glared at him.

"I'm going. I wouldn't want to keep you from your work. See you later."

She glanced up to see him disappear through the crowd. Their conversations had been the most thought-provoking, irritating and stimulating ones she'd ever experienced. And that didn't count how he'd made her feel when he'd kissed her. She had to think fast to stay ahead of him. Somehow that made her life more exciting and interesting.

Mark made one more circle around his patrol area along the parade route. He'd not worked patrol in three days and his muscles were telling him they had noticed. Busy at his practice, getting his patient load up, it required late hours to accommodate people coming in after work hours. As the newest man in the six-doctor general practice, it was his duty to cover the clinic for the hours that were least desirable.

He was pulled out of his thoughts by a boy of three or four standing in the middle of the street. The child looked lost. Mark parked his bike and scanned the crowd for some anxious parent. Finding none, he went down on his haunches in front of the boy. "Hello, there, are you looking for someone?"

"My mommy."

"Can I help you find her?"

The boy nodded.

Mark offered his hand and he took it. They started walking along the edge of the crowd, Mark looking for anyone who might claim the boy.

A woman clutching her cell phone stepped out from behind the barriers just ahead of them and hurried toward them. "Lucas, you shouldn't have walked off."

The woman looked at Mark. "I was talking on my phone and then he was gone," she said with a nervous little laugh.

Mark nodded. "I understand. Little ones can get away from you when you aren't paying attention."

The woman's lips tightened. She took her son's hand and left.

He went back to patrolling. Returning to Mobile so close to Mardi Gras season, he had social obligations to consider. He'd been king the year he'd left and now that he was back in town he was expected to attend certain events. He'd once lived for all the fanfare of the season but now it held no real thrill for him. Still, certain things were expected of him. He just wished doing so didn't bring on such heavy guilt.

Mark hadn't expected to find Laura Jo working the same parade as he was but he wasn't disappointed either. He'd missed their sparring. It was always fun to see how she'd react to something he said or did. Especially his kiss. He'd kissed enough women to know when one was enjoying it.

He wasn't disappointed with her reaction today, either. When he'd asked her about swooning over him he'd have to admit her pretty blush had raised his self-esteem. She had been one of those teens who'd wanted to be noticed by him. The sad thing was that he would've crushed her admiration with the self-centered attitude he'd wore like his royal cloak if he'd even noticed her.

Clearly he had noted the woman she'd become. There hadn't been another female who kept him on his toes or stepped on them more than she did. There were so many facets to her. He still didn't understand what made her tick. He couldn't count the number of times she'd been on his mind over the past few days despite his efforts not to let her intervene in his thoughts.

He compared the mother who'd been too busy talking on her phone to show any real concern for her child with Laura Jo's motherly concern over a skinned knee. She won. Laura Jo had seen the humor when he'd had to carry Gus. He could still hear her boisterous laughter. Under all that anti-society, I-can-do-it-on-my-own attitude, she hid a power to love and enjoy life.

From what he'd heard and read between the lines, she hadn't had much opportunity to take pleasure in life in a number of years. She been busy scrapping and fighting to keep Allie cared for. To go to school, then work and start a shelter. It had to have been hard, doing it all without family support. What was the deal with her family anyway?

No wonder she was so involved with the single mothers' house. She identified with the women, had been one of them. As if she didn't have enough going on in her life now, she was trying to raise funds to buy the house. Was there anything Laura Jo couldn't do?

Mark made another loop through his section of the parade route. He wasn't far from the med tent when he pulled over out of the way to let the parade go by. One girl in a group of dancers he recognized from other parades. She was limping badly. Seconds later, the girl left the line and collapsed to the curb.

To help her, he had to cross the parade route. He raised his hand and the driver of the next float stopped. Mark pushed his bike over to where the teenage girl sat. She was busy removing her tap shoe. Mark noticed that her foot was covered in blood.

He parked his bike and crouched beside her. The girl looked at him with tears in her eyes. "I just couldn't go any further."

It wasn't unusual to see members of the dance groups abusing their feet. Some of the dancers did up to four parades a day when it got closer to Fat Tuesday. More than once Mark had wondered how they kept it up. Almost everyone in the parades rode while these girls danced for miles.

"I don't blame you. That looks painful. How about we get you cleaned up and ease that pain?"

The girl nodded then started to stand. Mark picked up her discarded shoe and placed his hand on her shoulder. "The med tent isn't too far. Do you mind if I carry you? That foot looks too painful to walk on."

The girl nodded. Mark handed her the shoe and scooped her into his arms. The crowd parted so he could get through. "Would someone please follow us with my bike?"

A middle-aged man called, "I'll bring it."

Mark headed for the med tent a block away. As he walked people turned to watch. He was within sight of the tent when he saw Laura Jo look in his direction. It was as if she had radar where he was concerned. She seemed to sense when he was near. He would have to give that more thought later. He hefted the girl closer in his arms. This was turning into a workout.

Laura Jo moved away and when he saw her again she was pushing a wheelchair across the dirt and grass area between them. Mark faltered. The girl's arms tightened around his neck. The blood drained from his face as Mike crossed his mind.

When Laura Jo reached him, he lowered the dancer into the chair.

Laura Jo mouthed over the girl's head, "Are you okay?"

He nodded. But the look on her face had him doubting he'd convinced her.

"What happened?"

"Blisters."

"I'll get things ready." Laura Jo turned and hurried back toward the tent.

Mark let his hands rest on the handles of the chair for a moment before he started pushing. He wished he could have let Laura Jo do it. Bringing the wheelchair up on its two back wheels, he maneuvered it across the rough ground. When he arrived at the tent Laura Jo was waiting with a square plastic pan filled with what must be saline. He lifted the footrest off the chair. Going on one knee, he removed the girl's other tap shoe. Laura Jo then slipped the pan into position and the girl lowered her feet into the water with a small yelp of pain.

"Do it slowly and it will be less painful. It'll hurt at first but as soon as they are clean we'll bandage them and you'll feel a lot better. Are you allergic to anything?"

"No," the girl said.

Laura Jo then offered her a white pill and a small glass of water that had been waiting on the table beside them. "That should ease the pain." She looked at him. "I'll take care of her from here, Dr. Clayborn."

Had he just been dismissed? He had. Grinning at Laura Jo and then the girl, he said, "I'll leave you in the capable hands of Nurse Akins."

"Thank you," the girl said.

"You're welcome. I hope you get to feeling better. I'll miss seeing you in the parades."

The girl blushed a bright pink then looked away.

Laura Jo gave a dramatic roll of her eyes.

Mark smiled. He looked around to find his bike leaning against a nearby tree. He climbed on and prepared to ride off. He glanced back at Laura Jo. She looked away from caring for the girl's feet to meet his gaze.

He grinned. Maybe he could still make her swoon.

Two hours later, after the last parade of the day, he

pulled up beside the med tent. He would leave his reports of the minor injuries he'd handled with them. The city officials liked to keep a record of anything that happened during Mardi Gras season in order to plan for the next year.

Allie came running toward him. "Hey, did you bring Gus with you?"

"No, not today. I couldn't get him to ride the bike."

Allie giggled.

"Had any king cake this week?"

Allie nodded. "I even found the baby."

"Then I guess you're planning to take a cake to school."

"We're out of school today. It's our Mardi Gras break."

"Well, then, how about bringing me one? I haven't even had the chance to find the baby this year."

Laura Jo walked over "I don't think—"

Mark looked at her. "It just so happens that your mother owes me a favor."

"I do?"

"Anna."

Laura Jo's heart fell. She did.

"So how about you and your mother come over to my house tomorrow night and I'll fix sausage gumbo and you bring the king cake. Better yet, your mother can make it at my house." He looked at Laura Jo when he said, "She did say my kitchen was the perfect place to make a cake."

"Can we, Mommy? I want to see Gus. You don't have to work tomorrow."

"Great. Then it's all settled. I'll expect you at four o'clock."

"Do you two think I could say something since you're making plans that involve me?"

Mark looked at her and grinned. "Talk away."

"Allie, I think we need to take it easy while we have a day off. The next few days are going to be busy."

Mark leaned forward, making eye contact. "And I think that you owe me a favor that you are trying to welch on."

Laura Jo shifted from one foot to the other. She did owe him big for helping her with Anna, and the check, and Allie being in the parade. Even so, going to Mark's house again wasn't a good idea. "I thought you might be enough of a gentleman that you wouldn't stoop to calling in a favor."

He gave her a pointed look. "Sometimes you want something badly enough that the social graces don't matter."

She swallowed. The implication was that she might be that "something." When had been the last time she'd felt wanted by a man? It had been so long ago she couldn't remember.

Mark looked at Allie and grinned. "Manners don't matter when you're talking about king cake."

Allie returned the smile and nodded.

Why was she letting Mark talk her into it? Because the least she owed him was a king cake for all that he'd done for her. And she had to admit that deep down inside she'd enjoy cooking in his kitchen and spending time with him.

Mark couldn't remember the last time he'd looked forward to a king cake with such anticipation. He suspected that it had nothing to do with the cake and everything to do with seeing Laura Jo. She and Allie were due any minute. He gave the gumbo a stir. He'd missed the stew-type consistency of the dish while he'd been in California. As hard as he'd tried, he hadn't been able to get the ingredients to make good gumbo. What he had used had never tasted like what he was used to having when he was in Mobile.

He slurped a spoonful of gumbo off the tip of the ladle. It was good.

The doorbell rang. Should a man be so eager to spend time with a woman? For his own self-preservation he'd say no. With a smile on his face, Mark opened the door. To his amazement, Laura Jo smiled in return. He hadn't expected that when he'd given her no choice about coming to his home today. Allie brushed passed his legs.

"Where's Gus?" she asked as she went.

"He was in his bed, sleeping, the last time I saw him."

He liked Allie. He'd never spent much time around children but he found Allie a pleasure. She seemed to like him as much as he did her. What would it be like to be a father to a child like her? Maybe if he had Allie as a daughter he'd have a chance of being a good father.

"I hope Gus is prepared for this," Laura Jo said.

"I wouldn't worry about Gus. Can I take those?" He reached for the grocery bags she carried in either hand.

"Thanks." She handed him one of them. "I guess I'd better get started. It's a long process."

It occurred to him that she'd be anxious to get away as soon as she had met her obligation. He didn't plan to let that happen. "We have plenty of time. I have nowhere to be tonight—do you?"

"Uh, no, but I'd still like to get started."

"Okay, if that's the way you want it." To his astonishment, he said, "I'm going to take Gus and Allie outside to play. Gus needs some exercise." When had he started to think that he was capable of overseeing Allie?

"All right. Just don't let Allie get too close to the water."

"I'll take good care of her." He was confident he would. He headed in the direction of the living room.

Laura Jo watched as Mark left the kitchen after he'd placed the bag on the kitchen counter. He headed out as if he'd given her no more thought. For some reason, she was disappointed he'd not worked harder at encouraging her to join him and Allie. She was even more surprised that she trusted him without question to take care of Allie. Was it because she'd seen him caring for others or that she just innately knew he would see to Allie like she was his own?

Running a hand over the granite counter, she looked around the kitchen. It was truly amazing. If she had this kitchen to cook in every day, she might never leave it. But she didn't. What she had was a small corner one and it was plenty for her and Allie. Mark's kitchen reminded her of her childhood when she'd stood beside Elsie Mae, their cook, and helped prepared meals.

It was time to get busy. She planned to make the most of Mark's kitchen while she had it. Shaking off the nostalgia, Laura Jo pulled the bread flour and eggs out of the bag she'd brought. Over the next twenty minutes she prepared the dough and set it aside to rise.

Going to one of the living-room windows, she looked out. Allie was running with Gus as Mark threw a ball. Laura Jo laughed. Gus showed no interest in going after the ball. Seconds later Mark opened his arms wide and Allie ran into them. He lifted her over his head. Laura Jo could hear her daughter's giggles from where she stood. Her chest tightened.

Allie wrapped her arms around Mark's neck as he brought her back down. They both had huge smiles on their faces. Laura Jo swallowed the lump in her throat. The man had obviously won her daughter over and Laura Jo was worried he was fast doing the same with her.

She pulled open the door and walked out to join them. Allie and Mark were so absorbed in playing that they didn't see her until she had almost reached them. Seeing Allie with Mark brought home how much Allie needed a male figure in her life. Had she done Allie a disservice by not looking for a husband or keeping her away from her grandfather? Had she been so wrapped up in surviving and trying to take care of other mothers that she'd neglected Allie's needs?

"Is something wrong?" Mark asked.

"No, everything is fine."

"You had a funny look on your face. Was there a problem in the kitchen?"

"No, I found what I needed. Now I have to wait for the dough to rise before I do anything more."

"Then why don't we walk down to the dock?" Mark suggested.

"Okay."

"Come on, Allie," Mark called.

"So, do you boat or water-ski?" Laura Jo asked.

Mark stopped and looked at her. "You know, I like you being interested in me."

"Please, don't make more of a friendly question than there is. I was just trying to make conversation. You live on the water, were raised on the water so I just thought…"

"Yes, I have a small sailboat and the family also has a ski boat."

She and Mark walked to the end of the pier and took a seat in the Adirondack chairs stationed there.

"How about you?" he asked.

"I don't sail but I do love to ski." She watched the small waves coming in as the wind picked up.

"Maybe you and Allie can come and spend the day on the water with me when it gets warmer."

Allie ran past them to the edge of the pier.

"Be careful," Mark called. "The water is cold. I don't want you to fall in."

"You sure do sound like a parent."

Mark took on a stricken look that soon turned thoughtful. "I did, didn't I?"

"I don't know why you should act so surprised. You're great with kids."

A few minutes went by before he asked, "I know who your parents are but I can't remember if you have any brothers or sisters."

"Only child." Laura Jo wasn't pleased he'd turned the conversation to her and even less so to her parents. She didn't want to talk about them. The people who had been more interested in their social events than spending time with her. Who hadn't understood the teen who'd believed so strongly in helping the less fortunate. Who had always made her feel like she didn't quite measure up.

"Really? That wouldn't have been my guess."

"Why not?"

"Because you're so strong and self-sufficient. You don't seem spoiled to me."

"You do have a stereotypical view of an only child."

He shrugged. "You could be right."

Laura Jo kept an eye on Allie, who had left the pier and was now playing along the edge of the water as Gus lumbered along nearby.

"So tell me about growing up as a Clayborn with a big silver spoon in your mouth."

"I had no silver spoon that I can remember."

She gave him a sideways look. "I remember enough to know you were the golden boy."

"Well, I do have blond locks." Mark ran his hand through his hair with an attitude.

"And an ego."

They watched the water for a while before she stood and called to Allie, "Do you want to help braid the dough?"

"I want to do the colors," Allie said.

"Okay, I'll save that job for you."

Laura Jo headed back along the pier and Mark followed a number of paces behind her. As she stepped on the lawn her phone rang. Fishing it out of her jeans pocket, she saw it was Marsha calling and answered.

"Hey, I've just been given tickets to see that new kids' movie. Jeremy wants Allie to go with him. Would you mind if I come and get her?"

"I don't know, Marsha…" If she agreed, it would leave her alone with Mark.

"You mean you'd keep your child from seeing a movie she's been wanting to see because you're too afraid to stay by yourself with Mark Clayborn."

Put that way, it did sound kind of childish. But it was true.

After a sigh Laura Jo said, "Let me speak to Allie. She may rather stay here with the dog."

Laura Jo called to her daughter. Hearing the idea, Allie jumped up and down, squealing that she wanted to go to the movie.

"Okay, Marsha, but you'll have to come and get her. I'm in the middle of making king cakes."

"I'll be there in thirty minutes."

While they waited for Marsha to arrive, Laura Jo punched the dough down and placed it in the refrigerator to rest. She then cleaned Allie up so she'd be ready to go when Marsha arrived.

"Who's going to hide the baby if you leave?" Mark teased Allie.

"I bet Mommy will let you."

He looked over at Laura Jo. "Will you?"

"Yes, you can hide the baby." She made it sound like she was talking to a mischievous boy.

"Mark, will you do the colors for me too?" Allie asked, as she pulled on one of Gus's ears.

"I don't know if I know how to do those." Mark was sitting in a large chair in the living area with one foot on the ottoman.

"Mommy will show you. She knows how to do it all."

Mark met Laura Jo's gaze over Allie's head. "She knows how to do it all, does she?"

A tingle went down her spine. Leave it to Mark to make baking a king cake sound sexier than it really was.

Five minutes later there was a knock at the door. Allie skipped to it while Laura Jo and Mark followed behind her. Laura Jo stepped around Allie and opened the door.

"Come on, Allie," Marsha said. "We need to hurry if we're going to be there on time." Marsha looked at Laura Jo. "Just let her spend the night since she was coming to me early in the morning anyway. Enjoy your evening. Hi, Mark. Bye, Mark." With that, Marsha whisked Allie away.

"Does she always blow in and blow out with such force?" Mark asked.

Laura Jo closed the door with a heavy awareness of being alone with Mark. "Sometimes. I need to finish the cake and get out of your way."

"I invited you to dinner and I expect you to stay. Are you scared to be here with me, knowing Allie isn't here to protect you?"

"She wasn't protecting me!" Had she been using Allie as a barrier between her and men? No, her first priority was Allie and taking care of her. It had nothing to do with fear.

"Then quit acting as if you're scared I might jump you."

Laura Jo ignored his comment and headed toward the kitchen. She pulled the large bowl of dough out of the refrigerator.

"So what has to be done to it now?" Mark asked.

"Roll it out." She placed the bowl on the corner. "Will you hand me that bag of flour?"

He reached across the wide counter and pulled the bag to him. He then pushed it toward her. Leaning a hip against the cabinet as if he had no place he'd rather be, he asked, "So what happens now?"

"Are you asking for a play-by-play?" She spread flour across the counter.

"Maybe."

"I have to divide the dough." She pulled it apart and set what she wasn't going to use right away back into the bowl.

"Why're you doing that?"

"This recipe makes two cakes. Are you sure there isn't a basketball game on that you want to watch?"

"Nope, I like watching you."

Focusing her attention on her baking again, she dumped the dough onto the granite corner top. She reached into one of the bags and pulled out a rolling pin.

"You didn't think I'd have one of those, did you?" Mark asked from his position beside her.

"Do you?"

"I'm sure I do around here somewhere. I'd have to hunt for it."

"That's why I brought my own." She punched the dough flat with her palms then picked up the pin and started rolling.

"While I roll this out, would you find the cinnamon? It's in one of these bags."

"Sure." He walked to the other side of the room and pulled a bowl out of the cabinet. They each did their jobs in silence."

Heat washed over her. She was far too aware of him being near. All her disquiet went into making the dough thin and wide. "Would you also open the cream cheese? I set it out to soften earlier."

"Will do."

Laura Jo had never had a man help her in the kitchen. Her father had no interest in cooking, not even grilling. Phil had seen it as woman's work and never helped. It was nice to have someone interested in the same thing that she was. To work with her.

"I'm going to need the sugar. I forgot to bring any." Maybe if she kept him busy, he wouldn't stand so close.

"That I do have. Coming right up." Mark reached under the counter and pulled out a plastic container. "Here you go."

"Thanks." Laura Jo brushed her hair away with the back of her hand, sending flour dust into the air.

"Turn around," Mark said.

"Why?"

"Just turn around. For once just trust me."

Behind her there was the sound of a drawer being pulled open then pushed back.

"What are—?"

Mark stepped close enough that she felt his heat from her shoulders to her hips. Strong fingers glided over her scalp and fanned out, gathering her hair.

Her lungs began to hurt and she released the breath she held. Every part of her was aware of how close Mark stood. His body brushed hers as he moved to a different angle. One hand drifted over her temple to capture a stray strand. His warm breath fluttered across the nap of her neck. She quivered.

There was a tug then a pull before he said, "There, that should help."

He moved and the warmth that had had her heart racing disappeared, leaving her with a void that she feared only Mark could fill.

She touched the back of her head. He had tied her hair up with a rag. "Thanks."

"Now you can work without getting flour all in your hair."

He'd been doing something practical and she had been wound up about him being so close. She needed to finish these cakes and go home as soon as possible.

"Would you mind melting a stick of butter?"

"Not at all," Mark said in an all-too-cheerful manner.

Laura Jo continued to roll the dough into a rectangle, while keeping an eye on Mark as he moved around on the other side of the counter. "One more thing."

He raised a brow.

"Would you mix the cinnamon and sugar together?"

"Yeah. How much?" Mark headed again to where the bowls were.

"Like you are making cinnamon toast."

"How do you know I know how to make cinnamon toast?"

"Everyone knows how to do that," she said, as she finished rolling the first half of the dough. "While I roll out the other dough, will you spread butter on this one then put the sugar cinnamon mixture over that?"

"I don't know. All that might be out of my territory."

She chuckled. "I think you can handle it."

Over the next few minutes they each worked at their own projects. Laura Jo was used to making the cakes by herself but found she liked having a partner even in something as simple as a cake. She glanced at Mark. His full attention was on what he was doing. He approached his assignment much as he did giving medical care, with an effort to do the very best, not miss any detail.

She looked over to where he was meticulously shaking the sugar mixture on the dough from a spoon. "You know you really can't do that wrong."

"Uh?"

He must have been so involved in what he was doing he hadn't heard her. "Enjoy what you're doing a little. It doesn't have to be perfect."

Mark straightened. "This comes from the person who only laughs when my dog gets the best of me."

"I laugh at other times."

"Really?"

Was she truly that uptight? Maybe she was but she could tell that lately she'd been starting to ease up. Ever since she'd started spending time with Mark.

"Speaking of uptight, what's your issue with a wheelchair?"

CHAPTER FIVE

DAMN, SHE'D NOTICED. Mark had thought, hoped, Laura Jo
had missed or he'd covered his feelings well enough when
he'd seen a wheelchair, but apparently not.

Maybe he could bluff his way out of answering. "I don't
know what you mean."

Laura Jo was looking at him. His skin tingled. He
glanced at her. She had stopped what she was doing.

"Please, don't insult my intelligence," she said quietly.

He sighed before answering. "My friend who was in
the accident is now in a wheelchair."

"I'm sorry to hear that."

"Me, too." He put the empty bowl in the sink.

"What happened?"

"He was thrown from the car."

"Oh, how awful."

"It was." He needed to change the subject. "So what do
I need to do now?"

"Roll it into a log, like this." Laura Jo moved close and
started working with the dough.

He looked at the honey nape of her neck exposed and
waiting for him. Mike went out of his mind and all he
could think about was the soft woman so close, the smell
of cinnamon and sugar and the need to touch her, kiss her.

The wisps of hair at her neck fluttered as he leaned

closer. He touched the tip of his tongue to her warm skin. He felt a tremor run through her and his manhood responded. His lips found the valley and he pressed. Sweet, so sweet.

She shifted away. "Mark, I don't have time in my life to play games."

"Who said I was playing a game?"

"I have Allie to think about."

He spoke from behind her. "So you're going to put how you feel and your life on hold for Allie? For how long?" He kissed her behind the ear.

Her hands stopped rolling the dough. She stepped to the side so that she could turn to look at him. "What I'm not going to do is get involved with a man I have no intention of marrying."

Mark put some space between them. "Whoa, we're not talking about marriage here. More like harmless fun. A few kisses. Some mutually satisfying petting." He stepped back and studied her. "Are you always this uptight around a man?"

"I'm not uptight."

"The best I can tell is the only time you're not is when I'm kissing you or you're laughing at my dog."

"I wasn't laughing at Gus. I was laughing at you."

He took a step closer, pinning her against the counter. "No one likes to be laughed at. But what I'm really interested in is you showing me how you're not uptight. I want to kiss you, Laura Jo. Just kiss you."

She didn't resist as his lips came down to meet hers. His mouth was firm but undemanding as if he was waiting to see if she would accept him. When had been the last time she had taken a moment's pleasure with a man? What would it hurt if she did? Just to have something that was simple and easy between two adults.

Laura Jo wrapped her hands around his neck, weaved her fingers through his hair and pressed herself against his lean, hard body. With a sigh, she returned his kiss.

Mark encircled her waist and lifted her against him. His mouth took further possession, sending wave after wave of heat through her. He ran the tip of his tongue along the seam of her mouth until she opened for him. The parry and thrust of his tongue had her joining him. He pressed her against the counter, shifted her until his desire stood ridged between them.

Something poked at her bottom just before there was a loud thump on the floor. She broke away. Mark's hand remained at her waist. Her breath was shallow and rapid. She was no longer a maiden but she sure was acting like one. Her heart was thudding against her rib cage. She couldn't look at Mark.

When she did glance at him through lowered lashes, to her great satisfaction he looked rattled, too. He leaned toward her again and she broke the embrace before stepping away. "I need to get these cakes ready to put in the oven." She was relieved that her voice sounded steadier than she felt.

Mark looked for a second as if he might disagree but he didn't move any closer.

"I think I like the sugar you just gave me better than what is on a king cake."

She had to regain her equilibrium. The only way she knew how to do that was to go on the defensive. She placed her hands on her hips. "You haven't tasted one of my cakes."

"No, but I have tasted you," he said in a soft and sultry voice.

Pleasure filled her. Mark had a way of making her feel special.

"Why don't you spread the cream cheese on this cake while I finish braiding the other one?"

"Yes, ma'am."

Minutes later Mark dropped the spatula he had been using in the sink. Laura Jo placed the cake she was working with on a baking pan. She had been aware of every movement he'd made as he'd spread the creamy cheese across the thin pastry.

"While you finish up on this one I'm going to get us each a bowl of gumbo." Mark went to a cabinet and pulled down two bowls.

Laura Jo was both relieved and disappointed when he moved to the other side of the center counter. If Mark was close he made her feel nervous and if he wasn't she missed his nearness.

"We forgot to put the babies in." Laura Jo reached into a bag and brought out a snack-size bag with tiny hard plastic babies in it. Their hands and feet were up in the air as if they were lying in a crib, laughing.

"I'll put those in. I promised Allie I would. I keep my promises."

Mark joined her again and she handed the babies to him. They looked extra-small in his large palm.

"Turn around. And don't peek."

Laura Jo did as he instructed.

"Okay. Done."

Laura Jo started cleaning up the area. "You know, it doesn't have to be such a secret. Mardi Gras will be over in four days and we won't be having another cake until next year."

He met her gaze. "Well, maybe I'll ask for something besides cake if I find the baby inside my piece."

"That's not how it works."

"Then we could just change the rules between us."

Laura Jo wasn't sure she wanted to play that game.

"Are you ready for gumbo?"

"I can eat while these rise." She looked over at the cakes. "I had no idea this much work went into making a king cake."

"They are labor intensive but I enjoy it. Especially when I can make them in a kitchen like this one."

Mark filled the two bowls he'd gotten out earlier. "Do you mind carrying your own bowl to the table?"

"Of course not. I don't expect you to wait on me."

They sat across from each other in the small breakfast nook adjoining the kitchen. From there they had a view of the bay.

"This is delicious." Laura Jo lifted a spoonful of gumbo. "I'm impressed with your culinary skills."

"I think culinary skills is a little strong. It's not hard really."

"Either way, it tastes good." She was glad that they were back to their old banter. She'd been afraid that after their hot kiss, which had her nerves on high alert, they wouldn't be able to have an easy conversation. She rather enjoyed their discussions, even if they didn't always agree.

"How's Marcy doing?"

She looked at him. "Very well, thanks to you. She'll be coming home tomorrow."

"I didn't do anything but provide encouragement. I meant to go by to see them again but I had to work late on the days I wasn't patrolling parades."

"Ann really appreciated the one day you did check in on them. That was nice of you."

"I'm a nice guy."

He really was. She'd done him a disservice when she'd first met him. He'd proven more than once that he was a good person.

"So have you found the funding for the shelter yet?" Mark asked as he pushed his empty bowl away.

"We qualified for the grant I was hoping for but it requires we find matching funds."

"Well, at least you do have some good news." He stood, gathering his bowl. "Do you want any more gumbo while I'm getting some?"

"No, I'm still working on this." Laura Jo watched him walk away. He wore a lightweight long-sleeved sweater and worn jeans. He really had a fine-looking butt.

For a second she'd been afraid he'd ask her about going to the dance. A hint of disappointment touched her when he didn't. He probably had a date with someone else by now. She didn't like that thought any better.

They finished their dinner with small talk about the weather, parades and the coming weekend. Together they carried their bowls to the dishwasher. Mark placed them in it while Laura Jo checked on the rising cake.

"How much longer on those?" Mark asked.

"They need to rise to double their size. Then I'll bake them and be on my way. I can finish the topping when I get home."

"Oh, no, you won't. I want to eat some as soon as you get them done. Besides, I want to do the topping."

"You're acting like Allie."

"Did you think I was kidding when I told you that I liked king cake as much as she did? I haven't had any in a long time and I'm not letting you out of the house without a piece today. While we're waiting, why don't we go out on the deck and have a cup of coffee and watch the sunset?"

She wasn't sure if watching the sunset with Mark was a good idea but she didn't know how to get out of it gracefully. Those darned cakes were taking too long to rise for her comfort. "Make that another glass of tea and I'll agree."

"Done. Why don't you go on out and take your pick of chairs and I'll bring the drinks."

Laura Jo walked through the living area and out one of the glass doors. Gus got up from his bed and ambled out with her. She took one of the lounges, making sure it wasn't near any others. Having Mark so close all the time was making her think of touching him, worse, kissing him again. She needed to put whatever distance she could between them.

Gus lay at the end of the lounge.

"Here you go," Mark said, placing her glass and his mug on the wire mesh table beside her. He then pulled one of the other lounges up on the opposite side of the table. He stretched his long body out and settled in.

"You mind handing me my mug?"

With shaking hands, Laura Jo passed him his drink.

"This is the best part of the day. I miss this when I have to work late."

She had to agree. It was nice to just slow down and be for a few minutes. "Is working here a lot different from your clinic in California?"

"The patients' backgrounds are different but sick people are sick people."

"Do you regret leaving California?"

"I have to admit I like the slower pace here." Mark crossed his ankles and settled more comfortably into the lounge.

"I couldn't leave Mobile and move all the way across the country."

"Sometimes you do things because you don't think you have a choice."

She watched a bird dipping into the water after its evening meal. "I know about not having choices." Maybe in some ways they weren't so different after all.

They both lapsed into silence as the sun slowly sank in the sky.

Laura Jo took a sip of her tea at the same time a breeze came in off the water. She shivered.

Mark put his mug down on the decking and stood. "I'll be back in a sec."

He returned with a jacket in his hand and handed it to her. "Here, you can put this on."

She slipped her arm into one sleeve and Mark held the jacket for her to put the other in. He sat beside her again. She trembled again and pulled the jacket closer around her.

As the wind blew, a scent of spice and musk that could only be Mark tickled her nostrils. She inhaled. For some reason it was a smell she wanted to remember.

Again they lapsed into a relaxed silence.

As the daylight was taken over by the night, Mark reached over and took her hand, weaving his fingers between hers. It was strong, secure and soothing. Laura Jo didn't pull away. Didn't want to.

When the stars came out Mark said, "We need to go and put those cakes in."

Laura Jo started. She'd been so content she'd forgotten about having anything to do. Her hand being surrounded by Mark's added to that feeling. For some reason it made her feel protected, as if she weren't facing the world alone. She hadn't had that in her life for so long it had taken her time to recognize it.

Mark not only made her feel protected but she had seen his security in tangible terms. He was great with Allie. More than once he'd seen to it that she was safe and cared for and that made her happy. She'd also seen him showing that protection to others. He'd been there when she'd called for help with Anna and Marcy. There hadn't been a moment's hesitation on his part about coming. Not once had he acted like her having a daughter was an issue. In fact, he embraced Allie, included her.

Why was Mark the one man who made her feel that way? His background said he wasn't the man for her. She wanted someone who was more interested in her than what her last name had been. But hadn't he proved her background didn't matter? He'd shown his interest well before she had told him her maiden name was Herron.

She might have questioned whether or not he had become a doctor for the money and prestige but the Clayborns already had that. After she'd viewed him seeing to a patient she'd seen his concern was sincere. He was a man interested in caring for people. He had offered to help with the shelter and had proved it with his donation and medical care. How different could he be from Phil, who was the most self-centered man she'd ever known?

She slipped her hand out of his. "I'll bake the cakes. You should stay here. It's a beautiful night."

"I'll help you."

"It won't take me long."

"Do you promise to come back? Not disappear out the front door?"

Laura Jo smiled. "Yes, I'll come back."

"I'll be waiting."

She liked the sound of that. People didn't wait for her, they left her. Mark was starting to mean too much to her. Laura Jo put the cakes in the ovens. Thankfully, Mark had double ovens and she could bake them at the same time.

Still wearing his jacket, she went back outside to join him. If he hadn't stated his fear that she might leave she might have considered going home without telling him. Her attraction to him was growing beyond her control. She didn't trust herself around him.

As she passed him on the way to her lounge he sat up

and snagged her wrist. "Come and sit with me." He pulled her toward him.

She put a hand down next to his thigh to stop herself from falling.

"Mark…" she cautioned.

"I'm not going to jump you. I'd just like to have you close."

"Why?"

The light from inside the house let her see well enough his incredulous look. "Why? Because I'm a man and you're a woman. I like you and I think you like me more than you want to admit. You're as aware of the attraction as I am. You just won't admit it.

She looked down at him for a moment.

"All I want is to sit here with a beautiful woman and watch the stars. Nothing more. But if you don't want to, I'll live with that."

He made it sound like she was acting childishly. "Scoot over."

"If you're going to get bossy then maybe I need to re-consider my invitation."

She snickered and lay on her side next to him. He wrapped an arm around her shoulders and her head naturally went to his chest.

"Now, is this so bad?"

"No. I'm much warmer."

"Good. I'm glad I can be of service." Mark's breath brushed her temple.

"I can't get too comfortable. I don't want to burn the cakes."

"How much longer do they need to cook?" His hand moved up and down her arm.

"Another forty minutes."

He checked his watch. "Then I'll help you remember."

It took her a few minutes to relax and settle into her warm and cozy spot alongside Mark. The lights of Mobile glowed in the distance and the horn of an occasional seagoing freighter sounded. It was a lonesome noise, one that up until this minute she could identify with. Somehow she no longer felt lonely. As they sat in silence her eyelids drooped and closed.

The next thing she knew Mark was shaking her awake.

"We need to get the cakes out."

She jerked to a sitting position. "I'm sorry. I went to sleep on you."

"I'm not. It would be my guess you needed to rest after the week you've had."

Laura Jo couldn't argue with that. She struggled to get up.

"Let me climb out first then I'll pull you up," Mark suggested.

As he moved, his big body towered over her. She was tempted to touch him. Before she could stop herself she placed a hand on his chest.

"I'm squishing you?"

"No. I just wanted to touch you," she murmured.

He gave her a predatory glare. "Great. You decide to touch me when the king cakes might be burning. You need to work on your timing."

She nudged him back. "Let me up."

He hesitated a second before he took her hand and pulled her to her feet. "Let's go."

In the kitchen Mark peeked into an oven. He inhaled dramatically. "Smells wonderful."

"If you'll get your nose out of it, I can take it out." Laura Jo handed him a hot pad. "I'll get this one and you can get the other." Laura Jo pulled the golden-brown mound out of the oven and set it on the counter. Mark did the same and placed his beside hers.

Again he leaned over and inhaled deeply. "Perfect."

"I need to mix the icing and then we can put the colors on." Laura Jo found a bowl and added powdered sugar then water. She stirred them into a creamy white mixture. Using a spoon, she drizzled the icing back and forth over the top of the cakes.

Mark dipped a finger through the bowl and put it in his mouth. "Mmm."

She tapped the top of his hand when he started after the cake.

"Ouch."

"I believe you have a sweet tooth."

"I think you are sweet."

"I think you might flatter the cook in order to get your way. It's time for the colored sugar." Laura Jo picked up the food coloring she'd left on the other end of the counter. "We'll need three bowls."

Mark went to a cabinet and brought those to her. Laura Jo put granulated sugar in each of the bowls and added yellow coloring to one, purple to another and green to the last one. She mixed until each granule had turned the color. She sprinkled one color over a third of one cake. In the middle section another and on the last third another.

"Do you know what the colors stand for?" Mark asked.

"No self-respecting citizen of Mobile wouldn't know. Purple is for justice, green is for faith and gold for power."

"You are correct. Can we have a slice now?" Mark asked, sounding much like a child begging at his mother's side.

"You want to eat it while it's hot?"

"Why not?"

"I've just never had it that way. I've always waited until it's cooled."

"Well, there's a first time for everything." Mark pulled a knife out of a drawer and sliced a hunk off the end of one cake. Picking it up, he bit into it. "This is delicious. Allie is right, you do make the best cakes. I've never had one better from a bakery."

His praise made her feel warm inside. She cut a small section and placed it in her mouth. It was good.

"Hey, look what I found." He held up a baby.

"You knew where that was."

"I did not," he said in an indignant tone. "Just good luck."

Laura smiled and placed the items she had brought into bags. She needed to leave before she was tempted to stay longer. Being with Mark had been far more enjoyable than she'd found comfortable. What if he tried to kiss her again? Could she handle that?

"What're you doing?" Mark asked.

"I'm packing up."

"You don't have to go."

"Yes, I do. Do you have something I can wrap one of these cakes in? Allie will be expecting to eat some tomorrow."

Mark opened a drawer and handed her a box of plastic wrap.

She pulled out a length of wrap and started covering the cake. "Do you mind if I take your baking pan? I'll return it."

"I don't mind," he said in an aggravated tone, as if he knew she was dodging the issue.

"Are you running out on me, Laura Jo?"

She refused to look at him. "No, I've been here for hours and I was more worried about wearing out my welcome."

Mark took the wrap from her and put it on the counter. "I don't think that's possible. I believe you're running scared."

"I'm not."

"Then why don't you go to the dance with me on Tuesday night?"

"I've already said I can't." She reached for a bag and put the rest of the items she'd brought in it.

"I think it's 'I won't.'"

"Please, Mark, just leave it alone. I'm not going to change my mind. It's not because of you but for other reasons."

"Care to tell me what those are."

"I'd rather not. I need to be going." She pulled the bags to her.

"I'm a good listener."

"That's not the problem. I just don't want to talk about it. Now, I need to go."

Mark took them from her. "I'll get these. You can get the cake. I'll walk you to your car."

Laura Jo was a little disappointed that he hadn't put up more of an argument to her leaving. Had her refusal to open up about why she didn't want to go to the krewe dance put him off? Wasn't that what she wanted?

"I need to wrap your cake up before I go and clean up this mess."

"Don't worry about doing that. I'll take care of it. Theresa will be in tomorrow."

"Theresa?"

"My housekeeper."

Just another shining example of the fact they lived in two different worlds. "Well, I'm not going to leave anyone, including a housekeeper, this mess."

"I'm not surprised. It's in your nature to see to other people, make it better for them. Who makes things better for you?"

She hadn't ever thought of herself in that context but he might be right. She wouldn't let him know it, though. "I don't need anyone taking care of me."

"We might be perfect for each other because I'm no good at doing so," he said in a dry tone.

What had made him say that? He was always taking care of people.

She went to the sink, picked up the cleaning cloth and started wiping off the counter.

"Leave it." Mark said, taking the cloth and placing it in the sink. "I'll take care of it."

Laura Jo then picked up the cake and headed for the front door. Mark wasn't far behind. When they reached the car, he opened the front passenger-side door and placed the bags on the floor. He then took the cake from her and did the same.

She went to the driver's door and he joined her there. "Thanks for helping me with the cakes."

"Not a problem." Mark reached into his pocket and pulled something out.

Laura Jo could just make out with the help of the light from the porch that he was rotating the baby between his index and thumb.

"We had a deal."

Laura Jo had an uneasy feeling. Where was he going with this? "We did."

"I would like to collect now."

Every nerve in her hummed. Something told her that she might not like his request. "Just what do you want?"

Mark's lips lifted, giving him a wolfish appearance. He took a step closer, coming into her personal space.

Heat washed over her. She looked at him. In the dim light she couldn't see his eyes clearly but she felt their intensity.

"I want you to kiss me."

"What?"

"I want you put your hands on my shoulders, lean up and place your lips on mine."

He said the words in a form of a challenge, as if she would refuse. She'd show him. Placing her hands on his chest, she slowly slid them up and over his shoulders.

His hands went to her waist, tightening around her.

"Remember this is my kiss," she admonished him.

He eased his hold but didn't release her.

Going up on her toes, she took her time, bringing her lips to his. The tension across his shoulders told her Mark was working to restrain himself.

Taking his lower lip between her teeth, she gently tugged.

He groaned.

She let go and smoothed it over with the tip of her tongue. Slowly she moved her lips over his until she almost ended the contact.

At Mark's sound of resistance she grinned and moved her mouth back to press it firmly against his. She didn't have to ask for entrance, he was already offering it. Her tongue met his and danced but he soon took the lead. She'd been caught at her own game. It felt wonderful to have a man touch her. It had been so long. For Mark to be the one made it even more amazing. Wrapping her arms around his neck, she gave herself over to the moment. She wanted more, so much more.

* * *

Mark gripped Laura Jo's waist and pulled her closer. He pressed her back against the car. His hand slid under the hem of her shirt and grazed her smooth skin until his fingers rested near the prize. Wanting to touch, taste, tease, he had to remove the barrier. Using the tip of his index finger, he followed the line of her bra around to the clasp. When he hesitated Laura Jo squirmed against him. She wanted this as much as he did. Flicking the clasp open, he moved his hand to the side curve of her breast.

He released her lips and gave a small sound of complaint. Placing small kisses along her neck to reassure her, he skimmed his hand upward to cup her breast. His sigh of pleasure mingled with hers. He tested the weight. Perfect. Using a finger, he circled her nipple then tugged.

Her hips shifted and came into more intimate contact with his ridged manhood. He'd been aware of his desire for Laura Jo for a number of days but it had never been this overwhelming.

He pushed her bra up and off her other breast. Her nipple stood tall, waiting for his attention. That knowledge only fueled his desire.

Laura Jo cupped his face and brought his lips back to hers. She gave him the hottest kiss he'd ever received. Heaven help him, if she could turn him on with just kisses, what could she do to him in bed?

She ran her hands under his shirt and across his back.

When her mouth left his to kiss his cheek, he pushed up her shirt, exposing her breasts. He backed away just far enough to look at her. "Beautiful."

He didn't give her time to speak before his lips found hers again and his fingers caressed her breast. Thankful for her small car, he leaned her back over the hood. Her fingers flexed and released against the muscles of his back as she met him kiss for kiss. Standing between her legs, the heat of her center pressed against his. He pulled his mouth from hers. It went to the top of her right breast, where he placed his lips. Laura Jo shivered.

"Cold?"

"No."

His chest swelled with desire. What he was doing to her had caused the reaction, not the metal of the car. He lowered his mouth to her nipple and took it. Using his tongue, he spun and tugged. Laura Jo bucked beneath him.

Her hand went to the line of his pants and glided just beneath. She ran her hand one way and then the other before it returned to stroking his back.

She wasn't the cold fish she wanted him to believe she was. She was hot and all sensual woman. He smiled as he gave the other nipple the same devotion.

He wanted her here and now. In his driveway. On her car. But that wasn't what Laura Jo deserved. He wasn't that kind of man. She certainly wasn't that type of woman.

"Sweetheart, we need to go inside."

Mark saw her blink once, twice, as if she were coming out of a deep dream. She looked around as if trying to figure out where she was. He saw the moment she came back to reality and his heart dropped.

"Oh, God." She sat up and gave him a shove.

He stepped back and let her slide off the car.

She jerked her shirt down, not bothering to close her bra. "I have to go."

"No, you don't."

He stepped toward her and she stopped him with a hand. "I can't do this."

"Why not?"

"Because it is wrong for me on so many levels." She climbed behind the wheel of the car. "I'm sorry, Mark."

She couldn't have been any more sorry than he was. He stood there with his body as tight as a bike spoke, wanting to reach out to her. Laura Jo didn't even look at him as she started the car and headed out the drive.

It wasn't until the car stopped about halfway down that he knew she hadn't been as unaffected by what had passed between them as she'd acted. She had wanted him, too.

Guilt filled him. He had no business pursuing Laura Jo if he had no intention of the relationship going beyond what they had just experienced. He couldn't let it be more. He'd already proved he would run when the going got tough. Could he trust himself not to let them down, like he had Mike?

As her taillights disappeared, he turned and walked toward the house. All he had waiting for him tonight was a long, cold shower. He needed to stay well out of Laura Jo's life.

Laura Jo opened the door early the next morning to let Allie, Marsha and Jeremy in. Before Laura Jo could say hello, Marsha announced, "We've got a problem."

"Bigger than the one we already have?"

"Yep."

"Come on into the kitchen and tell me what's happened."

Marsha followed her while Jeremy rushed ahead and took the chair next to Allie.

Marsha sat in the other chair while Laura Jo got a bowl from the cabinet and placed it in front of Jeremy. She then sat down. "Okay, let me have it."

"I got an email from the city rep, saying that if we don't

get half the asking price in cash to them by the end of next week then there's no deal,"

This was worse than Laura Jo had expected. "That only gives us five days, and three of those are holidays," she groaned.

"I know. That's why I'm here. Do you have any ideas?"

Laura Jo propped her elbows on the table and put her head in her hands. "No," she said in a mournful voice.

"I do," Marsha announced emphatically.

Laura Jo looked at her. "You do?"

"You have to go to the knewe dance. It's our only chance."

Laura Jo stood and walked to the sink. After last night, going to the dance had become less about her past and more about her reaction to Mark. She had been so tempted to throw all her responsibilities and concerns into the bay and find paradise in his arms. She'd been lying half-naked on the hood of a car, for heaven's sake. The man made her lose her mind. She'd had to stop at the end of his drive in order to get herself together enough to drive. Her hands had still been shaking when she'd started across the bay.

She couldn't stand the thought of losing the best chance they'd had in years to have a new house. But if she went to the dance she'd have to resist Mark, which she wasn't sure she could do, and face her parents and the social circle she'd left behind. The one she spoke so negatively about. She would be going back with her tail between her legs and begging them to help her. No, she would be asking for help for the shelter. It had nothing to do with her personally.

"I'll call Mark. If he hasn't asked someone else to go, I'll tell him I'll go."

Marsha joined her at the sink. "I wouldn't ask you to do it if I thought there was another way." She put an arm around Laura Jo's shoulders. "The house is too perfect for us not to give it our best shot. I'd go but I don't have the same influence as you or Dr. Clayborn have."

"I know. I just hope it works." Maybe going would not only benefit the house but give her a chance to lay some ghosts to rest.

"Me, too." Marsha squeezed her shoulder.

What if Mark had already found another date? That thought gave Laura Jo a sick feeling. Then she guessed she'd be going to the dance by herself. Not only to face her past alone but to see Mark holding another woman. Neither experience appealed to her.

CHAPTER SIX

IT WAS MIDMORNING and Mark was at his office desk when the woman he'd been planning to ask to the dance informed him that he had a call.

Picking up the phone, he said, "Dr. Clayborn here."

"Mark, its Laura Jo."

Like he wouldn't recognize her voice.

"If you don't already have a date for the dance, I'd like to go after all," she finished on a breathless note.

He'd thought of little else but her since those minutes outside his home. She'd kissed him so thoroughly, leaving him in need of not only one cold shower but two. Laura Jo had completely turned the tables on him with those hot, sexy kisses. He'd only hoped to kiss her one more time but instead he'd been left wanting all of her.

"No, I haven't asked anyone else yet."

After the way she'd left last night, something bad must have happened regarding the shelter for her to agree to go to the dance with him. He didn't care, he wasn't going to question the gift.

"So I'm still invited?"

"If you would like to go."

"I would."

"So what changed your mind?"

"They've moved up the timetable on the shelter house and I've been left no choice."

"Well, it's nice to know it isn't because you might enjoy an evening out with me," he said in his best serious tone.

He had to admit it stung to know that she had no interest in being seen at the most prestigious event of the year with him. The only reason she had agreed to go was because she needed help finding funds for the shelter. She had made it clear on more than one occasion that she didn't want to go, so he could only imagine how desperate she must be to pick up the phone and call him. She wanted that shelter enough to take this bold step. What impressed him most was that it wasn't for her but for someone else.

"I'll pick you up at seven."

"Make it eight. I have to work the parade."

That figured. When did she ever take time for herself? He was going to see to it that she enjoyed the evening out with him if it killed him.

"I'll be there at eight, then. We'll make a grand entrance."

"That's what I'm afraid of. Bye, Mark." With that she rang off.

"Laura Jo, stop fussing, you look beautiful," Marsha nagged as Laura Jo pulled up on the dress that showed far too much cleavage for her comfort.

She'd found the evening dress at the upscale consignment shop downtown. Ironically, it was the same one her mother had taken all the family's outdated clothes to when Laura Jo had been a child. Her mother would say, "Maybe someone less fortunate can use these." Like people who were less fortunate cared whether or not they wore couture clothing.

"I'm only going to this thing to try to drum up funds

for the shelter, not to have men staring at me. I'll have to wear the green dress. Would you get it? It's in my closet."

Laura Jo hadn't had time to look any further for a more appropriate dress. She'd taken the first one that was her size and looked suitable. She hadn't even tried it on and had had no idea this one would be so revealing.

"Isn't the dress formal?" Marsha said, as if she were reassuring a child having a temper tantrum.

"Yes, but I guess I don't have a choice." Laura Jo looked into the full-length mirror one more time. The plunging neckline left the top of her breasts exposed. Each time she breathed she feared more than that might be visible. For a brief second the memory of Mark's lips pressed against her flesh made her sizzle all over. She inhaled sharply.

"Is something wrong?" Marsha asked.

She circled around and faced Marsha. "Don't you have a pink shawl? I could put it around my shoulders and tie it in front. That would fix the problem."

Marsha sighed. "I don't see a problem but I'll go get it. I think you're overreacting. The dress is perfect the way it is."

Laura Jo looked at herself again. Was she overreacting? If so, why? Because she was going to the dance with Mark or because she was afraid she couldn't control herself around him?

She studied the dress. It was midnight blue with the slightest shimmer to it. The material hugged her in all the correct places. Twisting, she turned so that she could see the back. It closed close to her neck so that it formed a diamond-shaped peephole in the middle. It was the loveliest detail of the dress.

"Mommy, you look pretty," Allie said from behind Laura Jo.

"Thank you, honey." She leaned down and kissed the top of Allie's head.

The doorbell rang.

"I'll get it," Allie said, running out of the room.

Laura Jo followed. Surely it was Marsha, returning with the wrap.

Allie opened the door and Mark stood on the other side. Their eyes met and held. Everything that had happened between them the night before flashed through her mind. His gaze slid downward and paused at her breasts.

They tingled and her nipples grew hard. Heat pooled in her middle. What was happening to her? Something as simple as a look from Mark could make her feel alive like no one else could.

Was he remembering, too?

"Doesn't Mommy look pretty?" Allie asked, looking back and forth between them.

Mark's gaze didn't leave her. Seconds later, as if coming out of a stupor, he said, "Uh, yes, she looks wonderful."

Laura Jo swallowed hard. She'd never felt more beautiful than she did right now as Mark admired her. The man was starting to get under her skin and everything about his idea of life was so wrong for her. Or was it? She'd better guard her heart tonight or he might take it.

Allie looked up at Mark. "You look pretty, too."

He did, in the most handsome, debonair and charming way. His blond waves were in place and his eyes shone. Dressed in his formal wear of starched white shirt, black studs and tailcoat, he took her breath away. She'd seen many men wearing their finest but none compared to the man standing before her.

"Thank you, Allie." He was still looking at her when he said, "Do you mind if I come in?"

"Oh, no, do." Laura Jo gave Allie a little nudge back into the hall. She stepped out of the way and let Mark enter.

"Come in and have a seat. I'm waiting for Marsha to bring me a cover-up."

"From where I stand, you look perfect just the way you are." His voice had a grainy sound to it that wasn't normal.

"Thank you." When had she become such a blusher? When Mark had come into her life.

"Have a seat while I get my purse. Marsha should be back by then." Laura Jo indicated a chair in their small living area.

There was a knock on the door and Allie ran to open it. Laura Jo trailed behind her. Her friend breezed in, breathless. "I couldn't find it. I must have given it away at our last clothes drive. Hi, Dr. Clayborn. You look nice." Marsha let the last few words spin out.

"Thank you. I was telling Laura Jo she looks great just as she is."

"I think so, too." Marsha said. She offered a hand to Allie. "Come on. It's time to go. Jeremy will be home in a few minutes."

Laura Jo picked up a small bag and handed it to her daughter. "I'll see you tomorrow afternoon. I'll be picking you and Jeremy up from school." Laura Jo kissed her on the head.

"Okay. Bye, Mark." Allie happily went out the door.

"Have a good time and don't do anything I wouldn't do," Marsha quipped with a wink.

"Marsha!"

Mark's low chuckle didn't help to lessen Laura Jo's mortification.

She turned to him. "You do understand I'm only going to the krewe dance because I need funds for the shelter. Nothing else can happen."

"You more than made it clear that the evening has nothing to do with my company. Are you ready?"

Had she hurt his feelings?

"Mark, I'm sorry. I didn't mean to sound so rude." She looked down. "After the other night I just didn't want you to get the wrong idea. I do appreciate you taking me to the dance. It's just that I have a difficult time with the idea and I seem to be taking it out on you."

"Maybe if you explained, I would understand."

She looked at him again. "It's because…I shunned that world years ago."

"Why?"

"I fell in love, or at least what I thought was love, with a guy who my parents didn't approve of. 'Not of our social status,' my father said. My parents were adamantly against the marriage. They told me Phil was after my name and money, not me. That he was no good. My father was particularly vocal about Phil being the wrong guy. He forced me to make a choice between them or my ex.

"I always felt like I was an afterthought to them. I never quite fit the mold they had imagined for their child. They spent little time with me when I was young and now they wanted to start making parental demands, showing real interest. I had always been more headstrong than they liked, so my father's ultimatum backfired.

"I told my parents if the man I loved wasn't good enough for them then I didn't need them. I chose Phil. Turned out they were right about him. He was everything they said he was and more. I said some ugly things to my parents that I now regret but I couldn't go running back. My pride wouldn't allow that. I had to prove to them and myself I could take care of myself. Live with my mistakes."

Laura Jo would never let Mark know what it took for her to admit her mistakes. No matter how many times or how sweetly Marsha had asked Laura Jo, she had never told her as much as she had just told Mark.

"You haven't spoken to your parents in all that time?"

"I tried to contact them after Phil and I got back from Vegas but the housekeeper told me Mother wouldn't take my call. I phoned a few more times and got the same response. I finally gave up."

"They really hurt you."

Laura Jo fingered a fold in her dress. "Yes. After I had Allie I had a better sense of what it was to have a child's best interests at heart. But after they'd acted the way they did when I called I couldn't take the chance that they would treat Allie the same way as they had me. I'll never let her feel unwanted."

"Maybe they've changed. They might be better grandparents than they were parents. You could try again. At least let them meet Allie."

She shook her head. "I think the hurt is too deep and has gone on for too long."

"You'll never know until you try. I could go with you, if you want."

"I don't know. I'll have to think about that. Let's just get through tonight, then I'll see."

"I'll be there beside you all night. We'll both put in the appearance to get what you need and to also satisfy my father. Then we're out of there."

To her surprise, he didn't sound like he'd been that excited about going to the dance to begin with. Had she made some judgment calls about him that just weren't true? He'd never once looked down on her, her friends or where she lived. Did his status in the area truly not matter to him?

She made a chuckling sound that had nothing to do with humor and more about being resigned. "We sound nothing like two people expecting to enjoy an evening out."

At the car, he opened the door, took her elbow and helped her in. At least if she had to go to the dance she would arrive in a fine car and on the arm of the most handsome man in town.

Mark settled behind the wheel and closed the door but didn't start the engine. Instead, he placed his hand over hers. Squeezing it gently, he said, "I can see by the look on your face that you have no hope of this evening ending well. Why don't you think positive? You might be surprised."

"I'll try."

"Plus you're starting to damage my ego by making me think I no longer know how to show a woman a good time." Mark started the car then checked to see if she was buckled in. She patted her seat belt and he backed out of the parking space.

"This doesn't have anything to do with you personally." She studied his strong profile in the dim light.

"Well, I'm glad to know that. I was starting to think you thought being seen with me was comparable to going to the gallows."

She smiled.

"That's better. At least you haven't lost your sense of humor completely." He pulled out into the street.

They rode down now crowd-free Government Street toward the port. The building where the dance was being held was located on the bay. Mark circled to the elegant glass doors of the historic building.

Mark stopped the car. He handed the keys to the valet then came around to open the door for her. Taking a deep fortifying breath, she placed her hand into Mark's offered one. It was large and steady.

"You're an outstanding nurse, mother of a wonderful daughter and an advocate for mothers, Laura Jo. You're more accomplished than the majority of the people here."

She met his look. His eyes didn't waver. He'd said what he believed. She drew confidence from that. "Thank you."

He pulled her hand into the crook of his arm as they walked toward the door of the building held open by another young man in evening dress. Slowly they ascended one side of the U-shaped staircase to the large room above. Mark paused at the door just long enough for her to survey the space.

People were standing in groups, talking. The room was narrow and long with a black-and-white-tiled floor. Round dining tables were arranged to the right and left, creating an aisle down the middle. The white tablecloths brushed the floor. The Mardi Gras colored decorations centered on each table were elaborate and striking.

The area looked much as it had the last time she'd attended a ball when she'd been nineteen years old and a lady-in-waiting. A month later she'd met Phil and her world had taken a one-eighty-degree turn. Back then she'd been a child of wealthy parents with her life planned out for her. When she'd broken away from her parents, she would never have guessed her life would become what it was now. Still, had she made a mistake by keeping Allie away from them? Her parents had faults but didn't she, too?

Just as eye-catching was the dress of the active men of the krewe. They were all clad in their Louis XVI brocade knee-length satin coats trimmed in gold or silver braid. On their heads were large hats that had one side of the brim pinned up with a plumed feather attached and matched the men's coats. Their pantaloons, white stockings and black buckle shoes added to the mystique. The women who were married to the members of the board wore equally ostentatious dresses, some of them matching their husband's. Otherwise, men and women were dressed in formal wear.

Were her parents here in all their finery?

Mark must have felt her stiffen because he placed his hand over hers, which was resting on his arm. "Let's go see and be seen."

They hadn't walked far when they were stopped by a man's voice calling, "Mark Clayborn, I heard you were back in town."

Mark brought her around with him. "Mr. Washington, how in the world are you?" Mark shook the man's hand and Laura Jo released his arm but remained beside him.

"I'm doing well."

"I heard about your father. He's recovering, I understand," the older man said.

"Slowly, but retirement is a must," Mark told Mr. Washington with ease.

"I imagine that's difficult for him. I'll make plans to get out to see him."

"I know he would like that."

When she started to move away Mark rested a hand at her waist. It warmed her skin. She was no longer worried about the people they might see. Her focus was on his touch.

Mr. Washington turned his gaze to her. Laura Jo knew who he was but had never met him.

Mark followed his look. "Mr. Washington, I'd like to introduce you to Laura Jo Akins."

Would he recognize her name? No, probably not. There were a number of girls in the south with double first names. Laura Jo wasn't that uncommon.

"Nice to meet you, Ms. Akins."

She forced a smile. "Nice to meet you, too." At least with her married name it wasn't obvious who she was.

"Laura Jo is a nurse at Mobile General and has started a shelter for abandoned mothers." Mark jumped right into helping her look for supporters.

"That sounds like a worthy cause," Mr. Washington said, as if he was really interested. "What made you decide to do that?"

Laura Jo wasn't going to lie. "I was an abandoned mother. My husband left me when I was pregnant. I have a daughter."

"So you know the need firsthand." He nodded his head thoughtfully.

"I do." Laura Jo lapsed into her planned appeal. Mark offered a few comments and the fact he had made a donation to what he thought was a worthy cause.

"Contact my office tomorrow and I'll have a donation for you," Mr. Washington assured her.

"Thank you. The women I'm helping thank you also."

Mark looked across the room. "Mr. Washington, I think it's time for us to find a place at a table for dinner."

"It does look that way. Good to see you, son. Nice to meet you, young lady."

As Mark led her away she whispered to him, "I never imagined it would be that easy."

"I don't think it will always happen that way. But Mardi Gras season is when people are having fun so they're a little more generous." He took her hand and led her farther into the room.

"You're right about coming tonight. As much as I didn't want to, it was the right thing to do for the shelter."

After they were stopped a couple of times by people Mark knew, he found them a table with two seats left near the front of the room. She still hadn't seen her parents.

Mark remained a gentleman and pulled her chair out for her before he took his own. She could get used to this. As ugly as she had been about coming to the ball, he'd still helped her get a promise of funds from Mr. Washington and was treating her like a lady. She owed him an apology.

He knew a few people sharing their table and introduced her. She recognized a number of other couples by their names but they didn't act as if they knew her. Still, she might run into some of her parents' friends. She looked around.

Mark whispered in her ear, "They might not be here."

Laura Jo knew better. They didn't miss a Mardi Gras ball. One more pass over the crowd and she saw them. They had aged well. There was more gray hair at her father's temples but her mother had a stylish cut and kept it colored. They both looked as elegant as they ever had for one of these events.

"What's wrong?"

"My parents."

Mark looked in the direction she indicated. "Why don't we go and say hello?"

"They won't want to speak to me. I said some horrible things to them."

"I bet that doesn't matter anymore. At least you could give them a chance. They may regret what happened, just like you do. You'll feel better if you do. At least you will know you made the effort. Come on, I'll be right there with you." He stood and offered his hand.

Laura Jo hesitated then placed her hand in Mark's. It was large, warm and strong. A new resolve filled her. No longer the same person she had been nine years ago, she could do this. Mark held her hand tight as they crossed the room. The closer they came to her parents' table the more her gut tightened. The sudden need to run splashed over her. She hesitated.

"You can do this." The small squeeze of her hand told her she wasn't alone.

Her parents looked up at them. Shock registered on their faces.

Mark let go of her hand and cupped her elbow.

"Hello, Mother and Daddy."

"We're surprised to see you here. We had no idea you were coming," her father said in a blunt, boardroom voice.

Well, he was certainly all open arms about seeing her again.

"Hello, I'm Mark Clayborn. Nice to meet you, Mr. and Mrs. Herron."

Her parents looked at Mark as if they weren't sure they had heard correctly. She was just relieved he'd taken the attention off her for a moment.

"Mark Clayborn, junior?" her father asked.

"Yes, sir."

Her father stood and offered his hand. "Pleasure to meet you."

Leaving her seat, her mother came to stand beside her father. "How have you been, Laura Jo?"

She sounded as if she truly cared. "Fine."

"I'm glad to hear that. I understand you've started some type of shelter."

How did they know about that? Was she really interested? "I have."

Mark put an arm around her shoulders. "Laura Jo has helped a lot of women who needed it."

It was nice to have someone sound proud of her. Not till this moment had she realized she'd been missing that in her life.

"Are they unwed mothers?"

At least her mother had asked with what sounded like sincere curiosity. "Some are but most have been abandoned. Those that have no family they can or want to go home to."

Laura Jo didn't miss her mother's flinch.

"That sounds like a worthwhile project," her mother finally said.

"It is," Mark agreed. "She's now trying to buy a larger place for the shelter to move to."

Laura Jo placed her hand on Mark's arm. She didn't want to go into all that with her parents. "I don't think they want to hear all about that."

When Mark started to argue she added, "How have you both been?"

"We've been well," her father said.

They were talking to each other like strangers, which in reality they were.

"I understand you live over in the Calen area."

"I do." Laura Jo was astonished that he knew that. Had they been keeping up with her when she'd had no idea? Did her parents care more than she'd thought or shown?

Her mother stepped toward Laura Jo with an imploring look on her face. "Will you tell us about our granddaughter?"

"You knew?" Laura Jo was thankful for Mark's steady hand steady on her elbow.

"Yes, we've known for a long time." Her mother's look didn't waver.

They had known and they still hadn't helped? Or they'd known that Laura Jo would throw their help back at them if they offered?

"Please, tell us about her," her father pleaded.

Laura Jo spent the next few minutes telling her parents about Allie. They seemed to hang on every word. Had they changed?

"Thank you for telling us," her mother said with a soft sigh when Laura Jo finished.

They were interrupted by the krewe captain getting the attention of the people in the room. He announced the buffet dinner was being served and gave directions about which tables would go first.

"We should return to our table," Laura Jo said.

It was her mother's turn to give her an entreating look. "Laura Jo, may we see Allie sometime?"

Laura Jo stiffened but she forced her voice to remain even. "I'll have to think about that. She knows nothing about you."

Moisture spring to her mother's eyes.

The table next to her parents' rose to get in line for their meal.

"I think it's time that we returned to our table, Laura Jo. It was nice to meet you both, Mr. and Mrs. Herron."

Mr. Herron blinked as if he had forgotten Mark was standing there.

"Thank you for coming over, Laura Jo. It's wonderful to see you."

Her mother sounded like she truly meant it.

"It's nice to see you, too." Laura Jo turned and headed back to their table on shaky knees.

Mark leaned in and asked, "You okay?"

"I'm good." She smiled. "Really good, actually. Thanks for encouraging me to speak to them."

He grinned. "Hey, that's what a good date does. So are you going to introduce Allie to them?"

"I don't know if I'm ready for that but at least I'll think about it."

"Sounds like a plan. Hungry?"

"Much more than I was a few minutes ago."

"Good."

They returned to their table and had to wait until a few tables on the other side of the room lined up and then it was their turn. Mark placed his hand at the small of her back again. As disconcerting as it was to have him touch her, he'd done it enough over the past couple of weeks that she'd grown to not only expect it but to appreciate the simple gesture.

They were almost to the buffet tables in the middle of the room when Mark jerked to a stop. She turned to question him about what was wrong. He stood looking in the direction of a group of people who were obviously together. His face had darkened. All pleasantness of a few minutes ago had washed away. One of the group was in a wheelchair. Did he know the man?

Mark quickly regained his composure and closed the gap between him and her.

"Are you okay?" she whispered when he came to stand next to her.

"I'm fine." He added a smile that for once didn't reach his eyes.

They stood in line for a few minutes, working their way to where the plates were stacked. A large floral arrangement was positioned where the tables intersected. On the four tables were shrimp cocktail, gumbo, salads of all types and prime rib, with a man serving that and desserts.

As they slowly filled their plates, Laura Jo saw Mark glancing toward the end of the line. She noticed the man in the wheelchair. This time Mark seemed even more uncomfortable about the situation.

As they went through the line Mark spoke to people. Thankfully everyone accepted her as his date and nothing more. Maybe she could get through this evening after all. She'd been a teenager when she'd last been at this kind of function. She had matured and changed since then.

During the meal, Mark spoke to the woman to the right of him. Laura Jo had a light conversation with the man in full regalia to her left. Once during the meal Mark gave her knee a reassuring squeeze. That little gesture said, We're in this together. She appreciated it. Except for Marsha, it had been her and Allie against the world.

She had finished her dinner when Mark got her attention and asked her to tell the woman he'd been talking to about the shelter. The woman told Laura Jo that she would like to help and how to contact her.

The conversation was interrupted by the captain announcing that it was time to introduce the krewe directors.

Laura Jo smiled at Mark and mouthed, "Thank you."

He put his arm around her shoulder and gave her a gentle hug and whispered in her ear, "You're welcome. See, it's not as bad as you thought."

"No, it hasn't been. Thanks to you."

He kissed her temple. "You can really thank me later."

Before she could react to that statement the captain started calling names and people were lining up on the dance floor that was acting as a stage.

It was her turn to feel Mark stiffen. She saw the man in the wheelchair Mark had looked at earlier propelling himself across the stage, while an attractive woman walked beside him.

She glanced at Mark. His focus was fixed on the man. "Do you know him?"

"Yes."

"He's your friend from the accident, isn't he?"

"Yes." The word had a remorseful note to it.

The next man was being introduced and she didn't ask Mark any more. With everyone having been presented, the crowd clapped in appreciation for the work the board had done on the dance.

The captain then asked for everyone's attention again. "The king and queen and their court have arrived."

There was a hush over the room as the first lady-in-waiting and her escort were introduced.

The young lady wore an all-white dress made out of satin and adorned with pearls and sparkling stones. Her white train trailed across the floor. It was heavy, Laura Jo knew from experience.

When she had designed her train so many years ago it had had the family crest in the center with a large, pale pink flamingo rising from it. The bird's eye had been an onyx from her grandmother's train when she had been queen. Each pearl and precious stone were sewn on by hand. It had been edged in real white fox fur. She'd worn long white gloves that had reached above her elbows. She'd been told she'd never looked more beautiful.

And this happened every year. The pomp and circumstance of it all still astounded her.

She and her mother had designed and planned her dress and train for months. They had even taken a trip to New York to look for material. A designer there had made the dress then it had been sent back to Mobile, where a seamstress that specialized in embellishments had added them. What she would wear consumed their family life for the entire year before Mardi Gras.

She had no idea what her dress and train had cost but she was sure it would have been enough to run the shelter for two or three months.

"I bet you were a beautiful lady-in-waiting. I'm sorry I didn't pay more attention," Mark whispered close to her ear.

She smiled.

The couple walked to the captain and his wife on the stage and curtsied and bowed, before circling back to the rear of the room. By that time another couple had moved forward. The entire court was dressed in white, with the females having different dress and trains that had their personal design. The escorts wore identical outfits. Each couple paid their respects and this happened eighteen more times.

From the court would come next year's king and queen of Mardi Gras. Since her grandmother had been queen, Laura Jo had been on track to be the queen the year she turned twenty-one. The king would reign the year he turned twenty-five.

She glanced at Mark, who was watching the stage more than the couples parading up the aisle. "I did notice you and you were a handsome king," Laura Jo whispered.

"Thank you, fair maiden."

Laura Jo giggled. She knew well that there was a private and public side to Mardi Gras. It all started around Thanksgiving, with all the coming-out balls for the girls. The society families held the balls and she'd been a part of the process. She'd loved it at the time. Now she looked back on it and saw how spoiled she been and how ignorant of the world. Not until she had gotten away from her parents' house had she realized how many people could have been helped with the money that had gone into just her dresses for Mardi Gras.

As the royalty came into sight, Laura Jo couldn't help but be amazed at the beauty of the couple's attire. No matter how many times she had seen this type of event, she was still left in awe. They wore matching gold outfits trimmed in gold. The king's clothing was adorned as much as the queen's. She had gold beads that came to a peak halfway up the center of her skirt. The bodice had swirls and curls covering it. They carried crowns on their heads that glittered in the lights. The king carried a diamond-headed walking stick while the queen held a scepter that matched her crown.

Laura Jo had forgotten the artistry and how regal their trains were. They were both at least twenty feet long.

Theirs, like those of the ladies-in-waiting, told a story of their life. The king's had his family crest with a hunting motif around it, which included an appliqué of a deer head. The queen's train was also appliquéd but with large magnolias in detail. Around the edge was a five-inch border of crystals that made it shimmer. The neckline had a collar that went from one shoulder to the other in the back. It stood up eight inches high. It bounced gently as the queen walked. It was made from a mass of light and airy bangle beads formed into magnolias and leaves, the centers being made out of pearls.

Their trains alone could buy a room in the house they were looking at for the shelter.

"How did it feel to be the man of the hour?" Laura Jo asked Mark.

"At the time, amazing," he answered in a dry tone.

CHAPTER SEVEN

WITH THE INTRODUCTIONS COMPLETED, everyone returned to their meals and the band struck up a dance tune. Couples moved toward the dance floor.

"Why don't we have a dance before we go and talk to a few more people about the shelter? I think we could both use a few minutes of fun." Mark stood and offered her his hand.

"One dance."

As they entered the dance floor he brought Laura Jo close. She fit perfectly. Wearing high heels, her head came to his shoulder. The band was just beginning the first notes of a slow waltz. Laura Jo put her hand in his and the other on his shoulder. His hand rested on the warm, creamy skin visible on her back.

"You know, I think I like this dress more now than I did when I first saw you in it." The words were for her alone.

She glanced up, giving him a shy smile. Seeing her parents again seemed to have taken some fight out of her. She had to have missed them more than she'd admitted. Leaning in, she put her head into the curve of his shoulder. Mark tightened his hold and slowly moved them around the dance floor.

Other couples surrounded them but for him there was only he and Laura Jo. For once he wished he could hold one woman forever. He'd never allowed himself to dream further but with Laura Jo anything seemed possible.

They were returning to their table when Mr. Washington approached. "I was telling a buddy of mine about the work your young lady is doing. He would like to pledge fifty thousand."

Laura Jo gasped.

"Baba McClure has had a little too much to drink already and he has pledged another fifty."

Laura Jo squeezed his arm.

"The thing is," Mr. Washington went on, "you'd better go over there and get something in writing or they may not remember in the morning."

"Do you have a paper and pen in your purse?" Mark asked Laura Jo.

She picked up the tiny purse she had brought. "I have a small pen. I'll ask at the registration table if they have something we can write on."

Mark watched Laura Jo go. She was soon back. Mr. Washington showed them across the room and introduced them to the two men and let Laura Jo take it from there. Despite wanting to distance herself from her background, she had a way of charming people that had been instilled in her. She soon had a makeshift agreement from both men and had promised she would see them the next day.

Both men groaned and asked her to make it the day after. Before they left the table she gave Mr. Washington a kiss on the cheek. "Thank you."

The eighty-year-old man beamed. "You're welcome, honey."

"Come on, I believe this deserves a victory dance." She pulled Mark to the dance floor. A fast tune was being played.

"I don't fast-dance." Mark pulled to a stop.

"What was it you told me? Uh…let go a little." Laura Jo started moving to the music. She held her hands out, encouraging him to take them.

He wasn't going to turn that invitation down. After a few dances, both fast and slow, he said, "I'm ready to go if you are."

"You're really not any more into this stuff than I am, are you?"

"No, I guess being in California for so long got it out of my system." And what had happened to Mike.

He had glimpsed Mike a couple of times across the room. They had never been near each other and for that Mark was grateful. Once he had thought his onetime friend might have recognized him. Dodging Mike didn't make Mark feel any better. He still couldn't face him. He used having Laura Jo with him as an excuse not to.

"Let's go," Laura Jo agreed. "But I need to stop by the restroom on our way out."

Mark was waiting at the exit when Mike rolled up.

"So was the plan to leave without speaking to me?" he asked, looking directly at Mark. "Running out again?"

He stood dumbstruck. His gut churned. If Laura Jo showed up, would she recognize what a coward he was?

"No," Mark lied boldly. If he could figure out how to leave without having this conversation, he would. "I hadn't realized you were here." Another lie. "It's good to see you." At least that had a small margin of truth.

"I'm not sure that's true." Mike's gaze hadn't wavered.

The ache in Mark's chest increased.

"I hear you're back in town and practicing medicine."

"Yes, I'm in a clinic in Spanish Fort and living in Fairhope." If he could just make it through some small talk, Laura Jo would show up and they could go.

"You always did like it at the summer house," Mike said.

Mark glanced toward the other side of the room. "How have you been? I'm sorry I haven't—"

A blonde woman with twinkling green eyes and a cheery smile approached. "I'd like you to meet my wife." He reached behind him and took the hand of the woman. "This is Tammy."

Mike married? "It's nice to meet you."

"And you, too. Mike has told me a lot about you." Tammy continued to smile but it no longer reached her eyes.

Like how he'd been the cause of Mike being in a wheelchair for life, or the fact he had run out on him when he'd needed him most, or maybe the part where he hadn't bothered to stay in touch, like he should have. Yeah, there was a lot to say about him, but none of it good. Or to be proud of.

Laura Jo walked up beside him. Could she see how uncomfortable he was? He took her hand and drew her forward. "Uh, this is my friend Laura Jo. Laura Jo, Mike and Tammy Egan."

"Hey, I remember a Laura Jo. She was a friend of my kid sister's. I haven't seen her in years." Mike gave her a searching look.

"You're Megan's brother?" Laura Jo studied Mike for a moment.

Great. Mike remembered Laura Jo when he himself hadn't. He truly had been a self-absorbed person in his twenties. Maybe in many ways he still was.

"Yes, and you're Laura Jo Herron."

She smiled at Mike. "Was Herron. Now it's Akins."

"No matter the name, it's good to see you again."

It was time to get out of there. Mark said, "Mike, I'm sorry, we're expected at another dance." Great. He was still running from Mike and lying to do so.

Laura Jo glanced at him but said nothing.

Mike rolled back and forth in his chair with the ease and agility of someone who had mastered the wheelchair. "I understand."

Somehow Mark was sure he did. All he wanted was to get away, forget, and find some fresh air. "Nice to see you again, Mike." Mark headed for the door. It wasn't until Laura Jo put her hand in his that he realized he had forgotten about her. He was running blind.

Mark didn't say anything on the way to his house. Laura Jo didn't either. They had both had an emotional evening. She let him remain in his thoughts, not even interrupting him to mention that he wasn't going toward her apartment. He didn't even register that he'd driven to his house until he'd pulled to a stop in his drive. "Why didn't you tell me to take you home?"

"Because I thought you needed someone to talk to."

How like her to recognize when someone was having trouble. He was in need, but of all the people he didn't want to look weak in front of it was Laura Jo.

"Let's go in. I'll fix us a cup of coffee." She was already in the process of opening the car door. Inside the house, she dropped her purse on the table beside the door, kicked off her shoes then headed straight for the kitchen. When he started to follow she said, "Why don't you go out to the deck? I'll bring it to you."

"Thanks. I appreciate it." He sounded weary even to his own ears.

"I'm just repaying all the times you've been there for me."

On the deck he sat in one of the chairs, spread his knees wide and braced his elbows on them. Putting his head in his hands, he closed his eyes.

Seeing Mike tonight had been as tough as it had ever

been. Mark had prepared himself that he might see him at the dance but that didn't make it any easier. It only added another bag of guilt to the ten thousand he already carried on his shoulders.

Now, with Laura Jo having seen his shame, it made the situation worse.

"Here you go," she said from beside him.

He raised his head to find her holding a mug and looking at him with concern. At least it wasn't pity. He took the cup.

She put the mug she still held on the table nearby and said, "I'll be right back."

Laura Jo returned wearing the jacket he'd offered her the night they'd made the king cakes. Picking up the mug she'd left behind, she took the lounge next to him. They sat in silence for a long time.

Finally Laura Jo said, "Do you want to talk about it?"

"No."

She made no comment, as if she accepted it was a part of him that he wouldn't share. Something about her being willing to do that endeared her even more to him and made him want to have her understand. "You asked me a few days ago about Mike being in an accident, remember?"

He didn't see her nod but somehow he knew she had.

"It was a night like tonight. Clear and warm for the time of the year. I had this great idea that we'd drive to the beach after the dance was over. After all, I'd be leaving in a few days for Birmingham to do my fellowship. My girlfriend, who was the queen that year, was having her last hoorah with her friends, so why not? Mike was going to ride with me and some of the other guys were going to meet us down there."

He swiped his fingers through his hair.

"I'd had a few drinks but I'd been so busy being king

I'd had little time to eat, let alone drink. Mike, on the other hand, had had too much. I told him more than once to buckle his seat belt. But he wouldn't listen. I was feeling wild and free that night. I knew I was going too fast for the road… Long story short, I ran off the road, pulled the car back on and went off the other shoulder. And the car rolled. I was hardly injured. Mike was thrown out. It broke his back."

"Oh, Mark."

He jumped up and started pacing. "I don't want your pity. I don't deserve it." Thankfully, Laura Jo said nothing more. "That's not the worst of it." He spun and said the words that he was sure would turn her against him. "I left. The next day I packed my bags, gave up my residency in Birmingham and accepted one in California. I've only seen him a few times since I watched him being put into an ambulance." He all but spat the last sentence.

Mark stopped pacing and placed his back to Laura Jo, not wanting to see the disgust he feared was in her eyes. She made a small sound of anguish. He flinched. His spine stiffened and his hands formed balls at his side. He hung his head.

Laura Jo felt Mark's guilt and pain ripple through her like the sting of a whip. How quickly and effortlessly Mark had worked himself past her emotional barriers. She cared for him. Wanted to help him past the hurt.

No wonder he was so hypervigilant about people buckling up in his car. Now that she thought about it, he'd even hesitated when he'd had to drive someone in his car. He found the responsibility too weighty.

She went to him. Taking one of his fists, she kissed the top of his hand and began gently pulling his fingers open until she could thread her own between his. She leaned her head against his arm. "It wasn't your fault, even if you don't believe it."

Mark snorted. "And it wasn't my fault that I was such a lousy friend that I ran out on him when he needed me most. That was unforgivable. But that wasn't enough, I've compounded it by years of not really having anything to do with him. I was closer to Mike than I was to my own brother. How could I have done that to him? Even tonight I was a coward."

"You know, it's not too late," she said quietly. "You're the one who has been telling me that."

"It's way past too late. How do I tell him I'm sorry I put him in a wheelchair while I still walk around?"

Laura Jo heard his disgust for himself in his voice.

"The same way I have to forgive my parents for the way they treated me. We have to believe people can change and grow."

He took her in his arms and looked down at her. "It's easy for someone with a heart as big as yours to forgive. Not everyone can or will do that."

His lips found hers.

Mark didn't ask for entrance. She greeted him. Welcomed his need. Her hands went to his shoulders. She massaged the tension from them before her fingers moved up his neck into his hair.

His desperation to lose himself in her goodness made him kiss her more deeply. She took all he gave with no complaint. There was a restlessness to his need, as if he was looking for solace. He pulled her closer, gathering her dress as he did so.

For tonight she could be that peaceful place if that was what he needed. Laura Jo tightened her arms around his neck and returned his kiss.

"I need you," he groaned. His lips made a trail down her neck.

Brushing her dress away, he dropped a kiss on the ridge of her shoulder. His tongue tasted her. The warm dampness he left behind made her quake. His other hand slipped under the edge of the back of her dress and roamed, leaving a hot path of awareness.

"And I need you," she whispered against his ear.

Mark pushed her dress farther down her arm. His lips followed the route of the material, leaving hot points along her skin. Laura Jo furrowed her fingers through his hair, enjoying the feel of the curl between her fingers.

He released the hook at the back of her neck and her dress hung at her elbows. Her breasts tingled with anticipation. His head lowered to kiss the top of one breast. He pushed the edge of her dress away from her nipple and took it into his mouth and tugged lightly. She shivered from the sensation. His tongue circled and teased her nipple until she moaned into the evening air.

When his mouth moved to the other breast he cupped the first one. The pad of his thumb found the tip of her nipple and caressed it. He circled her nipple with the end of his index finger until it stood at attention. He lifted the mound and placed a kiss on it.

Her heated blood rushed to her center and pooled there. She wanted to see and feel as much of Mark as he was of her. Her hands found his lapels and slid beneath them to his hard chest. There she worked his coat off. She wanted to touch him. Feel his skin. This had gone beyond giving comfort to a desire that was building into a powerful animal. It had been feeding and waiting since the first time Mark had touched her. The more she knew about him, saw him, felt his kindness, that longing had grown. Now there was no denying it or fighting it.

Mark's lips came back to hers as he shook himself out of his tux jacket and let it fall down his arms. Laura Jo's fingers went to the bow tie and released it, pulling it away and dropping it beside his jacket. His lips returned to her neck as Laura Jo removed first one stud and then another until she found his skin beneath his shirt.

The tip of her fingers lightly grazed the small patch of hair covering his warm skin. Yes, she'd found what she was looking for.

As Mark's mouth moved to hers for a hot, sinuous kiss, she yanked at his shirt, removing it from his pants. She wrapped her arms around his waist then she ran her hands over his back. She enjoyed the ripple of his muscles as they reacted to her touch. Would she ever get enough of touching him?

Mark gathered her dress, bringing it up until he could put his hand on her thigh. His fingers made circular motions along her bare skin. Slowly, his hand slid higher and higher until he ran his finger over the barrier of her panties at her core.

Laura Jo involuntarily flexed toward him. She'd never wanted a man to touch her more than she did at that moment.

With a growl of frustration, he set her on her feet. "I hope I don't live to regret this." He kissed her on the forehead. "Promise me you'll stay right here."

With heart pounding and body tight with need, Mark hurried into the house and scooped up the bedding in the extra bedroom. He grabbed two pillows, as well. With long strides, he walked back through the house. When he exited he was relieved to find Laura Jo waiting for him right where he'd left her. She had pulled her dress straps up over her shoulders. That was fine. He'd soon be removing her dress completely.

"What?" she murmured, as he came out of the house with his load.

"I want to see you under the stars."

He flipped the heavy spread out, not taking the time to make it neat. He lay down on his side and stretched out a hand in invitation for her to join him. His heart went to drumroll pace when she put her hand in his. This amazing woman was accepting him, even with all she'd learned about him.

She lifted her dress, giving him a tantalizing glimpse of her leg as she came to her knees before him.

Letting go of her hand, he used his finger to run a caressing line down her arm from her shoulder to her elbow. There he circled, then went to her wrist. He was encouraged by the slight tremble of her hand when he took it and eased her closer.

"Kiss me."

She leaned into him, pressing her lips against his. His hand pulled at her dress, bringing it up her leg. Gliding his hand underneath, he ran it along her thigh, moving to the inside then out again.

Laura Jo deepened their kiss.

His finger found the bottom of her panty line and followed it around to the back of her leg then forward again. She placed small kisses across his forehead and then nipped at his ear. He captured her gaze and watched her eyes widen as he slid a finger beneath her underwear at her hip. She gasped as his finger brushed her curls. He moved his finger farther toward her center and found wet, hot heat. His length strained to find release. She moaned against his mouth and bucked against his finger as he entered her.

"Mark." She drew his name out like a sound of adoration as she put her head back and closed her eyes.

When her hand grazed his straining length behind his zipper he jerked. The woman had him aroused to a painful point. The raw need that had built in him sought release. He feared he might lose his control and be like a teen in the backseat of a car as he fumbled to have all he dreamed of. Laura Jo ran her life with a tight rein and here she was exposing herself completely to him. That knowledge only increased his wish to give her pleasure.

"If you continue that I'm not going to be responsible for what I do," he growled. When had he been more turned on?

Laura Jo felt the same way. It had been a long time for her but she couldn't remember this gnawing hunger for another person that begged for freedom. She wanted to crawl inside Mark, be surrounded by him and find the safety and security she'd been missing for so many years.

He removed his finger.

She made a sound of protest.

"You have too many clothes on."

Could she be so bold as to remove her dress in front of him? She was thankful for the dim light. She was no longer a maiden. She'd had a child, gained a few mature pounds and things on her body had moved around. Would Mark be disappointed?

"Sit up on your knees, Laura Jo," he coached, as he moved to a sitting position.

Laura Jo did as he asked. As he gathered the fabric of her dress she shifted, releasing the long length of material from behind her knees. With it in rolls at her waist, he said, "Raise your arms."

She did so and he slipped the dress off over her head. Braless, she was exposed to Mark and the elements, except for her tiny panties. The cool air of the night licked her body, making her shudder. She was thankful for it because it covered her nervousness. She crossed her arms over her breasts.

"Please, don't hide from me," Mark said in a guttural tone filled with emotion. "You're beautiful. I want to admire you in the moonlight."

She'd been so absorbed in him she hadn't noticed there was a full moon. Slowly, very slowly, she let her hands fall to her sides. Mark's look started at the apex of her legs and traveled upward. He paused at her breasts. They were already prickly with awareness and had grown heavy. She looked down to see her nipples standing ridged from the cool air and Mark's hot gaze.

He cupped both breasts and she quivered.

"So responsive," he murmured, more to himself than to her. "Lie down. I want to touch all of you."

"But you still have all your clothes on," she protested.

He chuckled dryly. "If I don't remain dressed I might not be able to control myself."

"But I want to—"

"Later. Now I want to give you pleasure."

He nudged her shoulder then supported her until she lay on her back.

Laura Jo felt exposed, a wanton. She shuddered.

"I'm sorry, you must be cold." He leaned behind him and brought a blanket over them. "I hate to cover up all this beauty but maybe next time…"

Would there be a next time? Did she want more?

He rested his hand on the center of her stomach. Her breathing was erratic and shallow. He kissed the hollow of her shoulder. She pushed his open shirt off his shoulders. He finished removing it and threw it over his shoulder to the deck.

Her hand went to the nape of his neck. "I want to feel your skin touching mine."

"Ah, sweetheart…" Mark kissed her gently and brought her against his warm, inviting chest.

Laura Jo went from shivering to feeling warm and sheltered in the harbor of Mark's arms.

Mark lay down, bringing her with him. His mouth found hers. One of his hands went to her waist and shimmered over the curve of her hip and down her thigh and back up to cup her breast.

Her hands found his chest. She took her time discovering the rises and falls as she appreciated the breadth of his muscles as her hand traveled across his skin. Her palm hovered over the meadow of hair, enjoying the springiness of it.

He sucked in a breath.

She let her hand glide downward along his ribs and lower. He groaned when she brushed the tip of his manhood. With that he flipped the blanket off, letting it fall over her. In one smooth, agile movement he stood. He sat in the closest chair and proceeded to remove his socks and shoes. Seconds later his pants found the deck. He looked like a warrior of old as he stood with his feet apart, his shaft straight, with the moonlight gleaming off the water behind him.

Laura Jo bit her lower lip. This piece of masculine beauty was all hers for tonight.

She pushed away the blanket and opened her arms. Mark opened a package and covered his manhood then came down to her. She pulled the cover over them.

His fingers looped into the lace band of her panties and tugged them off. She kicked her feet to finish the process.

"Perfect," Mark murmured, as he kissed the shell of

her ear and his fingers traveled over the curve of her hip. "I want you so much."

Desire carried every word. She was wanted. Mark showed her in every way that she was desired by him. It fed her confidence. She arched her neck as his mouth traveled downward to the hollow beneath her chin, to the curve of a breast and out to her nipple. His hand went lower, where it tested and teased until she flexed.

Her core throbbed, waiting, waiting...

He slid a finger inside her, found that spot of pleasure and she bucked.

"So hot for me," he ground out, before placing a kiss on her stomach.

Mark said it as if he didn't think she could want him. Was the guilt he carried that heavy?

Laura Jo pushed him to his back. He made a sound of complaint. She slid on top of him and poured all she felt into making him feel desired. Positioning herself so that his tip was at her entrance, she looked into his eyes. Did he know how special he was to her? She pushed back and slowly took him inside her. His hands ran up and down her sides as his gaze bored into hers. She lifted and went down again.

Before she knew what had happened, Mark rolled her to her back and entered her with one bold thrust. His hold eased. "Did I hurt you?" His question carried an anxiousness that went soul deep.

"No, you would never hurt me."

He wrapped his arms around her as if he never wanted to let her go. When he did let her go he rose on his hands and pulled out of her to push in again.

She moaned with pleasure and his movements became more hurried. Her core tightened, twisted until it sprang her into the heavens.

A couple of thrusts later, Mark groaned his release to the starry night and lay on her.

Just before his weight became too much he rolled to his side and gathered her to him, twining his legs with hers. He adjusted the blanket around them.

"Perfect," he said, worshipful praise, before brushing a kiss over her temple.

Mark woke to the sound of thunder rolling in the distance. Laura Jo was warm and soft next to him. He shifted. Hard boards weren't his normal sleeping choice but with Laura Jo beside him it wasn't so difficult. He would have some aches in the morning but it would be more than worth it.

He moved to lie on his back. As if she couldn't be parted from him, she rolled in his direction and rested her head on his shoulder. She snuggled close. What would it be like to have Laura Jo in his life all the time?

Lightning flashed in the clouds. Thunder rumbled.

A hand moved over his chest. His body reacted far too quickly for his comfort. Could he ever get enough of her?

"What're you thinking?'

He tightened his hold and then released it. "That if we don't go inside we're going to get wet." The first large drops of rain hit the porch.

"I'll get the pillows. You get the blankets," she said, jumping up. He followed.

They scooped up the bedding and ran to the door, making it inside just before the downpour started. They laughed at their luck. They stood watching the storm for a few seconds.

"Oh, we didn't get our clothes." Laura Jo moved to open the door.

Mark grabbed her hand. "Forget them.

He dropped the blankets on the floor. "Leave the pillows here."

"Where're we going?" Laura Jo asked.

He gave her a meaningful look. "Like you don't know?"

When she only dropped one pillow he raised a questioning brow.

"I'm not used to walking around the house in the nude and certainly not with a man."

Mark chuckled. "I'm glad to hear that. But you have a beautiful body. You shouldn't be so self-conscious."

"Not everyone has thought that."

Her tone told him that she wasn't fishing for a compliment. Had her ex said differently? "Trust me, you're the sexiest woman I've ever seen. Come with me and I'll show you just how much."

She hesitated.

"You can bring the pillow."

Taking her hand, he led her to his bedroom. He was glad that he'd pulled the covers off his guest-room bed instead of his own. Something told him that if he gave Laura Jo more than a couple of seconds to think she'd be dressing and asking to go home.

Mark didn't want that. He made a point not to spend all night with the women he dated because he didn't want them to get any idea that there would ever be anything permanent between them. But he wanted Laura Jo beside him when he woke in the morning. He wanted her close until he had to let her go. For her own good, he would have to let her go.

He clicked on the lamp that was on the table beside his bed. Pulling the covers back, he climbed in, and turned to look at Laura Jo. "You have to let go of that pillow sometime."

There was a moment or two of panic that she wouldn't, before she slowly dropped it.

His breath caught. She'd looked amazing in the moonlight, but in the brighter light she was magnificent. Her husband had really done a number on her to make her believe she wasn't wanted. Mark sure wanted her more than ever.

"Move over."

He grinned. Laura Jo had gained some confidence. She found her place beside him. Where she belonged. But his feeling of ultimate pleasure quickly moved to the deepest depths of despair. He couldn't keep her.

Laura Jo gave him a look of concern that soon turned to one of insecurity. She slid her legs to the side of the bed.

"Oh, no, you don't. I'm not done with you." *Ever.* He rolled her to her back and kissed her.

Over the next minutes he teased, touched and tasted her body until he had her shaking beneath him. When he paused at her entrance she made a noise of disapproval. She wrapped her legs around his waist and urged him closer. He entered her and was lost forever.

Laura Jo woke up snuggled against Mark's hard body. She'd once thought he had none of the qualities in the man that she was looking for. She'd been so wrong. He had them all and more.

He was the opposite of Phil. When she had needed Mark to come help her at the shelter, he hadn't questioned it, just asked directions. He was good with Allie and she loved him. There had never been a question that he supported her cause with the shelter. He'd even been understanding about her relationship with her parents. He had been the support she hadn't had since she'd left her parents' home. Mark had become a person she could depend on, trust.

Her experiences with lovemaking had been about the other person doing all the receiving but Mark's loving had been all about giving, making sure she felt cherished. And she had.

She shifted until she could look at his face. His golden lashes tipped in brown lay unmoving against his skin. She resisted running her finger along the ridge of his nose. His strong, square jaw had a reddish tint of stubble covering it. She'd never seen a more handsome male in her life.

Her breath jerked to a stop. Oh, she couldn't be. But she was in love with Mark Clayborn!

"You're staring at me."

Her gaze jerked to his twinkling eyes. Could he see how she felt? Could she take a chance on trusting another man? She had Allie to consider. Had to act as if nothing had changed between them when everything had. In her best teasing tone she said, "You're so vain."

He moved to face her, propping his head on his hand. "That may be so but I did see you looking at me."

"So what if I was?" she asked in a challenging tone.

"Then…" he leaned into her "…I like it."

Putting an arm around her waist, he pulled her to him. His intention stood rock-hard ready between them. While he kissed her deeply, he positioned her above him and they became one.

CHAPTER EIGHT

AN HOUR LATER they were in the kitchen, working together to make breakfast. Laura Jo wore one of Mark's shirts while her dress hung on a deck chair, dripping, with Mark's jacket on another.

"I can't go home dressed in my evening gown," she mused, more to herself than to Mark.

"I'll find something around here that you can wear. Actually, I kind of like you in my shirt." He gave her a wolfish grin.

Warmth like the beach on a sunny day went through her. It was nice to be desired. It had been so long.

Wearing Mark's clothes and turning up in the morning instead of late at night in her evening gown was more than she wanted to explain to any of her neighbors. Allie deserved a mother who set a good example. More than that, she owed it to her not to become too involved with a man who wasn't planning to stay for the long haul. Mark had once said that marriage wasn't part of their relationship. Had that changed after last night? He'd said he wanted nothing serious. She had major responsibilities, which always meant some level of permanency. Either way, she had other issues to handle in the next few days. She would face that later.

"Butter on your toast?" Mark asked, as he pulled two slices out of the toaster.

"Yes, please." Waking up with Mark, and spending the morning doing something as domestic as making a meal, felt comfortable, right. Did he sense it, too? She liked it that he didn't expect her to prepare their breakfast. Instead, it was a partnership.

A few minutes later they sat across from each other at the table, eating. Mark wore a pair of sport shorts and nothing else. He hadn't shaved yet and the stubble covering his jaw was so sexy she was having trouble concentrating on her food.

"Do you have to work today?" Mark asked.

"No. I work tomorrow morning. But I have to go to the shelter, see Mr. Washington." She couldn't keep from grinning. "And pick up Allie and Jeremy from school."

"I have to work from noon to eight. Could we maybe have a late dinner?"

"Eight is Allie's bedtime. And it's a school night."

He hesitated, stopping his fork halfway to his mouth. Was he thinking about all that was involved in seeing her? She and Allie were a package and she wanted to remind him of that.

"What's your schedule for Thursday night?"

"Work morning then I have to see Mr. Washington's friend then Mr. McClure about their donations."

"That's right. You're supposed to get the house on Friday. We'll make it a celebration. Take Allie to someplace fun."

"That sounds doable. By the way, I don't think I said thank you for all your help with the shelter. We couldn't have done it without you. You're a good man, Mark Clayborn."

A flicker of denial came to his eyes before it changed

to something she couldn't name. He smiled. "Thank you for that, Laura Jo Akins. I think you believe it."

"And I think you should, too."

Mark had picked up his phone to call Laura Jo at least ten times over the course of the day. After returning her home, wearing a beach dress his sister-in-law had left there and one of his sweatshirts that had swallowed her whole, he had headed to work. He couldn't remember a more enjoyable morning. Laura Jo had just looked right in his kitchen. She was right for his life. The simple task of getting ready to leave for work, which turned out to include a very long shared shower, had been nicer when done with Laura Jo. He had it bad for her.

He picked up his phone. This time he texted her: How did it go with Mr. Washington?

Seconds later she returned, Good. Leaving now.

How like Laura Jo to say no more than necessary.

Unable to help himself, he typed, Looking forward to tomorrow evening.

She sent back a smiley face. He grinned. They had come a long way from the snarl that she had given him when they'd first met.

The next day, when he came out of one of the clinic examination rooms, he was told by the receptionist that there was a call for him. Was it Laura Jo? Was something wrong? His heart sank. Had she changed her mind about tonight? Mercy, he was starting to act lovesick.

"This is Dr. Clayborn."

"Hi, this is Marsha Gilstrap. Laura Jo's friend."

"Yes, I know who you are. Jeremy's mother."

"I'm calling because Laura Jo and I are getting ready to meet with the city about the shelter house. They have notified us at the last minute that they expect us to bring in the names of our board members. It has been only Laura Jo and I. Long story short, would you be willing to serve on our board? It would be for two years, with bi-monthly meetings. Would you be willing to serve?" Once again Marsha was talking like a whirlwind.

"Sure. Just let me know when and where I need to be." The shelter was a good cause and he would help Laura Jo in any way he could.

"Thanks, Dr. Clayborn."

"I thought we agreed to Mark."

"Thanks, Mark." With that she hung up.

That evening Mark drove straight from work to Laura Jo's apartment. He was looking forward to the evening far more than he should have been. Getting in too deep with Laura Jo could be disastrous. He wouldn't stay around forever and Laura Jo would expect that. But he couldn't help himself. He was drawn to her like no other woman he'd ever met.

Allie opened the door after he knocked.

"Hi, there." He went in and closed the door behind him. "Now that Mardi Gras is over, what do we need to look forward to next?"

"The Easter bunny bringing a large chocolate egg."

Mark nodded in thought. "Well, that does sound like something worth waiting for. Will you share yours with me?"

"Sure."

Laura Jo came up the hall. She wore nothing but a simple collared shirt that buttoned down the front and slacks but he still couldn't take his eyes off her. "Hello."

"Hi," she said, shyly for her.

He had gotten to her. She must be feeling unsure about them after the amount of time that had passed since they'd been together.

"Allie, would you do me a favor?"

She nodded.

"I'm thirsty. Would you get me a glass of water?"

As soon as she was out of sight Mark pulled Laura Jo to him. "What I'm really thirsty for is you." His mouth found hers.

Laura Jo had to admit that Mark had done well in choosing a place that would suit for a celebration and one Allie would enjoy. The pizza place was perfect. He'd even provided Allie with a handful of tokens so she could play games. Laura Jo was reasonably sure that this wasn't his usual choice of restaurant for a date.

"Thanks for bringing us here. Allie is having a blast." Laura Jo tried to speak loud enough to be heard over the cling and clang of the games being played and the overhead music.

"I love pizza, too," Mark said, as he brought a large slice of pepperoni to his mouth.

She liked his mouth, especially when it was on hers. His kiss at her door had her thinking of calling Marsha to see if Allie could spend the night then pulling Mark into her bedroom.

"So tell me what happened today about the shelter," Mark said, after chewing and swallowing his bite.

"I collected all the donor money." She grinned. "They didn't remember but when I showed them each the promissory note with their signature on it, both men called their accounting departments and told them to cut a check."

Mark chuckled. "Mr. Washington knows his buddies well."

"The only glitch is that the bank keeps throwing these roadblocks in our way. Today's was that we had to show we have a full board. It couldn't just be Marsha and I."

"Did you know she called me?"

"She told me afterward that she had. I would have told her not to if she had asked."

"Why?"

"I didn't want to put you on the spot." After the other night she didn't want him to feel obligated because of their one night of passion.

"It's not a problem. Besides being extremely attracted to one of the board members, I do think the shelter is a worthy cause. I'm more than happy to serve on the board."

Allie came running up. "I need one more token to play a game."

Mark handed her a token. "After you play your game, I want you to play one with me."

"Okay," Allie said, all smiles.

"Stay where you can see me," Laura Jo reminded her, before Allie ran back to a nearby game.

Mark leaned in close so that he was speaking right into Laura Jo's ear. "Is there any chance for you and me to have some alone time?"

"You'll have to wait and see," Laura Jo said with a smile. "There's one more thing about the shelter I wanted to tell you. Just before you picked us up, Marsha called. The city has decided to take bids for the house. They know of no one else who's interested but they want everything to look aboveboard so they have to offer it out for bids."

"Sounds reasonable."

"Yeah, but what if someone comes in and outbids us?"

He looked at her and said in a serious tone, "Then you'll just have to raise the money or find somewhere else. You now have new board members you can depend on to help you make a decision. You and Marsha won't be all on your own anymore."

She smiled at him just as Allie returned. "I'm ready to play."

"Are you ready to lose because I'm the best whack-a-moler you've ever seen," Mark announced as he puffed out his chest.

Laura Jo and Allie laughed.

He really was fun to be around. "Famous last words, the saying goes, I think," Laura Jo remarked. It had just been Allie and herself for so long. Was she ready to share their life with Mark? She smiled. Maybe she was.

"Come on, young lady," Mark said, taking Allie's hand. "Let me show you."

They arrived back at Laura Jo's apartment, laughing at something Mark had done while trying to best Allie at the arcade game. When they had gotten into the car to leave the pizza place, he'd looked back at Allie and then turned to her. Laura Jo had placed her hand on the seat belt and said, "Thank you for seeing to our safety."

He gave her a wry smile before he started the car but he seemed less anxious.

"It's bath- and bedtime," Laura Jo told Allie as they entered her apartment. "Why don't you get your PJs and the water started? I'm going to fix some coffee for Mark and I'll be right in."

Allie left in the direction of her room and she and Mark went to the kitchen. She took the pot out of the coffee-maker and went to the sink.

Mark came up behind her and took the pot from her, setting it on the counter. "I'll fix the coffee while you see to Allie. Right now, I want a kiss." He turned her round and gathered her close, giving her a gentle but passionate kiss.

Laura Jo's knees went weak. Her arms went around him and she pulled him tight.

"Mama, I'm ready," Allie called.

Slowly Mark broke their connection. He brushed his hips against hers and grinned. "I am, too."

Laura Jo snickered and gave him a playful push. "I'll be back in a few minutes. Behave yourself while I'm gone."

Ten minutes later, Mark walked down the hall in the direction of Laura Jo's voice. He stopped and stood in the doorway of the room where the sound was coming from. The lights were off except for one small lamp with a fairy of some sort perched on top. Allie lay in bed and Laura Jo sat on the side, reading a book out loud. He leaned against the wall facing them and continued to listen. Allie's eyes were closed when Laura Jo shut the book and kissed her daughter on the forehead.

His heart constricted. What would it feel like to be a part of their inner circle?

Laura Jo looked at him and gave him a soft smile. She raised her hand and beckoned him to join her.

His heart beat faster. This was his invitation to find out. But if he took that step he'd be lost forever. He couldn't take on the responsibility of protecting them. What if he failed them, like he had Mike? No, as much as it would kill him to do so, he couldn't tangle their lives up in his. He'd let them down. Hurt them, disappoint them at best. They'd both had enough of that in their lives.

Laura Jo's smile faded. He backed out of the door, walked to the kitchen and sat at the small table.

What had just happened? Didn't Mark recognize that she'd just offered her life and heart to him? He'd turned it down. Flat.

Laura Jo could no longer pretend this was a casual thing between them. She couldn't afford to invest any of her life or Allie's in someone who was afraid of their ability to share a relationship. She needed a confident man during the good as well as the tough times. Mark didn't believe he was capable of being that man.

Even if she believed in him and convinced him they could make it, Mark had to believe in himself. She couldn't take the chance of Allie experiencing that loss and devastation, the almost physical pain of believing no one wanted her, if Mark decided he couldn't do it. Allie wouldn't be made to feel as if she were a piece of trash being tossed out the window of a car. No, she wouldn't let it happen. Wouldn't go through that again.

She had to break it off before they became any more involved. Her heartache she would deal with, but her daughter's heart she would protect. Maybe with time, and many tears during the night, she would get over Mark.

Laura Jo found him a few minutes later, looking at his coffee cup as he ran a finger around the edge. She poured herself a cup of coffee she had no intention of drinking and took the chair across the table from him.

"This isn't going to work, Mark."

"Why?"

"Because I need someone who'll be committed to the long haul. I deserve your wholehearted love and loyalty. I won't risk my heart or Allie's for anything less. That is the very least I will agree to."

"You know I won't take the chance. What if I can't do it? I won't hurt you. I'm no better than your ex-husband. When things get too tough to face, I'll be gone. Just like him. I've done it before. I'll do it again."

"You're still punishing yourself for something that isn't your fault. Mike's in a wheelchair because of a choice that he made, not you. Your way of atoning is to remain uninvolved emotionally with anyone you might feel something real for. That translates into a wife and family for you. I can see that you care about Allie and I think you care about me, too. I've spent a long time not trusting my judgment about men. You got past that wall. You're a better man than you give yourself credit for."

He didn't look at her. Her heart ached for him but she had to get through to him. Make him start really living again. He deserved it. She loved him enough to do that and send him away if she had to.

"You can't create someone else's happiness by being unhappy. You can't fix what happened to Mike. Even if you had been wrong. What you can do now is try to be a better friend than you were back then.

"The problem is you have run from and hidden from the issue too long. You've left the subject alone so long that it has grown and festered to a point it's out of control in your mind. Based on what I saw from Mike the other night, he feels no animosity toward you. To me it sounded as if he just misses his friend. Face it, clean the ugliness away then you can see yourself for the person you are. Good, kind, loving, protective and caring. It's time for you to like yourself.

"I hope that one day you realize that and find someone to share your life with. It can't be Allie and I." Those last words almost killed her to say.

His chair scraped across the floor as he pushed it away from the table. He pinned her with a pointed look. His eyes were dark with sadness and something else. Anger? "Are you through?"

She nodded. She was sure she wasn't going to like what came next.

"I have issues, but you do, too. You carry a chip on your shoulder, Laura Jo. In the past nine years you have finished school on your own, raised a wonderful, happy child and started and helped to run a shelter for women, but still you feel you need to prove yourself to the world. You don't need your father and mother's or anyone else's approval. It's time to quit being that girl who had to show everyone she could do it by herself.

"You let your ex overshadow your life to the point it took me using a sledgehammer to get past your barriers. Laura Jo, not every guy is a jerk and doesn't face up to their responsibilities."

"Like you have?"

Mark flinched. She'd cut him to the core. But she had to get through to him somehow.

"I think I'd better go." He stood and started toward the door.

Shocked at his abrupt statement, she said, "I think it's for the best. Goodbye, Mark."

CHAPTER NINE

THE ONLY TIME Laura Jo could remember feeling so miserable had been when she'd taken Allie home from the hospital, knowing the child would have no father or grandparents to greet her. The pain had been heartbreakingly deep. She'd believed the scar had been covered over enough that she would never return to those emotions. But she'd been wrong.

They had rushed in all over again when Mark had walked out the door. The overwhelming despair was back. The problem this time was that it was even more devastating.

Looking back, she could see her goal when she'd been nineteen had been more about breaking away from her parents, standing on her own two feet and discovering what she believed in, instead of following their dictates. Turned out she'd let pride stand in her way all these years. It hadn't been fair to Allie, her parents or herself.

She appreciated Mark's fears, even understood where they came from, but she couldn't accept anything less than full commitment. Allie deserved that, and even she wouldn't settle for anything less.

Experience had shown her what it was like to have a man in her life who didn't stay around. She refused to put Allie through that. If she felt this awful about Mark leaving after they had known each other for such a short time, what would it have been like if they had been together longer?

The past had told her that the only way to survive disappointment and heartache, and in this case heartbreak, was to keep moving. It was Monday morning and Allie had school, she had to work.

Was Mark working the early shift? Moving around his big kitchen dressed only in his shorts? With them hung low on his hips? Bare-chested?

He'd called a couple of times but she had let the answering machine get it. If she spoke to him it would be too easy to open the door wide for him to come into her life. She just couldn't do that.

She groaned, afraid there would be no getting over Mark. She needed to stay busy, spend less time thinking about him. Forcing herself to climb out of bed, Laura Jo dressed for the day, making sure to have Allie to school on time.

Allie asked her during breakfast, "Why're you so sad, Mama?"

Laura Jo put on a bright smile and said in the most convincing voice she could muster, "I'm not sad. Why would I be sad?"

Allie gave her a disbelieving look but said nothing more. For that Laura Jo was grateful. She worried that she'd break down in tears in front of her daughter.

At midmorning, after just releasing a patient home from the ER, Laura's cell phone buzzed. Looking at it, she saw it was Marsha calling. It was unusual for her to call while Laura Jo was working. Something must have happened with the shelter.

"Hello. What's going on?"

"Someone has bid against us for the house. It's far over

what we have and I don't see any way for us to come up with that amount of money."

Marsha told Laura Jo the figure. They were doomed. The new house wasn't going to happen this time. "You're right."

"What we'll have to do is use the money we do have to refurbish the place we're in now and start looking for another place to buy. Sorry my call was bad news."

"Me, too, but I was afraid this might happen when the city opened it for bids. I'd prepared myself for it. We'll start making plans this evening when I get home."

Laura Jo hung up. The sting had been taken out of the loss of the house by the loss of Mark. With him no longer in her life, it made everything else feel less important. She and Marsha would deal with this setback somehow.

A week later, her heart was still as heavy as ever over Mark. If she could just stop thinking about him and, worse, dreaming of him, she could start to heal. But nothing she did except working on the shelter, seemed to ease the continuous ache in her chest.

She and Marsha had just finished meeting with a contractor about ideas for changes at the shelter when Laura Jo was called to the front. There a man dressed in a suit waited.

"Can I help you?" she asked.

"Are you Laura Jo Akins?" The man said in an official manner.

"Yes."

"I was instructed to personally deliver this to you."

He handed her an official-looking envelope. Was this some sort of summons?

Laura Jo started opening the letter and before she could finish the man left. What was going on?

Printed on the front was a name of a lawyer's office. Why would a lawyer be contacting her? She opened the envelope and scanned the contents. Her heart soared and her mouth dropped open in disbelief. She thought of telling Mark first, but he wasn't in her life anymore.

"Marsha!" she yelled.

Her friend hurried down the hallway toward Laura Jo. "What's wrong?"

She waved the letter in the air. "You're never going to believe this. My father has bought the house the city was selling and he has deeded it over to me!"

That night Laura Jo wondered about her parents' generosity. Had they had a change of heart years ago but she wouldn't let them close enough to say so? She had been surprised at the krewe dance to discover they knew some of what had been going on in her life. Had they been watching over her? There had been that school scholarship that she'd been awarded that she'd had no idea she'd qualified for, which had covered most of her expenses. Had that been her parents' doing?

She'd told Mark that people had the capacity to change. Had her parents? After speaking to them, she'd certainly seen them in a different light. She'd also told Mark that people could forgive. Maybe it was past time she did.

On Saturday afternoon, Laura Jo pulled her car into the drive of her parents' home. Allie sat in the seat next to her. Laura Jo had told her about her grandparents a few days before. She had asked Allie to forgive her for not telling her sooner, and had also told Allie that they would be going to visit her grandparents on Saturday. Later that evening, Laura Jo had called the number that she'd known from childhood. Her mother had answered on the second ring. Their conversation had been a short one but during it Laura Jo had asked if she could bring Allie to meet them.

"Mama, what're we doing?" Allie asked.

"I'm just looking, honey. I used to live here." That was true but mostly she was trying to find the nerve to go further. The last time she'd been there, hurtful words had been spoken that had lasted for years.

A few minutes later, she and Allie stood hand in hand in front of her parents' front door. Allie rang the doorbell. Her mother must have been watching for them because the door was almost immediately opened by her mother herself. Not one of the maids. Her father was coming up the hall behind her.

"Hello, Laura Jo. Thank you for coming." Her mother sounded sincere.

"Mother and Daddy, this is Allie."

Her mother leaned over so that she was closer to Allie's level and smiled. "Hi, Allie. It's so nice to meet you."

Her father took the same posture. "Hello."

Allie stepped closer to Laura Jo. She placed a hand at Allie's back and said, "These are your grandparents."

Both her parents stood and stepped back.

Her mother said in a nervous voice Laura Jo had never heard, "Come in."

It felt odd to step into her parents' home after so much time. Little had changed. Instead of being led into the formal living room, as Laura Jo had expected, her mother took them to the kitchen. "I thought Allie might like to have some ice cream."

Allie looked at Laura Jo. "May I?"

"Sure, honey."

"Why don't we all have a bowl?" her father suggested. When they were finished with their bowls of ice cream her mother asked Allie if she would like to go upstairs to see the room where Laura Jo used to sleep. Allie agreed.

Laura Jo looked at her father. "I don't know how to say thank you enough for your gift."

"We had heard that you were looking for support to buy it."

She should have known it would get back to them about why she'd been at the dance.

"It's a good cause and we wanted to help. Since we weren't there for you, maybe we can help other girls in the same position. I know it doesn't make up for the struggle you had."

It didn't, but at least she better understood her parents now. She had to share some of the fault also. "All those calls I made to Mom—"

"We thought we were doing what was best. That if we cut you off then you would see that you needed us and come back."

"But you wouldn't talk to me." She didn't try to keep the hurt out of her voice.

"We realized we had been too hard on you when you stopped calling. I'm sorry, Laura Jo. We loved you. Feared for you, and just didn't know how to show it correctly."

"You saw to it that I got the nursing scholarship, didn't you?"

He nodded. "We knew by then that you wouldn't accept if we offered to send you to school."

"I wouldn't have. It wasn't until recently that I realized that sometimes what we believe when we're young isn't always the way things are. You were right about Phil. I'm sorry that I hurt you and Mom. Kept Allie from you."

"We understand. We're proud of you. We have kept an eye on you both. You've done well. You needed to do it the hard way, to go out on your own. It took us a while to see that." Her strong, unrelenting father went on, with a catch in his voice, "The only thing we couldn't live with was not having you in our lives and not knowing our grand-daughter."

Moisture filled her eyes for all the hurt and wasted opportunities through the years on both sides. Laura Jo reached across the table and took her father's hand. Forgiveness was less about her and more about her parents. A gift she could give them. "You'll never be left out of our lives again, I promise."

Three weeks after the fact Mark still flinched when he thought of Laura Jo accusing him of being a jerk and not living up to his responsibilities. The plain-talking Laura Jo had returned with a vengeance when she'd lectured him.

She was right, he knew that, but he still couldn't bring himself to talk to Mike. That was the place he had to start. He'd spent over ten years not being able to face up to Mike and what had happened that night. Could he be a bigger hypocrite?

He'd looked down on Laura Jo's ex, taking a holier-than-thou approach when he'd been running as fast and far as Phil had when the going had got tough.

Every night he spent away from Laura Jo made him crave her more. He wasn't sleeping. If he did, he dreamed of her. The pain at her loss was greater than any he'd ever experienced. Even after the accident. He wasn't able to live without her. He'd tried that and it wasn't working.

He'd tried to call her a couple of times but she hadn't picked up.

Mark thought about Laura Jo's words. Didn't he want a family badly enough to make a change? Want to have someone special in his life? More importantly, be a part of Laura Jo's and Allie's world?

He'd been running for so long, making sure he didn't commit, he didn't know how to do anything else. It was time for it to stop. He had to face his demons in order to be worthy of a chance for a future with Laura Jo, if she would have him. How could he expect her to believe in him, trust him to be there for her, if he didn't believe it for himself? He had to get his own life in order before he asked for a permanent place in hers. And he desperately wanted that place.

Mark picked up the phone and dialed the number he'd called so many times he had it memorized by now. He'd been calling every day for a week and had been told that Mike wasn't available. Was he dodging Mark, as well?

He'd made his decision and wanted to act on it. It was just his luck he couldn't reach Mike. The devil of it was that he couldn't return to Laura Jo without talking to Mike first. She would accept nothing less. For his well-being as well as hers.

The day before, he'd received a call from Marsha. She'd told him how they had missed out on the house but then an anonymous donor had bought it outright and gifted it to them.

Mark was surprised and glad for Laura Jo. At least the dream she'd worked so hard for had come true. Marsha went on to say that she and Laura Jo no longer required a board but planned to have one anyway. Marsha wanted to know if he was still willing to serve on it.

"Have you discussed this with Laura Jo? She may not want me on it."

"She said that if you're willing to do it she could handle working with you on a business level. I think her exact words were, 'He's a good doctor and cares about people. I'm sure he'll be an asset.'"

Panic flowed through his veins. Laura Jo was already distancing herself from him. The longer it took to speak to Mike, the harder it would be to get her to listen.

Marsha said, "Look, Mark, I don't know what happened between you two but what I do know is that she's torn up about it. I love her like a sister and she's hurting. She can be hardheaded when it comes to the ones she loves. The only way to make her see reason is to push until she does."

"Thanks for letting me know."

The next day, when Mark had a break between patients, he tried Mike's number again. This time when a woman answered he insisted that he speak to Mike.

"Just a minute."

"Mark." Mike didn't sound pleased to hear from him.

"I was wondering if I could come by for a visit," Mark said, with more confidence than he felt.

"It will be a couple of days before I have time." Mike wasn't going to make this easy but, then, why should he. "I've been out of town and have some business I need to catch up on."

Mark wasn't tickled with having to wait, but he'd put it off this long so did two more days really matter?

"How does Thursday evening at seven sound?"

"I'll be here." Mike sounded more resigned to the idea than cheerful about the prospect. Mark couldn't blame him. His jaw tightened with tension from guilt and regret at the thought of facing him. He felt like a coward and had acted like one for years.

The next day an invitation arrived in the mail. It was to a garden party tea at the Herrons' mansion on Sunday afternoon. It was a fund-raiser for the new shelter. Had Laura Jo taken his advice and cleared the air with her parents? He looked forward to attending.

Two evenings later, Mark drove from Fairhope over the

bay causeway to Mobile. Mike lived in one of the newer neighborhoods that Mark wasn't familiar with. He hadn't slept much the night before, anticipating the meeting with Mike, but, then, he hadn't slept well since the night he'd had Laura Jo in his arms. He drove up the street Mike had given as his address during their phone conversation. It was tree-lined and had well-cared-for homes. He pulled up alongside the curb in front of the number that Mike had given him. It was a yellow ranch-style home, with a white picket fence surrounding the front yard. Early spring flowers were just starting to show.

Mark sat for a minute. He'd prepared his speech. Had practiced and practiced what he was going to say, but it never seemed like enough. If Laura Jo were here, she would say to just share what was in his heart. To stop worrying. Taking a deep breath and letting it out slowly, he opened the car door and got out. Closing it, he walked around the car and up the walk.

He hadn't noticed when he'd pulled up that there were children's toys in the yard and near the front door. Mike had a child?

Mark winced when he saw the wheelchair ramp and hesitated before putting a foot on it to walk to the door. His nerves were as tight as bowstrings. He rang the doorbell. Seconds later, Tammy opened the door.

"Mark, how nice to see you again." She pulled the door wider. "Come on in. Mike's in the den with Johnny."

She closed the door and Mark followed her down an extrawide hall to a large room at the back of the house.

Mike sat in what could only be called the most high-tech of wheelchairs in the middle of the room. A boy of about three was handing him a block and together they were building a tower on a tray across Mike's knees. "Mark. Come on in. Let me introduce you to my son, Johnny."

Mark went over to Mike, who offered his hand for a shake. "Good to see you again."

Mike dumped the blocks into a bucket beside his chair and then set the tray next to it. "Come here, Johnny, I want you to meet someone."

At one time Mike would have introduced him as his best friend. By the way he acted he wasn't even a friend anymore.

The boy climbed into his father's lap and shyly curled into Mike. He looked up at Mark with an unsure gaze.

"Johnny," Mark said.

"I think it's is time for someone to go to bed." Tammy reached out and took Johnny from Mike. "We'll let you two talk."

Mark watched them leave the room and turned back to Mike.

"I admire you."

"How's that?"

"Having a wife and family. The responsibility. How do you know you're getting it right?"

"Right? I have no idea that I am. I make the best decisions I can at the time and hope they are the correct ones. Tammy and I are partners. We make decisions together." Mike looked directly at him. "Everyone makes mistakes. We're all human and not perfect. We just have to try harder the next time."

Was that what he'd been doing? Letting a mistake color the rest of his life? If he couldn't be sure he'd be the perfect husband or father then he wouldn't even try.

Before Mark could say anything more, Mike said, "Take a seat and quit towering over me. You always made a big deal of being taller than me. Remember you used to say that was why you got the girls, because they saw you first in a crowd."

Mark gave halfhearted grin. Had Mike just made a joke?

Taking a seat on the edge of the sofa, Mark looked around the room.

"Why are you here, Mark? After all these years, you show up at my house now," Mike said, as he maneuvered his chair closer and into Mark's direct sight line.

He scooted back into the cushions. "Mike, I need to clear the air about a couple of things."

"It's well past time for that."

Those words didn't make Mark feel any better. "I'm embarrassed about how I acted after the accident. I'm so sorry I left without speaking to you and have done little to stay in touch since. Most of all, I'm sorry I put you in that damn chair." Mark looked at the floor, wall, anywhere but at Mike.

Moments passed and when Mike spoke he was closer to Mark than he had been before. "Hey, man, you didn't put me in this chair. I did. I was drunk and not listening to anything anyone said."

"But I was the one going too fast. I'd driven that part of the road a hundred times. I knew about that ninety-degree turn. I overcorrected." Mark looked up at him.

"You did. But I wouldn't have been thrown out if I'd worn my seat belt. I don't blame you for that. But I have to admit it hurt like hell not to have your support afterwards. I can't believe you did me that way."

Mark's stomach roiled as he looked at a spot on the floor. "I can't either. That isn't how friends should act." He looked directly at Mike. "All I can do is ask you to forgive me and let me try to make it up to you."

"If you promise not to run out on me again, and buy me a large steak, all will be forgiven."

Mark smiled for the first time. "That I can do."

"And I need a favor."

Mark sat forward. "Name it."

"I need a good general practice doctor to oversee an experimental treatment that I'm about to start. Do you know one?"

"I just might," Mark said with a grin. "What's going on?"

"I just returned from Houston, where they are doing some amazing things with spinal injuries. With all these guys coming back from war with spinal problems, what they can do has come a long way even from nine years ago. I will have a procedure done in a few weeks and when I return home I need to see a doctor every other day to check my site and do bloodwork. My GP is retiring and I'm looking for someone to replace him who Tammy can call day or night." He grinned. "She worries. Doesn't believe me when I tell her what the doctor has said. Likes to hear it from the doc himself."

"I'll be honored to take the job. I'll even make house calls if that will help."

"I may hold you to that."

For the next forty-five minutes, he and Mike talked about old times and what they were doing in their lives now. Mike had become a successful businessman. He had invented a part for a wheelchair that made it easier to maneuver the chair. As Mark drove away he looked back in his rearview mirror. Mike and Tammy were still under the porch light where he had left them. Tammy's hand rested on Mike's shoulder. That simple gesture let Mark know that Mike was loved and happy.

Mike had a home, a wife and child, was living the life Mark had always hoped for but was afraid to go after. All Mark owned was his car and Gus. He'd let the one special person he wanted in his life go. Ironically, Mike had moved on while he had stayed still. And he had been the one feeling sorry for Mike, when he had more in life than Mark did. He wanted that happiness in his life too and knew where to find it.

If he could get Laura Jo to listen. If she would just let him try.

LAURA JO COULDN'T believe the difference a few weeks had made in her life. It was funny how she'd been going along, doing all the things she'd always done, and, bam, her life was turned upside down by her daughter having a skinned knee. She'd worked Mardi Gras parades before but never had she had a more eventful or emotional season.

She scanned her parents' formal backyard garden. There were tables set up among the rhododendrons, azaleas and the dogwood trees. None were in full bloom but the greenery alone was beautiful. The different tables held canapés and on one sat a spectacular tea urn on a stand that swung with teacups surrounding it. People in their Sunday best mingled, talking in groups. The eye-popping cost to attend the event meant that the shelter could double the number of women they took in. Her parents had convinced her to let them to do this fund-raiser so that she could get the maximum out of the grant. She'd agreed and her mother had taken over.

How ironic was it that she had rejected her parents and they were the very ones who were helping her achieve her dreams? Her anger and resentment had kept her away from her parents, not the other way around. Forgiveness lifted a burden off her and she was basking in the sunshine of having a family again. She only wished Mark could feel that way, as well. She still missed him desperately.

Allie's squeal of delight drew her attention. Laura Jo located her. She was running down the winding walk with her new dress flowing in her haste.

"Mark," she cried, and Laura Jo's stomach fluttered.

She'd thought he might be here, had prepared herself to see him again, but her breath still stuck in her throat and her heart beat too fast. Each day became harder without him, not easier.

Already she regretted agreeing to let him remain on the board. Now she would have to continue to face him but he was too good an advocate for the shelter to lose him. At least, that was what she told herself. Somehow she'd have to learn to deal with not letting her feelings show.

When Allie reached Mark he whisked her up into his arms and hugged her close. The picture was one of pure joy between them.

Laura Jo had worked hard not to snap at Allie when she'd continued to ask about where Mark was and why they didn't see him anymore. Finally, Laura Jo had told her he wouldn't be coming back and there had been tears on both sides.

Mark lowered Allie onto her feet and spoke to her. Allie turned and pointed in Laura Jo's direction. Mark's gaze found hers, even at that distance. Her heart flipped.

He started toward her.

A couple of people she'd known from her Mardi Gras court days joined her. They talked for a few minutes but all the while Laura Jo was aware of Mark moving nearer.

He stood behind her. She'd know anywhere that aftershave and the scent that could only be his. Her spine tingled.

As the couple moved away Mark said in a tone that was almost a caress, "Laura Jo."

She came close to throwing herself into his arms but she had to remain strong. She turned around, putting on her best smile like she'd been taught so many years ago. "Hello, Mark, glad you could come."

"I wouldn't have missed it."

His tone said that was the truth.

"Marsha told me that you got the house after all. That's wonderful. With the grant and all the money you've raised, you'll be able to furnish it."

"Yes. My father was the one to outbid us. He then gave it to me."

His brow wrinkled. "You were okay with that?"

"I was. The women needed it too badly for me to use my disagreement with my parents against them. It really was a gift to me anyway. He wanted to make amends by helping other women going through the same experience I had."

Mark nodded. "It sounds like you and your parents worked things out."

"I wouldn't say that it's all smooth going. But I've forgiven them. We're all better for that. They want to see their granddaughter and Allie needs them. I don't have the right to deny any of them that."

"Mama, look who's here," Allie said from beside her.

Laura Jo hadn't seen her approach, she'd been so absorbed in Mark. She turned. "Who—?"

Allie held Gus's leash. Behind the dog sat Mike and next to him stood his wife. She looked back at Mark.

He smiled and turned toward the group. "I brought a few friends with me. I hope you don't mind?"

Did this mean what she thought it did? Mark had taken what she'd said to heart and had gone to see his friend. "Hello, Mike and Tammy. Of course you're welcome. I'm glad to see you again."

"We're glad to be here. This is some event. And I understand it's for a very worthy cause. I think we'll have Allie show us where the food is." Mike winked at Mark. "We'll see you around, buddy."

Laura Jo looked between them, not sure what the interchange meant.

"You're busy. I think I'll get some food also." Mark captured her hand. "When this is over, can we talk?"

A lightning shock of awareness and a feeling of rightness washed through her simultaneously. "It'll be late."

"I'll wait."

Mark sat in Mr. Herron's den, having a cup of coffee while he waited for Laura Jo. Her father was there, along with Allie and Gus. Mr. Herron had apparently noticed Mark was hanging around after the other guests were leaving and had taken pity on him by inviting him in for coffee and a more comfortable seat.

The longer Mark sat there the more nervous he became. Would Laura Jo listen to what he had to say? Would she believe that he had changed? Would she be willing to take a chance on him? He broke out in a sweat, just thinking about it.

She and her mother finally joined them. He stood. Laura Jo looked beautiful but tired. Had she been getting as little sleep as he had?

As if her mother knew Laura Jo needed some time alone with him, Mrs. Herron said, "Why don't you let Allie stay with us tonight? We can get her to school in the morning. She can wear the clothes she wore from home to here today."

"Is that okay with you, Allie?" Laura Jo asked.

"Yes. Can Gus stay, too?"

"I think you need to let your grandparents get used to having you before you start inviting Gus to stay," Mark said with a smile.

Ten minutes later, he and Laura Jo, with Gus in the backseat, were leaving her parents' house. She had touched her seat belt when he'd looked.

"Old habits are hard to break," he said in explanation.

"Not a bad habit to have," she assured him in a warm tone. That was one of the many things he loved about Laura Jo. She understood him.

"I hope you don't mind me taking Gus home. I don't want you to think I planned to lure you to my house. I just thought Allie would be glad to see him. I didn't think it all the way through."

"She was, and I don't mind riding to your house."

As they traveled through the tunnel Laura Jo remarked, "I've never known my parents to let a dog in the house."

"Gus does have that effect on people."

She went on as if more in thought than conversation, "Come to think of it, I've never seen my father invite another man into his private space."

"Maybe that's his way of giving me a seal of approval."

She pieced him with a look. "Are you asking for a seal of approval from my father?"

"No, the only seal of approval I'm looking for is from you."

She studied him for a minute before asking, "Are you going to tell me about Mike and Tammy or keep me in suspense?"

"It took me a while to admit you were right. Actually, I knew all along that you were. I just didn't want to admit it."

"So what made you decide to talk to Mike?" She had laid her head back and closed her eyes.

He hadn't planned to go into this as they traveled. But as usual Laura Jo had a way of surprising him. "Why don't you rest and I'll tell you when we get to my house?"

"Sounds like a plan."

By the time Mark pulled into his drive, Laura Jo was sleeping. Here he was, planning to bare his heart to her after weeks of being separated, and she'd fallen asleep. He let Gus out of the car and went to open the front door.

Going to Laura Jo's door, he opened it, unbuckled her and scooped her into his arms. She mumbled and wrapped her arms around his neck, letting her head rest on his chest. He kicked the passenger door closed and carried her inside.

He loved having her in his arms again. After pushing the front door closed, he went to his favorite chair and sat down. She continued to sleep and he was content just having her close.

Sometime later Laura Jo stirred. He placed a kiss on her temple and her eyelids fluttered open.

"Hello," she mumbled against his neck. Then she kissed him.

The thump-thump of his heart went to bump-bump.

Her lips touched the ridge of his chin, while a hand feathered through his hair near his ear.

His hopes soared. His manhood stirred. Had she missed him as much as he'd missed her? "Laura Jo, if you keep that up, talking is the last thing that will happen."

"So talk," she murmured, before her mouth found the corner of his. "I'm listening."

"Maybe we need to go out on the deck."

"Mmm, I like it here." She wiggled around so she could kiss him fully on the mouth.

His length hardened. If he didn't say what he needed to say now, he wouldn't be doing so for a long time.

"I can't believe that I'm doing this..." He pushed her away until he could see her face. She blinked at him and gave him a dreamy smile. "Why did you agree to talk to me? Was it because you saw me with Mike? You haven't answered any of my phone calls in the past few weeks."

"I hoped..."

"Hoped what? That I had changed my mind? Hoped you'd gotten through to me? Hoped there was a chance for us?"

"Yes," she whispered.

"Do you want there to be?"

By now she was sitting a little straighter and her eyes had turned serious. "Tell me what made you decide to go talk to Mike. When you left my place I didn't think you ever would."

"I went because I discovered that I was more afraid of something else than I was of facing Mike."

Her gaze locked with his. "What?"

"Losing any chance of ever having you in my life."

"Oh, Mark. I thought I had lost you forever until I saw you with Mike today. I knew then that you thought we had something worth fighting for. I've been so miserable without you." She took his face in her hands and kissed him.

"We've both been running from our pasts. I think it's time for us to run toward our future. Together."

His arms tightened around her. Their kiss deepened. He had to have her. Beneath him, beside him, under him. Forever.

Mark lifted her off him and she stood. He quickly exited the chair. Taking her hand, he led her to his bedroom. Putting his hands on her shoulders, he turned her around and unzipped her dress. Pushing it off and letting it fall to the floor, he kissed her shoulder.

"I've missed you so much it hurt."

"I felt the same."

He released her bra and it joined her dress. There was a hitch in her breathing when he cupped her breasts. She leaned back against him. As his hands roamed, she began to squirm.

She flipped around to face him. "I want you." Her hands went to his waist and started releasing his belt.

"No more than I want you."

With them both undressed, they found the bed and the world that was theirs alone.

Sometime later, Mark lay with Laura Jo in his arms. Her hair tickled his nose but he didn't mind. All was right with his world if she was in it.

Laura Jo shifted, placed a hand in the center of his chest and looked up at him. "Hi, there."

He looked at her and smiled. "Hey, yourself."

For a few moments he enjoyed the feel of her in his arms before he said, "I've worked for years not to become emotionally involved with anyone. I didn't think I could trust myself. Then along came you and Allie. I've been miserable without you both. I've always wanted a family and when a wonderful one was offered to me, like an idiot I turned it down. I won't do that again if the invitation is still open. See, the problem is that I've fallen in love with you."

With moisture in her eyes Laura Jo stretched up and placed a kiss on his mouth. "I love you, too, but are you sure that's what you want? What you can live with? I can't take any chances. It has to be forever. Kids or no kids. Good or bad days. Sickness or health."

Mark leaned forward so that his face was only inches from hers. "Until death do us part."

"I can live with that."

Her kiss told him she meant it.

* * * * *

Look out for Susan Carlisle's next Medical Romance™
HIS BEST FRIEND'S BABY
Available in June 2015
Don't miss the next installment of the
fabulous MIDWIVES ON-CALL *series!*

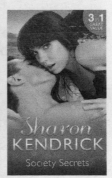

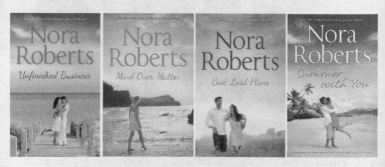

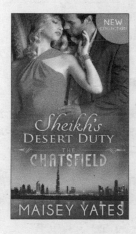

MILLS & BOON®

MEDICAL ROMANCE™

THE ULTIMATE IN ROMANTIC MEDICAL DRAMA